alone with YOU

USA TODAY BESTSELLING AUTHOR

ALY MARTINEZ

Alone with You
Copyright © 2024 Aly Martinez

Cover Design: Hang Le
Editing: Mickey Reed
Proofreading: Julie Deaton and Michele Ficht
Formatting: Champagne Book Design

A NOTE FROM THE AUTHOR

Warning: This book contains material that may be difficult for some readers including: grief, loss, PTSD, gun violence, suicide, and narcissistic abuse.

Mental health is a complex, difficult, and often misunderstood journey. While it would be nice if love could conquer all, reality isn't that simple.

It is important to remember that Truett and Gwen's story is a work of fiction.
Everyone has their own path to navigate,
but you don't have to do it alone.
Your life matters.

If you or someone you know is struggling, please reach out to:

The National Suicide Prevention Lifeline
1-800-273-TALK

alone with YOU

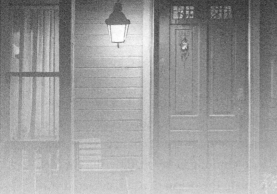

CHAPTER ONE

TRUETT

Death. It's life's only true constant. At any given second, someone was out there breathing their last breath. A heartbeat fading into silence. A soul escaping to a better place. At least that was what religious leaders and funeral directors would wax poetic about at services around the world.

I'd died once and it hadn't felt like floating through the clouds. There were no pearly gates. No bright light guiding me home. Not one fucking ounce of peace to be found.

But then again, I'd died failing the people I loved.

Dying was the most god-awful, heinous, and terrifying experience imaginable. Or so I'd thought—until someone had brought me back to life.

Surviving. Now that was one level of agony that could never be matched.

I was a prisoner. Like a storm hovering on the horizon, Death followed me. Day in. Day out. The Grim Reaper became my own personal stalker. Unfortunately for me, my name had yet to be at the top of his list. No, my fate was worse. I'd become something of his tour guide, sentencing everyone around me to his wrath.

Therapists and doctors alike assured me that Death wasn't a personified force chasing me around Earth. One even used the word *delusional* and asked if I'd considered medication. I shook a bag of pills at him and then not so kindly tossed his sorry-shrink-ass out of my house.

I wished I was delusional. I would have taken every fucking pill in existence if it could have made the horrors of my life figments of my imagination. I didn't honestly believe there was a mythical scythe-toting being lurking in my shadow. But for fuck's sake, something had to explain the ocean of pain I'd been drowning in for over half my life.

Call it what you will. Maybe I was cursed. Maybe in a different life I'd been a monster who deserved an eternity of torment. Regardless, delusion or karma, I wasn't leading anyone else to their graves. When Death finally came looking for me, I was going to be ready, eager, and *alone.*

Always *alone.*

Blindly slapping around my nightstand, I killed my screaming alarm. My heart raced, the rude awakening never getting easier.

"Fuck," I breathed as I pried one eye open. The sun streaming through my bedroom window blinded me. I let out a low groan and folded my forearm over my eyes, wishing I could block out my entire fucked-up life more so than the rays of the sun.

As I sat up and swung my legs over the edge of the bed, my back let out a loud creak. I kept myself in shape, working out virtually every day, but at forty-two, my body was all but revolting against me. I'd put it through hell in my twenties. Six years of jumping out of planes in the Army had done the real heavy lifting in the damage department, but I'd done my fair share of destroying it in other ways. Tequila had been my poison of choice for most of my thirties, but eventually I got my shit together. After that kind of abuse, I should have been grateful all I had were a few rusty creaks.

The aroma of freshly brewed coffee invaded my senses as I stood up and stretched. Thank God for auto brew. While sleeping naked was a definite perk of solitude, I'd learned the hard way that nudity and sloshing hot coffee did not mix. So, before leaving my room, I paused my pursuit of caffeination long enough to drag on a pair of sweats and a T-shirt.

The old house was noisy as I padded toward the kitchen. The hardwoods groaned under my weight, and even from the hall, I heard the fridge humming its pleas for retirement. From the air conditioner that sounded like it was following its dream of becoming a freight train to the horror-movie-worthy scream of my back door, everything needed an overhaul. My to-do list was almost two decades long.

Ah, the joys of home ownership.

Sipping my coffee, I got busy checking my daily voicemails.

"Hello, Mr. West, this is—" *Delete.*

"Hi there, I'm looking for—" *Delete.*

"Mr. West. Me again. If you could please—" *Delete.*

"Hey, asshole."

My finger hovering over the delete button stilled as I recognized Daniel's voice.

"It's that time of year again when the wife insists on throwing me a birthday party no matter how many times I've begged her not to."

I flipped my wrist and looked at the date on my watch. Shit. I'd totally forgotten that his birthday was coming up.

"Anyway, consider this your official invitation. No pressure or anything, but also, maybe show up and save me from three hours of small talk with people I don't like. We'll probably have enough food to feed a small country. So come hungry. Hit me back."

I tapped the trashcan icon and made a mental note to renew his annual beer-of-the-month subscription.

The last voicemail started playing immediately and I basked in the sender's frustrated tone.

"Mr. West, I *need* you to answer me. I—" *Delete.*

Amusing as it was, I did not have time for that shit. It was still early, but it wouldn't be long before my work phone started ringing.

Working with veterans was my passion, but it didn't matter how long they'd been in the civilian sector—they all still operated on military time. By zero six thirty, every single one of them had already finished PT, showered, shaved, and scarfed down some chow and was ready to kick the day in the ass. Myself included most of the time.

But today was different. Today was Wednesday.

And I had a date.

A massive smile stretched my face. I was far from being known as Mr. Cheerful, but I wouldn't say a grin was rare. Though, on Wednesday mornings, it was a permanent fixture.

Wednesday afternoons were a different story.

I dreaded them.

Agonized.

Turned myself inside out with stomach-churning anxiety.

But first, I got the morning—the sweet before the soul-crushing sour.

Ignoring the relentless ringing of my phone, I rushed through breakfast. Robotically, I went through the motions of preparing the usual: four scrambled eggs with yellow peppers, turkey sausage, a protein shake, and enough fresh fruit to open a produce stand. After that, it was a quick shower, a stop in the closet to get dressed for the day, and lastly, a drive-by at the coffee maker to snag my second cup of joe.

And then I was home.

Not home as in the building that had my name on the deed or the space where I laid my head each night. But truly home.

With her.

"Hey, baby," I cooed when her angelic face appeared on my computer screen.

She didn't immediately reply, as she was too busy playing with a set of plastic farm animals. I'd given them to her for her third birthday, but she'd only recently rediscovered them at the bottom of her toybox.

"Kaitlyn," I called at the same time her mother urged her to focus on the screen.

Her head popped up, brown curls bouncing wildly. "Oh, hey, Daddy."

My heart stopped at those two syllables. It didn't matter how many times I'd heard it. Each and every time she uttered the word *daddy*, it temporarily illuminated the black hole inside me.

"Hey, pretty girl. How was your week?"

Her round face hardened, and her brown eyes narrowed as though she were a surly teenager rather than my five-year-old princess. Leaning forward on her elbows, she put her button nose only a few inches from the camera. "This was the worst week ever!"

"Uh, oh," I mumbled, leaning back in my office chair. My girl loved to talk, and if this had been the worst week ever, I needed to go ahead and make myself comfortable.

"I hate school. Hate. It."

"Why?" I chuckled at her fury.

"First, they told us Mrs. Rowell isn't coming back to school. She had that stinky, rotten baby and forgot all about us."

"Hey," I scolded. "That's not nice."

She still hadn't moved away from the camera, so I couldn't see her face as much as up her nose. "Babies poop their pants, Dad! All of us in class use the potty like big kids. But nooooooo, Mrs. Rowell wants to stay home with that, that"—she paused for a half second before finishing with what had clearly become the foulest of all four-letter words—"*baby*."

Slapping on a face full of outrage, I whispered, "How dare she?"

"And then they made Mr. Ward our teacher!"

Now, I had no clue who Mr. Ward was, but the way her voice hit a pitch that was usually only audible to dogs, I knew it had to be bad. Who knew preschool could be so tumultuous?

"Yikes. Is he awful?"

"He's the worst!" she cried, finally leaning back in her chair so I could fully see her again. Her shoulders rounded forward in defeat. "I hate him. I don't even want to go to school anymore. But Mom said if I stop going now, I'll never be able to be a chicken nugget maker at McDonalds when I get older."

Ah, yes. My girl had dreams—big ones. For your average five-year-old, just working at McDonalds, where ice cream was on tap and the French fries were always hot, would have been the peak of success. However, my baby's eyes were set on the coveted and prestigious position of head chicken nugget maker. Hopefully when the time came, I could talk her into a slightly more lucrative career path, but until then, I just appreciated that she had goals.

"Oh, well, your mom has a point there, babe. School first."

She let out an exaggerated groan. "It's not fair. I just want Mrs. Rowell back."

My chest got tight as she pouted. Yes, I was fully aware that it was ridiculous, but I was nothing if not a sucker. "It's okay, baby. Mr. Ward might grow on you. Give him a chance."

Based on the purse of her lips, she was not convinced, but luckily for me, goldfish and Kaitlyn had the same attention span.

"Did I show you Fiona Iona yet?" She lifted a plastic tiger sporting a doll's tutu around its midsection toward the camera.

I smiled, my chest so full of love it physically ached. "She's beautiful," I whispered, my gaze locked on my little girl.

"She's a ballerina. Mom said she's going to get me some glue and pink glitter so we can make her shoes."

"Oh, wow, that sounds...messy."

"I don't think the glitter will work though, because she needs to be able to take them off when she goes to work."

"Ah, yes. Very wise. Obviously, she's a career tiger."

"Hang on. Let me show you her sister."

I didn't care about *Fiona Iona,* much less any of her siblings, but if Kaitlyn wanted to talk, you could be damn sure I was listening.

For the next fifteen minutes, I watched as she did a parade of her toys. She told me their names, nicknames, nicknames for their nicknames, and lastly, what she actually called them. I laughed as they became more and more ludicrous. My personal favorite was her gray stuffed horse. His name was Salty. His nickname was Pepper. His nickname for his nickname was Peppy. And what she called him? Well obviously, Woogity Boogity Salty Lillian Bogie West. At least she had given him our last name.

When her mother finally told her it was time for her to go, my heart wrenched. I had known it was coming. It was getting late and she had to get to school, but I hated saying goodbye. I'd see her again, but a week was a long time to wait. If I was lucky, I'd be able to squeeze in a few quick chats over the weekend. Though nothing compared to our Wednesday mornings together.

"I love you, Daddy!" She blew a dozen kisses my way.

I caught each and every one, pretending to press them all over my face. "I love you too, baby girl. Have a good day at school."

"Byeeeeee!" she sang as her face got really close to the camera again.

And then the screen went dark.

Just like the rest of my day.

Wednesdays. The best and the worst of it. Such was the definition of my life.

I stared at the computer for a few minutes, lost on how to move on with the rest of my day. But like clockwork, my phone started ringing all over again. That was my sign. My distraction for the next eight hours.

Recruiting in the civil sector was time consuming, tedious, and as close to being cupid as a mortal could get—professionally speaking of course. After almost a decade, I was damn good at my job. I'd never been the stereotypical fast-talking recruiter who wooed both companies and candidates by verbally painting a utopia of perfect matches. I took a slightly less orthodox—and a lot more realistic—approach.

Trust me, I liked a paycheck just as much as the next guy, and commissions were fantastic when I managed to place candidates in roles. But the people I worked with weren't the average twenty-three-year-old kid, fresh out of college, where the hardest part of their lives had been whether to visit Mommy's beach house or Daddy's yacht for spring break.

The men and women I worked with were combat veterans who had risked their lives to defend our country. They were usually transitioning into civilian life later in life after what had surely felt like ten careers in uniform. It was a scary transition; one I knew well. Those vets deserved more than to be guided into careers fast and carelessly. It was the companies who were paying recruiters. Qualified bodies in jobs were the goal. But fuck me, nothing drove me crazier than the lazy, half-ass work required to place a retired Sergeant Major in a managerial role he was going to find monotonous and mind numbing within the first three months.

That's where I came in.

I was no salesman, but I could research the fuck out of a candidate. Ya know, real wild, revolutionary shit like taking ten minutes to check their social media, reaching out to their previous chain of command, or hell, I don't know, maybe one phone call, soldier to soldier, that didn't have them reciting me their résumé. It wasn't rocket science, but the perks of working from home for six figures, a 401(k), five weeks of paid vacation, and full health benefits were enough for me to be cool with letting my boss assume it was.

Best of all, I got to escape my life for a solid eight hours. Focusing all my attention outward on someone else rather than the clusterfuck permanently rolling inside me.

It felt like part of my penitence. Helping soldiers and their families instead of failing them as I'd done all those years ago. I couldn't change the past. I'd been through enough therapy to have accepted that. But damn, every time I closed my eyes, I wished I could.

Well, at least until five o'clock, when everything went to hell.

Quitting time should have been celebrated. Even for me, when the only difference between on the clock and off the clock was relocating from my home office to my home couch.

However, on Wednesdays, I stayed at my computer as long as humanly possible, procrastinating on the inevitable and driving myself mad.

The clock never stopped. That damn minute display mocked me with each unyielding tick.

It was less than a mile from my house, though it might as well have been a fifty-mile death march for the way my heart pounded when it was time to leave.

Outside of my front door, my brain became hyper aware, a world of stimuli ricocheting inside my head.

The sun was too bright even on the cloudiest of days.

The cars passing sounded more like they were landing at an airport.

The metallic taste of blood flooded my mouth. It wouldn't be until later that I would figure out if it was because I had chewed a hole in my cheek or if it was merely memories that wouldn't let go.

I damn near hyperventilated walking down my driveway.

My lungs seized as I turned onto the sidewalk.

Lightheaded, vomit clawing at the back of my throat, ears ringing, I had to voluntarily constrict every single muscle to compel my legs to carry me away.

Those few blocks never got easier.

Every single Wednesday, I died inside as I made that trek.

And yet somehow, the trip home was always worse.

Alone.

Always alone.

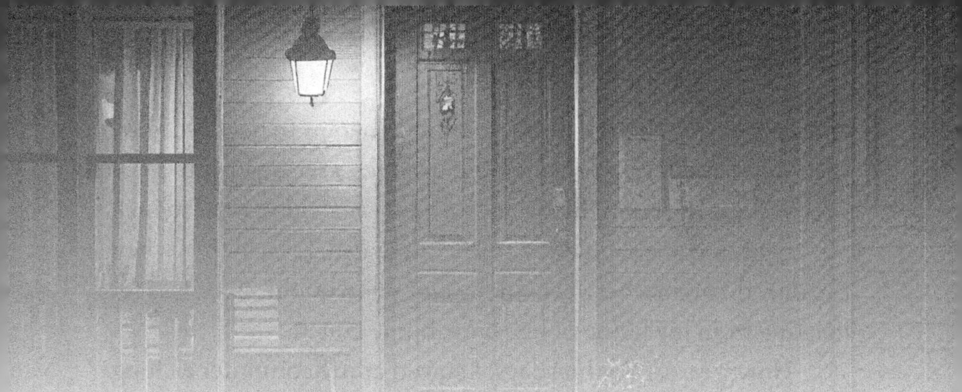

CHAPTER TWO

Gwen

"MOOOOOM!" DAPHNE EXCLAIMED, TURNING IN THE booth behind us, her blond hair whipping the shared backrest.

Her mother was sitting beside me, but as I saw my son holding her at straw-point with a spitball locked and loaded at the tip, I knew I was the mom she needed.

"Nathan Bryce Weaver, one blow and you will be knitting her a scarf tonight."

It was an odd threat to give an eight-year-old boy, but I'd learned that the typical punishments of taking away toys, video games, or screen time just didn't work for us. Mainly because my son didn't give a damn about any of the aforementioned pastimes.

Nate was a wild beast. He spent his days outside, attempting to cut down trees with butter knives, barefoot and shirtless, running beside the golf carts in our neighborhood (much to our HOA's dismay), or riding his bike off ramps he'd made using scraps of wood he'd collected from God only knew where.

I'd tried taking away his bike once. It backfired monumentally. Less than an hour later, I'd found him bouncing off the side of my house, teaching himself parkour. (Coincidentally, this was something I did not realize was actually a thing outside of an episode of *The Office*.) I was still paying the price for that mistake. Quite literally everything in my house had been jumped on, jumped off, or flipped over.

But what was I supposed to do? There was nothing else I could take away from him when he got into trouble besides fresh air, exercise, or, say...his legs. I had to get creative. A little forced mother-son bonding time did the trick.

When he'd dented my fridge rebounding off it, we'd spent an entire afternoon recreating a Bob Ross painting together. Nate was bored out of his mind, but you better believe he steered clear of anything breakable after that. So far, we'd scrapbooked pictures from the first year of his life, completed a one-thousand-piece puzzle, and we were only one up-past-his-bedtime away from finishing a gorgeous floral diamond art.

Truth be told, I loved when he got into trouble.

Something he knew all too well—hence the way his brown eyes flashed wide as he lowered the weaponized straw. "Jeez, Mom. I wasn't really going to do it."

His best friend and partner in crime elbowed him in the side. "Dude, you gotta be sneakier."

"Pike, stay out of it," Dylan scolded. Her back was to her son. Therefore, she never saw his eye roll. "Anyway," she said, tossing her napkin on top of a barely touched patty melt that, by the looks of the pooling grease, had left a lot to be desired. "Ohhh-kay, before a riot breaks out back there. Any chance you're going to tell us why you dragged us here? I know it wasn't for the food. Spill it. What's the big secret?"

Angela giggled musically beside me, her wilted chef's salad equally as untouched.

Dylan's eyes—which were Caribbean blue this week thanks to the miracle of colored contacts—narrowed. Leaning forward on her colorfully tattooed forearms, she hissed, "You hussy, you already know?"

"Of course I do." Little Miss Prim and Proper dabbed the

corner of her lips with a cheap paper napkin. True to its marketing, the red lip stain didn't budge. "I actually send texts that contain more than just links to TikToks. It's called a conversation."

Dylan scoffed. "Oh, yes, the daily updates on your period and what you're substituting for bread this week is far more riveting."

How these two had been friends since kindergarten, I would never understand. There was a story about them becoming besties after someone had pushed someone off a slide, but if I'd learned anything by becoming best friends with a set of lifelong best friends, it was that I usually "had to have been there" to understand the hilarity of their youthful antics.

They still tried to fill me in every chance they got. I'd seen plenty of photos of them growing up. Angela had looked exactly like a Barbie brought to life, clutching her pearls after she was crowned homecoming queen. Meanwhile, Dylan had home-pierced her nose, daith, and belly button all by the time she was sixteen.

They'd adopted me about eight years earlier, after we'd met at a birthing class. Nate, Pike, and Daphne had all been born over the span of four weeks. After that, the three of us bonded over the ups, downs, and flat-out disgusting perils of motherhood. Sitting on your couch, trying to figure out how to make a fussy baby fart, was infinitely better when you had company cheering you on. We were vastly different people though.

Angela was a Stepford Wife, reserved and proper.

Dylan was a jaded single mom, sarcastic and protective.

And I was… God, what was I? Anxious. Bitter. Broken. Those had all been more recent developments. At one point, I'd been witty and bold. I think? It was hard to remember anymore.

Regardless, I was trying to get back to that woman. Stepping out on my own after ten years of marriage had been terrifying. My marriage had fallen apart long before I'd actually left, but checking out emotionally was something completely different than braving a world I'd been manipulated into believing I couldn't make it in alone.

Not anymore. It was time for me to find strength where fear had once inhabited. To rediscover who I was when I wasn't forced into existing in a constant state of fight or flight. The best part was that I got to reinvent myself on my own terms, with my own goals, and I didn't have to ask permission from anyone.

Which led me right back to why I was sitting in a run-down diner with wobbly tables and peeling wallpaper, with my two best friends, our three kids, six plates of inedible food spread between two booths, and one dream to find myself again.

Smiling, I announced, "Welcome to The Rosewood Café. I'm Gwendolyn Weaver: owner, operator, and head chef."

Dylan curled her lip. "First of all, you are not using"—she lowered her voice so the kids couldn't hear her before finishing her sentence—"that *asshole's* last name anymore. Pierce is a perfectly good maiden name, and if you are against going back to that, I will wife you up myself just to get rid of Weaver. Secondly, I'm sorry. Did you say *owner*?"

Out of the corner of my eye, I caught Angela flashing her a scolding expression, which I'd learned translated to: *Be nice. Gwen is clearly on the verge of a midlife crisis slash mental breakdown.*

She was correct on both counts, but when starting over at forty-one, I assumed that was par for the course. I'd made that confirmation pretty clear when I'd chopped off eight inches of my hair, added blonde highlights to my natural mahogany, and pierced my nose with a tiny silver stud. (And no, I didn't let Dylan do it at home. Despite her begging.)

After all of that, a restaurant shouldn't be *that* shocking.

Dylan silently replied to Angela in yet another expression I was familiar with. This one read: *Are you going to handle this? Or am I?*

Neither of them needed to *handle* anything. I was perfectly capable of digging my own grave, lying in it for an extended period of time while brainwashing myself that it was a normal and brilliant phase in life, only to finally wake up, realize I'd gotten in way over my head, and then be forced to claw my way out fueled by nothing but regrets and tears. It was something of a pattern in my life, and I was nothing if not consistent.

Twisting the clear plastic cup with a red Coca-Cola logo rubbing off the front, I made a mental note to trash them immediately before confirming, "I did say owner."

"Of this restaurant?" Dylan lifted a single finger in the air. "Nay, this *hellhole*?"

"Yep, and I don't want to hear shit about it."

"I mean, *shit* is quite literally *all* I can say about it," she shot back.

I glared at her, but Angela quickly waded in, her freshly manicured nails patting me on the thigh under the table. "Ohhhhh-kay, let's take it down a notch. Maybe we should allow Gwen a few minutes to explain."

When I'd sent Angela a text telling her I'd bought a restaurant, she'd been stoked. Which was exactly why I'd texted her and not Dylan. Sure, I'd glossed over the fact that it was a diner still stuck in the nineties, complete with greasy linoleum and tattered booths. But I could see the promise hidden in those four walls. Currently known as The Grille, the soon-to-be Rosewood Café had been around since I was a kid. Surely that had to mean it at least had the potential to be successful. Maybe The Rosewood was having a midlife crisis too. Life didn't end because you had saggy boobs or booths. A little facelift and new accessories and she could look and feel fabulous again too.

Honestly, Old Rose and I were the perfect fit for each other. I'd fix her up physically, and she'd help me find my place in the world again. Win-win.

What else could my friends possibly want me to explain? "I bought a restaurant. I'm excited. Renovations start this weekend.

Ribbon cutting in four-to-six weeks. You're both invited. There. Explained."

"Great. Ribbon cutting. Awesome," Dylan deadpanned. "Any chance you want to touch on the part where you've never shown even the slightest interest in owning a restaurant before today?"

I arched a challenging eyebrow. "That is completely untrue. I managed three restaurants, and cooked at two before I met Jeff. And then remember when Nate first started preschool and I toyed with the idea of a catering business?"

"Right." She rolled her eyes. "But Jeff hated the idea of you working because then he couldn't lord it over you that he made all the money and thus had the right to control your every move."

It was my turn to speak with my eyes. I flashed them wide to yell, *Would you shut up! The kids can hear you.*

It could be said that neither of my friends was Jeff's biggest fan, but Dylan lacked the ability to bite her tongue. She never missed an opportunity to bash him. Both to his face and behind his back. A solid ninety-nine percent of the time, he deserved it. But I wouldn't stand for it to be done in front of my son.

Co-parenting with a narcissist was hard enough. I couldn't control what Jeff said about me on his weekends with Nate, but I'd vowed I would never sink to his level. Not just because his level was so low it could scrape the floor of the ocean, but rather because Nate was the only one who would suffer from that kind of toxicity. Jeff would always be his father, and I would always be his mother. We didn't work as husband and wife, but there was nothing I wouldn't do to make sure my son never felt the blowback of that failure.

Dylan immediately lifted her hands in surrender. "Sorry. Habit."

I sighed. "There's a lot of stuff I haven't shown interest in over the last decade. Myself being at the very top of that list."

Her eyes got soft with understanding, and Angela scooted closer to my side.

"But I've got to start somewhere. I know this place looks bad now, but I remember when The Grille had the best burgers and cheese fries in all of Belton. I mean, it wasn't difficult. There were, like, four restaurants here back then. But this was *the* place to be. There was a line out the door practically every day. And then…" I shrugged. "Life happened. For me *and* this place. Short of building a time machine, there's not much I can do about the me part of that equation, but I think it would be really therapeutic to prove to myself that it's possible to rebuild, reinvent, and come back better than ever."

Dylan blew out a ragged breath. "I hear you. I really do. But buying a restaurant seems like a big step. What if we just go on a shopping spree to redecorate your living room instead?"

"Well, that would be tough considering I just spent my life savings on what you seem to think is a dump."

She flinched. "Shit. I'm sorry."

Angela, who might as well have been the personification of rainbows and kittens, chimed in. "It's not a dump. It just needs a little TLC." She folded her hands over mine. "And you're not a dump, either."

"Thank you," I whispered. "I don't remember saying I was, but I do appreciate the sentiment."

"So it's done, then?" Dylan asked. "Papers all signed? Money and keys exchanged? No need to spend weeks convincing you that this is a fantastically horrible idea?"

"Yep. All done. The Grille closes on Friday, and then I have a demo crew coming in on Saturday to help me with the heavy lifting. I'm trying to save some cash by doing a lot of the easier renovations on my own, but I'm a one-woman show. So we'll see how that goes."

"Okay, then." Dylan leaned back in her seat. "No use harping on a done deal. Give me all the deets." She poked at her soggy bread. "Please tell me you're firing the chef."

I grinned. "Yep. All new kitchen staff. I'm aiming for an upscale café. Farm to table with everything fresh and locally sourced. A menu that changes quarterly, highlighting whatever produce is in season, and weekly specials that feature homestyle comfort foods. I want The Rosewood Café to appeal to every age and demographic, from the trendy twenty-somethings to mom and pop's Sunday supper."

"That's...a lot," Angela said, flashing me a tight smile.

"I know, but it will keep me busy. What's the old saying about idle—"

"Mooooom," Daphne interrupted.

My gaze sliced straight to my son.

Still holding the smoking gun—or in this case the straw—next to his mouth, he shouted, "I didn't mean to!"

Yes. *Shouted.*

At me.

In the middle of a restaurant.

I took a brief second to ponder if it would be more difficult to teach him to knit or crochet.

Narrowing my eyes, I whispered, "Did you just yell at me?"

"No! I mean...yes. Kinda. But it's Pike's fault. He made me laugh while I had the straw in my mouth! It just flew out and it didn't even hit her!"

Pike defended himself in an equally loud tone, and Daphne joined to referee the nuh-uh, ya-huh brawl.

Through the chaos, I heard the rumble of a deep baritone. The hairs on the back of my neck instantly stood on end.

"Shit," the man said, a loud clatter following the curse.

I turned in time to see a mammoth of a man lurch to his feet, water soaking his stomach and his lap.

Stunned, I stared at him. It was like that scene from *The*

Terminator when Arnold was in scan mode, searching his database for answers of what he was seeing.

After a few attempts, my frazzled brain identified him as none other than Truett fucking West.

It had been years since I'd seen him. The last time our paths had crossed, he'd been passed out drunk on the front lawn of a frat party. But he was a hard man to forget.

He was gorgeous. No denying that, but not in the traditional clean-cut, tailored-suit sense. He was more like the GQ version of a convict.

His dark-brown hair was the same military cut he'd been sporting since his high school JROTC days. Slightly longer on top now, but it was styled with a skilled hand. A thick beard peppered with the slightest bit of gray masked his face, but it was the tattoos covering both of his arms that truly gave him away. Judging by the muscles carved beneath the fabric of his shirt, time had been good to Truett.

His cold, distant brown eyes collided with mine, and while there was definitely a spark of recognition, his handsome face remained otherwise blank.

I sucked in a sharp breath as a chill over two decades old pebbled my skin. That was the Truett West effect. Only this time, it no longer held me captive.

The air seemed to thicken as a rush of emotions, long dormant, surged within me. Disdain. Anger. Bitterness. The laundry list could go on for a mile, but as I visually added up the one-plus-one of the situation where my son's spitball was responsible for the overturned glass and water dripping off his table, I couldn't very well lead with any of those. My emotional grid went with my old friend Indifference instead.

I grabbed the stack of extra napkins off our table and walked them over. As I stopped in front of him, it struck me how tall he was. I wasn't a short woman by any means, but he towered over me. His broad shoulders made him seem larger than the six foot three I knew him to be.

Extending the napkins his way, I issued a monotone, "Sorry about that."

He hummed an acknowledgement as he took the napkins and spread them across the table. His club sandwich swam in a pool of water, but given how bad the rest of the food had been, I assumed Nate had done him a favor.

I awkwardly stood there, waiting to do the whole, "Hi, how are you?" bit that was required when you ran into someone from your past. But not surprisingly, Truett said nothing.

Not as he flagged down the waitress for more napkins.

Not as he dried the bench seat.

Not even as he sat down, head straight, eyes forward, as if I didn't exist at all.

I blinked, waiting for him to say something. A simple hi or a lecture on disciplining my son would have been okay. Hell, even a "fuck off" would have worked.

He said nothing. I'm not sure why I was surprised. I'd spent over a year playing one-sided charades with that man. Silence was his preferred method of communication. Clearly *that* had not changed.

"Right," I mumbled. Rapping my knuckles on the table, I snipped, "Good talk as always." I walked away from Truett West no worse for the wear but pissed off all the same.

Nate, Pike, and Daphne were still arguing while Angela and Dylan tried to keep the peace. For a brief second, I considered allowing Nate to fling a few more spitballs in Truett's direction, but sometimes being a mom and setting a good example was seriously overrated.

I snapped my fingers before pointing at my son. "You." That one syllable was all I had to say to freeze him in his tracks. His mouth clamped shut and his face screwed tight, correctly reading the trouble he was about to be in. "We're leaving."

"It was an accident!" he argued.

But after the world's most infuriating and anticlimactic run-in with Truett, I was all out of patience. "Not another word, Nate, or you'll be helping me tie-dye beach towels too."

"Ugh," he groaned.

Grabbing my purse, I found our waitress pouring water for a table near the door and headed her way. Which just so happened to be right past Truett's table. This time, *I* pretended that *he* didn't exist. Because truth be told, he didn't exist anymore. At least, not the man I'd known.

"Excuse me." I paused, unsure what to call her. She was older, at least sixty, though she still looked amazing. Her gray hair was thick, pulled back into a bun, and her makeup was fresh and modern. When she'd introduced herself as *Cooter* despite her name tag reading Lucille, it made the conversation awkward really quick. Unwilling to call her—or anyone else for that matter—*Cooter,* I stuck with something a little more appropriate. "Ma'am. Would it be possible for me to pay our check now please?"

She grinned. "Sorry. No can do. Mr. Branning told us that if you ever came in, your food was on the house. Seems he made a pretty penny when he finally got you to take this train wreck off his hands."

I twisted my lips. "How…*kind* of him. But I still need to pay for my friends."

"Nope. I'm under direct orders from the boss. And I'm nothing if not an honest, loyal, hardworking, and very soon-to-be jobless employee." She arched an eyebrow. "You wouldn't happen to be hiring, would ya?"

"Oh, um, maybe? But I won't be reopening for at least a month or so."

"That's perfect! My daughter has been making me crazy to

come out and stay with her for a few weeks. I can't stand her husband, always chewing with his mouth open and drinking beer while tinkering with his motorbikes in the garage. But a vacation never hurt anyone. Trust me, you won't find a better waitress in Belton." Laughing, she waved a half empty water pitcher around the restaurant. "Nobody knows this place like I do, and you might be thinking that's not a good thing, but I didn't make the rules or the menu here. It's only my job to obey them and serve with a smile." She lowered her voice and leaned in close like she was about to tell me a secret.

Never one to turn down juicy gossip, I leaned in too.

"I've been here a long time," she said quietly. "I've had a front-row seat to a lot of mistakes Mr. Branning made through the years." She hooked her thumb over her shoulder toward the kitchen. "Like, say, hiring his delinquent son, who doesn't have a lick of experience making a PB and J much less managing a grill, as his head kitchen manager."

I hummed. "That would explain a lot."

"You need somebody on your team with experience. The good *and* the bad kind." Holding my gaze, she nodded at least a dozen times to really drive home her point.

She wasn't wrong. God knew I'd made my fair share of mistakes in life. Maybe having someone at my back who knew what *not* to do would save me a lot of growing pains in the figuring out what-*to*-do department.

From my purse, I pulled out a scrap of paper, a pen, and forty dollars. "Well, I'm assuming Mr. Branning won't be covering your tip, so this is for you. Give me your number and I'll call you tomorrow to see if we can work something out for when you get back from your vacation."

Her blue eyes twinkled as she snatched my offerings. Leaning on an empty table, she jotted down her information.

As I waited, I glanced back to see if Dylan and Angela had managed to calm the kids. They were all three sitting quietly in the booth, crossed arms and pouty faces. It seemed Nate wasn't going to be the only one in trouble when they got home.

I told myself not to do it.

My brain screamed for me to let it go and ignore him the way he had always done me.

But as if my eyes had a mind of their own, they flicked to Truett.

I could only see his profile, but the round of his strong shoulders as he hunched over the table revealed his anguish with a stark clarity. God, it was surreal to see him again. The city of Belton wasn't big by any stretch, and when our paths hadn't crossed over the years, I'd figured he'd long since moved away.

But there he sat.

No ring on his finger.

No family surrounding him with smiles and laughter.

Not even a friend sharing a meal.

Alone.

An odd pang of guilt hit me as I watched him peeling off the top piece of bread on each half of his sandwich, trying to salvage his sopping-wet meal.

I let out an audible groan, hating him that much more for making me feel anything other than disdain.

"Here ya go," Coot—um, *Lucille*—said, reclaiming my attention.

I took the receipt from her hand and tucked it into my purse. "Hey, can you do me a favor?"

"Anything, *Boss*?" She flashed me a wicked grin.

"Can you put that man's dinner on my tab too? And...maybe bring him a fresh sandwich?"

Curling her lip, she leaned around me and pointed at Truett. "That man?"

"Yeah. I feel awful that my son ruined his dinner."

She barked a laugh. "Oh, honey. That's not his dinner. And

trust me when I tell you that's no *man* over there, either. That right there is the hot gargoyle who takes up residence in that booth every Wednesday from six to seven p.m. He doesn't even eat the dang sandwich."

"What?" I breathed, swinging my gaze back to Truett. He'd placed the salvaged half of the sandwich on a dry napkin alongside two strips of bacon. "So, why does he order it, then?"

She shrugged. "I don't know. He's not a talker. He walks up here, waits for that specific booth, then I bring him out a club sandwich, no mayo, bacon on the side, and a water. He stays for a while, leaves cash on the table, and then disappears."

"He walks?"

"Yep. He only lives a few blocks up. Mr. Branning followed him home one night. Thought he was a creep or something, but he's harmless."

I'd been wrong about him leaving Belton, but the fact that he still lived in his mom's old house was beyond surprising. I'd figured he would have burned that place to the ground sooner than he'd make it his forever home.

Since he was so close, it made sense that he often came by for dinner. Except… "Are you sure he doesn't eat any of it?"

"Not a single bite. Mr. Branning once told me to quit wasting food and just put his sandwich in the cooler so he could resell it to him the following week. I wasn't about to do that to the guy. He's an odd duck but a good tipper." She nudged me with her elbow. "And besides, scamming your most loyal customers would fall under one of those bad kind of mistakes I could help you avoid after you hire me."

On instinct, I smiled, but with a pit forming in my stomach, I couldn't tear my eyes—or thoughts—off Truett.

I had so many questions, but if I'd learned anything, it was that I'd never get the answers from him.

After drawing in a deep breath, I held it for a long second, allowing the pain of the past and present to filter through my body.

And then I let it go. All of it.

My breath.

My curiosity.

My guilt.

Hell, I even managed to temporarily pack down my bitterness.

"Enough," I whispered to myself before flashing the waitress a grin. "Thanks for everything. I'll be in touch soon."

"I can't wait," she chirped.

Focusing on what truly mattered in my life, I walked back to my table and took my son's hand. Mad as I was, a warmth filled my chest as Nate's hand folded around mine.

Truett didn't fit into that equation, and I had every intention of keeping it that way.

It wasn't like I had time for yet another obstacle anyway. I still needed to gut a restaurant, remodel it from the ground up, tame my wild beast of a child, try not to have a texting brawl with my ex-husband, and then follow through on the promise I'd made to myself as a teenager to always live life to the fullest.

Though, in my experience, the last one might have been the hardest part of all.

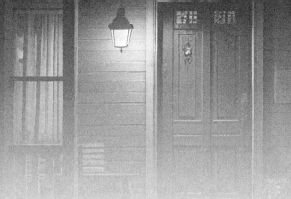

CHAPTER THREE

TRUETT

"THAT'S A FIFTY-DOLLAR BILL," I SAID, SLEEP STILL THICK in my voice. Holding my phone up in front of me to keep it in view, I poured a cup of coffee.

"What about this one?" the seeing-impaired gentleman on the other end of the app asked, holding up more cash in front of his camera.

"That's a five and the two on the counter are ones," I replied, padding down the hall to my office.

"Perfect." He set the money down. "Can I ask you one last thing?"

I sank down into my rolling chair and clicked the mouse to open my computer. My baby was already there waiting on me, her smiling face filling the screen. I lifted a finger for her to hold on a minute and then turned my attention back to my phone. "That's what I'm here for, sir."

His voice smiled. "And I appreciate that. You have no idea how nice it is to have volunteers like you."

I hated the praise. Loathed it. I wasn't a hero for helping people. If anything, it was a debt I owed society. One of many I'd never be able to repay.

"What was your other question?" I asked to refocus him—and myself.

A bag of coffee filled the screen on my phone. "Is this decaf? I won't be able to function by noon if I don't get some caffeine in me."

Boy, did I relate to that. I was going to need an entire pot to get through my day.

It was Wednesday again. My favorite dreaded day of the week. The last seven days had been… Oh, who was I kidding? It was always the same. Wake up. Eat. Work. Wait for Wednesday. Sleep. Wash, rinse, repeat. But this week, I had the near-impossible task of avoiding all thoughts of Gwen added to my list.

Nothing had ever been more exhausting.

"That is regular coffee, sir. You should be good," I answered.

"Great. Thanks again for your time."

"No problem. Have a good one." I ended the call and immediately clicked back to Kaitlyn. "Good morning, my love."

"Daddy, look!" She lifted a dead weed that could only barely be classified as a flower.

"Wow. That's gorgeous."

She giggled. "Mommy took me to the park yesterday and there were a bunch of white flowers but only *one* pink one. And *I* got it!"

I smiled, trying to fight back my disappointment. Damn. I wanted to take her to the park. When she had been younger, we had spent every Saturday morning there. Kaitlyn loved the swings. Though I was more partial to the slides. She was scared of how tall they were, so she would crawl into my lap and we'd go down together, laughing in harmony.

I longed for those days. Back when we had shared a roof and she was in the room next door, where I could tell her bedtime stories every night.

I should have been the one with her at the park that day.

I should have been there *every* day.

Instead, I whispered a sad, "That's great, baby. I'm glad Mommy took you."

Staring at her prize, she twirled the bent stem between her

fingers. "Do you think if I planted this in the backyard it would grow into a *huge* pink flower?"

"No." I chuckled. "Even if it would, Jazzy would dig it up."

She let out an adorable sigh. "Ugh, Jazzy would *totally* dig it up. Oh! Oh! Guess what else we saw at the park?" She waited exactly zero seconds before blurting out, "A kitten! It was soooo widdle and cutie cute, cute, cute. It was hiding in the bushes and meowed at me and everything."

"Oh, yeah? Did you meow back?"

She laughed loudly and the camera shook as she put her elbows on the table. Closing her eyes, she let out a sound that was more of a chirp. "Meow. Meow. Meow." Her eyes popped open wide, all bright and sparkling, filled with untamed curiosity. "But then the mommy cat was rude and kept grr'ing at me like this." She blew a dramatic hiss through her teeth. "So I couldn't pet it."

"That was probably wise. Can't have you bringing home rabies."

She looked off screen and shouted, "What? Why?"

Her mother's muffled voice came through my speaker. "Come on. Tell Daddy bye. We need to go. I have to be at work early today and I still have to stop and get gas."

My stomach sank. God, I hated when our chats were cut short. I looked forward to time with her all damn week; a few minutes just wasn't enough.

One could say her mother and I didn't have the best relationship, but immeasurable amounts of love had once existed between us. It would have been easy for me to be mad about her stealing Kaitlyn away early. But I'd been raised by a single mother. I knew firsthand that solo parenting could be a difficult balancing act. Especially since I couldn't be there to help.

I think that was always the hardest part. Every day, I wished like hell things could be different. Maybe if I was a better man. Maybe if I'd chosen a different profession. A different city. A different, well, any-fucking-thing and maybe I would be hugging her goodbye before school rather than saying it to a damn screen.

I silently chastised myself. Coulda, shoulda, woulda never actually changed anything. Yet night after night, I went to sleep hoping it would.

My smile was skillfully locked in place as my daughter looked back at the camera and said, "I gotta go, Daddy. I love you lots and lots." Using both hands, she blew kisses.

I caught every single one before replying, "I love you too, sweetheart. More than you'll ever know."

"Byyyyyyeeeee." She waved, and then she was gone all over again.

I didn't move for several minutes. The day was all downhill from there and I was nowhere near ready to tackle any of it. For a while, I seriously debated crawling back into bed. Then I decided against it when I realized that it would only give me time to think—the most dangerous pastime of all.

Besides, I couldn't risk my thoughts inevitably drifting to Gwen.

Gwen.

Fucking Gwen of all people.

I'd been so rattled after seeing her I couldn't focus. Even after she'd left, my mind had been a hurricane of empty thoughts. What the hell had she been doing at The Grille in the first place? I'd spent an exorbitant amount of time and money there over the years and had never once run into her. Something I was profoundly and overwhelmingly grateful for.

But there she was.

Time changed people. A fact I knew better than most. It was still surprising how different she looked. Sure, she was beautiful. I was crazy, not blind. But I couldn't fathom why she'd cut her hair and added those bits of blond. They suited her nicely, but back in the day, we couldn't go anywhere without women stopping her to gush over her long chestnut waves. And that nose ring? What the hell was that about? The woman I'd met in high school wasn't edgy in any shape or fashion. I could still feel the sting of the tongue lashing she'd given me when I'd gotten my first tattoo.

I hadn't recognized the women she was with at the restaurant or how many of the three kids were hers, but there was no denying that little boy with the dark hair. He looked so much like her it had rendered me speechless.

Not that I had anything to say.

When it came to Gwen, the chasms of the past were far wider than the English language could ever bridge. Hell, even trying would have been downright disrespectful.

Suddenly, work and all the distractions that came with it sounded more enticing than ever.

Without another thought, I got busy.

Phone calls.

Virtual meetings.

Pretending I cared when a colleague called to bitch about our boss.

There was a turkey sandwich and a midday cup of coffee in there somewhere, but for the most part, it was a pretty standard day.

And then it was six o'clock.

My therapist had once told me that the hardest part about leaving my house was putting on my shoes, but that was a Mount Everest–sized load of bullshit.

The hardest part was spending every single second of the week dreading it.

And then coming home, knowing I had to do it all over again.

I was Sisyphus, and going to that diner every Wednesday was my rock to push up the hill.

Until suddenly my hill disappeared.

I could barely breathe as I stood under the tattered awning in front of The Grille and read the note taped to the door.

Dear Valued Customers,

Our family has been honored to serve you over the last three decades, but it is with a heavy heart that we must close our doors. Life has taken us in a different direction, but we will never forget the memories made at The Grille. Thank you for being a part of our story.

All our best,

The Branning Family

"No," I whispered, panic hitting me like a tidal wave.

My throat closed and my mind spiraled as I tried to make sense of what was clearly written out in black and white directly in front of me.

There must have been a mistake. I peered through the window and saw all the tables pushed into the corners with the chairs stacked on top. The lights were on. That had to mean something.

I pounded my fist against the glass door.

The Grille couldn't close.

The Grille could not fucking close.

Frantic, I tugged on the handle.

It was Wednesday at six o'clock. And the door was *locked.*

Lightheaded, I desperately shook the door, trying and failing to force it open. "No, no, no, no, no," I chanted. "You can't be closed. Come on, come on, come on."

Every muscle in my body strained as I considered ripping the whole damn door off the hinges.

It would probably set off an alarm.

The cops would show. More than likely arrest me.

But I'd be sitting in that booth when they did.

Worth it. So fucking worth it.

I backed up, prepared to put my foot through the glass—consequences be damned—when a pair of brown eyes suddenly saved me.

Again.

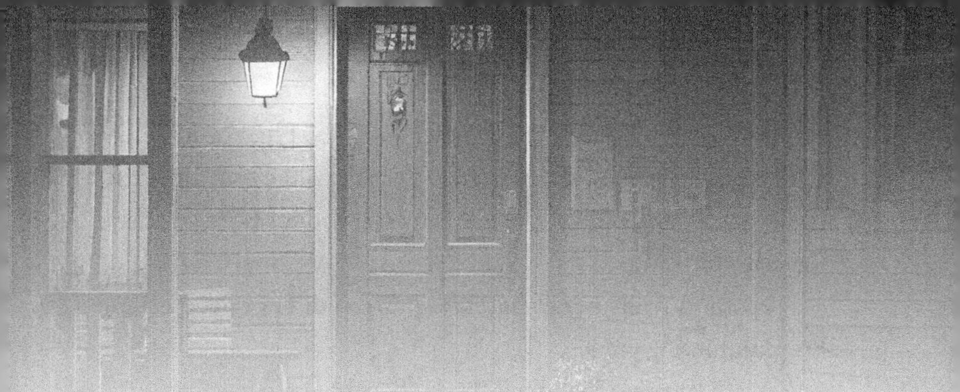

CHAPTER FOUR

Gwen

TYPE.

Delete.

Type.

Delete.

I squirmed in my chair, my damn bra suffocating me. When would I ever learn not to shop online? Nothing ever fit right. Mediums were either extra-smalls or extra-larges. But if I ordered an extra-large aiming for a medium, I'd end up with a Barbie dress. Meanwhile, if I went the other direction and purchased the extra-small, it would swallow me. It made absolutely no sense.

And forget about returning stuff! I mean, seriously, who had time for that? I had multiple packages of misfit clothing in the back of my car that just toured around town with me until the return windows closed. I made the best of it though. Some of my favorite summer dresses were supposed to be shirts.

That bra was a next-level torture device. Yet it was still the most comfortable part of my current situation. Sitting in the shoebox-sized office at the restaurant, I was composing the perfect gag-inducing text to my ex-husband. I hated asking that dickhead for help, but despite my best efforts, I had not yet unlocked the science to clone myself.

The demo crew I'd hired to help me gut the restaurant had

canceled on me not once, but twice. Luckily, I had been able to find another team on short notice. Unluckily, the only time they had available was on the same day my son had to stay after school for math tutoring.

Math tutoring my ex had said our son did not need despite his plummeting grades.

Math tutoring that my ex had refused to help pay for.

Math tutoring that my ex would no doubt allow Nate to skip if he had to be even mildly inconvenienced with picking him up.

So, once again, I had to get creative.

The thing with communicating with a narcissist is that, no matter what you're saying, you're always stupid. They, of course, are smarter. Truly, an expert in all fields from child rearing to classifying the color of the sky. It was wild. Even when they were wrong, they were still right, and the mental gymnastics and abuse used to make sure you understood that they were superior to you in every facet was utterly impressive—and totally fucked up.

It took years for me to see through Jeff's constant cycle of love bombing, manipulating, and gaslighting to recognize that I wasn't always the problem in our relationship. I wasn't stupid or naïve. I didn't enjoy drama. And his *yes* did not hold more weight than my *no*. But, after having been married to him for over a decade, I'd learned a few lessons in manipulating the manipulator.

Jeff loved to be the hero. His ability to save the day fed his ego and gave him something to lord over me should he ever need an ace up his sleeve to play against me.

At the current moment, I didn't give one single shit how many aces he had. We were divorced. The game was over. I had my own deck of cards now.

So there I was, typing my text:

Hey, Jeff. I may have bitten off more than I can chew with this restaurant.

It was total bullshit, but it would give him satisfaction to think I was struggling without him.

I know, I know. You were right.

I dry heaved just typing that.

Can you do me a huge favor and pick Nate up from tutoring tomorrow? If not, no worries. I can always ask Dylan.

A little competition with my best friend, who he hated with a passion, never hurt.

With my finger hovering over the begging emoji to really sell it, I jumped when a loud banging sounded at the front of the restaurant.

I grabbed the mace connected to my keys. Belton was about as low crime as a suburb got, but as a single woman who spent a lot of nights working alone, I was ready to protect myself if need be. My pulse spiked as I listened. The rattling and banging continued. I figured it was a diner who hadn't read the sign, and they would go away soon enough, but as I waited, the noises got louder.

Shit. Was I being robbed? I didn't even have a cash register yet. With my luck, it was a former customer of The Grille there for redemption after being given a life-threatening case of food poisoning.

Dammit. Why hadn't I prioritized the new security system?

Oh, right. The budget.

I inched toward the office doorway, my lungs burning as I held my breath. A million what-ifs ravaged my nervous system. And then suddenly, a familiar voice broke through the chaos.

"Come on, come on, come on," he chanted.

My shoulders sagged.

Of course.

Of.

Fucking.

Course.

Truett.

I'd lived an entire lifetime without running into him. Twice in a week only seemed fitting.

Frustrated beyond reason, I marched to the door. He had stopped trying to get inside, but unfortunately, it didn't appear as though he was leaving. Through the glass, his gaze collided into mine with the force of a freight train. His face was ashen, his eyes wide with a panic that shattered the barrier between us. I tried to steady my breathing and reject the tsunami of emotions crashing over me.

My instincts screamed for me to reach out and soothe whatever demon had overtaken him.

Experience, on the other hand, told me that attempting to help Truett West was the definition of insanity. Experience also begged the question of why I would even care to try.

With our eyes locked, I forced my feet to stay planted, my hands remaining firmly at my sides, my finger still poised on the mace. Despite every intention to remain detached, my heart pounded in my chest—no doubt echoing his own.

I hated that he still had that effect on me. More, I hated that I *allowed* him to have that effect on me. I placated myself with lies about it being human nature to have such a visceral reaction to another human in distress. Empathy was never a bad thing.

Unless it became toxic.

Absorbing the emotional grid of others came with a price.

A price I would never be able to afford when it came to Truett.

I couldn't do this. Not today. Not tomorrow. Not ever. Fuck my instincts, there was only one way to end it—cruel as it might have been.

"What the hell are you doing?" I snapped through the glass.

His reply was muffled. "Someone locked the door."

"Uh, yeah. Me."

His thick brows drew together. "What?"

I wasn't sure if he actually couldn't hear me or if he just

couldn't get it through his thick skull, so I unlocked the door and shoved it open with hopes of making this entire interaction as brief as possible. "The Grille is *closed*."

The crinkle of his forehead deepened. "Then what are you doing here?"

"Well, I was trying to work until you decided to scare the shit out of me."

His chin jerked to the side—confusion stacking on top of confusion. "You work at The Grille now?"

I did not know the man standing in front of me anymore, but I was relatively certain he hadn't lost his ability to read through the years. Stabbing a finger at the sign on the door, I repeated, "No, because The Grille is *closed*."

Glowering, he spoke slowly, enunciating every other word. "Then *what* are *you* doing *here?*"

I was almost impressed that he still had attitude left in him. However, it was aimed at me, so I rolled my eyes. "I bought the place. It will be closed for renovations for the next month or two, but keep an eye out for The Rosewood Café's grand opening. Now, if you'll excuse me, I need to get back to well…anything that is not standing here with you."

I started to close the door, but he caught it with his palm against the glass only inches from my head. The faint smell of his cologne assaulted me. In that moment, my olfactory senses unlocked the power of time travel, transporting me back to a day when that scent had meant safety, comfort…*happiness*.

Now, though, it felt like a knife to the chest. My stomach rolled as I fought the urge to punch him for being such an imposter. He had no right to still smell like Truett. This guy would never be man enough to fill those shoes.

"Back up," I demanded.

"A month or two?"

"I said back up!"

He didn't move. He stood there looming over me, his chest rising and falling with labored breaths. "I can't wait that long."

"Well, you don't exactly have a choice. Try that place on Oak Street or something."

"I can't go to Oak," he growled. Yes. *Growled.* Like he was some kind of bear I'd just run into in the woods.

I couldn't remember the survival skills on black bears versus grizzly bears off the top of my head, but I had a lot of experience with disrespectful men. "I don't give a shit where you go as long as it's out of my face." Using both hands, I yanked on the door, but he didn't allow it to budge.

"Wait," he begged.

"For what?" The fissures in my heart burned as I struggled to keep them closed. "What exactly am I waiting for now, Truett?"

He had the good sense to look sheepish, but I didn't let it slow my fury.

"Don't get me wrong," I said. "I'm really impressed that you finally figured out how to speak in full sentences. But you can fuck all the way off if you think I'm going to take even one more second of your bullshit. I did wait. I waited for *years.*" I changed my tactic, so rather than pulling on the door, I pushed it open wider.

His hand fell away, but he caught it with his foot. "Okay, okay. I'm sorry."

I'm sorry.

I'm sorry.

He could have pissed on my shoes and angered me less.

"Don't you dare utter those words to me," I seethed.

Absolute understanding slashed his face. "You're right. I just…" The bob of his Adam's apple was barely visible under his beard, but his desperation was palpable. Flicking his gaze off to the side, he dragged a shaky hand through the top of his hair. "I just need to come in and sit down for a few."

"What part of closed do you not understand?"

"I'm not asking you to be open. I'm asking you to let me come inside." His dark eyes came back to mine—the overwhelming intensity stealing my breath, but not my fire.

"You have to go," I stated.

"I won't bother you. I swear."

"It's not about you *bothering* me. This is weird, Truett. Really freaking weird, even for you."

It was a low blow, but what was I supposed to do? He was too close, and not because we were only inches apart, fighting for control of the same door. No, he was too close because Truett West was currently sharing the same timeline as me. He was the past and I was barely surviving the present without those two worlds colliding.

"Gwen, come on."

"*No.*"

His wild eyes shifted from side to side. "You won't even know I'm here. A few minutes and I'll be out of your hair."

"Sure, until next week." I cocked my head to the side. "Wednesdays. That's your thing, right? You come up here, don't eat a club sandwich, and then head back to that godforsaken house."

He sucked in a sharp breath. "How do you know that?"

"Because people talk. Especially when it's about creepy shit that makes them uncomfortable, just like this entire conversation right now."

He shook his head rapidly. "You don't understand."

"You're absolutely right. And I don't care to understand, either. I have a whole life to get back to, and quite honestly, I can't believe you, of all people, are standing here arguing with me about it. Riddle me this, True. When exactly did leaving me become a problem for you? Because you were damn near a professional not too long ago."

A myriad of emotions washed over his face, pain prominent in each one. The truth hurt. It sure as hell had destroyed me. He hadn't given one single fuck back then, so I figured he wouldn't mind if I offered him the same courtesy.

He didn't reply, and when the silence stretched, I couldn't stop the bitter laugh that escaped my throat. Not that I'd tried hard—or honestly at all. The entire situation was beginning to feel more and more like a bad case of déjà vu.

Fuck it then.

Fuck it now.

Fuck it all.

"We're done!" I snapped, my frustration boiling over.

At my outburst, he jerked so violently he stumbled back a step.

With the door freed from his blockade, I wasted no time pulling it shut—the lock clicking with bone chilling finality.

Rushing forward, he placed both palms to the glass and stared at me with a torrent of emotions storming in his eyes. "Please don't do this."

"Go home, True."

"Gwen, please."

"Jesus, what the hell is wrong with you? Just go home."

And with that, Truett exploded.

"I can't!" he boomed, his deep baritone echoing off the glass. "You don't have to like me or understand me. Or, fuck, even care about me. But please, just let me come inside."

My throat got tight, and for a brief moment, my frustration waned. I did care about him. Or I had back when I'd existed in a magical land filled with beauty, invincibility, and fairy tales—also known as youth.

The problem was I didn't live there anymore. I'd grown up, even if he hadn't.

Desperation flickered in his eyes like a dying flame as I stared at him.

As a people pleaser by nature, I had caved way too many times in my life.

With Truett.

With Jeff.

With the whole damn world, which seemed hell-bent on keeping me down.

But not this time.

The Rosewood was my fresh start. A new life, a new path, a new me.

This was my future, and Truett West didn't exist there.

"I'm sorry," I said, speaking the two words from our past that would never stop haunting me.

I saw the verbal blow hit him, his whole body absorbing the shock. It sucked to witness, and I hated that I had to be the one to cause it, but I had nothing left to give. My cup was already empty, so I wasn't about to let him stab another hole through the bottom.

With my chin held high, I walked back to my office and shut the door.

There was no more banging or yelling.

No more arguments or pleas.

I wasn't sure how long Truett stayed after that, but a few hours later, as I locked up for the night, I felt nothing but relief when the only thing waiting for me outside was a full moon.

CHAPTER FIVE

TRUETT

Eighteen years earlier…

PEERING DOWN THE SCOPE OF MY RIFLE, I USED MY shoulder to wipe the sweat from my neck. Nothing in my training had prepared me for the suffocating heat of an Iraqi summer. The windows of the dingy apartment had been covered with screens to obscure our presence. An occasional breeze would blow through, offering me a reprieve from the oppressive heat. Those moments were few and far between, so the majority of the time, it felt like someone had replaced my blood with lava.

Ya know, real comfortable shit.

My rickety chair echoed through the room as I shifted my weight, trying to ease the pain in my back. I'd been perched on the edge for so long my ass had fallen asleep.

"Jesus, Cherry. Keep it down. It sounds like you're having a seizure over there," Nutz whispered from the secondary window a few feet away.

With five years enlisted, a Ranger tab, and the newest member of one of the most elite reconnaissance teams the Army had to offer, I was far from a cherry. Though, being that it was my first deployment, the nickname came with the territory. Before Cherry, I had been strapped with the wild creativity of "Dubs" since my last name started with a W. Now, I'd be Cherry until the day I retired.

"Shit, my bad. I didn't realize anyone could hear me with you over there breathing like an asthmatic wild boar," I deadpanned while continuing to scan the street below.

Focused. Always focused.

The Army didn't pay me to fuck off, though being in an abandoned apartment with trained professionals who knew to keep their voices barely audible helped when it came to a little banter.

Steve-O joined the conversation from the door at our six, where he was keeping watch on the interior stairwell. "Both of you smell like a fucking wild boar who's been dead for a week."

He was not wrong. It had been days since any of us had taken a real shower. With five men in full kit sweating our balls off, it smelled exactly as rancid as one would expect. Possibly worse.

For three days, our team had taken up residence inside that apartment. We had been sent to conduct a low-vis operation on the building across the street. It was a known meeting place for several high-value targets, and we had been tasked with collecting intel on anyone who so much as glanced at the door as they passed.

So far, the operation had been a bust. There hadn't been a single soul entering or exiting the property. The neighborhood felt like a ghost town with the exception of the occasional elderly local who had been too stubborn to leave their war-torn home.

Long story short, it was as hot as the sun's asshole, fragrant as a rotting corpse, and boring as fuck.

Otherwise, it wasn't too bad.

Don't get me wrong. We'd all have rather been at home with a cold beer and a hot woman, but I could think of worse company than the guys on my team.

As the room returned to a watchful silence, I reflected on the odd family we'd become—not bound by blood but by shared experiences and the unspoken promise to watch each other's backs no matter what. We leaned on each other during the good times, the really-fucking-good times, and the occasional bad time, which would inevitably turn into the aforementioned really-fucking-good times after we'd attempt to solve our problems by going downtown and drowning them in alcohol. It was something of a tradition for us. And something we were all looking forward to when we got back home. Deployment was dry—the best thing to ever happen to our pickled livers.

Nutz was my brother in every way other than DNA. We'd grown up together. He was older by a few years, but when he joined the Army, it wasn't long before I followed in his footsteps. His real name was Nathanial, but he'd more than earned his nickname. He liked to play it up that he'd been dubbed Nutz because he was this crazy wild card who should never be crossed. Truth be told, his ball sack had fallen out of his PT shorts one day during sit-ups.

If we were keeping the whole family dynamic going, Steve-O would have been the weird overachieving cousin who made everyone else look bad at the family reunions. If the Army had a school for it, chances were Steve-O had already completed it. The man was a *stud*. More so in the gym and the classroom than with the ladies. I shit you not, Wyatt looked exactly like Steve-O from the MTV show *Jackass*. Less charming if that was humanly possible.

He didn't have nearly as many tattoos as the TV star, but the ones he did have were equally as embarrassing. Like, say, the words "fuck me" he had inked in giant black letters on his lower stomach like his cock was wearing a crown. Yes. I'd seen it. Like it or not, communal showers were a way of life in the military.

The fun in our dysfunctional family came from Thomas Lindy. He would have been the estranged second cousin who only showed up to weddings and funerals but still managed to be everyone's favorite. Married with three kids, he hadn't been around for many of our nights of debauchery, but when he was there, it was guaranteed to be legendary. He'd been dubbed Skytrash after one bad jump on a free-fall operation. Honestly, it didn't take much for shit to stick in the military.

Rounding out our family tree was Sergeant Rhodes. He was that weird uncle who you loved but also kind of scared the shit out of you. His smooth Southern accent wasn't fooling anyone—that was no gentleman. He was a beast in every facet. None of us dared to call him any-fucking-thing other than, "Roger, S'arnt."

So yeah, we were all miserable, thousands of miles away from home, and missing family and friends, but good company made for a good time.

"Uh oh, Nutz," I said quietly, my eye never leaving the scope of my weapon. "I think you might have a stalker."

"Huh?" he replied.

"I can't be sure, but she definitely looks like one of the girls you used to sneak into the barracks."

"You gotta be more specific. Kilo's first-floor window saw more traffic than a parade route. I used to tell the ladies it was the VIP entrance."

I chuckled. "Look for yourself. Three o'clock, short little blonde."

His kit rustled as he shifted his weight, turning his binoculars down the street. "What the hell are you talking about? That's just the old dude out walking his—oh, you son of a bitch."

A grin split my lips as I feigned innocence. "What? It's a cute dog."

"Yeah, I'm sure that's what you meant, fuck face."

Steve-O chuckled. "He does have a point. You really need to up your standards. You're embarrassing us all."

Nutz scoffed. "I don't know who you're calling embarrassing. Have you looked in the mirror recently? Your lips are big enough to suck your own cock without having to bend over."

"You sound jealous," Steve-O retorted.

"Yeah, I'm jealous of people that have a real wingman. How am

I supposed to up my standards when your ugly ass is always standing behind me at the club like a damn scarecrow in a field of hotties."

I bit my cheek, desperately trying to suppress my laughter. God, I loved riling them up. Who needed television when you had this kind of entertainment?

I couldn't see him, but I felt his presence as he entered the room.

"What the hell's all the noise about?" Sergeant Rhodes rumbled.

"Steve-O runnin' his mouth, S'arnt," Nutz replied.

"Don't blame that shit on me. Cherry was the one who called your girl a Golden Retriever."

"Whoa, whoa, whoa. I did no such thing." I smirked. "Golden Retriever would have been a compliment. That right there's a grade-A mutt."

Steve-O laughed while Nutz let out a mumbled string of curses.

"All right, shut it, and keep it low. Anything new?" Rhodes asked.

"No, S'arnt," I replied. "We have the same elderly civilian male out for his daily stroll with his dog, but besides that, nothing to report."

He hummed approvingly. "Good. If it stays that way, the GFC will be good to EXFIL tonight. This is a waste of our time."

My shoulders sagged in relief. Thank. Christ. Getting back to the FOB wasn't the same as going home, but it was a hell of a lot better than this shit.

"Cherry, take a break and get some chow," Rhodes ordered. "Steve-O, take over for him. Skytrash just woke up. He can man the stairwell."

"Roger, S'arnt," we whispered in unison.

My muscles ached as I sat up straight, stretching from side to side. I wasn't sure if I was actually hungry or if I'd become Pavlov's dog and the act of stretching had signaled that it was time to eat. Either way, I was suddenly starving. Like a well-oiled machine, as soon as I stood up, Steve-O slid into my seat, adjusted the rifle, and then put his eye to the scope.

With sleep still thick in his voice, Skytrash appeared in the doorway and asked, "So what's your fine dining today, Cherry? Pizza? Lobster? Kung Pow Chicken?"

That all sounded amazing, but it was going to be some brittle crackers with cheese spread, M&Ms, and whatever the hell travesty of a protein the MRE gods had handed me as we'd packed to leave. Luckily for me, I'd always been a mind-over-matter guy. The brain was a hell of a weapon. With enough concentration, I could pretend my mystery meat was tikka masala and boom, I had gourmet cooking in the middle of a world conflict.

"Oh, for fuck's sake," S'arnt rumbled. "Can we not do this? I had tuna in my MRE. The smell alone made me want to shit myself."

Steve-O's shoulders rounded with a gag. "Damn, tuna in this heat? That should be against the Geneva Conventions."

"Unfortunately, I'm not a prisoner of war, so that doesn't apply to me. But I'm in no mood to listen to your cherry-ass wax poetic about a ribeye while he's choking down cold chili mac."

I shrugged. "Fine. Suit yourself. I just figured, with it being tradition and all, we wouldn't want any bad juju right before we get out of here."

He stared at me for a long second, his jaw ticking at the hinges. None of us were sure if it was OCD or superstition with him, but he was a staunch creature of habit. With a suffering sigh, he crossed his monster forearms over his chest. "Just fucking get it over with."

His window of his patience would be short, so I rushed out with, "A burger from The Grille."

His dark brows climbed his forehead, while Nutz and Steve-O let out a groan.

"Like a backyard grill?" Skytrash asked.

Nutz beat me to the response. "No. It's a grease pit that asshole swore had the best burger on the East Coast. Talked about it nonstop for weeks. Over a long weekend, he convinced me and Steve-O to road-trip it back home with him so we could experience it too. We drove ten hours, refusing to eat anything to save room for this godly burger."

"Let me guess, it was a frozen patty?" Skytrash deadpanned.

"We don't know," Nutz continued. "This idiot didn't bother to call home or, say, check the Jersey weather in the middle of January before we left. By the time we got there, a huge winter storm had taken out The Grille's power, so while they were still open, they couldn't cook anything. Essentially, we drove twenty-plus hours round trip for a club sandwich and a bag of chips."

That was all *mostly* true. The burger at The Grille was fucking amazing. They were so addictive I'm pretty sure old man Branning laced them with narcotics. Though I'd yet to piss hot on a drug test, so maybe not. Mainly, I'd just needed to get home that weekend and wanted a little company for the drive. With the storm approaching, I'd worried about my mom's ancient generator being able to keep the house warm. It wasn't my fault they were gullible. I mean seriously, who the hell drove ten hours for a burger?

"You two can talk all the shit you want, but it was a damn good club sandwich," I lied.

"What do you expect? We were starving. I'd have eaten S'arnt's biohazardous tuna at that point," Steve-O shot back. "It didn't even have the bacon on it. That is *literally* the only ingredient that upgrades dry-ass ham and turkey to club level."

I waved them off. "Ah, quit your bitching. You should be thanking me. That was a damn good trip. Minus Steve-O's shitty-ass music."

Nutz scoffed, but Steve-O was quiet.

Eerily quiet.

Too quiet.

The hair on the back of my neck stood on end as the whole room went on alert.

"Whatcha got?" S'arnt asked.

"I'm not"—he paused—"sure exactly. Hey, Cherry, this guy one of your regulars?"

"The guy with the dog?" I asked. Snagging my binoculars, I went and stood next to Nutz so I didn't crowd the rifle. "Yeah, that's him. He walks his dog every day at thirteen thirty. Cleans up his shit and everything."

"He usually got a phone open like that?"

The air in the room went static. Not that I needed oxygen as I zoomed in on his hand. My stomach wrenched as I saw the camera on the phone peeking through his sprawled fingers.

Aimed directly at us.

"Oh, fuck," I breathed.

"S'arnt!" Nutz called, louder than we'd spoken in days. "We got a black sedan coming in hot from the southeast."

"Oh, fuck," I repeated as all the puzzle pieces in my head snapped into place, each one feeling like a rusty dagger carving my soul.

The phone.

His timing, right at shift change and the only time we were all in the room together.

Cleaning up after his dog so he could linger to take pictures.

Clearly, we hadn't been the only ones running surveillance.

And somehow, I'd completely missed it.

"West!" S'arnt barked. Not Cherry. *West.* "Get on the sat phone with the TOC. Tell 'em we've got a black sedan traveling at a high rate of speed in our direction, and stand by until I can get a count of occupants and weapons."

"Roger, S'arnt." Adrenaline rocketed inside me as I raced from the room. My heavy footfalls echoed as I ran into the bedroom across the hall and snatched up the satellite phone. I spoke with an urgency, sharing the pertinent details, but I had no idea what I was saying.

My training had taken over as if the Army had installed an autopilot inside me, but my mind was a million miles away.

How had I missed the phone?

How the fuck had I missed him carrying a goddamn phone?

I'd never doubted my abilities as a soldier before, but after that, I'd never be able to trust myself again.

"Vehicle's not slowing, S'arnt!" my brother called.

Then it was my cousin. "What the fuck is this guy doing?"

Then my second cousin. "There's four occupants, and I see two AKs, S'arnt!"

And lastly, my uncle. "Take out the driver."

I didn't remember much after that. I think they fired. I prayed every night to a God that I wasn't sure existed that they were at least able to defend themselves.

Those four men were the best of the best.

They were heroes.

They were my *family*.

And in the blink of an eye, as the car slammed into the front of the building, detonating on impact…

They were gone.

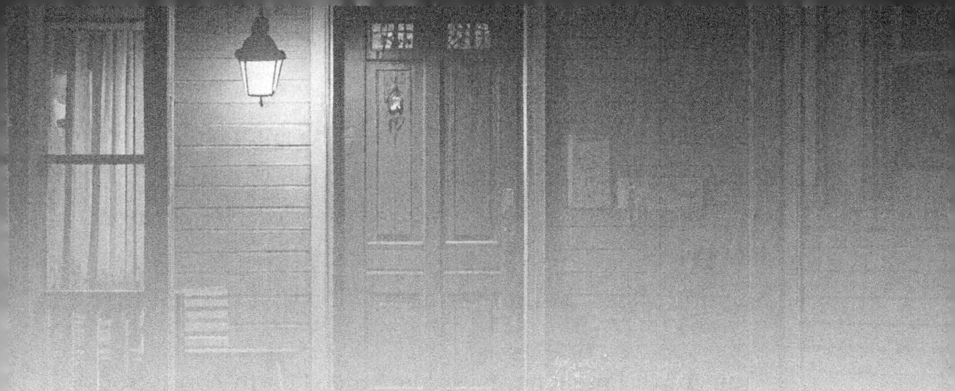

CHAPTER SIX

Gwen

WITH AN INFURIATING LOOP OF HOLD MUSIC PLAYING in my ear, I paced the peeling linoleum of The Grille.

Yep. Two weeks later, it was still The Grille and not The Rosewood thanks to yet another contractor flaking on me. It was truly astounding how hard it was to pay someone to show up and work. I could have just left the door unlocked and let the local teenagers loot the place quicker—and most definitely cheaper.

A gentle rap at the door caught my attention. I glanced up to see Cooter—I mean, Lucille —standing on the other side, an umbrella held over her head. I barely recognized her with her long gray hair flowing over her shoulders. We'd been in contact a few times since that day at the diner. I'd texted to let her know her job was secure, and she'd called to let me know she'd spent one weekend at her daughter's house before her "mouth breather of a son-in-law" had made her run for the hills. So she was back in town if I needed help sooner than planned. It was a kind offer, something that I was learning was not uncommon for her.

"Open up. I come bearing gifts," she said, lifting a Tupperware container filled with what I could only identify as something chocolaty.

Unfortunately, the gift wasn't the professional with a toolbelt that I needed or even the bottle of wine that I wanted, but I was never one to turn down chocolate.

After unlocking the door, I shoved it wide. "Hey, what are you doing here?"

She tipped her chin at the phone. "Sorry. I didn't mean to interrupt."

"You aren't. I'm on never-ending hold with my contractor's office. Come on in. Get out of that rain."

"You don't have to tell me twice." With the click of a button, she closed her umbrella and left it outside the door.

She looked amazing in a stylish pale-pink T-shirt dress cinched at the waist with a thin brown belt. I, on the other hand, was in my best comfort chic of yoga pants and a stained T-shirt. Whatever. Tearing down bathroom stalls didn't exactly require formalwear.

Her lip curled as she scanned the dining room. "You should probably fire that contractor when he answers. It doesn't look like he's done anything around here."

"Oh, he hasn't. That includes stepping foot inside the building for any reason other than to pick up the deposit check. It's starting to feel like hiring a reliable contractor is nothing more than an urban legend."

She carried the container to one of the tables I'd pushed into the corner and set it down. "That's men for ya. Always playing games, even with their work ethic."

"True, but I don't know of any women in the construction business. Do you?"

"Nope. Don't know any women with a dick, either, which is why I never got remarried."

A loud laugh bubbled up my throat. "I like the way you think."

"And I like the fact that you didn't get all prickly when I said dick."

I shrugged. "Half the world has one."

Carefully, she took two of the stacked chairs off the table and set them on the floor. "And it sounds like all the contractors in this town *are* one. Have a sit-down and fill me in on this renovation run-around you've been dealing with. Call it sixth sense or female intuition, but I just knew you needed some of Coot's famous brownies."

Shifting the phone to my other ear, I lifted the edge of the Tupperware and peeked inside. "Oh, wow," I moaned as I took in the most amazing brownies topped with caramel sauce, pecans, and white chocolate chips. "With the day I've had, I'm going to need at least three."

"Girl, you can have 'em all. With a figure like yours, I was worried you'd be one of those calorie counters who can't eat sugar or orgasm."

I slanted my head. "Do those two things usually go together?"

"In my experience, almost exclusively."

I laughed again, relishing in the much-needed moment of levity. "Thank you. I really appreciate this."

"Anything for you, Boss." She winked.

A woman's voice finally cut through the elevator music. "Ms. Weaver?"

"Yes! I'm here." I lifted my finger in Lucille's direction, asking for a second. "Yes, I was on hold for Ryan Meeker."

"Sorry, but Ryan is already gone for the day."

"Uhhh, was he gone before I spent twenty minutes on hold?"

She ignored my sarcasm and replied with all the charm of a doorknob. "It's six o'clock. What do you expect? Just give him a call back tomorrow."

"No, thank you. He was supposed to be here with a whole crew to clear out my restaurant *today*."

"And just like I already told you, they got tied up at another jobsite this morning. We'll get you back on the schedule for some time next week."

Screwing my eyes shut, I pinched the bridge of my nose. I could not afford another delay. Whether the restaurant was open or not, I had bills to pay. Power, water, insurance. Those things didn't stop.

"Why were they even at another jobsite today? You told me they'd be here at seven this morning and it's now six p.m. Eleven freaking hours later."

"Ma'am, I'm going to need you to watch your language."

My chin jerked. "Freaking isn't a cuss word."

"Oh really? So what exactly does freaking mean, then? Is it something you'll be doing on your darn way to heck?" She scoffed. "I can read between the lines, ya know."

I pulled the phone away from my ear and stared at it incredulously. What in the nonsense hell was this woman talking about? I opened my mouth to give her a piece of my mind that she wouldn't have to read between any lines but managed to stop myself. I'd always been a firm believer in the whole catching-more-flies-with-sugar-than-vinegar thing. Besides, I was shit at confrontation. I talked a big game but would probably end up sending her flowers and an apology the next day.

Filling my lungs, I held my breath as I did a mental search-and-rescue for my patience. This was not the time to lose my shit, my contractor, and more than likely my deposit too. "Okay, you're right. I'm sorry. I'm just a little frustrated. That's all."

"Oh, hell no!" Lucille exclaimed just before she snatched the phone from my hand. "Listen up. You've got exactly twelve hours to get that contractor to my doorstep or I'm calling my lawyer. He's a real class act with a penchant for courtroom dramas. He makes Perry Mason look like a teacup poodle."

Oh, sweet Jesus.

"Lucille," I hissed, frantically trying to get the phone back.

She swirled, swatting me away as she continued her rant. "What do I look like to you? Google? Search up Perry Mason on your own damn time. Right now, you're on *my* clock. Twenty-four hours, I tell ya! You've been giving us the runaround for too long, and my girl here might be too nice to say it, but when you mess with the bull, you get the horns. And guess what, baby? I've been horny my whole life."

"What the fuck?" I whispered.

Lucille never slowed. "Oh, you heard me right. We expect him here first thing in the morning, tools in hand, shirt off."

Shirt off? Dear God, forget about my deposit. I was going to have to flee the country after this.

I grabbed her arm. "What are you doing?"

She covered the speaker of the phone and whispered, "This contractor of yours is hot, right?"

"No!"

She looked at me like I'd suddenly grown snakes for hair. "Why the hell wouldn't you hire a hot contractor?"

"Because I don't care what they look like as long as they do the damn job."

"How's that working out for you?" She shook her head in disappointment and then uncovered the speaker. "Never mind. Shirts are required. However, considering the inconvenience, I think a little discount is in order—say, twenty percent?"

My ears perked and I immediately stopped trying to retrieve the phone. Embarrassment be damned, my deflating checking account could definitely use a break.

"Hey," I whispered, waving frantically to catch her attention. "Tell her you've got connections at the Better Business Bureau."

She beamed at me with pride. "Oh yeah, laugh it up now, honey. If my lawyer doesn't bury you, my connections at the BBB will. I'll wait while you Google that one too." She paused. "Uh huh, right. Then you already know how damaging something like that could be for a small business. Do you really think Mr. Meeker is going to be able to pay your salary after I flip his business belly up?" She sucked in a sharp breath. "Then as his wife, you really understand the ramifications of bankruptcy. I promise you, I am not a woman you want to mess with."

I bit my lip to stifle a laugh. Note to self, Lucille could be scary.

With my fingers crossed and my hopes high, I waited anxiously as she listened, her silence broken only by the occasional, "Uh huh."

Finally, after what felt like an eternity, she flashed me a triumphant grin. "Absolutely, I'll be here at seven tomorrow to speak to him directly. Just tell him to ask for Cooter." Her face got tight. "Yeah, seriously. That's my name. Write it down. C-O-O-T-E-R. Got it? Mmhm. You have a good one too. Bye bye, now."

As if she hadn't just gone full Tony Soprano, she casually ended the call and handed me back the phone. "They'll be here in the morning."

"And the discount?"

"Ten percent is the best she could offer, but I'll be here tomorrow to chat with ugly contractor Ryan myself. Should be able to get that up to fifteen percent, no problem."

Dollar signs flashed in my eyes. Ten percent was a lot of money when you were already spending a lot of money, but fifteen sounded a hell of a lot better. "Oh my God, Lucille!" Bouncing on my toes, I wrapped her in a tight hug. "That was amazing."

"All right. Calm down now. You're wrinkling my dress."

I released her, but my smile was permanent. "Sorry, sorry. I just… Wow. I'm impressed."

She popped a shoulder. "Now that you own the place, you gotta remember the goal isn't just to be the squeaky wheel. It's to get the *whole* oil change."

"I'm not completely sure what that means, but I'm sure it's sage advice. You are seriously the best. Brownies and a discount? You better be careful or I'm going to have to promote you."

She waved me off. "Ew, no. Management is not for me. You can keep that nightmare all to yourself."

"Gee, thanks."

She patted me on the shoulder as she passed me. "Now listen, I gotta get out of here. I have a date."

"Ohhhhh, do tell." I followed her to the door.

"A lady does not kiss and tell." She paused dramatically. "We screw and tell. I'll fill you in when I see you in the morning. Don't forget. Seven a.m."

My loud laugh echoed off the glass. "You're one of a kind, Lucille."

"I feel like I'm talking to my pastor when you call me Lucille. That's going to be really weird when we're talking about scrumping in the morning."

Dear lord, this woman was amazing and insane. Dylan was going to love her. I pulled the door open, holding it with my back so she could pass. "Sorry about that. I just know another Cooter, so it's easier for me to call you Lucille." With an awkward laugh, I made a mental note to brainstorm a nickname for her that wasn't slang for vagina. "Be careful. Stay safe. Use a condom."

"Yes, ma'am." The rain had picked up again, so she opened her umbrella before stepping out to avoid the leaks in the awning. "Oh, don't you worry, I—shit."

"What's wrong?" I followed her gaze across the street.

A swirl of contradictory emotions made my stomach sink the moment I saw him.

Fucking Truett.

I knew there was a chance he'd come back this week. I'd prepped a whole "stalking is illegal" speech and everything. I was going to read him the Riot Act, tell him to take a hike, and then threaten to call the cops if need be.

However, the moment I saw him, my anger transformed into a vile brew of guilt and pity. Logically, I knew that my buying The Grille wasn't the reason for the anguish so thick in his body language it made my chest ache even from a distance. But the poison still coursed through my veins regardless how hard my brain tried to formulate the antidote.

Clad in a black jacket with gray panels on its sides, he had the hood drawn tightly around his face. It looked like he was shielding himself from more than just the weather. As if somehow those synthetic fibers could block out the entire world, hiding him in plain sight. His hands were buried deep in his pockets while his drenched jeans clung heavily to his legs. The spring weather had warmed, but there was no way he wasn't freezing in those wet clothes.

And for what? To follow some Wednesday dinner routine in a grease pit that had sucked even before it closed?

"Damn," Lucille whispered. "I was really hoping the hot gargoyle had found a new place to perch by now."

"Me too," I replied.

"Just leave him be. He'll leave eventually."

I nodded absently, never tearing my gaze off him, my mind swirling in a million different directions. Why, how, and what-the-fuck warred for the forefront of my thoughts.

"See ya in the morning." She gave my arm a squeeze before she walked toward the side parking lot.

That should have been the end of it. After the stunt he'd pulled the week before, I had every right to be pissed. Livid even. There was no reason I shouldn't have walked back inside, locked the door, and then carried on with my life—without him. God knew that was what he'd done to me.

My feet never moved though.

I was supposed to be angry.

I was supposed to hate him.

I was supposed to feel a sick sense of relief that he was exactly as miserable as I'd once hoped.

But as my chest tightened, I unfortunately learned that emotions didn't always follow the path you paved for them.

CHAPTER SEVEN

TRUETT

IT WAS RAINING. WHY THE FUCK WOULDN'T IT BE? KARMA had really pulled out all the stops for me over the last few weeks. Closing The Grille, having Gwen buy it, what next? Sink hole under my house? Gangrene in the hand I jerked off with? The options were limitless. With the way my life worked, I should have been grateful it was only a little rain and I hadn't been struck by lightning yet.

Though the day wasn't over. Still plenty of time for the universe to fry my ass.

I was well aware that I looked like a fool sitting on that bench as the clouds emptied around me. Hell, even cockroaches were smart enough to hide during a storm.

Not me though.

Not on a Wednesday.

After a lifetime of chaos and agony, predictability was the only thing that kept me sane—if you could even call me that.

I thrived on routine—every minute having a purpose. A therapist had once told me it was about control. He couldn't have been more wrong. It was about survival.

I could handle the days. Wake up, workout, eat, work. Easy enough. It was the freedom in evenings that I struggled with the most.

Mondays were straightforward. I'd fire up the grill in my backyard, the aroma of sizzling chicken breasts filling my senses—a practical and completely mundane start to the week. Post-grilling, I'd meal-prep lunches for the next few days and then settle into the corner of my tattered couch until Netflix lulled me to sleep.

Tuesdays had their own elements of excitement. The night would highlight Chinese delivery while I'd distracted myself by spinning online slots on my phone—the hum of ESPN in the background giving me the illusion of company.

The rest of the week was a series of slightly tweaked redundancy.

But Wednesdays were different. They were sacred. The Grille was my last remaining anchor to the real world. Each week, when I took that first step out of my house, I'd feel a flicker of hope—however misguided as it might have been.

Don't get me wrong. I hated my weekly outings with the intensity of a thousand suns, but it was a predictable torture and therefore comfortable agony.

I didn't know how to function without Wednesday nights. Would Thursdays even exist without them?

Would I?

I told myself not to go. To respect Gwen's wishes and stay away. But call it obsession, habit, or muscle memory, at six p.m. on the dot, fueled by nothing more than a mixture of dread and necessity, I walked to a restaurant where I was no longer welcome.

Desperation gave me a delusional tunnel vision. I'd honest-to-God convinced myself that when I arrived everything would be as it should.

The Grille would be open.

My booth and a club sandwich would be waiting for me.

And the confrontation with Gwen had been nothing but a nightmare fabricated by my self-loathing subconscious.

But reality, as always, had a different script.

Hell-bent and determined, I fought the urge to knock on the door and attempt to convince her to let me inside. It would have no doubt turned into a rerun of the week before, but it was worth a try. Wednesdays were always worth a try.

But at what cost? At *whose* cost?

I watched her through the window as she paced back and forth, her phone pressed to her ear. With her forehead crinkled and her lips pursed, she was downright pissed. It was an expression I recognized well. When we were younger, I'd all but permanently painted it on her face.

Pained memories tore through me. What the fuck was I doing? How could I be such a selfish prick? Gwen had put up with enough of my bullshit to last a lifetime. But there I was, literally and figuratively dragging it right back to her doorstep.

How was that fair to anyone but me?

Despite my every waking moment saying otherwise, I wasn't living in a nightmare.

The Grille wasn't open.

No booth awaited me, no sandwich—just the cold, unyielding rain echoing my failures.

With my tail tucked, I dodged puddles as I walked across the street, hoping and praying she wouldn't see me. She could go about her life, and I could go about mine. Though I had no fucking idea what that looked like without Wednesdays.

So there I was, sitting on the bench, staring at what used to be my weekly sanctuary, the bitter taste of nostalgia souring my stomach, when I heard footsteps approaching.

My gaze flicked up and I found Gwen trotting toward me, a plastic cafeteria-style tray held over her head, shielding her from the elements.

"What are you doing?" she asked, her tone surprisingly gentle, if not resigned.

I shifted uncomfortably, wishing I'd taken the time to prepare a lie. "Just hanging out."

She slanted her head. "Right. Who could resist such a beautiful evening?"

A reluctant smile tipped my lips—the absurdity of the situation not lost on me. "It's perfect if you need to, say, test a new water-resistant jacket."

"Oh, okay, then. That makes total sense. For a second there, I thought you were stalking me."

I swallowed hard and avoided her gaze. "I just…needed to be here, but I didn't want to bother you."

She barked a laugh. "Yeah, making me feel bad while you sit out here getting soaked is *so* much less invasive."

My back shot straight. "I wasn't trying to make you feel bad. I was actually trying to avoid *being* the asshole for once. Staying out of your way seemed like the way to go."

"Not coming would have been the way to go."

Feeling like a scolded child, I peered up at her and shrugged. "I don't know how to not be here."

"Why? What's so special about this place? I knew you used to like their burgers when we were growing up, but the food has been shit for a while. You avoided this place like the plague after…" She paused and peered down at her pink sneakers. Her gorgeous brown eyes came back to me, begging for answers in the most heartbreakingly familiar way. "I just don't get it. Help me understand."

I clenched my fist, tension running through my body. That was the one thing I'd never be able to give her.

I didn't want her to understand.

I didn't want her to know.

I didn't want her anywhere near the shitshow that lived inside my head.

"I don't know," I mumbled like the fucking coward I was.

Her humorless laugh was filled with frustration. "Right. Of course not. How silly of me to even ask the question."

"Gwen, I—"

"So what, then? Every Wednesday, you're just going to sit out here, rain, sleet, or snow, acting like the town's newest statue until I reopen the restaurant?"

Pulling my hands from the pockets of my jacket, I reached under the hood and scratched the back of my neck. "Well, I'm hoping it doesn't snow in March, but honestly, I don't know. I haven't made it that far." That was the truth. I had no idea if it would even feel like The Grille when she reopened. That was a whole mental breakdown I was saving for a different day. "Look, go back inside. You shouldn't have to deal with this. I just couldn't stay at home tonight."

"You shouldn't be in that house any night," she shot back so fast I barely understood her. A groan rumbled in her throat as she aimed her gaze anywhere but at me. "Get up. Let's go."

"I'm fine. Seriously."

"You're not fine, Truett," she snapped, frustration bubbling over. "You're sopping wet and on the verge of catching pneumonia. I don't have anything to make a club sandwich, but I can at least get you dry and out of the rain."

I stared at her, the weight of her invitation sinking in more slowly than the cold had seeped into my bones. A surge of hope pulsed inside me as I tried to make heads or tails of her offer.

On one hand, it was exactly what I needed.

On the other, I was right back to that whole at-what-cost debate.

"Are you sure you're okay with that?" I asked.

"Nope. But I don't know what else to do with you."

Funny. I didn't know, either. "I'm—" I started to say *sorry* but managed to stop myself. "I apologize. This isn't your problem."

She once again interrupted me. "Unfortunately, that's not true. You're here. You're wet. You aren't leaving, are you?"

I shook my head, water dripping from my beard.

"Right. Then that apology is worth about as much as me wasting my breath telling you to go home. You usually stay until seven, right?"

I nodded.

"Okay. Well, it's getting late. So let's get this over with." With that, she turned on a toe, lowered the tray, and jogged across the street.

I stood there for several beats, watching her, wondering if following her was the right thing to do.

It was for me. I knew that to the core of my soul.

But for her…

"Let's go, True!" she called over her shoulder as she pulled the door open. "This offer expires in ten, nine, eight…"

She didn't make it to seven before I sprinted after her.

"Here," Gwen said, offering me a stack of towels. "Don't mind the stains. They're clean, I swear. Give me your jacket and I'll hang it up in front of the hand blower in the bathroom. It probably won't dry in time, but you won't be dripping all over the place, either."

With an eerie awe, my gaze trailed around the empty restaurant. The Grille had never been crowded, but with the absence of the clatter from the kitchen, waitresses wandering about, and the scent of grease filling the air, it felt stagnant and unsettling. The booths still lined the walls, but the tables had been pushed to the side, chairs stacked on top, giving the space the illusion of being bigger.

It was odd the way everything felt so right yet so damn wrong.

"True," Gwen said, snapping her fingers in front of my face. "Did you hear me?"

"Yeah, sorry." I made quick work of removing my jacket, and then I traded her for the threadbare towels that either needed a bottle of fabric softener or a firepit STAT.

She pointed to the corner booth. "That one's yours, right?"

A lump formed in my throat as I nodded.

"Go sit down. Do whatever it is that you do." She offered me a tight smile. "You need a drink or anything? I've got some coffee in the back. It's not a club sandwich, but it might help warm you up."

I walked over to the booth and dragged the tips of my fingers across the top of the laminate table. The way my pulse spiked and dread pooled in my stomach comforted me immediately. "That'd be great," I rasped, barely able to get the words out.

She eyed me curiously—a million questions poised on the tip of her tongue. To her credit, she asked none of them. And, as if I didn't already owe her a massive debt of gratitude, for that alone, it grew.

"I'll be right back," she said, disappearing down the hallway.

While she was gone, I did my best to dry off, but it was like trying to drain the ocean with a spoon. Eventually I gave up and spread the towels out across the booth's bench seat with hopes that I could at least avoid leaving a puddle.

And then, like Sisyphus, I took my position behind my boulder.

My body trembled as I slid into the booth. On contact, the flames of the past engulfed me. Frantic, I gasped for air, but my lungs no longer seemed to be able to process oxygen. That was okay. I didn't deserve it anyway. A vise cranked down on my ribs, agony tearing through my soul in a way that made my bones feel like they were being shattered, one by one.

The weight of my failures crushed me.

The pain was so great the room spun, so I closed my eyes to

keep the nausea at bay. It was the wrong move. So fucking wrong. Without my sight, I couldn't anchor myself. The sound of gunfire assaulted me. I sucked in a sharp breath, wishing the bullets would finally hit me and release me from this perpetual hell once and for all.

And suddenly, like a ding as the elevator arrived at its floor, everything just…

Stopped.

"You still take your coffee black?" she called from the distance.

Gwen.

Gwen.

Dear God…Gwen.

My eyes popped open. The flames of my hell suddenly extinguished as though they had been doused by a sudden downpour.

How did she do that?

Why did she do that?

I looked at my watch. I still had thirty minutes to go. I hadn't paid my dues yet.

I wasn't done.

I wasn't—

My traitorous heart slowed as I watched her round the corner holding two Styrofoam cups of steaming coffee.

Usually, my pain was a relentless force, clinging to me long after I'd left The Grille. But now, it was gone. Had she fucking stolen it?

I thought back to when I'd run into her a few weeks earlier. Sure, I'd been shocked to see her and gotten distracted. Running into a gorgeous woman did that to a man. But it wasn't like this. Was it?

Shit, was it?

I swallowed hard, the most confusing mixture of anger and elation swirling inside me. I had a penitence to pay, but as a chill spread across my skin, it was a welcome—albeit undeserved—reprieve from the searing heat of the flames.

I tracked her every step as she approached the booth.

"Black?" she repeated.

"Yeah," I rumbled, my voice filled with gravel.

She placed a cup on the table. I didn't immediately reach for it, knowing my hands would still be shaking. Or would they? I glanced down at my lap.

Shit.

They were as still as a brain surgeon's. Which was exactly who I was going to need to see after this mindfuck. A lobotomy had never sounded so good.

I drew in a deep breath, and fuck me sideways, it was slow, even, and steady.

It was wrong.

All fucking wrong.

I shot to my feet, a different kind of panic slamming into me. "I have to go."

Her lips twisted to the side. "It's not seven yet."

That was exactly the problem. I needed to get home and figure out what the hell was going on. I couldn't think with her so close. I couldn't do *anything* with her there.

My anxiety skyrocketed as long purposeful strides carried me to the door. I had to get the fuck out of there. I fumbled with the lock, trying to get it open so I could make my escape. Dear God, I'd spent two weeks trying to get inside, and now, I couldn't get out.

Gwen appeared at my side. "Hey, relax. Let me get it."

It opened with the flip of her wrist, and I was like an Olympic sprinter in the blocks, ready to bolt. Her palm landed on my forearm, stopping me dead in my tracks. Jesus. My own fucking legs wouldn't operate around her.

"Are you okay?" she asked, worry etched in her face. I hated myself that much more for carving it there.

"Yeah," I lied. "Thanks for letting me come in."

She shook her head, completely unconvinced. "Truett, I—"

I covered her hand with my own and gave it a squeeze. "Really. I'm good."

She didn't believe me. Or understand. Or know how to help. And I loathed the fact that I'd seen those expressions from her so often that, even after all this time, I still recognized them.

I also recognized the moment she resigned herself to the reality that there was nothing more she could do.

Slowly, as if trying to delay the inevitable, her hand slid from under mine. "Okay. Have a good night."

"You too." With that, I shoved the door wide open and took off through the rain.

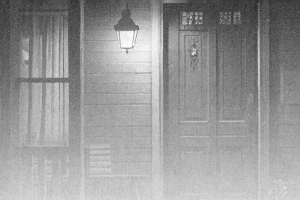

CHAPTER EIGHT

Gwen

“COOTER!” DYLAN LAUGHED WILDLY, CAREFUL NOT TO spill her latte on Angela.

“What?” Lucille feigned innocence from across the booth. “I’m sorry, but if I have to search through a forest to find the tree, I don’t want it.”

Angela crinkled her nose. “I hear some women like *au naturel*.”

“Not this one,” Lucille replied, lifting her Starbucks cup across the table.

Dylan did not leave her hanging and met her in the middle for a cheers. “Me either! If I have to brave razor burn and ingrown hairs to tame the hairy gremlin, he damn sure better do the same.”

“A hairy gremlin? Really, Dylan? I did not need to know that,” Angela scolded, disgust painted all over her face. Sliding out of the booth, she looked at me. “Do the restrooms still work? I suddenly feel the need to gouge my eyes out.”

I laughed. “Yes, and you’ve got three thrones to choose from too. I ripped out the stall dividers already.”

“Perfect.” Her heels clicked toward the hall.

“Oh, come on, Ang,” Dylan called. “Don’t be such a prude!”

Angela flipped her the middle finger before disappearing into the women’s restroom.

Dylan batted her lashes at Lucille. “She loves me.”

"I get it," she replied. "You two remind me of me and my sister. I swear she was born with a stick up her ass. She always acts scandalized by a little girl talk, but the woman's got six kids. She's no stranger to a dick if you know what I'm saying."

Lucille leaned into my side as they howled with laughter. Fighting and failing to suppress a smile, I shook my head, debating if they were a match made in heaven or hell. Probably a little of both depending on the day.

An alarm on Lucille's phone interrupted their hysterics. Never breaking the conversation, she picked it up, hit redial, and put it to her ear. "Razor burn? I got my gremlin hair lasered off years ago. I'll give you my girl's number. It didn't hurt too much until she got to the assh—hey there." She lifted a single finger at Dylan and then spoke into the phone. "It's me again. Any update? Uh huh. Yep. Okay, talk to you soon." She put the phone back on the table and hit the button on her screen to start the timer again. "She says they're only a few minutes out, but I swear, if they keep this up, they're gonna be doing this job for *free*."

"I'd rather just pay at this point," I muttered.

It was a full house that morning. Unfortunately, that did not yet include a crew of construction workers.

I'd slept like shit, tossing and turning. My mind had alternated between my strange interaction with Truett and anxiety over what I was going to do if the demo crew no-showed again. Around five, I gave up on sleep and decided to hit the gym. The new trending workout clothes I'd ordered after one too many glasses of wine had finally arrived, and I put them on, hoping a new 'fit would help me kick off the day right.

No such luck. In true TikTok Shop fashion, the legs of my shorts were uneven and my shirt was too big yet somehow simultaneously too short. I wore them anyway. It seemed more practical than tossing them into the graveyard of returns in the back of my car.

I drove to the gym but never got out. As I stared through the windows, watching the early birds pounding out miles on the treadmills, all I could see was Truett running away like he was being chased by demons. And worse, I feared he really was.

After that, I skipped going home to change and went straight to the restaurant so I could squeeze in a quick video call with Nate before school. It was his dad's long weekend, and that meant five full days without my little man. Nobody made me laugh like Nate, and that morning was no exception. By the time we hung up, I felt more refreshed than a full night's rest could ever provide.

As promised, Lucille had met me there bright and early with coffee in hand, ready to steamroll a contractor. However, when the crew hadn't arrived by 7:05, she started blowing up their office. The same woman from the night before assured us that the crew was just running a little late. Ever the bulldog, Lucille called back every five minutes to check their status. I had to give her credit for persistency.

Around eight thirty, Dylan and Angela had surprised me with breakfast. Unwilling to admit my renovation woes already, I'd been avoiding their questions in our text thread. This was their not-so-subtle way of checking up on me. They brought donuts, so I didn't complain.

It was now past nine, and despite all the promises from the contractor's office, I was starting to believe the day was a wash.

"Hey, Gwen," Angela called. "Whose jacket is this?"

My head whipped in her direction as she reappeared holding a black-and-gray raincoat.

Awesome. Just what I needed. The whole clusterfuck with Truett was not a subject I was eager to revisit. I didn't know what to say even if I wanted to explain it. He'd begged to come inside. Sat in the rain to be nearby. And then, when I'd finally given in, he'd bolted. It made no sense whatsoever. And quite honestly, as he'd raced away, I'd kinda, sorta, maybe, *absolutely* taken it personally.

Had I done something or said something to upset him?

And if not, what did it say about me that in less than five minutes my potential stalker was already done stalking?

Yeah, okay. Maybe neither of us made sense.

But it was done. Over. He was fine. Or so he'd claimed.

End of story...ish.

"Uhhh. Yeah. That's mine." I slid out of the booth and tried to grab his jacket, but she turned, holding it out of my reach.

"You don't wear a men's extra-large," she argued.

"I like my raincoats baggy. So what?"

"You do not," Dylan said, snapping her fingers for Angela to pass her what had clearly turned into exhibit A in this interrogation. "Do you have a new man you aren't telling us about?"

"What? No!" I defended. Diving forward, I banged my leg on the corner of the booth and almost knocked Angela over in an effort to prevent Dylan from getting her hands on it. For all I knew, she had an emergency DNA kit in her purse. I'd witnessed her track people down on Facebook with less information. That was one self-proclaimed detective I did not want to challenge.

She eyed me suspiciously. "Then why are you acting like such a weirdo right now?" As if a lightbulb went off in her head, all humor evaporated. "I swear to God, if that is Jeff's jacket and that asshole was here, I'm going to lose my shit."

Angela gasped, slapping a hand over her mouth, pure horror showing in her blue eyes.

I swung an incredulous scowl between them. "Seriously? Jeff? I'd rather amputate my own leg and then swim with sharks."

"Wait, wait, wait," Lucille interjected. "The hot gargoyle's name is Jeff?"

Dylan shivered. "Not if you're calling him hot."

Continuing the cacophony of confusion, Angela inquired, "Who's the hot gargoyle?"

Lucille smirked. "The piece of man meat who was wearing

that jacket last night. Did you happen to take off any more of his clothes? Because that's the screw-and-tell I'm going to need to hear."

And because there wasn't enough chaos in that room, there was a knock at the door. Our heads turned in unison.

"About damn time!" Lucille exclaimed.

A lanky middle-aged man in jeans and a red polo with sunglasses propped up in his sandy-blond hair smiled and waved from the other side of the door. It wasn't my contractor, but I assumed he was part of the crew. And even if he wasn't, as long as he could wield a sledgehammer, I was about to put him to work.

As I walked to the door, I dropped the infamous jacket on the seat of Truett's booth, praying for a little out-of-sight, out-of-mind reprieve.

"Hey," I greeted, opening the door. "Are you here to start the demo?"

The man's face was friendly and warm, like a father figure even though he wasn't much older than I was. "Uh, no. I'm actually here to talk to you, Gwen. Mind if I come in?"

My eyebrows furrowed at his apparent familiarity. "That depends. Talk to me about what?"

He passed me a business card. "My name is Taggart Folly. I'm with Flat Line Productions. I was hoping I could speak with you about a documentary we're filming on the Watersedge Mall shooting."

A sharp breath lodged in my throat. It had been years since anyone had uttered those words to me. Most people spent a considerable amount of energy tiptoeing around the subject. Surely, I'd misheard him. "What did you say?"

His smile never faltered. "I'm sorry about showing up like this. We've been trying to reach you for quite some time. I went by your old address and Jeff Weaver told me you'd be here. I hope it's okay that I stopped by."

I stared at him in disbelief. Of course, Jeff had told him how to find me. What better way to slay me than to send a hitman he didn't even have to pay.

His gaze lifted over my shoulder. "If now's not a good time, I'm happy to come back later."

Now wasn't a good time.

Later wouldn't be a good time, either.

Never was probably the only good.

I'd spent too many years clawing my way out of that darkness. Therapy. Meditation. Yoga. I'd done it all. There was no way I was going to risk unraveling the progress I had painstakingly achieved for the sake of a fucking documentary.

Squaring my shoulders, I handed him back the card. "You have the wrong person."

"See, I don't think I do. I've spoken with other survivors and—"

"I'm *not* a survivor," I seethed.

"Everything okay?" Lucille called.

My body shook with anger, but I tamped it down in the name of professionalism. "Yeah, I was just about to see Mr. Folly out." Stepping over the threshold, I forced him to back away. Waiting until the door was fully closed, I spoke with my voice low and my tongue sharp. "First of all, I find it disturbing that you thought ambushing me about the most traumatizing day of my life would be acceptable in *any* regard. But to do it when you so obviously have no idea what the hell you're talking about." I shook my head. "You disgust me."

His smile changed, or maybe I finally saw through the façade. It wasn't kind or warm—this man was one hundred percent cold and calculating. "What exactly is it that you think I don't know, Gwen?"

Every. Fucking. Thing.

"For starters, one Google search would tell you I wasn't in the mall that day."

"Maybe not. But you were there. We have the recording of your nine-one-one call."

The hairs on the back of my neck stood on end—a suffocating mixture of anger and pain filling my chest. I channeled the anger—it was easier to process. "Then you have already received the only statement you will *ever* get from me. Get the fuck off my property before I have the police escort you away." With that, I turned on a toe and started back inside.

My fingers had barely brushed the handle when his words hit me like a hand grenade.

There was no deafening blast, no flying debris, no physical destruction. But his question tore through me with devastating effects.

"Do you still keep in contact with Truett West?"

The world shrank around me like plastic wrap, stealing my ability to breathe. Fire flooded my veins, and the pressure in my chest felt like a vortex trying to separate me from my soul. I spun around so fast my head swam. "Excuse me?"

He tipped his head. "We haven't been able to reach him, either. I just figured—"

"Stay away from him!" I exploded, rushing forward. "Under no circumstance are you allowed to contact him. Do you understand me?"

He peered down his nose at me, his expression neutral but still grotesquely arrogant. "We believe his narrative would be crucial to our film."

"His narrative?" I hissed. "This isn't fucking fiction. People died that day. Even the survivors. Nobody walked out of that mall unscathed. Are you seriously standing here, telling me that you want to dredge that up, for what? Morbid curiosity? Entertainment?" I pressed up onto my toes and got in his face. "*Money*?"

His reaction to my outburst was so nonplussed it felt robotic. "We're trying to raise awareness about gun violence."

"You don't need Truett for that! Watersedge happened eighteen years ago. There have been dozens of tragedies since then. Go dig up those graves."

I didn't hear the door open before Dylan's arms circled around my waist from behind, restraining me.

"What the hell is going on out here?" she barked.

He lifted his hands placatingly and aimed his dry response at her. "I was just asking a few questions. I didn't mean to stir up anything."

"Bullshit!" I yelled, fighting against Dylan's hold. "A Goddamn documentary will stir up *everything*. Some people just want to forget."

"That is precisely what we're worried about," he challenged. "People have already forgotten. This documentary will—"

"Destroy him!" I boomed, finishing his statement. "This fucking documentary will absolutely *ruin him*, and I'll be honest there isn't much of that man left to begin with. Leave. Him. *Alone*."

Angela stepped in front of me, blocking my path and more than likely an assault charge. "This conversation is over. You need to go, sir."

He held my gaze over her shoulder. "Don't you think a hero should be celebrated?"

"What is there to celebrate?" I shouted. "Forty-eight people died in that mall."

"There were over a hundred others who escaped because of Truett West," he countered. "Given the amount of unused ammunition found on the scene, that was a miracle. We believe that's the story people need to hear."

"It's not a story! It was real life and real people and…and—" An onslaught of emotions crashed over me. I sagged against Dylan, keeping my legs under me by sheer force of will as memories shredded me.

How could something that happened so long ago suddenly

feel so raw? Agony pierced through my anger, causing tears to fill my eyes. "It destroyed us all. But especially Truett. Don't make him relive this. He will not come out the other side."

He stared at me, his posture remaining resolute and uncaring. "Maybe if he cooperates, we can finally get him the help he so obviously needs?" He tipped his chin. "Just think about it."

"Fuck you!" I yelled.

His slimy grin stretched as he lowered his sunglasses, and then casually strolled to a white BMW in the side parking lot.

Dylan didn't fully release me until his taillights had disappeared around the corner.

"Jesus," Lucille whispered. "What was that about?"

Angela turned to face me. "Are you okay?"

I stared at her without seeing, my mind spinning in a dozen different directions, all of them starting and finishing with one man. "I have to go," I whispered.

Dylan moved into my side, hooking her arm with mine. "Yeah, come on. Let's get you inside."

I snatched it away, fear engulfing me. "No. I have to *go*."

Her forehead crinkled. "That asshole's gone. You don't have to go anywhere."

Oh, but she was wrong.

So fucking wrong.

"He's not gone! He's gonna go to Truett." I darted inside and snatched my phone off the table and his raincoat from his booth. "I have to warn him."

They all called my name.

Dylan begged me to wait.

Angela offered to go with me.

But just before I left, I pointed to the booth in the corner and looked at Lucille. "If the contractor gets here, nobody touches that. Do you understand me?"

She gave me a sharp nod. "Loud and clear, Boss."

CHAPTER NINE

TRUETT

“Then she walked out with the coffee and everything just went. . .*quiet.* I couldn’t feel anything.”

“And the problem is?” Daniel’s face was so utterly incredulous it was almost insulting. No, strike that. It was totally insulting. The asshat was wearing a teal button-down tucked into pleated khaki slacks and he had the gall to look at *me* like I was the *ridiculous* one.

“Were you listening to anything I said?” I shoved a hand through the top of my hair and continued to pace a frenzied path through my living room.

“I listened all night actually. Got a set of blue balls to prove it.” He topped off his coffee and then put the carafe back on the warmer. “Any chance you could maybe not have a nervous breakdown on my birthday next year? When you called, Amber was just getting to the good stuff. And when you’ve been married as long as we have, birthdays are the *only* time you get the good stuff.”

I rolled my eyes. “You might be the worst psychiatrist in existence. I can’t believe people actually pay you for this shit.”

He barked a laugh. “You get what you pay for, asshat. And newsflash, you don’t pay me a penny.” Casually strolling past me, he walked to my tattered brown couch and sank down. The cushion let out a squeak, and without missing a beat, he reached into the crack and pulled out one of Kaitlyn's plastic ponies. "But if you want my professional opinion, I think this could be a healthy step for you."

I stopped and planted my hands on my hips. "In what realm of the universe is me losing my mind considered healthy?"

He tossed the pony into the toy basket beside the couch and then propped his yuppy-ass loafers on my coffee table. "Uhhh, I think we are a few years past the word 'losing.'"

"Remind me why I let you come inside again?"

He stared off into the distance, stroking his freshly shaved chin, and looking every bit as stupid as his wardrobe. "Perhaps my top-notch banter? Dashing good looks? Razor-sharp wit?" He swayed his head from side to side. "Or maybe because I'm the only friend you have."

He was not wrong there. Isolation didn't leave a lot of time for socializing. Luckily for me, Daniel had been born into his role as my best friend. He was seven years younger than me, strapped with the same deadbeat dad. We hadn't grown up together, but when I became a teen, I found myself seeking him out. I took him under my wing and tried to be the father figure we never had. Despite our different upbringings, we shared an unspoken bond. Through late-night conversations, a mutual love of football, and a competitive edge that bred a natural sibling rivalry, we got close.

He lived almost two hours away now, so we didn't see each other all that often anymore. Which, given my curse, was probably a hell of a lot safer for him.

I'd always found it amusing that he had grown up to be a head-doctor while I'd turned into a head-case. I had a whole team of therapists and medical professionals I could have reached out to in regard to Gwen's apparent superpower over me. Though Daniel would always be my first call. I must have sounded like a maniac on the phone, because he had already been standing on my front porch at eight a.m., ready to use his fancy degree to fan my flames.

It was only fair that he gave me a heavy dose of bullshit first.

I shot him a scowl. "You done cracking jokes yet?"

"Probably not."

"Awesome. Should I bend over to make it easier for you to kick me in the ass?"

He set his coffee on the end table, managing to fit it perfectly inside one of the stained water rings. "All right. All right. Let's just take a deep breath."

"That's the problem," I rumbled. "I *can* breathe, and I have no idea how to stop it."

"From a medical standpoint, I'm going to advise you *not* to stop it. The body usually revolts against asphyxiation."

"But I know how to handle that. I've been suffocating for years. Then suddenly, last night, I wasn't." I shook my head. "No, no. That's not true. I was definitely suffocating when I got home. But when I was sitting in that booth with her there…I, I…" I scrubbed a hand over my beard and fought to keep the emotion out of my voice. "I think she broke me. Forever."

"Hey," he said, all trace of humor gone. "I think you're framing this wrong. This is black-and-white thinking. You're assuming that because it happened once it's *always* going to be that way. There is no truth to be found in *always* and *never*."

It was a bald-faced lie therapists had been trying to shove down my throat for years. In my experience, *always* and *never* were far more factual than the torturous *maybe* and *possibly*. Those words implied that life was like a coin and every situation had two sides. Heads, everything works out. Tails, you fail everyone you love.

But my coin was one-sided.

It *always* had been.

That would *never* change.

Those were the facts.

I kept those thoughts to myself in order to avoid a twenty-minute lecture on faulty thinking patterns.

"What am I supposed to do now?" I asked.

He leaned forward and put his elbows to his knees. "I don't know. Maybe it's time to change the routine."

"No," I clipped, the idea knotting my gut. "There's gotta be another way."

"There are a lot of different ways, actually. I get why you go there every week, and a few years ago, I agreed. But it's time, Truett. You need to work on radical acceptance of the things you can and cannot change. Slicing the wounds open every week, even for just an hour, will never allow you to heal."

I don't deserve to heal. I didn't dare say that out loud, either. He'd have been all over the big D-word.

To avoid eye contact—and his shrink clairvoyance—I started pacing again. "Fine, okay. Let's pretend she didn't break me. The Grille's closed now. What if, when she opens up again, it's not the same?"

"Then we're right back to radical acceptance. You can't change what happens to The Grille. You can only control how you react to it."

If I had a nickel for every time someone had preached the same message, I could *maybe, probably,* find a coin that would finally land on heads. I wasn't holding my breath.

Intertwining my fingers, I rested my cradled hands on the top of my head and continued the step-step-turn routine. "Blah, blah, blah. I could have gotten that shit off a pamphlet at the VA."

"And if you had, I wouldn't have needed to forgo my birthday blowjob and then cancel my morning patients so I could come here and repeat it to you *again.*"

Guilt consumed me. Not about the blowjob. Fuck that. But I hated to be a burden. My issues were my own. As much as I leaned on Daniel, I never wanted to interfere with his life. I was so fucking proud of the man he'd become. He had an amazing wife, two handsome little boys, and a successful career that afforded him a lifestyle we could have only dreamed about when we were younger.

Unlike me, he *deserved* every single bit of that and more.

Drawing in a deep breath, I finally sat down on the other end of the couch. My heart didn't slow, nor did the panic leave my body, but I plastered on a smile. "Shit, I'm sorry."

He patted me on the shoulder. "You know I'm here for you no matter what, right? Day or night. It doesn't matter. I just wish I could drill a hole in your head and force this into your brain."

I chuckled. It wasn't real, but it was what he needed to hear in order to release him from duty. "So just to recap, you're against asphyxiation but cool with at-home brain surgery?"

Victory sang in my veins as his eyes lit with humor. "Don't worry. I did a whole eight-week rotation in general surgery during med school. I'm *totally* qualified."

"Well, next time, bring a drill. Who knows, a hole in my head might be exactly what I need."

His smile fell before I was able to finish the thought.

"I didn't mean it like that," I assured.

His scrutinizing gaze searched my face. "Are you having thoughts of self-harm again?"

"No," I stated clearly and honestly. "Those days are long gone. I promise. You're stuck with me until I'm old, gray, and incontinent. Okay?"

"You positive?"

I rested my hand over my heart. "I swear."

It burned the way he melted with such staggering relief. "Good. Though you've already got some gray in your beard. Is this your subtle way of telling me you're shitting your pants now too?"

I laughed, and it was finally genuine. Daniel was good like that.

Nothing had been solved. I had no clue what I was going to do next week when Wednesday afternoon rolled around, but that wasn't his problem. The sooner he left, the sooner I could keep it that way.

"All right, time for you to go," I announced, rising to my feet.

"Nah, I've got a few more hours. I don't have any patients until after lunch."

"Must be nice, but I have to get back to work, so maybe you should head back and see if Amber's up for some belated birthday *good stuff.*"

His mouth gaped. "Are you seriously kicking me out?"

"Yep!"

"Oh, come on!" His voice was so whiny it made me grin. He had MD behind his name and he was still the same kid trotting behind me, begging to be included. "I drove all the way down here. Let's order in some breakfast. I'm starved."

"I already ate." Giving him my back, I walked to the door.

"Come on. We never get to hang out."

I unlocked the deadbolt and gave the doorknob a twist. "I don't hang out on Thursdays. You know the schedule."

"News flash, Truett. You created the schedule. You can change it too." He continued to argue, but his footsteps sounded behind me.

"Sorry, bud." I swung the door open and then immediately suffered a heart attack. "Fuck!" I boomed, tripping over my own damn feet as I lurched back, barely catching myself on the doorjamb.

Gwen froze on the second step, my raincoat in her hand at her side, her eyes wide with surprise. "Sorry. I didn't mean to scare you."

She did more than scare me. Seeing her there terrified me for more reasons than I could count.

Even in the middle of a mild cardiac arrest, I couldn't stop my gaze from trailing down her body. Tight black athletic shorts clung to her toned thighs. One leg of the fabric was curiously longer than the other, but they hugged her in all the right places. A bright-pink tank top gaped at the sides, revealing a glimpse of her sports bra. And while it didn't appear that it was supposed to be a cropped top, it fell one delicious inch above her waistband. They were simple workout clothes. Not even particularly revealing ones at that. But dear God, she made my mouth dry.

I'd installed a doorbell camera long before they became a suburban accessory. It sent an alert to my cell phone when it detected motion at my door. I had never needed a warning more than when she nervously peered up at me while toying with her ponytail over one shoulder. Too little too late, my phone buzzed in my pocket when she made it up the final step.

At least the vibrations snapped me out of my drooling stupor.

"What are you doing here?" I asked accusingly.

It was a dick move, but she wasn't supposed to be there.

Not anymore.

"You got a few minutes?" she asked. "I need to talk to you."

That did not sound good.

I didn't have the chance to respond before Daniel ducked around me, sporting a shit-eating grin. "He has nothing but time, actually."

Her face stretched into a smile.

Wide.

Bright.

Breathtaking.

Aimed at him.

Twist the fucking dagger, why don't ya.

"Danny?" She gasped.

The jackass stepped directly in front of me like I'd become the invisible man. "Technically, I go by Doctor Daniel West now, but yeah, you can still call me Danny."

Gwen dropped my jacket like it had developed a case of leprosy, and all but launched herself into his arms. I, on the other hand, secured a life in dentures, clenching my teeth so hard it was positive they'd shatter.

Dr. Shithead lifted Gwen off her feet and spun her in a circle, nearly taking my knees out with her dangling legs. Last I'd checked, we were not in a countryside field in Austria with Julie Andrews singing in the background. Was spinning seriously necessary?

I would not punch my brother.

I would not punch my brother.

"Damn, it's good to see you again, Gwennie."

Gwennie?

Fucking Gwennie?

Okay, maybe just one punch.

I propped my shoulder against the door frame, trying to play the role of cool and casual. Then on every half spin, when I was positive Gwen couldn't see me, I leveled my brother with a glower that I hoped scalded his skin.

He eventually got the message—or, knowing that pansy, he just got dizzy—and set her on her feet.

"Wow," she breathed. "Look at you, all grown up. A doctor too?"

He flexed a puny bicep. "Yeah. I had to make a plan B when the whole professional wrestling thing didn't pan out."

I couldn't have rolled my eyes harder without causing permanent injury.

"You really tried to do that?" she asked.

"I'm a buck fifty soaking wet with the athletic ability of a sloth. Teenage dreams die hard in reality." He hooked his thumb over his shoulder—and oh look, I existed again. "He got the brute and I got the brains. Fair split, I guess."

I shoved his shoulder harder than necessary. "Perfect. Then maybe you should use your brains to figure out how to get the hell out of here."

Teetering off-balance on the edge of the top step, he flashed Gwen a teasing grin. "I guess I'm leaving now. I hear you bought The Grille? Maybe when you reopen, I can stop by so we can catch up."

"I would love that."

"All right, then. It's a date."

Oh, yeah, I was going to punch the shit out of him later and I didn't give one fuck that Amber would probably light my house on fire for maiming his pretty little face.

"See ya, Truett," he called over his shoulder.

As little brothers do, he drove me up a wall most of the time, but life was too fragile to ever allow him to leave like that.

"Hey!" I jogged down the steps after him. "'See ya, Truett'? That's it?"

He slanted his head, his lips twitching. "You looked like you were about to take a baseball bat to my knees. I figured I should run while I still can."

I dragged him into a hard hug. "Don't be ridiculous. You know I'd aim higher than your knees."

He barked a laugh and patted me on the back. "Love you, brother."

"Love you too. Thanks for coming down."

Holding my shoulders, he leaned away and caught my eye. "Any time and *every* time. Promise me you know that."

I lifted my middle finger and shot him the bird. "Scout's honor."

"Good. Now, try to act normal. There's a woman who is actually willing to talk to you on the porch. Don't screw this up."

I slapped him on the back of the head. "You know, it's funny. I suddenly don't feel guilty for costing you that blowjob last night."

He laughed all the way to his black Cadillac parked on the street. I didn't watch him leave as I was already heading back to Gwen.

She was holding my jacket again. "Wow. That was a blast from the past."

"Mmm," I hummed. "Seems to be a lot of that going around recently."

Her gaze came back to mine, the joy vanishing from her face the instant our eyes met.

Awesome. That didn't slay me at all.

"Here," she said, extending the jacket in my direction. "You left that last night."

"Yeah, I realized that about two blocks too late." I draped it over the shoe rack just inside the door. "Thanks."

"You mind if I come in?" she asked.

My back snapped straight, my entire body becoming rigid.

Shiiiiiiit.

CHAPTER TEN

Gwen

NOSTALGIA HAD ASSAULTED ME THE MINUTE I SAW THAT small brick house with the white railing. Memories flooded my system—good, bad, incredible, horrendous, euphoric, soul shattering, and everything in between. Seeing Danny again had been a nice reprieve from the pressure mounting in my chest. But as much as I would have liked to have forgotten, I wasn't there for a reunion.

"We need to talk," I said to Truett. "Inside would probably be best."

Indecision stormed in his eyes. "Things are kind of a…mess right now."

"I'm not worried about the cleanliness of your home. I promise I didn't bring my white gloves to check for dust." I started inside, but he sidestepped, blocking my path. I barely managed to keep from running into his barrel chest.

"You can't go in there," he snapped.

I wanted to ask why. I quite literally had to purse my lips to keep the words from flying out. But it wasn't my place to question him. When I'd seen him alone at the diner, I'd assumed he didn't have a family. But maybe I'd been wrong. He didn't wear a ring, but he could have had girlfriend or something. It was early, but for all

I knew, he could have been having a party or…an orgy. With his brother? Yuck. Never mind. None of my business.

I swallowed hard and tried not to think about the latter. "Am I interrupting something?"

"No, it's just—" He quickly pulled the door shut. "Let's sit out here."

I glanced around his porch. It wasn't big by any means, but it would have comfortably fit two rocking chairs or a bench swing. As it was, it was empty, not a potted plant or woman's touch to be seen. Not that I was checking for that or anything. It was just an observation.

He scrubbed his hands on his faded jeans and then pressed a palm to my back, ushering me toward the stairs. There was something so comforting about his touch—a familiarity my body recognized immediately.

As if teaching me how to sit, he slowly sank down on the top concrete step, and then he peered up at me expectantly to follow his lead.

Fucking hell, this was not where I wanted to drop this bomb on him. Not that inside the house—especially *that house*—would have been any better, but privacy would have helped.

He patted the space beside him. "Come on. The fresh air will be nice."

Yeah. Until that damn producer pulled up, bombarding him with arrows disguised as questions. Shit. Truett would have been a sitting duck on that front porch.

Nerves reignited inside me. I swung my head from side to side, searching up and down the street. "Can we sit on the back porch? Or stand in the backyard? Or…behind the bushes? Or…" I didn't realize I was knotting my hands until he reached up to still them. For some reason, that too felt comfortable. I had no idea how to process that.

His eyes bored into me with a tangible intensity. "What's wrong?"

I considered myself a damn good actress. God knew I'd had enough practice hiding my emotions from Jeff through the years. You didn't survive a narcissist if you didn't master the ability to smile even when they were breaking you.

But not with Truett. I'd never had to hide with him, and it seemed my body remembered that on instinct too.

Telling him this was going to feel every bit as good as kicking a puppy.

But why *me*? Why did I have to be the one to break this news? I didn't have the best success rate when it came to Truett. Too many times, I'd tried to keep him from falling apart. Too many times, I'd failed. Too many times I'd sacrificed parts of myself in the name of helping him. Yet there I stood, cracking open the history books all over again, when I'd sworn all the pages had already been shredded.

"Gwen," he prompted, his patience waning.

Rip off the Band-Aid, Gwen. Just rip it off.

And then get the hell out of there and back to real life in the present.

I didn't sit down next to him. That would have taken too much time, and I feared if I didn't spit the words out right away, I'd be trapped on that porch forever. "A producer named Taggart Folly visited me today. They're filming a documentary on the Watersedge Mall."

"What?" he snarled, shooting to his feet. His brown eyes flashed a scary shade of dark as he took the step up, closing the space between us.

My breath hitched and my nose stung. This was so fucked up. So fucking fucked up. Eighteen years later and we were back at that house, facing the repercussions of that damn mall.

My body hummed as he loomed over me—tiny sparks prickling my skin as if it had fallen sleep and finally awoken. I told myself it was nerves and had nothing to do with the man in front of me. Lying to myself was far easier than processing that clusterfuck.

I tried to keep the shake out of my voice as I answered him. "He said he'd spoken to some of the survivors. Then he asked if I still kept in contact with you."

"That motherfucker." Truett stabbed a hand into the top of his hair, the muscles on his neck straining the fabric of his black T-shirt. "What kind of questions did he ask you?"

"Nothing really."

Murderous, he stared down at me. "That's not an answer."

Eying him cautiously, I hesitated. I'd expected this to go over like a knife to the gut—surprise, pain, panic. But the all-consuming rage emanating from him was unexpected—and oddly intoxicating.

"Start at the beginning," he ordered. "No more of the 'nothing really' shit. I want to know every word he dared to speak to you."

My brain fired off roughly four million smartass retorts in response to him ordering me to do anything. But when I spoke, my traitorous mouth overrode my brain. "He knocked on the door and asked if he could talk to me."

"Were you at The Grille?"

"Yeah."

"Alone?" He ominously inched closer—and truthfully there wasn't a whole lot of *close* left for him to inch.

His proximity clouded my thoughts, but I managed to shake my head.

"Did you let him inside?"

"No."

"Good girl," he whispered, his breath feathering across my skin, leaving a trail of chills down my neck. "And after that?"

I couldn't breathe, his hypnotizing gaze holding me captive. "I told him no and then lost my mind on him for digging up the past."

His jaw clenched. "And how did he take that? Did he get aggressive or loud? Because I swear to God, Gwen, I will—"

"Hey," I whispered. "It's fine. He was a dick but nothing I couldn't handle."

He glanced off to the side, mumbling, "Fucking piece of shit."

I rested a hand on his chest, his heart pounding beneath it. "He's gonna show up here, True. You need to be ready."

His gaze snapped back to mine. "Oh, I'm fucking ready. I wish that spineless leech would drag his ass to my door. I told him months ago to stay out of Belton. It's bad enough they call me every goddamn day. Leaving messages morning, noon, and night. But showing up like that? You better believe I'm gonna shut that bullshit down real fast."

A staggering betrayal stopped me cold. "You knew about this?"

"Journalists have been trying to get their talons into me for years. Folly's not nearly as original as he thinks. He's just a bigger asshole than most. I'll call my lawyer and see what we can do to stop him from coming back."

I blinked at him—annoyance roaring to life and thankfully silencing the hum he'd caused inside me. "Why didn't you tell me?"

His forehead crinkled. "What?"

I shoved at his chest, forcing him back. "Why didn't you warn me? I was blindsided today when he showed up. And you know what? All I was worried about was *you.* I ran all the way over here panicking that you were going to lose your mind. I should have known something was up when you pulled that sexy voodoo hypnotism shit."

He quirked an eyebrow, but I was on a roll, so I ignored it.

"What the hell was the point in the cranky caveman routine? This wasn't news to you. You've known for months and never thought to mention it?" I shook my head and crossed my arms over my chest.

Okay, so maybe I was more than annoyed. I was flat-out pissed.

And worse, this jackass smiled.

At me.

Those perfect lips curled at the corners of his mouth. It was a masterpiece and so classically Truett it made me want to kick him. That was also another lie I told myself. What I really wanted to do to his mouth definitely started with a K, but with him, it would have been the worst four-letter word possible.

The kick was safer.

"You done yet?" he asked.

Like the mature adult I was, I mocked, "You done yet?"

His smile grew. "You were worried about me, huh?"

I scoffed. "Truett, you've had a panic attack every time I've seen you the last few weeks. Yeah, it's safe to say I was worried."

That made his smile fall, and much to my dismay, it didn't feel nearly as good as I'd hoped. Actually, it made me feel like a total jerk.

"Shit, I'm sorry," I muttered.

He hung his head. "You don't have to apologize for the truth."

"I don't have to be rude about it, either."

The side of his mouth hiked as he peeked up at me through thick lashes. "That's true too. You can be pretty rude."

I leveled him with a glare, but it only succeeded in making the other side of his mouth hike too.

He moved to the step and sat down again. Tipping his chin to the spot beside him, he bargained with, "Humor me for a few minutes? No panic attacks this time. I promise."

My shoulders sagged as the anger ebbed from my system. I had a laundry list of things to do. A contractor to harass. A restaurant to demolish. But against my better judgment, I sank down beside him.

The stairs were only so wide, and he was a big guy, so I was extra careful not to touch him.

Reading me like a book, he interlocked his fingers and rested his elbows on his thighs in an effort to make himself smaller. It worked to an extent. Our bodies weren't touching, but there was still a connection that had nothing to do with the physical.

"I didn't know you would want me to warn you," he said. "We hadn't spoken in years, and after the way things ended, I thought me reaching out to you would be even worse than someone like Folly."

He had a point. A few weeks earlier, I'd have chosen an entire documentary crew showing up on my front lawn with a mariachi band at three in the morning over a phone call from Truett. I couldn't put my finger on why that had changed. Given how my emotions had been a pendulum of highs and lows since he'd made a reappearance in my life, I wouldn't say it fell under the "time heals all wounds" category. Maybe over the years, I'd callused over enough that the mere sight of him didn't rip open the scars of my heart anymore.

Or maybe Jeff had shown me how awful the people who claimed to love you could really be to the point that Truett didn't seem so bad anymore.

The thought made guilt churn in my stomach. There was no comparison between a monster and a man.

I tugged on the hem of my stupid shorts, trying to make the legs the same length. Anything for a distraction. "I shouldn't have blamed you for that. It's not your responsibility to keep me informed."

"I can do it from now on though."

I couldn't tell if it was a statement or a question, but I decided to let him off the hook either way. "Don't worry about it."

"I do though. I can't explain the whole 'sexy voodoo hypnotism shit' as you so eloquently called it." His face warmed playfully, and I was struck, not for the first time, by how damn handsome he was.

My cheeks heated, so I looked down to hide my blush.

He swayed toward me, pointedly bumping me with his shoulder. "But the cranky caveman thing was because I'm livid he went to you. I'll figure something out so you don't have to worry about that asshole again." He held my gaze, a fierce determination blazing in his eyes, sealing his promise.

I believed him wholeheartedly. Contrary to the dense tattoos and thick ropes of muscle, Truett had always been something of a gentle giant. He was older now, but somewhere inside him was still the same kid who'd once pulled over on the highway to pick me a bouquet of wildflowers when he couldn't afford anything else for our anniversary.

But gentle did not equal a pushover. When it came to his family and friends, Truett had the heart of a warrior and the ruthlessness to match. I found it interesting that I still fit into either of those categories for him.

I'd sworn to myself I wouldn't ask him any more questions. I'd learned the hard way just how futile that could be. But on that step, it seemed he'd finally found his voice. I hoped like hell that meant I could finally use mine too.

"How are you doing, True? Like *really* doing?" I prepared myself for the same cookie-cutter responses he'd given me since the day he'd come home from his first and only deployment. *I'm fine. I'm okay. I'm hanging in there.* But for the first time in almost two decades, he spoke words that I didn't need a therapist to decode.

"I guess that depends on who you ask." He looked down, becoming fascinated by his bare feet. Meanwhile, I was just fascinated with him. "My therapists check in with me weekly and my doctor makes house calls. I'm pretty sure that's not normal."

"Truett," I breathed, wishing like hell I'd stuck to my no-questions policy. The weight of gravity suddenly crushed me. "You still don't go out in public? But…I saw you…at the restaurant…in the rain."

He blew out a ragged breath, slowly peeking up at me. He tried to smile, but it was wholly sad—and completely heartbreaking. "Once a week I go to The Grille, but recently my ex-wife bought it and promptly shut it down."

"Oh, God," I whispered, my lungs suddenly on fire. Whether it was a voluntary reaction or not, I couldn't be sure, but I immediately reached for him. Resting my hand on his thigh, I gave him a squeeze. "I didn't know. I swear I didn't."

"I know," he mumbled. "How could yo—"

"Holy shit! You're Truett West." Lucille's voice broke through the moment.

My head popped up to see Dylan and Angela standing beside her on the sidewalk.

Dylan was sporting her usual skeptical curiosity.

Angela looked apologetic.

And Lucille, well... Clearly, they'd filled her in, because she appeared unapologetically starstruck. "I've been serving Truett West for years and didn't even know it." She planted her hands on her hips. "You know, you could have told me. I would have given you a discount. Heroes should never have to pay full price."

I gasped, but it was too late. The H word had been released like a bag of venomous snakes.

Truett went solid, his thigh becoming granite. "I'm not a fucking hero," he seethed, rising to his feet.

And she didn't stop there. Fucking Lucille could not read a room even if she was the only one in it. "Sure you are. You saved all those people at the mall. You should be proud."

Oh, fuckity fuck. Proud was the only word worse than hero.

I stood and stepped in front of him, not sure if I was protecting him or her. "Lucille!" I yelled. "Please stop talking."

"Get the fuck away from my house," Truett snarled from behind me. His anger was so palpable I could feel the vibrations on my back.

"Go back to the restaurant," I urged, flaring my eyes at Dylan and Angela in a plea for help.

They jumped into action, tugging on her arms.

"All right. Gwen's fine. Everything looks good to me. Let's go," Dylan said.

Lucille argued, "Did I say something wrong?"

"Just come on," Angela hissed, dragging her away.

I could still hear her arguing as they disappeared down the street when I turned back to Truett. "I'm so sorry about that."

His mouth was a hard slash as he stared over my shoulder in the direction they'd left. And just like that, he was gone again. Still standing in front of me, but this was the version of Truett West who had abandoned me after six years of marriage.

"You should go," he grumbled, never meeting my gaze again as he turned toward the door.

"Wait," I called as I hurried after him, but his impenetrable walls were already locked in place.

He yanked the door open and stepped inside.

Then, in the mother of all role reversals, I used his trick and caught the door with my foot. "Wednesday," I told his back. "I'll be there from noon until late, so come whenever you want. Okay?"

He didn't move.

Nor did he reply.

But the way his strong body relaxed told me he'd heard me.

No sooner than I moved my foot did the door slam in my face.

Yeah. I knew that version of Truett West all too well.

And I fucking *hated* him.

CHAPTER ELEVEN

TRUETT

Eighteen years earlier...

A river of blood carved its path at my feet as I sat frozen—ass on the tile, back to an overturned table—the past melding into the terrifying present.

The world around me blurred, paralyzing memories so vivid and relentless holding me captive.

In my head, I heard Nutz shout, "*Vehicle's not slowing, S'arnt!*" The echo of his voice was as clear as if he stood beside me. A vise cranked down on my chest, making every breath more and more difficult until I longed for the reprieve of suffocation.

I was trapped in a war zone, the sound of cries and moans echoing around me.

"*What the fuck is this guy doing?*" Steve-O yelled.

My heart pounded in my ears, each beat feeling like the strike of a sledgehammer.

My skin crawled, every nerve ending firing on high alert.

"*There's four occupants, and I see two AKs, S'arnt!*" Skytrash shouted over the chaos.

I couldn't move—my limbs heavy, rooting me in hell.

"*Take out the driver,*" S'arnt ordered.

Gunfire—real or imagined—rocked me to the core. I flinched, curling tighter into myself.

Each second stretched into an eternity as I waged war with my mind.

I wasn't back in Iraq.

But I was living an even more inescapable nightmare.

At six three, two twenty, I was trained in every form of combat the Army had to offer. But as I sat in that mall food court, bodies strewn around me, a gunman on the loose, killing everyone in his path, I was nothing but a helpless child, trapped in my own mind.

Suddenly, a man got up and darted toward the double glass doors. There was no point in running. They'd been chained together, trapping us like wild animals ripe for the hunt.

With one single gunshot, the man dropped to the floor. I slapped my hands over my ears to block out the sounds.

I couldn't focus, but I desperately tried to use the grounding techniques they'd drilled into me during countless therapy sessions.

Five things I could see: lifeless eyes, bullet casings, abandoned shopping bags, terrified faces, the red-stained sneakers of the dead man beside me.

Four things I could touch: my shaking legs, splintered wood, the cold tile, so much blood.

Three things I could hear: footsteps of a madman, muffled cries, death-rattled breathing.

Two things I could smell: acrid gunpowder, metallic blood.

One thing I could taste: every single one of my failures.

This wasn't happening.

Not again.

My whole body jerked when another gunshot sounded, marking the end of another life. My stomach rolled, bile crawling up the back of my throat.

I couldn't do this.

I wasn't scared of dying, but I wouldn't be able to survive the aftermath of this.

I didn't *want* to survive the aftermath.

Just as I'd convinced myself to stand up and volunteer as his next victim, two kids sprinted toward the pizza place. The lanky boy was older, no more than sixteen, while the girl with red ringlets couldn't have been older than ten. I assumed they were siblings, but why hadn't their parents stopped them? I answered my own question as I watched in horror as they held hands, leaping over bodies as they ran.

"Hey!" the gunman yelled.

I nervously leaned forward to see how far away he was. They had a decent head start, but bullets didn't need to be close to hit their mark. He gave chase, the spray of his gunfire narrowly missing them.

I scanned the area, frantically searching to see if anyone was going to help them. They were kids; somebody had to do something. Somebody had to—

My heart stopped as her brown gaze collided with mine through the glass doors.

Gwen.

Oh, God, Gwen.

Seeing her there, knowing she could be next—that was a kind of helplessness I would never be able to forget.

"Truett!" she screamed from outside the mall doors. She had a cell phone held to her ear in one hand, the other balled in a fist, pounding on the glass.

I blinked, panic engulfing me. Glass wasn't bulletproof, and pressed up against it, her whole body was vulnerable. She might as well have been wearing a target.

If he saw her. . . .

If he fucking saw her, I had no doubt he would—

Like a guillotine in my mind, a sharp blade of reality fell, severing the past's grip over me. As my mind slowly transported me back to the present, my instincts roared to life.

No fucking way I was going to let anything happen to her.

I'd failed them. *All of them.* I would not let Death take her from me too.

I glanced back in time to see the gunman follow the kids into the kitchen of the pizza place, momentarily leaving the dining area unguarded.

I could have run—others did, escaping deeper into the mall.

But when another gunshot rang through the air, it was like a match to my central nervous system. Adrenaline exploded inside me as I clambered to my feet. I paused to steal one last glimpse at the most beautiful woman I would ever see.

I didn't have a weapon or body armor, but I was determined to take that maniac down no matter the cost. There was no guarantee I'd survive—mentally or physically. That very well could have been the last time I ever saw her.

My chest ached as I took in her tear-stained cheeks. I wanted to tell her I loved her and, no matter what she thought, I had loved her every minute of every day since she was sixteen years old and walked into my math class wearing a smile that branded my soul. Nothing would change that. Not even death.

Though, after everything I'd put her through, those words would have been purely selfish. She was moving on. No matter how much it destroyed me. I'd all but forced her hand.

My list of failures was already a mile long when it came to Gwen. No way I was adding to that in what was more than likely my final moments on earth.

I'm sorry, I mouthed to her.

Her eyes flashed wide, understanding donning on her face. "Truett, no!" she screamed, pounding even harder on the door.

All these people were trying to get out, and my Gwen was out there fighting like hell to get inside.

She was scared.

So fucking scared.

But that was quite literally the only thing I could fix for her anymore.

With blood roaring in my ears and a new resolve coursing through my veins, I took off toward the pizza place, hell-bent on ending this nightmare once and for all.

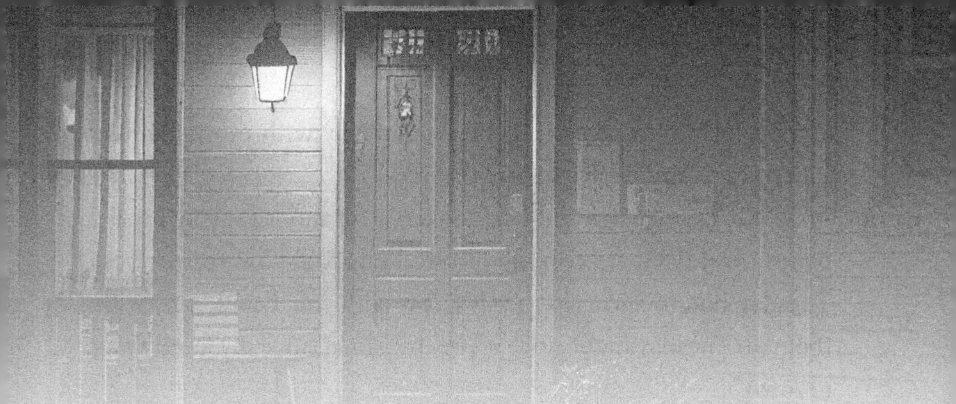

CHAPTER TWELVE

Gwen

"But, Mom," Nate whined through the phone. "Dad already bought tickets!"

I ground my teeth and dropped the paint roller in the tray.

When we'd separated, Jeff and I had agreed to fifty-fifty custody, because neither of us liked the idea of being away from our son for a full week. My therapist had recommended we try a 5-2-2-5 schedule. This meant I had Nate on every Monday and Tuesday, and Jeff got him every Wednesday and Thursday. We alternated weekends, which bled into our regular days, giving us each two five-day stretches with him per month. It had been a tad confusing at first and taken some getting used to, but it'd been over a year now. There was no way Jeff had magically forgotten our schedule when he'd purchased two tickets to a Monday night Yankees game.

It wasn't the first time he'd pulled this crap, either. Jeff was a habitual line stepper who would rather berate me for being "crazy" and "selfish" than simply ask for permission *before* making a commitment to our son. He had nothing to lose. I, on the other hand, was forced to either be the bad guy and tell Nate no or give up a day with my son.

I shifted the phone, pinning it against my ear with my shoulder, and used both hands to refill the paint tray with more primer. "Sorry, bud. You'll have school that day."

"No, I don't! Me and Dad looked it up and it's spring break. Nanny and Papa are coming into town too. He has to work on Tuesday, but he said as long as it's okay with you, I could stay with them on Tuesday night since it's been so long since my family was in town."

Oh, look. He'd made plans for Monday *and* Tuesday, using his family as an excuse to manipulate me into saying yes rather than just asking. Oh, and it was not lost on me that Nate had used the term 'my family.' It wouldn't surprise me if Jeff was holding up cue cards during this call.

"Mom, please. Please. Pleeeeeeease!"

Thankfully my son couldn't see me, because I rolled my eyes so hard it probably would have registered on the Richter scale.

Yes, this was a gross overstep on Jeff's part, but, after all the shit he'd pulled, a father-son trip to a baseball game was the least of my worries.

"Just let me think about it, okay? Maybe I can talk to Dad about trading days with me or something." *Right after I wasted my breath talking to him about boundaries and respect.*

"Wooohooo!" he shouted.

"Don't start celebrating yet. I did *not* say yes."

"But you will, 'cause you're the best mom in the whole wide world."

"Okay, now you're just sucking up."

"Maybe." He laughed wildly and it filled my chest with happiness. Little moments like that were what kept me going—no matter how hard things got.

"All right, buddy. I have to get back to painting. I'll see you on Friday, okay?"

"Okay. I love you. Infinity times infinity."

My grin stretched. "Oof, that's a lot. But I still love you more. Infinity times infinity *times infinity*."

I waited, knowing exactly what was coming. I'd laughed so hard the first time he did it it'd cemented itself as part of our routine.

He rushed out with a giggled, "Plus one. I win." Then he hung up without so much as a goodbye.

Grinning like a fool, I put the empty primer can down and slid my phone into the pocket of my paint-stained yoga pants. I'd never been more eager to get back to work on The Rosewood.

Yes. It was finally The Rosewood.

In a miracle of all miracles, the contractor had fulfilled his promise and The Grille was officially gone.

The kitchen had been gutted.

Linoleum floors peeled up.

Wallpaper torn down.

Just my luck, we'd discovered water damage in the kitchen that had seeped into the dining room. Lucille had negotiated me a sweet discount, but I'd still had to dig even deeper into my shoestring budget to have some of the studs and sheetrock replaced.

And that wasn't the only expense that had snuck up on me. The ventilation system needed a total overhaul to bring it up to code, and the walk-in cooler didn't get cold enough to meet food safety standards.

How The Grille hadn't been shut down at least a dozen times, I would never understand, but it was my pain-in-the-pocketbook now.

Despite the fact that I'd padded the budget for the unexpected, that pocketbook had emptied far more quickly than I'd prepared for. Unless I wanted to kick off entrepreneurship in a mountain of debt, I was going to have to use some good old-fashioned elbow grease and finish the renovation on my own.

Needless to say, there would be *a lot* of YouTube tutorials in my future.

Snagging the empty primer can, I walked to the parking lot to toss it into the dumpster. The company my contractor had rented it from was late hauling it away, so I was making the most of it.

"Shit!" I yelled as I turned the corner, slamming directly into Truett's chest.

I hadn't been positive he'd take me up on my invitation to come back. There was a part of me that hoped he wouldn't. But I also knew a different part of me would have marched down there and dragged him out of that damn house by his ear if need be.

I ached knowing he'd locked himself away from the world. Solitude had always been his go-to coping mechanism, but all these years later? How was that even possible?

I'd spent a lot of time over the last week, revisiting the past, both consciously and in my dreams. Sometimes we were kids again, young and carefree. Others, we were fighting; his silence making my ears ring as I begged him to talk to me.

Much to my own frustration, I'd thought about him over the years—birthdays, anniversaries, and such. How could I not? Nobody forgets their first love.

Unfortunately, the same could be said for their first heartbreak too. It didn't matter that it had been over eighteen years since he'd served me with divorce papers. The pure disdain I felt for that man had kept my thoughts of him fleeting and extinguished all curiosity of where life had taken him.

But deep down, I'd assumed life had taken him *somewhere*.

Now, as he stood there on Wednesday night, his face blank, no reaction, and his eyes glued to the remnants of The Grille hanging out of the dumpster, I wasn't so sure.

"Jesus, True. You have to stop scaring me all the damn time."

Emotionless, he looked down at me. "Technically, you scared me last week."

I rolled my eyes. Leave it to Mr. Personality to point out the semantics. "Why are you out here? I left the door open so you could come inside tonight."

"You gutted it?" he asked, his voice timid as if he didn't want the answer.

I tossed the primer can into the dumpster. "If you'd have seen the mess we pulled out of there, you'd be asking me why I didn't set it on fire and collect the insurance money."

"It's gone? All of it?"

I crossed my arms over my chest. "That depends. Who are you?"

His eyebrows drew together. "Huh?"

"Who are you tonight? The nice guy sitting on the porch, cracking jokes, or the one who slammed the door in my face?"

His lips thinned. "I guess that also depends. Is Cooter here?"

I couldn't help the smile that stretched my mouth. "You call her Cooter? With a straight face?"

"I don't call her anything, but that's how she introduces herself every damn time she sees me. And let's be real, the woman is a loon. Cooter might be the only name appropriate for her."

"Touché," I replied.

He scrubbed a hand over his bearded jaw. "But to answer your question, I don't know who I am any night, Gwen. Especially recently."

"Why recently?"

"You mean besides the obvious?" He gave me a pointed head-to-toe that I assumed was supposed to be teasing, but for reasons I refused to acknowledge, his scrutiny caused my face to heat.

Okay, that was a lie. My whole damn body heated.

Quickly turning away before he could see the color in my cheeks, I started toward door and waved for him follow. "Lucille isn't here. But consider yourself warned, she is working for me now. I had a long talk with her the other day, so she knows to keep her mouth shut from here on out."

"Appreciated," he mumbled, his footsteps sounding behind me.

I stopped at the door and turned to meet his gaze again. "Look, if you can play nice, so can I. Deal?"

As soon as he nodded, I swung open the door and stepped aside to allow him a clear view inside.

His inhale was sharp as he froze in the doorway, beautiful disbelief etched on his face.

I'd been there every day for a week, so I was used to the changes already. I tried to imagine seeing it through his eyes. The space appeared smaller now that it was empty. The bare concrete floors and half-primed walls only added to the illusion of desolation, yet in the corner, a single booth stood as the lone beacon of familiarity.

"Gwen," he rumbled, so much packed inside that single syllable it caused chills to pebble my skin. "You kept it?"

I popped one shoulder. "What kind of host would I be if I invited you here and then expected you to sit on the floor?"

He didn't move for a long second, his dark gaze locked on the booth. As his breathing sped and the muscles at the base of his neck swelled, I couldn't tell if he was relieved or terrified.

Nerves erupted in my stomach as I suddenly felt like I'd done something wrong. Shit, had I kept the wrong one?

"Truett," I prompted.

"Thank you," he choked out. "You have no idea what this means to me."

Wasn't that the damn truth.

Fortunately for him, compassion didn't require understanding. "You're welcome." I reached out and gave his forearm a lingering squeeze.

His palm covered mine so fast it was as if our hands had become magnetized. We were north and south, total opposites, connecting together in the most natural way possible.

I hated that it felt right.

I hated that I'd craved that connection for the majority of my life.

But most of all, I hated when he let me go—in the past and the present.

Slowly, as if he were afraid it was nothing more than a mirage, he walked over and trailed his fingertips across the tabletop. A gentle laugh escaped his throat, a sound both tender and bittersweet, as if he were welcoming home an old friend. The reunion felt so personal I debated if it was wrong to watch. However, as Truett slid into the booth with a profound reverence, I found myself unable to look away.

He drew in a shaky breath, his head lolling back as if he were absorbing a necessary nutrient he'd long been deprived of.

And then in the most confusing moment of my life, I was struck by a thought so rancid it burned my throat.

In that booth, Truett seemed at home.

A place he had once found with me.

Nope. Nope. Nope. I was not going there. I was doing a good deed, not driving a bulldozer into the past. I needed to remember that—for both of our sakes.

I shook my head in a frenzied effort to dislodge whatever insanity had caused garbage to spew all over my frontal lobe. "Is it going to bother you if I paint?"

His eyes popped open, and for a brief moment, he appeared disconcerted. "Where? In here?"

I pointed to the full paint tray a few steps away. "That was kinda the plan."

His eyes shifted from side to side. "Oh. Yeah. That's fine."

But he didn't say it in a tone like it was *fine* at all. He said it like he was disappointed.

And because the past few weeks hadn't been enough of a colossal mindfuck, I was somehow disappointed that he was disappointed by the idea of my presence in my own damn restaurant.

Sweet baby Jesus in a manger. I needed to schedule an appointment with my therapist ASAP.

It was already after six and my aching muscles had a hot date with my bathtub and a glass of wine before bed. I didn't have the time to analyze Truett's emotional grid. Paint was drying and my brain was rotting. Time to get back to work.

The next hour was strange. Actually, strange was a gross understatement. It was epically strange. *Twilight-Zone*-meets-*Black-Mirror* strange.

I put my earbuds in and blasted my favorite early 2000s R&B playlist, effectively ending any possible conversation, but out of the corner of my eye, I watched him.

Fidgeting.

Shifting.

Closing his eyes.

Opening them.

Shaking his head.

His lips moved with mumbled curses, and he cracked his neck, wrists, fingers, and everything else with a joint.

He was so obviously uncomfortable, and I couldn't figure out why he didn't just leave.

And then I'd catch him watching me.

Eyes soft.

Body relaxed.

An almost imperceptible smile lifting one side of his mouth.

There was something so undeniably beautiful about that man's smile, no matter how slight it might have been.

I tried to focus on the task at hand, but more than once, I found myself painting over the same area while spying on him with my peripheral vision.

Me watching him. Him watching me. Me watching him

watching me. It was a ridiculous cycle of Peeping Toms, trying to out peep each other.

Eventually, I ran out of primer and went to grab one from the storage room.

When I returned, his booth was empty.

His quiet departure should have been a relief. We didn't have to do the whole awkward goodbye where we stood there, debating between the hug or handshake before landing on a curt nod and uncomfortable smiles. But I would have taken awkward any day over the hollow ache in my chest as I stared at that empty booth.

I glanced at my watch.

7:01 and Truett West was a ghost all over again.

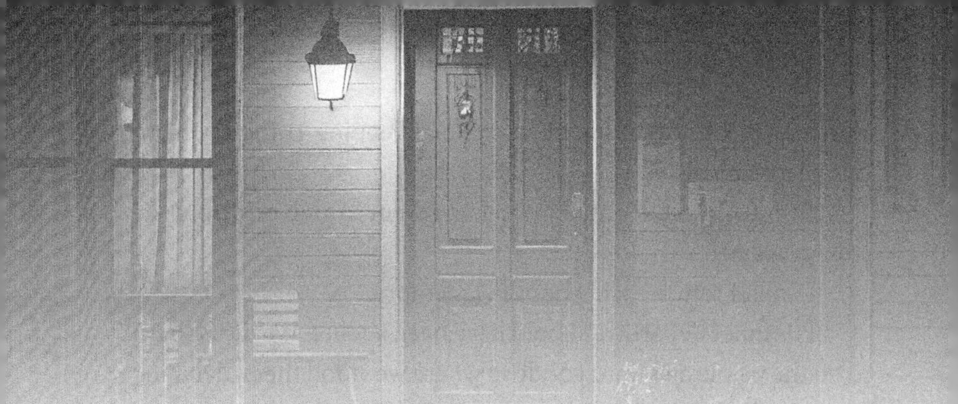

CHAPTER THIRTEEN

TRUETT

"I have to go, but I miss you!" Kaitlyn said.

My heart wrenched as I set my coffee on my desk and sighed. "I miss you too, baby."

"Maybe I can come see you soon."

I grinned. "That would be incredible."

The camera shook as she bounced with excitement. "Mommy said I would have to fly on a plane. I've never done that!"

"You would love it. The clouds are awesome."

Her eyes flared wide. "Oh, can I touch the clouds in an airplane?"

I chuckled. "No, but you get to eat pretzels and drink juice."

Propping her hand under her chin, she wrinkled her nose. "I wonder what clouds taste like?"

In an effort not to break her heart with the answer, I shifted gears. "Aren't you supposed to be getting ready to leave?"

"Kaitlyn Haven West," her mom called from somewhere in the distance. "You better have your shoes on already."

Kaitlyn flashed me an eek face. "Uh oh! Gotta go, Daddy. I love you." She blew kisses and I caught each and every one of them.

"Love you too, baby. Have a good day at school!"

"Byeeeeeeee," she called.

I sagged in my office chair. My sweet portion of the week was officially done, so I waited for the paralyzing sour of what was to come that afternoon to engulf me.

While the week had passed with a predicable familiarity, nothing was the same anymore. I was going crazy, pent up like a volcano ready to erupt. I'd been short with everyone at work. Shit that had always been annoying—but pretty typical in my line of work—suddenly felt like sandpaper to my patience. I'd shredded three résumés, rejected two job offers, and hung up on the hiring manager when they included free water in the break room as part of their benefits package.

Okay, fine. They deserved that one, but I was usually more professional about it.

I knew it was bad though when I got annoyed with a visually impaired caller who spent a few extra minutes venting about the similarity of the packaging with sugar-free and regular pudding. Again, nothing unusual there. Well, nothing besides the fact that Gwendolyn Pierce had stormed into my life, rocking me to the core, and I was acting like a petulant child because I had no idea how to cope with it.

Ha! Imagine that. Me. The king of coping mechanisms—both healthy and royally fucked up—yet a five-eight brunette had thrown me completely off-kilter.

Unfortunately for me, her ability to hijack my emotions with that mysterious calm she unknowingly wielded like a weapon was only one of the tools in Gwen's arsenal. I was in no way prepared to sit there for an hour, being assaulted by her hips swaying as she subtly danced to whatever god-awful music she'd had playing in her headphones.

Ogling wasn't usually my thing, but the woman had curves I ached to brand with my fingerprints. And that was just the back of her. The front was even more torturous.

Her plump lips as her tongue snaked out to dampen them.

The curve of her delicate collarbone.

Her golden skin flashing from under the hem of her tank top when she'd stretch to paint the top of the wall.

It made me a creeper, but I'd had an entire internal debate on which part of her I wanted to taste first.

Spoiler alert: Her nipples won. Whoever had designed that bra, so damn thin I could see her perfect peaks through her baby-blue tank top, either deserved a national holiday in their honor or to be thrown in prison immediately. I couldn't decide which.

Fuck me. I tried not to stare. Really, I did. But in a cruel twist of fate, when I closed my eyes, instead of transporting me to my own personal hell, my brain taunted me with memories of her head thrown back in ecstasy as she rode my cock. It was nothing short of a miracle that I'd escaped that restaurant with my zipper still intact.

So I did what I always did: I ran. My feet pounded the pavement, each step echoing like a desperate heartbeat as I raced back to my house. It was my safe space, where I could sift through my thoughts in peace and quiet and then pretend that my world hadn't been completely upended.

A few weeks earlier, that booth had a forcefield around it. I could block out everything. Waitresses taking orders. Customers chattering. The bell over the door. Cooks clanging utensils in the kitchen. I heard none of it.

But no matter how hard I tried, I couldn't block out Gwen.

I'd spent the past week waffling back and forth on how to handle Wednesdays moving forward. My routine was ruined, but the thought of giving up and staying home made my skin crawl. The only other option was to spend yet another evening gawking at my ex-wife. That came with a different set of challenges though. I could not afford the water bill for another week of marathon cold showers.

So between damned if I do and damned if I don't, I was stuck. No place to go, no way to stay away.

After a long debate, in which I vetoed all commentary from my cock, I decided to give it another shot. Maybe Gwen wouldn't be working in the same room with me this time. The restaurant wasn't big, but there were places where she wouldn't be directly in my line of sight—and thus obsession.

I just needed to be there, destroy myself, pay my penitence, push my rock up the hill, and then come home. Gwen should not have been a factor in that.

Though as I got ready that afternoon, I spent extra time in front of the mirror, trimming my beard and styling my hair. I'd dug through the back of my closet to find my good jeans and a fitted Henley I hadn't worn in years. I passed on my go-to Chucks in lieu of a pair of black retro motorcycle boots that I didn't tie in order to keep the look casual, but then I spent an exorbitant amount of time making sure my pants legs settled on top, purposefully messy.

When it was all said and done, even I had to admit I cleaned up pretty nice. And wasn't that a fucking waste. Delusion was my drug of choice, but this was a lot even for me.

What the hell did I think was going to happen? Gwen would see me looking half decent, forget that I was a master-level head-case, and then fall naked into my lap?

I didn't even want that.

Actually, I did. *Desperately.*

But what would have been the point? So I could disappoint her again? Abandon her? Break her?

I was a rat-fucking-bastard for even thinking about it. Neither of us needed an instant replay of the catastrophe that was the end of our marriage. If I was any type of man, I would have left her the hell alone and not bothered her with more of my bullshit.

But in a real-life showing of Jekyll and Hyde, I couldn't stop myself.

I berated myself as I stood at my front door with my hand on the knob.

I opened it anyway.

I trembled with both anticipation and guilt as I walked down my front steps.

I never slowed as I headed toward the restaurant.

I saw my cowardly reflection in the glass door—my eyes hollow with regret.

Yet, when her innocent gaze lifted to mine, a wave of something I vaguely remembered as happiness washed over me.

I should have kicked my own ass right then and there.

Instead, I walked inside.

To her.

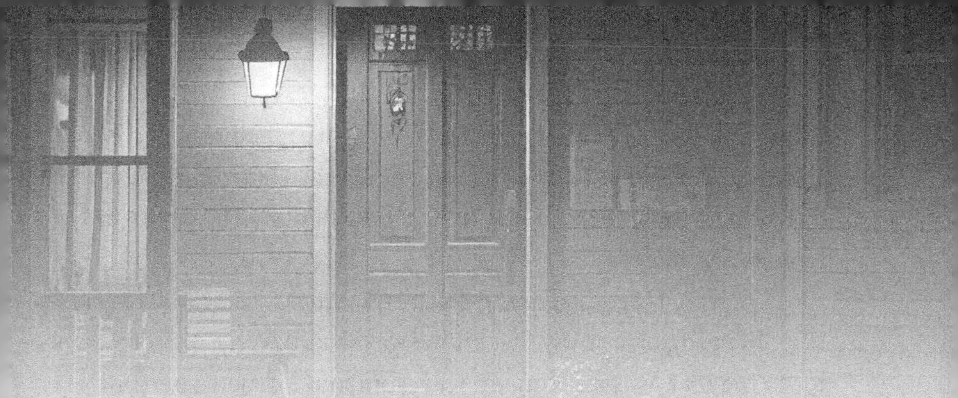

CHAPTER FOURTEEN

Gwen

“Hey,” I said, wiping my dusty hands on my shorts as I strolled toward the door.

“Hey,” Truett replied without making the first attempt to hide his gaze as it perused my body.

Normally, I would have called him out on such a blatant appraisal had I not been doing the exact same thing.

Holy hell, the man was downright edible. Dark jeans hung low on his hips, and a gray Henley hugged his muscular shoulders. His thick biceps waged war against the fabric while his abs tapered down to a trim waist. He’d trimmed his beard. Not a shave by any means, but it was now short enough to reveal the sharp angles of his jawline.

Truett had already been gorgeous, so this was like gorgeous squared and I did not have the mental capacity to compute that. For a mere mortal like myself, it was overwhelming and a bit unfair. Wearing braided pigtails and cut-off denim shorts, I looked like I should be starting my farm chores, while he was obviously on his way to audition for the next superhero film.

Something was off though. This wasn’t just something he threw on for a casual Wednesday at his favorite diner. Nobody could pull off jeans and a T-shirt like he did, and from what I could tell, that hadn’t changed over time. This was different though. His jeans were dressy, lacking signs of everyday wear and tear, and his shirt was far from upscale elegance, but his chiseled body made it red-carpet ready. It was the same with the boots—classic yet intentionally rugged.

Oh, yes. Truett had dressed up for *someone*.

The pang of jealousy that hit me was absurd. What did it matter to me if he was meeting up with someone? Truett's personal life was none of my business or concern. He hadn't been mine in nearly half my life. I'm pretty sure the dibs I'd called on him in eleventh grade had expired by now.

And yet, even as I told myself all of that, I still blurted, "You look nice. You got a date later?"

His lips twitched as he stepped deeper into the room, his boots thudding softly against the unfinished floor. "Not that I'm aware of. I don't meet a lot of women in my living room."

Damn, that was sad, and it shouldn't have felt like a relief. "Shit. Sorry."

Ignoring my apology, he picked up a stray tile spacer from the floor and turned it in his fingers. "What about you? Some lucky country boy taking you to the hoedown?"

"Yep, Billy Bob's picking me up on his tractor and everything."

He smirked. "So tractors are what's doing it for you these days?"

"Psh. Actually, nothing's doing it for me these days. I'm kind of on an expedition of self-discovery right now. Men suck. Present company included."

"Fair assessment." Still turning the spacer between his dexterous fingers, he wedged his other hand into his back pocket. "What does this 'expedition of self-discovery' include? Are we talking incense and crystals or LSD?"

A laugh bubbled from my throat. "Neither. This is more the kind where you get a divorce, pierce your nose, dye your hair, and spend your life's savings on a run-down restaurant. Though, now that you mention it, it's not often a person can say LSD would have been the smarter choice."

His smile.

Dear God, the smile that stretched across his mouth was yet another exponent to the sexiness equation I couldn't compute.

And worse, why did I suddenly want to?

"You cut your hair too," he stated, a slight tilt of his head giving his words a playful edge. "I like it."

I hit him with a side-eye. "You liar. You used to beg me not to cut my hair."

He pressed his palm against his chest, feigning innocence. "What? I never."

"Oh, really." I propped my hand on my hip. "You once bribed my hairdresser to cancel my appointment and then replaced all the scissors in the house with safety scissors."

"First of all, the safety scissors happened to be on sale. And hello, Coupon Queen, I thought you liked it when I was thrifty."

I rolled my eyes, fighting to suppress my smile.

"Secondly," he continued. "It wasn't a bribe."

"So you just happened to send her husband a gift card for a couple's massage that had to be used on the specific day of my appointment or it expired?"

"What was I supposed to do? I missed Kyle's birthday."

"You never met Kyle!"

He erupted into deep, rich laughter and I couldn't help but join him. It was nice to remember the good times. It hadn't all been doom and gloom with us. Once upon a time, our lives had been full of laughter and sarcasm. We'd poked at each other relentlessly, until one of us got annoyed. Then we made love, slow and tender, ensuring nothing was ever taken to heart.

We'd had a good life.

A beautiful life.

It was easy to forget how incredible we'd been together when our relationship had met such a tragic demise. Hate was easier. Or at least I missed him less when the memories were tainted with anger and resentment.

When we sobered, there was a moment of silence, both of us staring at each other, grinning like a pair of fools.

For once, he was the one to speak first. "I wasn't lying about your hair. You look amazing, Gwen. Head to toe."

"You too. If more women knew about that shirt, there would probably be a line in your living room."

Great. Now I was flirting.

With my ex.

More specifically, *Truett.*

Outstanding.

I cleared my throat and ignored his wolfish grin. "Anyway, come sit down. Sorry about the mess. I left you a path to the booth."

He glanced around at the floor's half-completed state. From the center of the room, smoky porcelain tiles spread outward, giving way to bare, gray concrete closer to the walls. Tools lay scattered, and little spacers stuck up from between tiles like a garden of plus signs.

"You did all this?" he asked, a hint of pride in his voice.

"Yep. A few friends came by earlier and helped me lay out the pattern, but they had to get their kids from school. So it's just been me for the last few hours."

"What's all that?"

I didn't have to follow his gaze to know what he was asking about. In the mouth of the hallway, beside my rented power tool, was a small mountain containing at least $200 worth of rubble.

A wry smile tugged at the corners of my mouth. "Most people cut tile the boring way, but you know I like a challenge, so I made it into a game called 'How Many Tiles Can I Break While Learning to Work a Water Saw.'"

He did a slow blink. "Wow. New game and you've already mastered it. Any chance you're planning to do a mosaic?"

"I wasn't, but a few more boxes of tile and that might be my only option."

"You want some help?"

"And risk ruining your date clothes? No, thanks. Besides, I've made it this far. Might as well see it through. You go sit down and do your thing. If you're still here when I finish cutting, you can watch me play 'Bankruptcy Tetris', where I try to make all the pieces fit."

"Just remember, measure twice and cut once."

I batted my lashes. "Thanks, but I'm currently using the far superior 'measure twelve times and cut twenty-four' method. It's a trade secret amongst professionals like myself."

He laughed again and I honest-to-God couldn't remember the last time he seemed so. . .unburdened. Seeing him happy mended holes in my heart that I hadn't realized still existed. It was like sand pouring over a bed of rocks, the grains seeping into the empty spaces, filling a hidden void. Nostalgia curled around me, bitter-sweet and tender, bringing back memories of when things were simpler and we were both carefree. I hadn't been able to admit it to myself in years—self-preservation and all—but I missed that version of Truett. Achingly so.

"I have a little something for you," I announced, turning toward the kitchen.

"For me?" he asked, his voice full of surprise.

"Yep. Go sit. Be careful not to trample my plus signs."

"Plus signs, right. Gotcha," he muttered as we both navigated the narrow strip of concrete in opposite directions.

When I returned less than a minute later, he was in his booth, peering down at the table. His head popped up when he heard my approach. A smile still graced his handsome face, but it disappeared as I placed the plate in front of him.

"Order up."

"What is that?" he asked, leaning away like he feared it might suddenly sprout legs and launch at his jugular.

"A club sandwich, no mayo, bacon on the side. That's what you order, right?"

"Yeah, but…" he trailed off, shaking his head.

I didn't understand what that sandwich meant to him any more than I did the booth.

I wanted to though. I'd always wanted to understand him.

Unfortunately, Truett had locked himself in his own mind long before he'd locked himself in that house. I wasn't delusional enough to think cold cuts and dry bread held a magical key to free him.

He looked up at me, conflict etched into his face. "You didn't have to do this."

"No, but it's part of your routine, and I'm about to subject you to an hour of me cussing while intermittently blasting your eardrums with a saw. It was the least I could do."

He shook his head again, his lips parting as if to speak, but no words came out. God, what I wouldn't have given to spend five minutes inside that man's head—to find the dam blocking his ability to express himself and level it with a sledgehammer, freeing him from his self-made prison once and for all.

Some battles weren't mine to fight though. I'd learned that the hard way.

I rapped my knuckled on the table. "Stay as long as you'd like. I need to—"

"Will you sit with me?"

My heart stopped, the flutter in my stomach stealing my breath.

I sat in that booth every day. Making phone calls, paying bills, building my menu. It was the only table left where I could spread out and work.

But I'd never sat with *him*.

I didn't need to understand why that booth or sandwich was so special to recognize that his invitation was huge.

And if it wasn't huge to him, it sure as hell was to me.

"Um..." I bought myself a second to think by glancing over my shoulder. The place was a disaster and I'd be lucky if I made it home by midnight with as much tile work as I had left to do.

The easy and obvious answer was no.

But it was Truett.

"Of course." I made a move toward the opposite side of the booth but stopped in my tracks when he slid over to make room for me beside him.

I stared at him—his expression open and welcoming, not a hint of doubt or discomfort marring his handsome face. It was as if my place beside him was a given. And damn it if that wasn't my version of the club sandwich—a seemingly simple gesture that carried such profound depth.

My nose stung as I accepted his offer. The booth squeaked under our combined weight as I slid in beside him. He was far enough away that our bodies didn't touch, but a comfortable warmth radiated between us. The silence that followed was both familiar and charged.

It was crazy how perfectly comfortable I'd been standing beside the table, the proximity only changing by inches, but sitting beside him in that booth felt so personal and intimate it unnerved me. I faced forward, knotting my hands in my lap, unsure what to do or say.

Was there going to be a conversation during this little visit? Or was he expecting me to sit there while he fidgeted and grumbled the way he'd done the prior week? Suddenly, cutting tile didn't sound so bad.

"You didn't have to do all this," he said.

I flashed him a forced grin. "It's just a sandwich, True."

He angled his body, putting his back to the wall so he was

partially facing me, and drew in a deep breath. "Sure. But it's also a booth, and letting me invade your space each week, and… Well, mainly I just appreciate you not telling me to go to hell the first night I showed up here."

"Actually, I'm pretty sure I did do that."

He chuckled and I turned, hooking my leg up on the bench so I could face him too. I think it was also an unconscious effort to create a barrier between us, but it backfired monumentally. He wasn't as far away as I'd thought and my lower leg pressed against the length of his thigh. Before I had the chance to shift and apologize for bumping him, his hand came down landing on my knee.

His touch closed a current, electricity sparking inside me. It was both painful and euphoric. I couldn't decide if I wanted to cry or rage at the unfairness of the world, because in over eighteen years, never had a man's touch felt so right.

His face flashed dark and ominous, but not like his usual storm. Raw need and desire stared back at me.

"How do you do this to me?" he rasped almost painfully. "*Why* do you do this to me?"

"It's just a sandwich," I repeated, knowing good and damn well that wasn't what he meant.

"It's not though. It's *you*."

I swallowed hard, unsure if he considered me being me a good thing or not.

Until…

Leaning toward me, he brushed a braid off my shoulder, his fingertips trailing across my neck. A chill raced down my spine as his gaze locked on my mouth, his tongue snaking out to dampen his lips.

I knew that look. Oh my God, did I know that look.

He was going to kiss me. And I was suddenly terrified I was going to let him.

I hated him.

Supposedly.

Allegedly.

Shit, did I still hate him?

I was all too aware how talented his lips were. It had been a lifetime since anyone had kissed me like he did. Jeff had never ignited me like Truett. In a way, it was why I'd married him. Jeff was a controlled burn rather than the wildfire of the man in front of me.

"Truett, please," I breathed, but I didn't know if it was a plea for his mouth or his mercy.

His fingers curled around the back of my neck. "Please what?"

Back up.

Kiss me.

Never come back.

Stay.

Oh fuck it…

"Ki—"

That was all I got out before a flash exploded through the room. In the next second, I was tackled to the floor. His hand cradled my head to soften the blow, but my back hit hard on the edge of the tile, the spacers digging into my shoulders as his heavy body crashed on top of me.

Trying to make sense of what happened, I struggled beneath him.

"Stay down," he hissed in my ear, another flash detonating through the room.

His dead weight suffocated me, so I squirmed beneath him. "I can't…breathe."

He pushed up onto his elbows a fraction, allowing my lungs a taste of oxygen that was immediately stolen when I caught sight of his ashen face.

His gaze flicked in every direction, searching without seeing. Panic and confusion etched deep lines across his forehead, and the corners of his eyes crinkled. He was literally on top of me, our bodies flush head to toe, but mentally, that beautifully broken man was a million miles away.

And it absolutely destroyed me to imagine where he could have been.

"True," I whispered.

Another flash jolted him.

Dammit, what the hell was going on? It wasn't the horrors that he more than likely had playing in his mind, but I couldn't figure out what it was to reassure him otherwise.

The sun had started to slip below the horizon, but it wasn't dark out yet. The flashing was too interspersed to be passing headlights, and there was no sound, so I ruled out lightning too. Craning my neck, I searched the front windows, desperate for an answer. When another flash illuminated the restaurant, I was able to track it and caught sight of a figure just outside, holding what looked like a camera. And not a cell phone or the compact type a tourist would carry. This was the tool of a professional, and it was aimed directly at us.

Fury ignited within me as the camera slowly lowered, revealing Taggart fucking Folly behind the lens.

What the hell was he doing? Did he really think sneaking around and taking pictures was going to make us suddenly catch a case of the warm and fuzzies and cooperate with his documentary? Then again, maybe after the way I'd behaved during our last interaction, he'd realized he didn't need us to cooperate at all.

While I owned the restaurant, I didn't own the sidewalk. It wasn't illegal to take pictures on public property, and with all the windows up front uncovered, we had no illusions of privacy. Whatever photos he snapped were fair game for him to use however he saw fit.

We had to get out of his view. If he had a camera, he probably had video too. Never had Truett been more vulnerable than he was in that moment, lost in the past. I wouldn't allow that asshole to profit from his pain.

I fought to free myself from under Truett, but he held me tight, not allowing me to budge.

In a voice so full of gravel it felt like road rash as it traveled over my skin, he pleaded, "Stop fucking moving. I can't lose you too."

I can't lose you too.

It felt like a kick to my gut, and I immediately redirected my focus. My anger morphed into featherlike gentleness. "True, baby, look at me."

His gaze instantly slid to mine, the desolation on his face stripping me bare.

"You're okay. It's just the flash of a camera."

His eyes remained unfocused, the past refusing to abate. "What?"

"It's the documentary guy taking pictures through the windows. There's no danger, baby. I promise."

His breathing shuddered, his mind not yet ready to release him. My Truett was in there though, fighting his way back, because this time when I moved, he allowed me the space to free my arms.

I hooked one arm around him, my palm resting on his back, pulling him impossibly closer as if I could bring him back by sheer force of will. I slid my other hand over his bearded cheek and into his hair, smoothing it down. "You're safe, True."

His eyes slowly began to focus, a glimmer of recognition returning. "Are you safe though?"

My lungs seized. Four words and my heart shattered before piecing itself back together, fuller than before. He was forging his way back from hell and *I* was his first priority.

Damn, why did that feel so good?

Maybe because I hadn't been a priority to anyone—even myself—in years.

I continued to stroke his hair and managed a weak smile as I replied, "Yeah, baby. I'm safe. We're both safe. Everything's okay."

For once, I didn't feel like it was a placating lie.

My back ached.

I was still struggling to breathe under his immense weight.

And who knew how much footage Taggart Folly already had of us or what he planned to use it for.

But I would have happily stayed on that floor, wrapped in his arms, for the rest of the night.

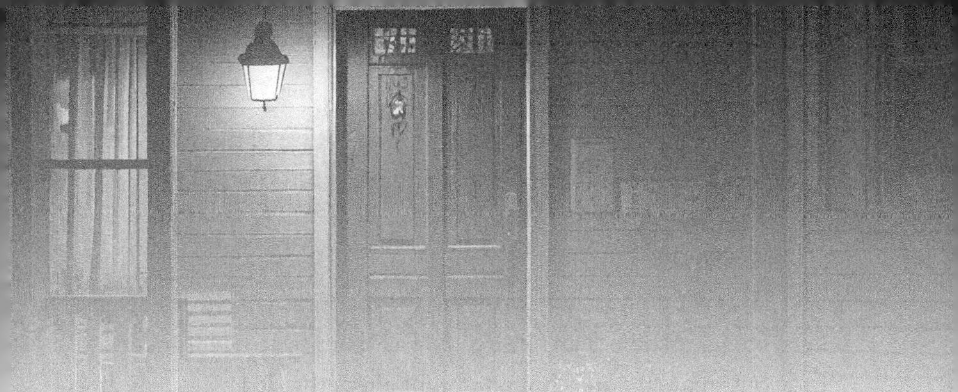

CHAPTER FIFTEEN

TRUETT

FIVE THINGS I COULD SEE: GWEN'S LASHES BATTING OVER concerned eyes; Gwen's lips as she whispered to me; Gwen's braids curling over her shoulder; the curve of Gwen's neck, tense and strained; Gwen's flushed cheeks, burning with urgency.

Four things I could touch: Gwen's hands, clutching me desperately; Gwen's cheeks, pink and perfect; Gwen's chest rising and falling with rapid breaths; Gwen's legs, tangled with mine.

Three things I could hear: Gwen's voice, frantic and soothing all at once; Gwen's breath, quick and shallow in my ear; the sound of Gwen's hand gliding over my hair.

Two things I could smell: Gwen's perfume, a faint hint of lavender and something uniquely her; Gwen's sweat, a tangible mix of fear and adrenaline.

One thing I could taste: Dear God, how I wanted to taste her.

As my mind cleared and my heart slowed, she filled my every sense, grounding me in a way I'd never been able to master on my own. That calm—*her calm*—was like a lifeline, wrenching me from the dark, tumultuous waters flooding my mind.

"We're safe, True," she repeated, and even as the flashing continued from outside, I believed her. Mind, body, and soul. Because, fuck me, I'd always been safe with her, even if I hadn't been able to offer her the same.

"It's Taggart?" I asked, trying to make sense of the situation.

"Yeah. He's out there taking pictures."

"Of us?"

"I guess."

How was it humanly possible for that piece of shit to be an even bigger asshole than he already was? He'd been a nuisance before, but this was something different altogether. I'd called my attorney after his last surprise visit, and he'd sent a letter to Flat Line Productions warning them of our intent to take legal action should the harassment not stop. Either Folly had gone rogue or Flat Line felt like hemorrhaging money in a messy lawsuit.

Flat Line was a successful production company with countless awards and a reputation to uphold, so I was banking on the former. Though the speed in which Folly was changing tactics—from phone calls and emails to stalking and picture taking—was starting to unnerve me.

Desperate men made desperate decisions.

Now that he'd dragged Gwen into his circus, the concern of what he'd try next made my vision flash red.

It had to end, and if it meant keeping her safe, I was all too happy to be the man to do it.

Pulling her up with me, I surged to my feet. "I'm gonna kill him."

"Truett, no," she hissed, still clinging to my front.

Soaking in one last moment of her warmth, I hesitated for a beat, and in that brief amount of time, his camera flickered like a strobe light.

Oh, yeah, Folly was long overdue for a lesson on boundaries.

With one arm around her hips, I lifted her off her feet and turned, setting her out of my path. "Stay here and don't come outside no matter what. Do you hear me?"

She hurried in front of me, her palm landing in the middle of my chest. "You can't go out there."

I laughed without humor. "You wanna bet?"

"No, True. You *can't*. He's trying to bait you."

I cracked my neck, my hands clenched tight at my sides. "Well, then consider me caught. Hook, line, and sinker."

"Please, just think about this for a second. Yes, he's a dick. We know that. But we can handle this in a way that doesn't involve you getting arrested and me having to figure out how to bake a file into a cake." She waved her free hand out to the side. "I mean, look at this place. I don't have time for a side quest right now."

As mad as I was, my lips hitched. Jesus, she was ridiculous—and gorgeous, and sexy, and...*everything*. "A side quest?" I teased.

She nodded, not a lick of humor showing on her face.

Dammit, she was serious. That was cute too. "A side quest where you'll learn to bake a file into a cake?"

She shrugged. "I'm not sure if that's still a thing in prison, but maybe you can use it to pick a lock or something?"

"What, so I'm MacGyver now?"

"If you don't commit a murder in front of my restaurant, you can be whoever you want."

Your man again? I managed to keep that little kick in the pants to myself, but I was far from convinced that Taggart Folly deserved to keep the heartbeat in his chest.

"This is insanity, Gwen. Tracking you down and asking for a statement was one thing. I didn't like it. But that was his right. Just like it was your right to say no. But this..." I swung my arm out and pointed at the front windows, his flash going off again as if I'd summoned it. "Taking pictures of you? This is too damn much."

Her gaze cut to the side. "I agree, but I don't necessarily think it's me he's taking pictures of." Apology filled her beautiful face when she looked back up at me. "I hate to say this, but without you, I'm nothing but part of the supporting cast for him. He *needs* you and he's going to stoop to whatever level necessary. Drama sells, True. It doesn't matter to him if he gets footage of you spiraling out of control like a madman or sitting down on a couch, having a civil discussion."

My whole body locked up tight. "Are you saying I should cooperate with this prick?"

"Hell no!" Her fingertips curled against my chest. Her palm was no longer a blockade to stop me, but a tether holding me close. "But that's exactly what you'd be doing if you go out there right now. He's on public property and can take whatever pictures he wants no matter how invasive we think they are. *Technically*, he's not doing anything wrong."

"Bullshit. What he's doing is wrong in *every* way. He may not be breaking any laws, but if he's going to pull a stunt like this, he better be ready for me to break a few."

"That's what he wants though. We have to ignore him. Even just telling him to fuck off gives him soundbites to use. You losing your cool is not going to solve anything."

"It would sure as hell make me feel better though."

She sighed. "Yeah, it would make me feel better too, but that would only be temporary, and whatever he gets on you will be forever. He wants a piece of you, but he can't take it unless you give it to him. Don't give him this." Her hand slid up my chest, and when she spoke, it was the sound of my every nightmare—and my sweetest dream. "Please, True."

Her calm iced the rage in my veins. It felt like an out-of-body experience as I stared down at her. Gwen. *My Gwen.* Her hand on my chest, standing in front of me, my name tumbling from her mouth as if it had been created for no other purpose.

Thousands of days had divided us. Hell, we'd spent more time apart than we ever had together. But in that restaurant with her, it was as if time had collapsed in on itself, seamlessly connecting the past to the present.

God, I'd missed her.

Resting my hands in the curve of her hips, I pulled her toward me. It was only an inch, but my body roared for the whole mile. It didn't help matters that her eyes heated as they flicked to my mouth. And worse, she arched her back, brushing her full breasts across my chest.

I was not strong enough for that kind of temptation. Or honestly, smart enough, either, because I wasn't positive the temptation went both ways. When it came to the fine art of reading a woman's body language, I was grossly out of practice. For all I knew, the heat in her eyes was a burning desire to slap the shit out of me and the arch of her back was a wince of pain from when I'd tackled her out of the booth.

Jesus, how was my dumb ass considering making a move after that giant cyclone of fuckery?

I forced myself to release her. "You're right. I won't kill him."

The joy I felt as her eyes dimmed when I stepped away would have landed me the role as CEO at Asshole International.

I fucking loved that she felt it too. Whatever it was between us, the pull, the need, the desire. It was still there. And with that knowledge, my smile was so big I was going to have to ice my face when I got home.

Misinterpreting my grin for mischief, she shot me a scowl and added, "You also can't punch him, or kick him, or egg his car, or—"

"Hey! I have never egged anyone's car, thank you very much."

She arched a scolding eyebrow. "Or shoot a potato through his window, or put a snake in his toilet, or put Nair in his shampoo, or duct tape his boots to the ceiling right before an inspection, or sneak laxatives into his coffee, or—"

"Okay, okay!" I lifted my hands in surrender. "Do you forget anything?"

"Not after as many times as I listened to you and Nathanial repeat the same stories over and over again."

Nathanial.

Nutz.

Fuck.

Another flash came from outside, the light punctuated by the sound of Gwen's palm slapping over her mouth. "Oh my God," she mumbled from behind her hand before lowering it. "I am so sorry. I shouldn't have said that. I know you don't like to talk about him—or any of them."

I didn't.

I couldn't.

Especially in the beginning when I'd still raked myself over the red-hot coals with my every breath. However, therapists were relentless and eventually forced me into discussions. Nothing pissed me off more than the old convo starter of, "Tell me about the men you lost."

I didn't just lose *men.*

I lost my *best friends.*

I lost my *family.*

And then I lost *myself.*

It had taken years for me to see past my grief. I didn't get over it, or forget, or even learn to live with it properly. I simply put a plan into action to control it so I didn't drown in the sea of self-loathing. Once a week. One hour. Total earth-shattering despair. And currently, I was even failing with that.

So as I stood there, his name hanging like a million arrows frozen in the sky, apologies pouring from her mouth, I braced for the avalanche of pain.

But there was nothing.

No dagger lodged in my heart.

No bile clawing up my throat.

I wasn't transported to hell at all.

That was until I saw the first tear roll down her cheek. Now that fucking gutted me.

"No," I whispered, rushing forward to drag her into a hug. "Don't cry."

She came willingly, wrapping her arms around my waist, her fingers gripping the back of my shirt. "I'm so sorry. I shouldn't have brought him up."

Jesus, how the hell was *she* apologizing to *me*?

I cupped my hands around the sides of her neck, and gently tipped her head back. "Gwen, baby. You never have to apologize to me for talking about him. For fuck's sake, I should be the one apologizing."

"I know you don't talk about them. It just kinda slipped out."

Using my thumbs, I wiped the salty streaks from her cheeks and offered her a sad smile. "No. I don't talk about them a lot, but that shouldn't stop you. He was your brother. You didn't fail him. I did."

"Don't say that." She shifted, shaking my hands off her neck, but it wasn't for space. She got closer, her breasts pillowing between us as I wrapped my arms around her midsection.

With her whole body flush with mine, everything inside me relaxed, my mind slipping into a peace and security I'd never been able to give her after my deployment. Knowing I'd gone to war with her brother and had to look her in the eye, break her heart, and acknowledge that I was the reason he didn't make it home was more than I could bear.

Failing my guys was the heaviest burden I could have imagined at that time, but I couldn't even escape the guilt at home. I'd listened to her cry, night after night, her tears slicing through me like a hurricane of razor blades. Her kindness rather than hatred burned like alcohol dousing my gaping wounds.

So I'd shut down. Unable to escape the past, impossible to function with her in the present.

And still, when she'd think I was sleeping, she'd curl up behind me, taking the comfort I couldn't provide her. I fucking hated that, in those moments, I found overwhelming comfort too. One I would never deserve. At least not from her.

It got to the point that I'd felt wrong for being as grief stricken. Nutz and I had been thick as thieves, but she'd lost her only sibling. If she wanted to scream his name from the rooftop, she sure as hell shouldn't be apologizing to me about it.

Nathanial Pierce, AKA Nutz, loved his baby sister and would have kicked my ass up and down the East Coast for making her cry. He had been as protective as big brothers came. I'd feared he was going to rush the altar when Gwen and I had gotten married.

When someone finally managed to unlock the secrets of time travel, that would be the exact day and time I would program into my DeLorean. Gwen in a white sundress, a daisy in her hair. Me in a pair of khaki pants and a white linen shirt I'd found at Goodwill, more love than I knew possible filling my heart. The two of us standing under a makeshift arch I'd built from scraps of two-by-fours covered in flowers from her grandma's garden. Our immediate families seated in folding chairs in her parents' backyard, looking on with a mixture of concern and resigned disapproval.

But it was by far the happiest day of my life because it marked the beginning of *our* life—*together*—and everything that I naïvely thought would come with it.

My life started that day when I slid my ring on her finger.

And years later, when she dropped that same ring at my feet, my life ended.

The sweet and the sour.

The beginning and the end.

Happiness only truly existed in the space in between.

"Hey," she whispered, dragging me back to the present. "Maybe that's enough talking for today."

I forced a smile, but it couldn't have looked any more real than it felt. "Yeah."

"We should go anyway. We're sitting ducks in here. I bet he has enough pictures to make a special edition flipbook to go with his stupid documentary."

I swallowed hard to clear my throat. "I'll reach out to my attorney again and see what we can do to stop him from coming back."

"All right. Let me just clean up really quick and I'll drive you home so you don't have to walk back with him out there."

"That'd be great."

My body screamed when she backed away, but in my life, letting Gwen slip from my fingers was a necessary evil, so I had no choice but to let her go.

As she swirled around the room, unplugging things and turning off lights, I cleaned up the tools on the floor. I glanced up in time to see her toss the club sandwich into the trash.

I never ate them. Hundreds of club sandwiches had met their demise because of me.

But that one? Gwen had made it for me.

And like everything else we'd shared, it would forever be nothing but a memory.

CHAPTER SIXTEEN

TRUETT

Hoping to fool Taggart into believing we were still at the restaurant, Gwen left the dining room lights on as we ducked out the back door. Using the key fob, she unlocked her white midsized SUV before exiting the building, motioning for me to get inside. Instead, I stayed by her side as she locked the restaurant, not willing to leave her vulnerable for even a second.

Not surprisingly, her car was a mess. Not dirty, just cluttered. Such was life with that crazy, beautiful woman. Books of paint samples covered the passenger floorboard, three stainless-steel water bottles balanced between two cupholders, and a gym bag blocked the seat.

"You can toss all that in the back," she said, climbing in behind the wheel.

"It's good to see the old grab-and-toss routine is still a prerequisite when riding with you."

"I find it keeps out the riffraff." She flashed me a side-eye as she pressed the button to start the engine. "Or at least it did until now."

Chuckling, I made quick work of moving the bag and relocating one of the water bottles to the cupholder in the door. I slid the seat all the way back before joining her inside. As she pulled out of the parking lot, turning right to avoid Taggart on the main road, I bent over and collected the sample books, stacking them neatly before tucking them into the pocket on the back of her seat.

"You still a neat freak?" she asked playfully.

"I find I'm heavier on the freak these days, but yeah, I like to keep things organized."

She laughed, shaking her head.

The drive was quiet and mercifully short. My mind wandered to a time when Gwen and I had spent a lot of time together in a vehicle similar to this one. Mainly with the back seats folded down—naked, fogging up the windows, ravaging each other's bodies.

I performed the herculean task of keeping my cock from entering the chat, but it was my water bill that was going to suffer the consequences of those memories after yet another cold shower when I got home.

Not bothering with the driveway, she stopped at the curb in front of my house and kept the car idling.

Thank you for the club sandwich.

Thank you for the ride.

I'm really sorry about tackling you tonight.

Goodbye.

I'll let you know what my attorney says.

Any and all of those would have been the appropriate thing to say before getting the hell out of her car. Instead, I sat there, a sense of dread swirling inside me. The leather seat creaked as I shifted uncomfortably, glancing at the dimly lit dashboard and then back at her.

It wasn't lost on me that she was doing the majority of her renovations alone rather than paying professionals. I'd seen firsthand the primer she'd rolled on too thick in spots and then too thin in others. That tower of tile she'd broken had to have cost her a pretty penny, while the majority of her tools had rental tags from the local hardware store. Don't even get me started on when she mentioned Bankruptcy Tetris. It was all I could do to keep my eye from twitching.

I had always been a firm believer in not paying someone for a job you could do on your own, and I respected the hell out of her for taking on a project of that size. But she needed things done, and if I had any intention of sleeping for the next week, they needed to be done faster than she could do on her own.

"I don't want you going back there for a while," I stated. "I'll order blinds first thing in the morning and get someone scheduled to install a new security system. I'll let you know when everything is set up."

"You're kidding, right?" She turned toward me, her hand gripping the steering wheel.

Turning my body in my seat, I faced her, my expression hard. "Not in the least. Taggart's spiraling."

"He's trying to get a story. He'll eventually learn that we aren't going to talk, get bored, and scurry off to the next person. Hopefully it will be Caven Hunt, who will spend a bajillion dollars to get him locked up for an unpaid parking ticket Taggart got in high school."

"I wish. I called his woman the other day. She said they hadn't heard a word from Taggart yet. Guess he's not as stupid as I thought."

Shock registered on her face. "You talked to Caven's woman?" As she turned fully to face me, her seat belt pulled tight across her chest, dividing her breasts into split screens of seduction.

Fuck me. In the confines of that car, I was barely focusing as it was. I did not need the seat belts plotting against me too.

I cleared my throat and forced my eyes to lock onto hers. "It's more like she talks to me, but yeah. I know her."

Her mouth fell open. "Do you talk to Caven too?"

"Fuck no. I'd rather not talk to Red, either. But the woman is relentless. I lied to her a while back and told her I go to the diner on Saturdays so she can't ambush me anymore. Best decision I ever made. Now, can you please just promise me you won't go back to the restaurant until I've had a chance to get some guys in there?"

"Sure," she replied, chipper and cheery. "But first, let me say one thing." She angled her upper body over the center console, bringing her face within inches of mine, and slowly enunciated the word, "No."

God bless America. Two fucking inches closer and she would have breathed that into my mouth. "No. What?" I asked when my ability to comprehend the English language failed me.

She—thankfully for my brain and unfortunately for my desire to strip her naked and bury my face between her thighs—leaned away. "Truett, be real here. I can't just stop going to the restaurant. That's my job, and money is tight as it is. If I don't open soon, things will go belly-up before I even get my feet on the ground. I appreciate the concern. Really, I do, but I have bigger fish to fry than a producer-turned-paparazzo."

"Which is why I said I'll handle it. It won't cost you a penny."

"Yeahhhhh, that's not happening, either. No offense, but I'm not accepting investors at the moment."

"What are you talking about? This isn't *Shark Tank*. It's free money."

She rolled her eyes. "What is it with men thinking the answer to every woman's problem is for them to strut in with a fist full of dollar bills and save the day?"

"That's not what I'm doing."

"No? Then why didn't you ask me about blinds and a security system before magnanimously announcing that you were going to handle it?"

"Because currently you have neither."

"I also don't have bathroom stalls or a cash register, but I don't see you worried about those."

"Those aren't safety concerns. Right now, anybody can walk by and see you inside alone, shaking your ass in those tiny black shorts and the pink tank top that gapes open every time you bend over."

She arched a knowing eyebrow. "Are we discussing the men walking by or the man sitting in at the booth inside?"

Busted! Though I'd caught her doing a little creeping of her own that night, so at least I wasn't the only one. "All I'm saying is—"

"I don't need you to say anything," she snapped. "I'll handle it. I always do."

I clamped my mouth shut so fast I bit the inside of my cheek. I didn't think she'd intended for those words to be a TKO punch. But that was exactly how they landed.

Gwen was easily the strongest woman I had ever met. With me traveling for military training or stationed halfway across the world, she'd had to figure out an entire life on her own. And then again, when I'd forced her to start over after she'd lost her brother, she'd grabbed life by the horns with such strength and grace that I truly believed I'd done the right thing by letting her go.

I sighed, guilt filling my veins. "I just want to help."

"And I get that. Which is why I kept the booth and made you a sandwich tonight. But maybe find a way that isn't throwing money at a problem when I have no idea if and when I would be able to pay it back."

I ground my teeth, fighting the desire to argue. Or more likely, say fuck it and hire a full crew to show up at her restaurant first thing in the morning. She'd get pissed. That was nothing new, but then what? We wouldn't go home together, bickering about who was right. We wouldn't make love long into the night where I could show her just how determined I was to make sure nothing, and no one, ever touched her because that was what a man did to protect his woman.

She wasn't mine anymore, no matter how deep that cut me.

Resigned, I sank deeper into my seat and dropped my head

against the headrest. The leather was cold and unyielding against my skin. "You're right."

She smiled. "I know."

"I just worry about you," I confessed.

"I know that too."

"But I'll cool it with the money thing. Though that's not to say, I'm not going to spend a shit-ton of cash. Because, heads up, I'm about to drop a small fortune in attorney's fees to rain legal hell over that bastard. But I'll try to keep my worries from overflowing onto you so I don't cross eighty-four thousand boundaries in the process."

Her face lit, a soft smile curling her mouth. "Just eighty-four thousand?"

"I was lowballing it, hoping you wouldn't notice."

She laughed, soothing my soul. In the span of less than an hour, my emotions had been on a full-tilt roller coaster, and that was saying a lot for a Wednesday.

I'd smiled. I'd laughed. I'd lusted. I'd panicked. I'd raged. I'd marveled. I'd hoped.

Little did I know, the ride was far from over.

"Listen, before you go, we need to talk about next week."

"What about it?" I asked.

She reached into the back seat to retrieve her purse. After setting it on the center console, she dug inside, saying, "I'm not even sure if you'll want to come back after that shitshow tonight, but in case you do, I had this made for you." She extended a single silver key in my direction.

A grin radiated through my body as I took it from her hand. "Is that the key to The Grille?"

"The Rosewood," she corrected. "But yes, and I'm trusting that you can use this responsibly and I won't show up one day to gold-plated blinds and a million-dollar security system."

"Wow. Clearly, you have not seen my paystubs. I hate to break it to you, Gwen. Despite the lavish mansion before you, I am no millionaire. You were going to get faux wooden blinds and an alarm that came with a monthly bill—addressed to you."

She laughed. "Damn, now I'm regretting saying no."

I waggled my eyebrows. "It's not too late."

"Truett," she warned.

I lifted my hands in surrender. "Okay, okay. I'll drop it."

"Good. Now, back to what I was saying. I can't meet you at the restaurant next Wednesday."

My stomach dropped as if I'd been hurled from the top of a skyscraper. The freefall happened in slow motion as my mind frantically tried to figure out a way to make it stop.

"Why not?" I blurted more loudly than intended.

She sighed, glancing out the window before meeting my eyes again. "It's a long story, but I had to switch days with my ex-husband so he can take our son to a Yankees game."

I carefully schooled my features so I wouldn't look like even more of a basket case than I'd already proven myself to be. "Oh, okay. Makes sense."

"Hey," she whispered, seeing right through my act. "That's why I gave you the key. You can still come on Wednesday. Just let yourself in, and lock up when you leave."

I should have been elated. I'd spent the last week dreaming of just such a situation. If she wasn't around, I wouldn't have to worry about that magical calm of hers and I could get back to my routine. That was exactly what I wanted—what I *needed.*

Yet the blood drained from my face, disappointment hitting me like a freight train. Two weeks. It was going to be *two weeks* before I saw her again?

A rusty dagger twisted in my stomach. I loved my Wednesday mornings, but fuck me, for the last few weeks, whether I was willing to admit it or not, a part of me looked forward to the afternoons too. I was conflicted, confused, and totally uncomfortable with the loss of predictability. But it was Gwen. I'd been starved for her for far too long, and just a taste of having her back in my life had made me an addict.

Desperation swirled inside me, but what was I going to do? I couldn't very well ask her to hire a sitter and sacrifice time with her son so I could get my weekly fix.

Hell, with as hot and cold as I'd been recently, she probably needed a break from me and made up the whole baseball thing to buy herself a night of peace and quiet. The thought burned like I'd face-planted into a pile of embers, but I couldn't blame her. I was giving myself a first-class case of whiplash too.

The fact was, just like with the booth, the sandwich, and now the key, Gwen had been going out of her way to make life easier on me. I couldn't repay her by panicking and making her feel even an ounce of guilt for spending time with her kid.

This wasn't her problem.

I wasn't her problem.

Forcing a smile, I lifted the key. "Thanks. I appreciate this."

"No problem. Don't lose that. It cost a solid three dollars, and now that I have to add blinds and an alarm to my to-do list, I might have to mortgage my house to replace it."

Pulling my house keys from my pocket to add the new one to the ring, I tried to lighten the mood—*my mood*. "Oh, so you can spend money on me, but I can't spend it on you?"

"Three dollars is a far cry from—" She abruptly stopped talking when she caught sight of the key chain dangling in my fingers.

It was a picture of Kaitlyn when she was around two, sitting on my lap. We were both laughing, her mouth wide open with surprise. I was looking directly at the camera, tickling her sides. So much happiness filled that cheap three-by-two plastic keychain that I hadn't been able to get rid of it even when the corners started to chip.

Gwen reached out, catching it in her palm as she leaned

forward to get a better view. A massive smile split her face. "Oh my God, that is such a cute picture."

"Thanks," I mumbled, pulling it away and tucking it back into my pocket. "I appreciate the drive home."

"No problem."

I reached for the door handle, everything inside me screaming not to open the door. "I guess...I'll see you in a few weeks?"

"Hopefully it will look like a real restaurant by then."

"I'm sure it will. You're doing a great job. It's going to be amazing."

Pride lit her eyes. "Thanks. I needed to hear that."

An awkward silence fell between us, the weight of unsaid words and unresolved feelings hanging heavy in the air.

"Well, goodnight, True," she said, and I could have made it up, because it was what I wanted to hear, but I swear there was a tinge of regret in her voice.

"Goodnight, Gwen," I replied, opening the car door and stepping out.

I watched her drive away, the taillights disappearing into the night before I headed up the front steps.

The warm evening air gave way to my air conditioning when I stepped inside, but a sweat broke out across my brow when I closed the door behind me. My heart raced as I flipped the light on and then stood in the foyer scanning my house. It was the exact same as it always was, and my old couch called to me from across the room.

If I followed the routine, that would have been my first stop. I'd sit down. Take a deep breath, remind myself that I was home, safe, and all was right with my world again.

Only this time, everything felt so fucking empty. I slid down to the floor, my back pressed against the front door. As I stretched my legs out, I accidentally kicked the shoe rack, causing mine and Kaitlyn's sneakers to tumble off into a messy pile. And if that wasn't symbolic of the mess my life had become, I didn't know what was.

I buried my face in my hands, feeling more lost than ever. My home was my sanctuary, yet everything suddenly felt wrong. For the first time in God knew how long, I didn't want to be in that house.

I wanted to be with Gwen. Back at the restaurant, laughing—or hell, even arguing and dealing with that prick Taggart. And now, I had to wait two weeks to see her again?

Fourteen days?

Half a fucking month?

What the hell was I supposed to do for that long without her?

Oh, right, the same thing I'd been doing for almost two decades—Existing alone.

Always alone.

But what if I didn't want to be alone anymore? The thought was equal parts terrifying and liberating.

I dug my phone out of my pocket before pulling up Daniel's name in my contacts. He'd know what to do. I hadn't pressed the call button before his words filtered through my mind, causing a wave of panic to crash over me.

"News flash, Truett. You created the schedule. You can change it too."

CHAPTER SEVENTEEN

Gwen

"So, how much do you think it's gonna cost?" I asked, trying to keep the frustration out of my voice.

The older gentleman I'd found on Google under the search "People who hang blinds and actually show up in Belton, NJ" quirked a furry gray eyebrow. "Well, that depends. What kind of budget are we looking at?"

"Cheap," I said flatly.

His tape measure snapped shut, and he looked at me with a curious smile. "How cheap are we talking?"

"Clearance that has been marked down at least a dozen times, because while they are super trendy and fit my vision perfectly, they are just taking up space in a warehouse and will soon be discarded and I can pick them up off the side of the road for free."

He chuckled. "That's a nice thought, but, baby doll, there's no such thing as clearance when it comes to custom blinds."

I let out a groan, and not only because he called me baby doll.

Just my luck. The restaurant's windows were a patchwork of mismatched sizes, none of which were standard, so picking up blinds off the shelf at the home store and hanging them myself was out of the question.

"Look," he said, lifting his clipboard and retrieving the pen from behind his ear. "If you want my advice, I'd spend a few extra dollars on something that will last. With these windows as thin as they are, you might be surprised how much blinds can cut down on your heating and air bill, especially if you plan to open for lunch." He shuffled a few inches to the side, standing in direct sunlight. "The sun rises that way. If you stand right here for more than a second or two, it's going to feel like dining on the sun. You planning to put tables here?"

I wasn't *planning* to put tables there. I'd already bought them. I nodded.

"Now, we do offer sunshades that are pretty economical. A lot of the restaurants around here use 'em."

I shook my head. "No, I need something that's *not* see-through."

"That narrows it down. Let me get back to the office and I'll send over some options. When's your opening date?"

I laughed, shaking my head. "Who knows. Few more weeks at least. But I really need to get something up by next Wednesday."

It was his turn to laugh, except I didn't find any humor when he said, "A few weeks I can do. Next Wednesday? Not a chance."

"Damn," I whispered.

He was right. I could feel the rays of the sun penetrating through the windows. If it was already this warm during spring, I could only imagine how sweltering it would be at the peak of summer.

With one last hopeful smile, I asked, "And just to make sure I heard you correctly, you don't have a dumpster out back that is unattended after dark and filled with blinds that could even remotely fit my windows?"

Mr. Budget Blinds shook his head as the corner of his mouth tipped up. "Doll face, if we did, I wouldn't even make you wait until nightfall to go get 'em." He tucked the clipboard under an arm and extended his hand toward me. "I'll get this quote over to you as soon as possible."

With an inward groan, I shook his hand before leading him to the door. "Thank you for your time. Have a nice day."

"You too, sweets."

I rolled my eyes at the term of endearment and turned to go back inside, but something down the street caught my attention.

"What the…" I muttered to myself, squinting against the sun.

Lumbering down the sidewalk, arms full of who knew what, a pack mule resembling Truett West made his way toward me.

Holy shit.

While I was frozen in place with the door half open, the cool air breezed past me. My instincts had me panicked. He didn't leave his house except for on Wednesdays. At least that was what he'd told me. But his long legs took purposeful strides, far too slow for something to be wrong.

I waited until he was within earshot before shouting, "Have I been transported to an alternate universe?" I checked my watch to verify that it was in fact not only noon, but Thursday as well. "Truett, you do know yesterday was Wednesday, right?"

His stormy brown eyes narrowed from above what appeared to be a stack of dusty newspapers balanced on his forearms while two plastic grocery sacks hung from his hands. He grunted a reply I couldn't begin to understand.

"Okay, so an alternate universe where you don't speak English, apparently."

Louder this time and enunciating each word, he repeated what I assumed he'd said the first time. "If this was an alternate universe, I'd have bought a wheelbarrow. Can I get a little help?"

I hurried toward him, meeting him in the middle of the street. "What's all this?"

"Newspaper to cover the windows." He waited for me to open the door and then unceremoniously dumped the stack of papers on a corner of the floor that had yet to be tiled. He stretched his back from side to side and then took the bags from my hands and made his way toward his booth. "Before you say anything, this cost me next to nothing."

Sidling up next to him, I eyed him suspiciously as he began unloading the contents of the bags. The smell of garlic and ginger wafted up.

"Is that Chinese food?"

He turned and proudly presented me a wax paper bag. "That it is. These spring rolls were exactly three dollars. So your gift of the key cancels them out." He dropped the bag onto the table and pulled out a round black plastic bowl crammed with food. "I got garlic vegetables with white rice for you. Sesame chicken and ham fried rice for me. All for the low, low price of buy-one-get-one-free." He waggled his eyebrows. "I had a coupon. I'll let you guess which item was free."

I recognized the logo on the bag. "You went all the way to China Wok to get that?"

"Nah, I had it delivered. But I was stingy with the tip, so you can't have that on your conscience, either." He finished pulling the rest of the food from the bag and then flipped it upside down, dumping out the packets of sauce and chopsticks before sliding into his side of the booth. "Let's eat before it gets cold."

My stomach growled, ratting me out before I had the chance to lie and tell him that I wasn't hungry. Not counting the untouched club sandwich, it had been forever since we'd shared a meal together, much less from our favorite Chinese hole-in-the-wall. I'd avoided it like the plague since our divorce, unwilling to open Pandora's box of positive memories. But damn, he knew me well. They had the best spring rolls, and my mouth watered just thinking about taking a bite.

I stood there for a beat, but he didn't slide over so that we could share the same side of the booth again. A pang of disappointment hit me as I slid in across from him. Then he went to work opening the dishes and passing out the duck sauce he knew I couldn't resist.

"Just so you know, I feel worse knowing some poor delivery kid got stiffed because of me."

His shoulder raised slightly. "That might have been a lie. I tipped him just fine."

I teasingly gasped. "A lie? Now I can't believe anything you say. Was there even a coupon or did you"—I clutched my invisible pearls—"pay full price?"

He snapped his fingers and pointed at me. "See, I knew you were going to say that." Digging into his back pocket, he retrieved a paper and then unfolded it. "So I brought the doorhanger they left last week as proof." He pointed to the square missing amongst various other coupons. "No money spent on you, I swear."

I turned, the vinyl of the booth squeaking as I looked to where he had dropped the stack of papers. "Okay, what about the newspapers?"

"They've been in my garage so long I'm scared to actually look at the date. This isn't a man trying to rescue you with a fist full of dollar bills. Just a man who took the day off and needed some lunch. I figured, what better place to have lunch than across from you?"

I fought the urge to once again remind him that I didn't need his help. But what would have been the point? Walking a fine line, he'd done as I'd asked and not spent any money. Worst case, I'd owe him less than twenty bucks. I didn't like the idea of being in debt to him at all, but whether I understood it or not, I did like the idea of spending time with him.

"Fine," I relented. "But I'm going to need you to share some of that sesame chicken with me."

His neck snapped back, confusion furrowing his brow. "Well, now I'm the one convinced we're in an alternate universe. Since when do you eat meat?"

I chuckled, snagging a piece of the sticky meat with my

chopsticks and waving it in the air. "Since Dylan dragged me to a steakhouse for her birthday right after I had Nate. My hormones were crazy and I swear I must have been anemic or something because one look at her medium-rare steak was all it took for me to send my house salad back in exchange for a T-bone."

I popped the chicken into my mouth, my eyes fluttering shut as I moaned, "God, I forgot how good their food is."

After what could be considered an inappropriate amount of pleasure from a single piece of chicken, I opened my eyes to see what was *definitely* an inappropriate amount of pleasure staring back at me. Truett's eyes were zeroed in on my mouth.

My cheeks heating, I let my tongue dart out to moisten my lips, not letting the way his nostrils flared escape my attention. "Ahem." I cleared my throat, trying to find something to say, anything to ease the burn that was starting to bloom in my chest. Switching to a fork, I stabbed a broccoli stalk from my bowl. "I do still love veggies though."

"Nate, huh? You named him after Nathanial?" His smoldering grin morphed into one that was soft, sweet, and damn if that wasn't sexy too.

Most notably, Truett had said his name and managed to keep the color in his face all at the same time.

I chewed quickly, hurrying to answer him before he shut down. "Yes and no. I went with Nathan. I didn't want him to ever feel like he was born with shoes to fill, but we call him Nate for short." I swallowed hard, searching his face for any trace of pain that told me I should change the subject to something easier, lighter, like, I don't know, capybaras or facts on otters holding hands. But there was nothing to be found other than love and a hint of nostalgia.

"I like it. He would too." He cleared his throat, wiping his mouth with a cheap napkin, and then said, "He was the dark-haired boy that day I first ran into you, right?"

"Yep. The spitball king belongs to me."

He chuckled. "Any of the other two kids yours?"

"God, no. Those other hellions belong to my two best friends, Angela and Dylan." I grinned. "Don't get me wrong. I love those monsters like they're my own, but the three of them together is chaos." Nerves fluttered in my stomach as I found the courage to ask, "What about you? Kids?"

He glanced down at his lap and patted a lump of keys in his pocket. "Just the one for me."

I nodded. "Why mess with perfection, huh?"

"Right," he said simply before digging into his food.

For several minutes, we continued to eat in comfortable silence, though it took a boatload of effort to stifle my reaction when I bit into the crispy spring roll. When I saw that there was only one piece of chicken left, I caught the lip of the bowl with my fork and pulled it across the table toward me, my lips pursing playfully when he shot me an incredulous look.

"What?" I quipped before popping the last bite into my mouth. "You said you'd share and then you went and ate it all."

The napkin that was in his hand dropped onto the table and he leaned back, stretching his arms out to the sides before folding them behind his head. "If I'd known you weren't a vegetarian anymore, I'd have brought more to share. Seems like there's a lot I don't know about you anymore."

I pushed the empty containers away and rested one forearm on the table, using my other to prop up my chin. "I could say the same about you. You said earlier you took the day off. I don't even know what you do for work."

He shifted, his biceps flexing with the action, the tattoos moving almost like they were alive on his arms. My mind wandered to what they would look like without the confines of his shirt. Had he gotten more ink over the years? There'd been a day when I'd had them memorized and spent hours blindly tracing them in the dark as we lay naked in bed, sweaty and sated.

When his biceps flexed again, this time one after the other, I knew I'd been caught. I tore my stare away and sputtered, "You, uh, you were saying?"

"I hadn't said anything yet." He grinned wolfishly. "But *you* asked what I do. I'm a corporate recruiter. Specifically for veterans. I help them transition into civilian life, find jobs that suit them rather than based solely on what they did while they were in."

It didn't surprise me one bit that Truett had found himself in a career like that. He'd always been passionate about the military, even after he'd been medically retired. It sounded like the perfect job for him.

"You work remotely?"

He nodded. "What about you? What were you doing before you decided to revamp this place?"

I looked around at the mess. What had I been doing all the years before I dove headfirst into the sinkhole of restaurant ownership?

"I was being a wife. A mother. A cook. A maid. A chauffeur. A zookeeper for Nate. A punching bag for Jeff."

"A what?" he growled, his aura no longer relaxed, but tightly coiled, ready to snap.

"No, no. Not a literal one. He never laid a hand on me. That was a poor choice of words. I only meant that my ex was, and still is, an ass of epic proportions. The very definition of a narcissist, and I was usually the target of his bad moods." I reached across the table, resting my hand over his clenched fist, and squeezed his fingers, trying to bring his focus back to me, "True, I know that look. And I'm telling you I'm okay. I wasn't for a while, but I am now. I promise."

His eyes blazed with fury desperate to escape, but with nowhere for it to go, he unclenched his fist and laced his fingers with mine. "I know shit ended bad with us, but you wouldn't lie to me about that, would you? You'd tell me if he ever hurt you, right?"

"He hurt me, True. We were together for ten years. Some were worse than others, but he didn't hurt me in the way you're thinking. I swear."

His eyes searched my face, looking for any signs I was downplaying the truth. When he found nothing, he visibly relaxed. "Is that why you bought this place? After your divorce?"

"Yeah. When I realized that I needed a career and had a hole in my résumé over a decade wide, I decided to take a leap and used the mall settlement money to buy the place."

His eyes widened as he sucked in a sharp breath.

"I know, I know. I vowed to never touch that money. But I figured using it to start over, for myself, for Nate, that couldn't be wrong, could it? Now, I'm not so sure that it was the smartest choice, but what I lack in talent, I make up for in feral determination." I let out a short laugh. "Or lunacy, not sure which."

"You have more skills, more talent, more everything, than any person I know." His voice was gravelly, the sincerity in each word painfully clear.

"That pile of tile over there would probably beg to differ." I moved to pull my hand from his.

His grip tightened and he leaned in across the table. "Let me help you with this place."

I shook my head, the spell almost broken. "No. I didn't tell you any of that to garner sympathy. You asked what I'd been up to. Putting my life back together, one step at a time, was the answer."

His frustrated breath blew across my face, but his hand still held tight to mine. "Why won't you let me help you?"

I couldn't properly explain it to him. I didn't want to. So I went with the abridged version. "I don't like owing people."

His brow furrowed as he scoffed, "I'm not a loan shark. No money involved. I'm just offering my services."

My stomach dipped at his words, although the services he was offering were probably not the ones that flashed through my mind. I wiggled my hand free from his and pushed to my feet, my tired legs protesting the move almost as loudly as my mind. "What services are you offering exactly?"

He slid out of the booth and wandered to the water saw. "For starters, I can finish this tile job. Hell"—he bent over and picked up a scrap from my pile of misfit ceramic—"I could probably salvage half of these."

I crossed my arms over my chest. "I hate to break it to you, but it's not as easy as it looks."

"Don't you remember when I redid Grandpa Jack's floor in his fishing cabin? He said it looked so good he insisted I pull up the hardwood in Aunt Shelly's house and replace them with his exact same tile."

I groaned at the memory. "Those wood floors were gorgeous. I have no idea how he convinced her to rip them out."

"They were rotting. Gorgeous wasn't going to keep her from falling through to the basement and breaking a hip. Look, when you live in a house as old as ours, everything has to be fixed or replaced at least twice."

I jolted when he called it *our* house.

It had been our house. After his mom passed away, he'd inherited it, but we'd been living there for years even before that. We'd had grand plans of raising our family in that house. Growing old in that house. Spending a lifetime together in that house.

Instead, uniformed military members had shown up to my door in that house, rocking my entire world.

I'd shed more tears than I'd thought a human could ever produce in that house.

My husband had told me he wanted a divorce in that house.

I had been gutted and forced to give up on my soul mate inside that house.

There hadn't been *our* anything in almost two decades, but especially not that house.

I didn't have the chance to correct him before he walked over, stopping directly in front of me.

"I'm not trying to rescue you. I know you can do this on your own and it will turn out absolutely incredible. But you mentioned you're running behind schedule to open on time, and I'm offering free labor. Nothing more." His body hovered so close to mine that it made a chill roll down my spine. His dark eyes held me hostage as I considered his offer—and how it would feel to press my lips to his.

"It's going to take more than an hour on Wednesdays to get this place done on time."

He smiled, and sweet Jesus, he swayed even closer. "It's Thursday, Gwen. And I've got all night."

I had so many questions.

What had suddenly changed, allowing him to venture out of his safe haven?

Was it only Wednesdays and Thursdays now?

Could he go other places too?

But most of all, why the hell was he so damn close, and why did I want him even closer?

"Okay," I breathed, afraid to say more.

"Okay?"

I took a small step back, desperately needing to clear my head. "Yeah. I'm not in any position to turn down free labor. But just know that you helping does not obligate me to help you move, or do yard work, or shovel snow in the winter. You are volunteering and I'm not accepting it as much as just not kicking you out."

A lazy smile split his lips, victory dancing in his eyes. "That seems fair."

"All right, then. Where do you want to start?"

For the next several hours, we worked side by side. He spread the old newspapers, which we noted were from two thousand ten, over the windows while I handed him pieces of tape and made sure to point out all the areas that might need more adhesive. Once he was satisfied that Taggart wouldn't be able to take any more pictures, we moved on to the floors.

He expertly cut the tiles on the first try while I tried not to stare as tattoos danced over his muscles.

As the day went on, we talked about nothing in particular. I filled him in on my farm-fresh, family-dining vision of The Rosewood, and he begged me to add my "world famous" tortellini ranch salad to the menu. It was only world famous to him, but it felt good that he'd remembered. I'd teased him when I found out he still had his old motorcycle in his garage, despite the fact that he no longer had a valid driver's license. And then we fell awkwardly silent when he reminded me that Nathanial had helped him build it and that was the only reason he kept it.

After that, we kept things surface level. He told me about his job and some of the men he had helped find new careers, and I told him stories of my online shopping horrors.

He smiled—a lot.

I think I smiled more though.

Throughout the day, I'd caught glimpses of longing in his eyes, felt the magnetic pull between us, and heard the way his voice caught every time he said my name. I tried to ignore the way my body reacted, keeping my distance from him as much as possible. But it was a futile effort, and more times than I could count, he'd walk behind me, squeezing my hip as he passed.

Just as he'd promised, he managed to get almost the entire floor laid by the time the sun began to set. I rocked back onto my heels as I pushed to my feet, my knees sure to be bruised in the morning. But for the first time since I'd decided to take this on, I looked around and felt proud.

"Wow, that tile looks amazing."

Truett finished bagging the trash and nodded as he appraised his work. "It does look good. You're welcome."

I laughed, the sound coming from deep within. "I don't recall saying thank you yet."

"That smile on your face is all I need."

My stomach dipped in all the best ways. "Let me get my stuff and I'll drive you home."

"Don't worry about it. I can walk. I need to stretch my legs a bit anyway. For a minute there, I forgot I'm not twenty anymore."

"Do you think that's a good idea? Just because we haven't seen Taggart doesn't mean he isn't out there waiting for you."

He shrugged. "My guess is he's been watching me enough to know I only come here on Wednesdays. If not, he probably got tired of reading the Dear Abby columns taped to the windows and took off."

"Maybe she had some advice about how to not be a dickhead and he took it to heart."

Truett laughed, and the sound sent a rush of warmth through my bones.

"You have your son this weekend?" he asked.

I shook my head. "Nope. It'll just be me, a bottle of wine, and a few gallons of paint all weekend."

He paused, one hand on the door, and turned to face me. "I have to work tomorrow. But I'm all yours Saturday."

His words caught me off guard. "Saturday?"

"Yep, the day after tomorrow. Usually people's favorite day of the week. Mine's Wednesday, but Thursdays are already starting to grow on me. Maybe Saturday will too."

"Is that something you want to do? Come paint and grout and run the risk of electric shock as I try to install the light fixtures in this dump? With your ex-wife? On a Saturday?"

His free hand cupped my chin, his thumb rough as it brushed across my cheek. "The Gwendolyn Pierce standing in front of me may not be the same Gwen I was once married to. She may eat steaks now, she may not be able to cut a fucking tile straight to save her life, and she may have an insulting amount of confidence in my handyman abilities. But the Gwen of the present is still singlehandedly the only person I would want to spend my Saturday with. And stop calling it a dump. You've done some amazing things here already. I have no doubt that, when we finish, it's going to be nothing short of incredible."

God, why did that feel so good?

His use of *when "we" finish.*

The fact that he wanted to be there.

The fact that I wanted him to be there too.

The smolder of desire that had been kindling in my chest all day ignited. Before my logical brain could douse the flames, I blurted, "Were you going to kiss me in that booth yesterday?"

His hand slid down the column of my throat, his thumb resting at the base, my heart beating wildly beneath it as I anticipated his answer.

What was I anticipating? I didn't know.

What did I want his response to be? I didn't know the answer to that, either.

All I knew was that, if he didn't say something soon, it was possible I would spontaneously combust right there at the door of my restaurant.

"I don't think you asked me the right question, Gwen."

Out of all the possible answers he could have given, that wasn't one I'd expected. "I'm sorry?"

"Yesterday in that booth was past Truett. He doesn't exist anymore. The only person here with you right now is present Truett. Maybe you should ask that question to him."

My lips parted; my throat suddenly dry as I realized what he was saying to me. We'd spent the whole day comparing and contrasting the past and present. We weren't the same people anymore—for better and for worse. So it made sense that he wouldn't want to answer a question that was aimed at a man who was no longer there.

I placed a hand on his chest, letting the strong thrum of his heart settle me, and whispered, "Are you going to kiss me now, True?"

"I've been waiting all fucking day for you to ask me that." He hooked his arm around my waist and crushed my body to his, mere seconds before his lips came down over mine.

My body came alive as his tongue moved with mine, our mouths dancing together, synchronized in perfect rhythm. It was both so familiar yet so foreign.

My fingertips curled into his shirt, and I pressed up onto my toes so that I could loop my arm around his neck, pulling him closer to deepen the kiss. The taste of him, the scent of his cologne tinged with the saltiness of sweat, and the way his arm flexed as he held me tight were intoxicating and I found myself wanting nothing more than to get drunk on him.

Why had it been so long since I'd felt this? Better yet, what could I do to ensure that I never lost this feeling again?

He groaned, the deep timbre of lust and desire reverberating through me, and in that instant, I snapped back to reality.

I was kissing Truett.

A man I'd loved so fiercely.

The same man who had broken my heart, shattered it into a million pieces. Pieces I was still trying to put back together.

I broke our seal and stepped away, my lungs filling with the oxygen I'd deprived them, my mind swirling with indecision.

What was I doing?

Oh, God. *What was I doing?*

"I…uh," I said, still trying to catch my breath. "I'm not sure we should be doing that."

His lips tipped in a grin. "Really? Because I was just thinking we should have been doing that every day for the last twenty years."

Shit. I felt that too.

He gave my hip one last squeeze before turning to shove the front door open. "We still good for Saturday morning?"

I should have said no and nipped what would surely turn into a fiasco of epic proportions in the bud.

I couldn't make out with Truett and then just casually hang out with him on Saturday.

Had I suddenly developed a case of amnesia?

Apparently so, because when I opened my mouth, a shaky, "Yeah," came out.

He smirked. "Good. I'll see you then." He shut the door and then spoke a muffled command through the glass, "Make sure you lock up."

Stunned and dazed, I stared at him, but he didn't walk away until I finally flipped the deadbolt.

CHAPTER EIGHTEEN

TRUETT

Eighteen years earlier…

"WHY AREN'T YOU DRESSED? THE FUNERAL STARTS in twenty minutes." Disbelief coated her words as they echoed loudly in the open space of my living room. It was a stark contrast to the silence I'd been sitting in for the last few hours. "Truett, look at me."

I kept my gaze aimed at the unraveling thread I'd been picking on the arm of the couch.

I couldn't bear to look at her. I'd seen more than enough when she'd shoved my front door open and marched inside.

Heels, black with straps around her ankles.

Tanned legs.

A black dress that hit just above her knee and cinched at the waist.

A thin silver chain resting against the column of her smooth neck, its cross flush against her breastbone.

Small hoops in her ears, hidden by the long dark waves of her silky hair as it rested over her shoulders.

Makeup applied strategically to hide the dark bags under her eyes.

Red-rimmed eyes that hit me like acid raining from the sky.

No. I couldn't look at her again. I'd seen enough of her tears to last me a million lifetimes.

Hope replaced the exasperation in her voice. "Did you lose track of time or something? We're going to be late."

I hadn't lost track of anything. I could tell down to the very minute how long it had been since the world had come to a screeching halt.

I wasn't dressed because I wasn't going.

Plain and simple.

I shook my head, my eyes still trained on the corner of that ratty brown couch, the one she hated but I couldn't bear to part with. Especially now.

Her heels clicked on the wood floor as she walked over to me before sitting on the coffee table in front of me. Her words were unfairly patient as she spoke. "I know this is going to be hard for you. But I need you there. I can't do this by myself."

She wouldn't be by herself. Her family would be there. Her parents, who thought I was every bit of the fuck-up I'd proven myself to be, would mourn beside her, grief-stricken and shattered.

They would all be better off if I never showed my face again. At least then I couldn't destroy their family any more than I already had.

"Please," she begged. "I need you. I've been a mess. I keep alternating between crying and throwing up. I haven't eaten or slept in days. And for some reason, all I can think about is how dark it's going to be when they lower the casket into the ground." Reaching out, she stilled my hand, the tiny diamond on her engagement ring catching the light.

I'd long since tucked my wedding band into the darkest depths of my closet. And even still, that was sometimes too close.

"Talk to me," she urged.

I pulled my hand away. I couldn't speak, my throat raw from

the screams that had woken me out of a fitful sleep every night that week.

Besides, there wasn't anything left to say.

Not a single word that left my lips would change the facts of how gravely I'd failed her.

I kept my gaze down, the seconds stretching into minutes.

She needed comfort, to be held, to be reassured she'd find a way to mend her broken heart. But I was broken too—past the point of repair—so I didn't have those promises to offer her.

Her pain eventually turned to frustration, or anger, or...I don't know, everything in between.

"Say something, dammit!" she roared, pushing to her feet.

My head snapped up on instinct, and just as I'd feared, tears poured from her eyes, igniting my soul like a match to a pool of gasoline.

She carried a pain so heavy it distorted her face as she leveled me with a glare. "You're not doing this to me. Not today. Get your ass up, go get dressed, and let's fucking go."

"No." My voice was hoarse, the word barely more than a croak, but the way she flinched, I might as well have screamed.

"What do you mean, no? This isn't optional. Get up."

I shook my head.

"Get. *Up*."

I scrubbed a hand over my face but made no effort to stand.

"You know what? Fine. Just like always, I'll do it my-fucking-self." With mumbled curses, she stomped down the hall into a bedroom that had once been ours. Reappearing a few seconds later with my suit in her hand, she threw it onto the couch beside me. "Put it on."

I had no intention of wearing that death suit, but she didn't give me a chance to refuse before she started tearing my T-shirt over my head. Her hands were rough as she struggled to shove my arms into the sleeves of the white dress shirt.

I didn't fight her, but I didn't cooperate, either. "Gwen, stop," I rumbled.

Using her body, she tried to wrestle it around my shoulders. "You're not fucking doing this to me. Not today. Put the Goddamn shirt on!"

"Gwen, stop," I repeated, attempting to catch her frenzied hands, but she was a swirling cyclone of grief.

"You can walk away from me. Abandon me. Feed me to the wolves during the most difficult time of my life. I don't care anymore. But you are going to this funeral even if I have to drag your ass there myself." Giving up on my shirt, she snatched up my slacks and then went for the waistband on my sweatpants.

Losing all patience, I shot to my feet. "Stop!"

"I can't!" she screamed back, only inches from my face. Dissolving into a fit of sobs, she collapsed to the floor, wedged between my couch and coffee table. Wails tore from her throat, her shoulders rolling with gags.

And all I could do was stand there staring at her, knowing it was all my fault.

"I'm sorry," I choked out, tears streaming down my face.

"Bullshit. You wouldn't do this to me if you were sorry."

"Gwen..."

Sobs racked her shoulders. "I hate you. I hate you so fucking much. I wish this was your funeral instead."

"I do too!" I exploded.

Her head popped up and she stared at me for a long second, her chest heaving, her bloodshot eyes swimming with tears. "You coward."

I jerked from the verbal blow, but she wasn't wrong. "You think I don't know that! You think I don't live with that knowledge every fucking day of my life?"

"I don't know anything anymore, Truett. Least of all you." With that, she drew in a shaky breath and climbed to her feet. Her hands shook as she reached down to her wedding rings, sliding them off with a finality that crushed me. Holding my stare with a disdain I would never forget, she dropped them, one by one, onto the floor at my feet. "I would have loved you for the rest of my life. But, now I will hate you for the rest of yours."

She turned on a toe, walking the long way around the coffee table so she didn't have to pass me.

My body screamed for me to stop her, to beg her to make this nightmare end as only she could, but my feet never budged.

The door swung inward, and from my spot in front of that godforsaken couch, I watched as she stepped into the sunshine, her head held high in false bravado, taking every happy memory this home had ever held with her.

I told myself to open my mouth and say something, any fucking thing before I lost her forever.

Don't go.

I need you.

I'm so fucking sorry.

But, much like myself from that point forward, those words stayed locked inside.

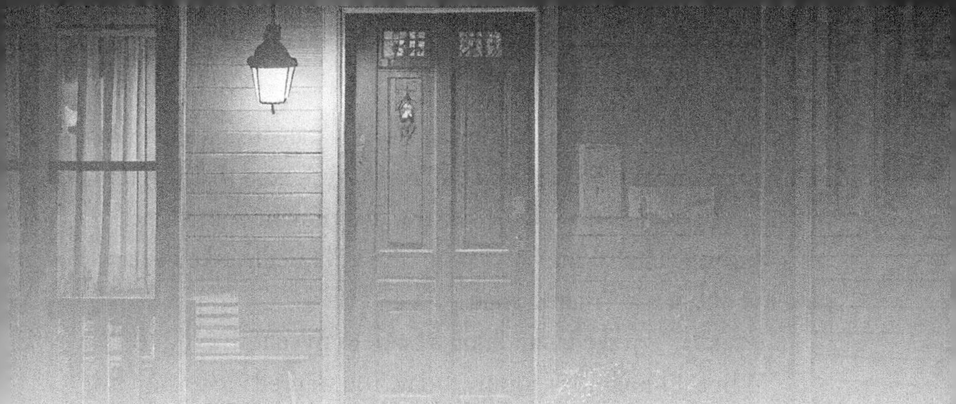

CHAPTER NINETEEN

Gwen

I STARED AT THE STACK OF PAPERS IN FRONT OF ME, WILLING myself to pick up the first one. It was just past three o'clock, and all I had accomplished for the day was walking through the front door and turning the lights on.

I hadn't replied to the vendor emails that had been in my inbox for days, checked the budget spreadsheet for the week to make sure I was still on track—or no more off track than usual—or even dived into finalizing the menu.

What I had managed to do while sitting in Truett's booth was think about the man who had somehow managed to set my head spinning all over again.

"I've been waiting all fucking day for you to ask me that."

That sentence had been echoing in my head all day. Well, that and what had happened after.

His mouth on mine.

His beard deliciously scratching my chin.

His massive body engulfing me, setting me on fire in ways that I had forgotten were possible.

The way it felt so good, so natural, so…everything.

I'd not only let him kiss me, I'd asked him to.

And if I was being honest, I wanted more.

It was that realization that had me reeling.

I hadn't been thinking straight. I was no longer using any form of logical thought when it came to Truett West. And that was terrifying, because I'd barely survived the first time he ruined me.

"Sugar, whatcha doin' just sittin' there?" Lucille asked, snapping me out of my Truett trance.

"Jesus H!" I jerked, clutching a hand to my chest.

"Whoa. Somebody's jumpy today. You wanted me to stop by at three, right?" She walked across the restaurant, a gorgeous emerald-green skirt brushing her knees, and slid into the opposite side of the booth. She dropped her ridiculously large purse onto the floor beside her.

"Yeah. Sorry. I'm just a little out of it today."

Her shrewd gaze appraised me, but she didn't press any further. Flicking her gaze to the stack of papers in front of me, she asked, "You started without me?"

"If you count gathering the papers, then yeah. Otherwise, no."

She slid the stack of applications toward her and snatched the first one from the top of the pile. "Jenny Cooper. Nope." Tossing the application to the floor, she picked up the next one. "Mabel Dean. Absolutely not."

Just like the one before, that paper fluttered to the floor.

"Ah, Eddie Jackson. He's not bad. Maybe." She set that application to the side, and then a hearty laugh escaped her throat. "This is a joke, right?" She waved a paper toward me. "Shawn Tully? No way in hell." She crumpled the paper into a ball before throwing it onto the ever-growing pile of rejected applicants.

"Stop," I protested. "You're not even reading their experience. We don't exactly have a ton to choose from."

I'd put a "help wanted" ad in the paper and a sign on the door a few days earlier, and while the first day had me excited thinking I'd be fully staffed in no time, the applications had trickled off since then. With Lucille's automatic rejections, it was looking like she and I were going to be running the whole place by ourselves.

Just add that to the world's most overwhelming to-do list.

"I don't need to read their experience. I've lived it. Jenny job hops. That girl has worked at every single restaurant in this town, including this one. *Twice.* She'll schmooze ya, make you think she's gonna be the best employee ever. Then one day she'll have some drama with her oldest kid's baby daddy and not be able to come in. The next day it'll be the same thing, except with the baby's dad." She lifted her finger in the air to amend. "Not the same man, either. Then it'll be her middle kid causing trouble at school and she has to leave to go pick him up 'cause he got suspended. That one has a different daddy too and he works outta town, so he's no help."

"Single moms need jobs too," I told her. "Us women need to stick together."

"Correct. You didn't let me get to the part where she steals money from the register and gives out free food to every person she so much as went to preschool with."

"Say less." I bit my bottom lip.

"And then there's Mabel. She's at least a hundred years old. That woman has lost all of her marbles if she thinks she can do anything in a restaurant other than sit at a table and aggravate the customers while she talks about her bunions and her ancient cat that refuses to die."

I couldn't help my giggle. "How is that any worse than the story you told me about your last colonoscopy?"

"Girl, I'm just letting you know what you have to look forward to in a few years. Besides, you weren't trying to eat breakfast when we talked about that. You think anyone's gonna want an order of pancakes with a side of cat vomit stories?"

I cringed. "Okay, pass."

"Exactly."

I chuckled. The best thing about Lucille was that it didn't matter what the hell she was saying. She said everything with a straight face and more conviction than a preacher on Sunday morning.

Whether she was talking about bodily functions or space travel, she just said it matter-of-factly and then acted surprised when you were shocked. She had no filter and I kind of loved that about her, because I could trust that she'd always give it to me straight.

She continued to explain her rigorous hiring techniques. "And don't even get me started with Shawn. That man is a whack job. Conspiracy theories, baby goats, and baseball are his entire life. With a side of being an ass to his ex-wife and his oldest son. I'd sooner set myself on fire than work alongside him." Her lips set into a firm line as she crossed her arms over her chest and settled back in the booth.

"And another pass." I grabbed the remaining papers and counted them. "That leaves us with six people. That's not enough to operate a food truck, much less an entire restaurant."

She pulled the papers from my hands, flipping through them before quickly discarding four more. "Nope, that leaves us with two. Don't worry though. These two could probably run this place with their eyes closed."

I let out a frustrated sigh and dropped my forehead to my palm. "Great."

Lucille dug her phone from her purse. "Let me make some calls. I know a few people who might be up to a little change of scenery."

Oh, wonderful. We were poaching employees from other restaurants now. Surely that would endear me to the rest of the local businesses.

I didn't stop her though.

As she paced around the restaurant with her phone to her ear, barking like she was collecting money for the mob, my mind drifted back to Truett.

He'd be back the next day to help again, and there was so much to be done, but all I could think about was that the only work I wanted him to do was on me.

"Earth to Gwen." Lucille snapped her fingers inches in front of my face as she slid back into the booth. "Where'd ya go?"

"Nowhere," I muttered.

Her sharp eyes roamed my face for point two seconds before she blurted, "You get laid last night?"

"What? No!"

"Well, what happened, then? And don't even try to tell me you're thinking about renovations. No paint has ever made a woman get stars in her eyes like that."

I had stars in my eyes? Fan-freaking-tastic.

"I do not have stars in my eyes. I don't even know what that looks like outside of cartoons." I looked away quickly, my cheeks heating.

"Mmhm, sure." She leaned across the table and used one finger under my chin to turn my head back to face her. "Stars. Blush. And a glow. Don't tell me you didn't get laid."

I swatted her hand away. "I didn't!"

"You know butt stuff still counts, right?"

"Oh my God!" I groaned. "Can we drop this?"

"Sure," she chirped. But she didn't move on or change the subject. She just sat there staring at me, tapping her pink fingernails on the table.

I did need somebody to talk to. A woman who called herself Cooter was probably a horrible choice when it came to the romance department, but she was there.

"Let me ask you a question."

Her whole face lit. "Now we're getting somewhere."

I rolled my eyes. "You ever been married before?"

"Three times." She settled back in her seat and crossed her arms over her bust. "First one was when I was eighteen. Lasted about eight seconds. Realized that I didn't really enjoy ironing a man's pants while studying for an algebra test. Though I didn't really learn my lesson, either. Four years later, I was walking down the aisle again. This time to an older guy who I thought hung the moon. Turns out he was just a good actor until he got that ring on my finger." She made a sour face and stuck her tongue out. "He gave me my babies, but besides that, he was a nasty, miserable man. Nothing I did was ever right. Meals were overcooked one day, undercooked the next. House was never clean enough. I wasn't ever dressed up enough for him. Blah, blah, blah. The list just went on and on and on. Then, one day he just keeled over, right there in the plate of lasagna that he'd just complained didn't have enough sauce. Dead as a doornail."

All I could do was blink at her. She'd just told me a lifetime of trauma like she was recapping a movie. "I'm so sorry. I had no idea."

She waved a hand in my direction and laughed. "Oh, please. Nothing to be sorry about. It was a long time coming."

I swallowed hard. "When you say long time coming, you didn't...like, off him, did you?"

She barked a laugh. "I mean, I probably had a hand in it. Cooking up all that greasy bacon he demanded. But to answer your question, no I didn't *off him*. It was a heart attack."

I let out an audible sigh of relief, making her laugh again. "What about husband number three?" I asked. "Third time the charm?"

At the mention of her third husband, her face softened, and for the first time since I'd met her, I caught a glimpse of the vulnerability she seemed to keep hidden.

"Lewis," she said softly. For several moments, she didn't speak, her gaze fixed over my head, dreamily. When she brought her attention back to me, the softness was replaced by her quirky grin. "That man was a pain in my ass. Cantankerous, loud, and annoying as hell. Don't even get me started about how horny he always was. That man couldn't keep his hands off of me." She waggled her eyebrows and chuckled. "I can't blame him. I'm a card-toting member of the AARP, but I still got it."

"You do," I agreed wholeheartedly.

Her face got serious. "But I miss him every single day. He passed away a few years back. Left me a mountain of money, but I'd give it all away to have my Lewis back."

"That's really sweet."

"Yeah. He was a good one. I had to look past a lot of flaws, but he treated me like a queen. My biggest regret was that I didn't meet him when I was younger. He didn't have any kids, but he always treated mine as his own. He left them each a gas station when he died."

"A gas station?"

"Yup. He owned a string of them. My kids all got one. Then he left the others to me."

"Wait, you own gas stations? As in plural?"

"Nah. I sold them all. What was I gonna do with ten Texacos?"

My jaw slacked open. "Ten? What the hell were you doing working at The Grille?"

"I liked to keep myself busy even before I lost him. You heard the part about him being cantankerous, loud, and annoying as hell, right?"

I nodded. "I guess it's good that you're not in this for the money. At the rate I'm going, I may end up having to pay you in IOUs and eternal gratitude."

She grinned. "You gonna tell me what the sudden interest in my personal life has to do with why your head's been in the clouds today?"

I chewed on my bottom lip, my mind jumping back to Truett. "Hypothetically speaking. Let's say you started spending time with your ex." I paused and held up a hand. "Just casually. Except, then it became not so casually and you started to feel a spark. Let's call it chemistry, maybe? I don't know."

She quirked an eyebrow. "You have my attention."

"So, let's pretend that this ex kissed you."

Her eyes flashed wide, a playful grin splitting her mouth. "Now, you're talking."

I shot her a glare, and she rolled her eyes before motioning for me to continue.

"What if when that happened—you know, when he kissed you—you liked it? *A lot.* So much so that it freaked you out and now you can't stop thinking about it or him and focus on anything you're supposed to be doing?"

"Well." Her lips twisted as she tried not to smile. "Hypothetically speaking, 'cause that's what this is, right? Just a pretend scenario that didn't actually happen?"

"Right. Exactly. Did *not* actually happen."

"Okay, then. *Hypothetically,* if ex number one kissed me, I probably would like it. He was a great kisser and a decent guy."

"Mmhm. Okay."

"And, *hypothetically,* if ex number two kissed me, I would probably assume I was in hell, since he's dead and that is surely where he is. So I would be pretty upset, 'cause I'm no saint, but I don't think I'm headed down south."

I grinned. "I dunno. Maybe you'll be the first ever Saint Cooter."

Her laughter erupted from deep in her throat. "Wouldn't that be a trip?"

"What about ex number three?" I pressed.

That soft smile returned. "I'd give anything to kiss Lewis one more time. He wasn't perfect, but he was mine." She propped her elbows on the table. "I guess what I'm saying is that I can't answer this *hypothetically*. 'Cause I've heard some stories from Dylan, and she will run over me with her car if I condone you making out with your kid's dad."

My stomach churned at the thought of ever kissing Jeff again. "No. Not him."

Her eyes bugged out of her head as she animatedly slapped

the tabletop. "I knew it! You kissed the hot gargoyle! Holy shit, girl. I need details."

I groaned as I squeezed my eyes shut. "It was good. I mean… It was better than good. It was incredible in every cheesy cliché you've ever thought. Toe-curling. Heart-stopping—"

"Panty-melting?" she interrupted.

Truett's mouth could definitely be defined as panty-melting.

"Yes. That. But what am I thinking, opening that can of worms again? My life is a mess right now. I don't have time to add a train wreck on top of that."

"That's fair. But I guess you need to figure out why that chemistry is still there. Why did you two get divorced anyway?"

I sat there for a minute. A dozen reasons sat on the tip of my tongue, but that was just it. I knew the reasons. I knew the circumstances. I knew the trauma. But I had no idea why leaving me had been the answer to all his problems.

"I don't know," I admitted.

She leveled me with a side-eye. "You don't know? All these years and you never asked?"

"Oh, I asked. A million times. Over and over until I could barely breathe. He just never answered me."

Her eyebrows shot up. "Then I think you're talking to the wrong person here. Clearly that mouth of his is working now. It might be time to throw a few hypotheticals his way."

I sagged in the booth. She had a point, but a part of me was afraid of the truth.

Had I been too cold after he had come back from his deployment?

Had the sight of me reminded him of everything he'd lost?

Or had I meant so little to him that discarding me had been easier than letting me in?

My old friends, Anger and Resentment, flickered inside my chest.

Damn, how was I right back in a situation where I was willing to take whatever scraps of Truett he was willing to give me? One ounce of affection and I was a teenage girl again, lovestruck and smitten.

"You're right. This is dumb. I shouldn't even be entertaining something with him."

"Girl, stop putting words in my mouth. I didn't say all that. I'm just saying, you have to figure out if he's your version of husband one, who you didn't give a fair shake; husband two, who was a total shitbag and doesn't deserve to ever taste you again; or husband three, the one who slipped away far too soon and you'd give anything to have him back. Because I'll be honest, if there is even a speckle of a chance that he's your husband number three, it's worth a conversation to figure it out."

I stared at her. This woman was crazy on every level, including the one where she doled out sage relationship advice by using her *three* ex-husbands as examples.

But she wasn't wrong.

I wasn't sure she was right either, though.

"I'll talk to him," I relented.

"Good. And don't be chintzy on the details next time. I should have gotten a call the second his tongue exited your mouth."

I laughed until the sound of the door caught my attention. I'd forgotten to lock it when she'd arrived, but luckily it was only Nate who came barreling inside.

"Mom!" he shouted, a huge smile on his face and his bookbag bouncing on his back.

"Hey, buddy! What are you doing here?" I checked my watch, worried that I had the day wrong. Nope. Definitely Friday.

He launched himself into the booth, tackling me with a bear hug.

I managed to wrap my arms around him, catching us both

before we fell against the wall behind me. I kissed the top of his head, his brown hair smelling of grass and sweat. "Ew, you stink."

He giggled as he pushed off of me. "We got extra recess today for winning the school fundraiser. And then when Dad picked me up, he opened the sunroof. It was sooooo cool."

Right on cue, Jeff waltzed in the door, wearing his signature polo shirt and penny loafers that had gone out of style at least twenty years earlier. Brushing his blond hair to the side to cover his receding hairline, he stated, "That parking lot is horrendous. I scraped the shit out of my car on the way in. Good luck not getting sued over that when you open up this dive."

"And hello to you too," I mumbled. I patted Nate's thigh. "Lemme out, buddy."

He slid out and dropped his bookbag onto the floor. "I'm hungry! You have any chips in the kitchen?"

"I think so, but so help me God, if you touch any of the tools in there, you will be bedazzling the ribbon for our opening ceremony. There's a thousand-piece gem set I've been eyeing with your name written all over it."

"Yes, ma'am," he grumbled.

I grinned as I watched him disappear into the kitchen.

My smile fell as I turned back to face my ex. "What brings you two by?"

He acted as though he hadn't heard me as he made a lap around the dining room, his lip curled into a sneer.

I couldn't quite explain it, but when he stopped in front of me, it made my skin crawl. Actually, that was completely explainable. My skin crawled whenever I so much as heard his voice. Though, my reaction this time was due to his proximity to that booth—Truett's booth.

"This place is a fucking wreck. What half-bit contractor did you hire? Did you even check his references? The primer is sloppy and this tile is awful."

My blood began to simmer as I stared at him, irritated at his unannounced visit and downright pissed at his appraisal of the hard work Truett and I had put in. But this was not a fight I was interested in starting, so I swallowed the frustration in the name of ending this conversation as quickly as possible. "Is everything okay? What are you and Nate doing here?"

Still ignoring my questions, he planted his hands on his hips. "I told you they weren't going to take a woman seriously. I'll put in a call tomorrow. It looks like you've been condemned from outside with all the newspaper on the windows."

I ground my teeth. He had always been an asshole, but hearing him insult the newspaper Truett had carried down the street, just to ensure that I was safe from Folly's prying camera lens, sent me over the edge.

"I do not want you to call anyone," I seethed. "What I want is for you to tell me what the hell you're doing here and then leave."

He eyed me with his own secret recipe of arrogant disgust. "Why are you always so dramatic? Mind cooling it with the cusswords? My son's here."

My back shot straight. He cussed like a sailor, but oh yes, me saying *hell* was going to corrupt our son who was in the other room. I could not roll my eyes hard enough.

Lucille cleared her throat. Sticking a hand out, she said loudly, "I don't think we've met. I'm Cooter."

Like the complete prick he was, Jeff looked at her outstretched arm before tipping his chin up, refusing to shake her hand. "Your parents should be arrested for naming you that."

When her mouth fell open, I quickly took a step between them, hoping to end the violence before it started—though I made a mental note to circle back around to that comment should I ever find myself in a room with the two of them while my son was not in earshot.

"For the last time, what's going on?" I snapped.

Jeff plastered on a condescending smile, evil Hyde morphing into Jekyll. "I was just trying to look out for you. I could have this place ready for you to open in no time."

"Thanks," I said dryly. "But I've got it under control."

"Suit yourself. Look, I've got a last-minute business meeting in the city. I'll be back in time for a late dinner. So don't let him eat too much junk." He tucked a hand in his pocket and shouted toward the kitchen. "Nate-man. Be back in a bit."

"Wait. What?" I looked around, projects I needed to tackle evident in every corner of the room. "You can't just drop him off. I have a lot to do today and he's going to be bored out of his mind here."

Jeff had the absolute gall to look confused. "Are you saying you don't want him?"

"I didn't say that," I hissed.

"That's what it sounded like to me. Funny, I'd do anything to spend more time with my son. He's always my first priority. My mistake for assuming he'd be yours too."

The sheer hypocrisy of Jeff dropping Nate off with me so he could go to work while expecting me to cancel work to spend time with my son was astounding. But this was nothing new. Hypocrisy and gaslighting were his preferred methods of communication.

"Of course I want to spend time with him. But I'm not on call for you twenty-four-seven. I'm working here too."

He arched a challenging eyebrow. "I'm not sure we can call sitting on your ass gabbing work, but sure. Whatever you have to tell yourself." He pulled his phone from his pocket. "I'll call my sister. I'm sure she'd be happy to help you out today."

Help me out?

Help *me* out?

It took everything in me not to explode on this prick. But I'd learned he feasted like a tick when he was able to set me off. Cool, calm, and firm was the only way to fight his toxicity.

I painted on a smile. "Nate can stay, but I want him overnight too. I'll drop him off on my way to *work* tomorrow. And maybe next time, give me a little heads up before showing up here out of the blue."

He barked a laugh. "You might want to reread our custody agreement. It's my night with him, Gwen."

"And it's your *day* with him too. But here you are, asking me for a favor. If I'm sacrificing a full afternoon of work, I'm going to make the most of it and take him to do something fun on a Friday night."

He scoffed. "Like hanging out with Dylan and her spawn?"

I shrugged, knowing that keeping him in the dark would drive him up the wall. "Maybe. Maybe not."

He stared at me for a second, and I just smiled, giving nothing away. "Fine. But don't forget I have him on Monday *and* Tuesday. I don't want you popping up with some excuse and screwing up our plans."

Lucille snorted, and I began to make my way to the door before Jeff could engage her again.

"I already agreed and put it in my calendar." I pushed the door and held it open for him.

He took his time leaving, his eyes roaming the space, no doubt looking for something else to comment on. Sure enough, just as he stepped across the threshold, he paused to say, "You're not putting in more booths like that, are you? It's outdated and frankly, looks like shit."

It took every ounce of restraint I had not to kick him in the dick. "Have a good night, Jeff." I pulled the door closed with probably more force than was necessary. "Jesus," I breathed, twisting the lock on the door.

"Wow, the hot gargoyle must have really screwed up. You went from Mr. Tall, Quiet, and Tattooed, who is a solid twelve on a bad day, to marrying Mr. Shrimpy Loafers, who is about a negative three on his best day."

"Shhhhhh!" I whisper-yelled. "Nate's gonna hear you."

She shrugged but dropped her voice. "Kid's gonna have to learn his dad's an ass sooner or later."

Right on cue, Nate rounded the corner of the kitchen, his arm elbow-deep in a bag of kettle chips. "Who's an ass?"

"Don't say ass," I scolded.

"What? She said it."

"She's an adult. You are *not.* Now, quit being rude and go introduce yourself."

He eyed her for a second, then walked over and offered her his crumb-covered hand fresh out of the chip bag. "Hi."

She didn't bat an eye before shaking it. "Hey, little man. I'm Cooter."

I sighed. "Nate. This is *Miss Lucille* and she's going to be working with me. Please don't repeat *anything* she says."

"That's probably best," she told him before pinning me with a glare. "Uh uh. No way. I'm not Miss. *Or* Lucille. I'm Cooter. I only let you get away with calling me Lucille because you're my boss. Though, if you need him to be more respectful or whatnot, he can call me Saint Cooter."

Nate roared with laughter as I choked at the thought.

Before I had the chance to argue or come up with a better alternative, Nate shouted, "Nice to meet you, Saint Cooter!"

The two dissolved into a fit of laughter, and as I watched an unlikely friendship bloom between them, I decided I had bigger fish to fry than what my son called the crazy lady who'd taken a liking to me.

"I'm starving," I announced. "Let's get out of here and grab a pizza. Saint Cooter, you're welcome to join us for a large pepperoni with extra pineapple."

Lucille made a face like I'd just offered her a bowl of dog food, but she wrapped her thin arm around Nate's shoulders. "Kid, you ever had hot wings before? We'll leave that nasty pizza for your mom, and I'll introduce you to some real food."

I quickly gathered my things, racing to catch up to the two peas that were already in a pod, vowing to get there early the next day so I could actually check something off my to-do list before Truett arrived.

Or, more than likely, just sit around and obsess about our kiss until he showed up and I could obsess about him in person.

CHAPTER TWENTY

TRUETT

“Wow, you’re here bright and early,” Gwen said as she opened the door.

I chuckled awkwardly, keeping to myself that I’d been up since five because we hadn’t established a time to meet. I’d been so hyped about seeing her again this was actually my third trip to the restaurant that morning, waiting for her to arrive.

Fuck. Me. Two days without seeing her had been torture.

If breaking my routine and branching out of the house on days other than Wednesday had me off-kilter, that kiss had sent me into orbit. On Friday, I’d been shit at work, unable to focus knowing she was just down the street. I couldn’t see the restaurant from my house, but like a sap, I ate lunch on my front porch that day, hoping that the rows of homes dividing us would heed to my desperation and magically disappear so I could catch one single glimpse of her.

I ached to see her again. One taste hadn’t been enough. Though, there was no such thing as enough with Gwen.

I’d put my shoes on no fewer than a dozen times on Friday afternoon. Once, I even made it to the end of the driveway before convincing myself not to go.

She’d wanted that kiss just as much as I had, and the passion that had sparked between us when our lips touched could have set the world on fire. But her hesitance when she'd backed away was the only thing that had kept me from going to her. She needed time.

To think.

To remember.

To come to terms with the fact that something profound still existed between us.

Time was no match for a love like ours—even if tragedy had been a hurdle I'd failed to overcome.

"And good morning to you too," I replied, fighting the urge to drag her into a hug.

She was gorgeous standing there in a pair of tight pink athletic shorts and a black tank top that hugged the swell of her breasts. Her hair was down, hanging just below her shoulders, and she'd changed her nose ring from a flat silver stud to a tiny pink gem that somehow unlocked the sacred middle ground between sexy and cute. I hadn't been a fan of her piercing at first, but I had to admit it had grown on me.

Music played softly as she closed the door, locking it behind me. However, the second that lock clicked, an awkwardness blanketed the room.

My eyebrows furrowed as I looked down and found her fidgeting with her shorts.

Fuck. She was nervous.

"Everything okay?" I asked.

"Yeah. I, uh, just didn't expect you to be here so early." Her voice was flat as her eyes scanned the room, landing on everything but me.

Double fuck.

"We've got a lot of work to do. No time like the present." *Or the four hours I'd been stalking you before that.*

She finally tilted her head back to peer up at me, an emotion I couldn't quite put my finger on clouding her eyes. "Yeah. It's gonna be a long day. You sure you're up for this?"

"I've never been more ready for something in my life." When I'd formulated the thought, I'd meant it in relation to getting my hands dirty and whipping that restaurant into shape. But the moment the words came out of my mouth, the double meaning was not lost on me.

She winced and sucked her bottom lip between her teeth.

Triple fuck.

Okay, so maybe that kiss hadn't gone as well for her as it had for me.

"Can you help me move some boxes in the kitchen?" she asked, walking away.

"Sure." I followed after her, hoping like hell I was reading her wrong. I came to an abrupt stop as soon as I walked through the swinging door. "Wow," I breathed.

She must have had a big delivery since I'd been gone, because it had only remotely resembled a kitchen when I'd left on Thursday. Now, brand-new stainless-steel appliances gleamed under the bright overhead lights. A massive commercial range dominated one wall, its burners and oven doors untouched, still covered in a plastic film. The prep station, expansive and orderly, stood in the center like the heart of the kitchen. All that was missing was the hustle and bustle of culinary excellence.

"This is incredible."

Whatever was going on with her at the moment couldn't mask her pride. "Right?"

The song playing through the Bluetooth speaker ended, fading into another slow, melancholy melody—each note dripping with sorrow and regret. The atmosphere in the room grew heavier as the somber tune filled the air. It was a far cry from her normal chaotic compilations ranging from of Outkast to *NSYNC.

"What's going on with your playlist today? I feel like we should be at a funeral, not prepping for world restaurant domination."

It was a joke.

Something I'd hoped would lighten the mood and engage her in a bit of friendly banter.

I had never—in my entire life—been more wrong.

A sharp burst of laughter erupted from her lips, but her face held no humor. "And how the hell would you know anything about funerals, Truett?"

My chin jerked to the side—and not just because of her sudden outburst. Her tone was downright scathing.

I lifted my hands in surrender, belatedly realizing the nerve I'd struck. "I'm sorry, I—"

"For fuck's sake, can you say anything besides I'm sorry?"

I clamped my mouth shut, confusion crinkling my forehead. "Gwen, baby, I—"

Her eyes flashed wide. "Don't do that. Don't *baby* me with your sexy voodoo hypnotism shit."

I swallowed hard, desperately trying to follow the bouncing ball of her emotions and failing in spectacular fashion. Drawing in a deep breath, I made sure to keep the frustration out of my tone as I pleaded, "Look, can we just take a second to breathe? Maybe talk this out? I genuinely don't understand what's happening right now."

She threw her hands up in the air, slapping them against her thighs as she brought them down. "Me either. That's always been our problem. I don't understand *anything*. You kept me in the dark for so long, and now you're back, kissing me, making me question my entire life. How am I supposed to process that when I still don't even know why you left me?"

Infinity fuck.

I blinked at her, the boulder of guilt I carried with me at all times becoming so heavy it crushed my chest. She deserved answers, the truth, and most of all, closure. It was something I knew she'd been waiting for, so her question might have come out of left field, but it was no surprise.

Still, I couldn't speak. Couldn't find the words to string

together that would explain the why's of the past. Probably because there was no real explanation. At least, none that made sense to a sane person.

"I don't know," I said, like a coward.

"Then how the hell am *I* supposed to know?" she shot back, her body shaking with anger. "The past happened, Truett. No kiss in the entire fucking world will fix that. And now, I'm just expected to, what? Get over it? Jump back into your arms? Welcome you back into my life?"

I stared at her, my silence enraging her all over again.

"You know what. This was a bad idea. You should go." She turned on a toe, marching through the dining room, straight toward her office.

I stood there like an idiot, watching her go. It was the day she'd left me all over again. That day in my house, when she'd dropped her rings on the floor and I'd let her leave without one single ounce of explanation. My legs hadn't moved that day. My mouth failing to fight. My mind telling me lies.

I'd be damned if I made that mistake again.

With long strides, I followed after her. That damn office was the size of a shoebox, only big enough for a few filing cabinets, a desk, and a rolling chair. But as I stepped inside, it felt infinitely smaller as the distance between us, measured in mere inches, charged the air.

"I'm sorry," I told her back.

She whipped around, ready to tear into me for offering yet another hollow apology, but I looped an arm around her hips and tugged her off-balance. She collided with my front, her hands landing on my chest, anger still blazing in her eyes.

I didn't let her get a word out before finishing with, "I'm sorry I didn't talk to you back then. I'm sorry I couldn't be the man you needed me to be. I'm sorry I gave up on our family. And I'm sorry I didn't fight harder, because I have missed you every fucking day since you walked out of my life. *That* is what I mean when I say I'm sorry."

She clamped her mouth shut, her gaze darting around my face as she tried to process what I was saying. I'd only had her back—if you could call it that—for a few weeks, but the fear of losing her again gnawed at me relentlessly. It was finally enough to break through the deepest recesses of my mind, where I kept the truth locked away, shackled and imprisoned to prevent it from stripping me bare.

"I didn't hurt as much when I was with you," I confessed. My voice was barely above a rasp, yet it was all I could manage. Saying the words aloud, to *her*, was as painful as it was a welcome relief.

Her eyes narrowed. "What?"

"Back then… I hated myself. I didn't deserve to feel better. But when I'm with you, even now, I can breathe. I don't know what it is, but something about you has always softened the agony, making it so I don't feel like I'm suffocating."

She blinked, pursing her lips. Her mouth opening and closing like a fish out of water. "Let me make sure I've got this right. I made you feel *better*, so you thought the best thing to do was divorce me?"

I knew how it sounded. The age-old copout—"It's not you, it's me"—given to placate a breaking heart. But it was the God's honest truth.

"After the mall—"

"No!" she snapped, slapping a hand over my mouth. "Don't you dare try to use that as an excuse. You were gone long before the mall."

Her chest heaved and her face was full of rage.

But.

She.

Didn't.

Back away.

That had to mean something. She could hate me all she

wanted—it was a sentiment we shared. But she was still with me, though I feared my time was running out.

I gathered her tighter in my arms, shifting her so our bodies were flush head to toe. "I felt like I was a fraud taking comfort from you. Your brother had just died, something I'd caused."

"You didn't cause it," she argued. "Stop acting like you drove that car into the building. Nate knew what he was signing up for. He was proud to put on that uniform. He was proud to serve beside *you*."

I shook my head. "I missed the cell phone, Gwen. They'd been watching us for days, and I missed it."

"And he missed it too," she seethed. "They all missed it, Truett. You weren't standing in that building alone."

"I know… I mean, I know it now. I was the only one who survived. There was no one else to blame."

She narrowed her eyes. "You think they would have blamed you…for surviving? They loved you too, you know. Especially Nathanial."

I swallowed hard. "I know that too. It's taken a lot of time, and I think I'll always feel responsible, but it's manageable now."

"Yeah, well, it could have been *manageable* without you kicking me to the curb for"—she lifted her hand in a pair of air quotes—"making you feel better."

"You needed to grieve, not take care of me."

"What I needed was my husband," she fired back.

"I know, but I couldn't be that man for you. I died over there, Gwen. Not physically, but part of me never came back. And then when I got home…it didn't feel so unbearable with you. And that was not something I was ready for. I felt like a monster, and you coddled me like a child. All your hugs and kisses and reassurances."

Tears filled her eyes, anger being replaced by rejection. "Then why didn't you tell me that? I would have stopped."

"Because you weren't doing anything wrong. Please hear me

when I say this. You were the most incredible wife any man could have asked for. Strong and steadfast. Patient and understanding. You did *everything* right. But I wasn't ready for that. Up until a few weeks ago, I still didn't think I was ready." I dipped forward, brushing my nose with hers. "But then you came to me after Folly showed up. I acted like a horse's ass that day, but you kept the booth. *For me.*"

Her breath hitched, and her tongue snaked out to dampen her lips. "I could tell it was important to you."

"It is. Do you remember that big winter storm, when I drove up to make sure the old generator was working because I was scared the power was going to go out and you guys would freeze to death while I was hundreds of miles away?"

She silently nodded.

"I promised the boys burgers, but the power was out, so they served us club sandwiches instead." The memory pinched my chest, but she was too close for it to cause any real pain.

Understanding hit her face, and she fisted the front of my shirt. "Oh, God. You sat there with them?"

"I've been coming here for years and sitting in that booth to torture myself. One hour. I'd allow the memories to shred me. I'd see their faces. Hear their voices." I leaned away to catch her eye before finishing. "*All* of them."

Her lids fluttered shut in a pained understanding. "Truett, that's just torture."

"That's exactly why I did it. I needed to hurt." The confession burned my throat. "But then you showed up and I can't do it anymore. I come here. I sit down. I try to let the past devour me. And then I look at you and everything just...gets quiet. I was completely freaked out at first. Pissed that you'd stolen something so rightfully mine. But if I'm being honest, when we're together, the only penance I ever want to pay is to you. So yeah, Gwen. I'm sorry. I'm so fucking sorry."

I stood there, staring into her eyes, knowing I'd only given her half of the story when it came to that booth, but I wasn't sure she'd ever be ready for the rest. I wished like hell I could forget it on a damn near daily basis.

"I don't know what to say," she whispered. "This is crazy, Truett. I spent eighteen fucking years without you. And you're telling me I lost the love of my life over a miscommunication?"

"No. *I* lost the love of *my life* over a miscommunication. You lost me the day you kissed me goodbye in front of the barracks. I wasn't the same man who came home, and then everything just got so much fucking worse." I laughed without humor. "This may come as a surprise, but I'm still not okay. I don't know that okay even exists for me anymore. In the name of transparency, you need to know that I'm convinced I'm cursed. Everybody I love dies. And yes, deep down, I know it's not real, but I'm still terrified to have you back in my life. But I have no idea how to let you go again, either."

Conflict danced across her face, her long lashes fluttering as she stared at me, incredulous. "And there it is."

"What?"

"You're already planning to let me go again."

I shook my head adamantly. "No, I'm not."

She shoved at my chest. "Yes, you are. You just said you have no idea how to let me go again. Why is that always a fucking option for you?"

I held her tight, unwilling to release her and prove her right. "It's not. I never wanted to leave you."

"But you did!" she roared, the pain in her voice searing through me. "You shut me out, Truett. I could have helped you. Dammit, I *wanted* to help you."

"No one could help me. I would have just dragged you down with me. I wasn't going to force you into a lifetime of misery right alongside me."

"But you did," she repeated. "You wrecked me. I didn't think

I would ever recover. I spent years asking myself what I could have done differently. Wondering if you ever even cared about me. I was trapped in a purgatory where life moved forward yet stood still."

I flexed the arm that was still wrapped tightly around her waist and dropped my face so that our eyes met. "Well, that's where we differ. My life never moved forward from you. Not a single day has passed that you haven't been on my mind. I've spent countless hours replaying the sound of your laughter, remembering the weight of your head on my shoulder, the way your eyes would light up when you talked about a funny story you heard at work. Every morning has been nothing short of agony when I wake up without you curled into my side. The nights are sometimes worse as I collapsed into our bed, wanting nothing more than to steal a kiss in the dark and hear your whispered declarations of love before we drifted off to sleep tangled in each other's arms."

Our faces were inches apart, her breaths short and ragged, matching my own.

"Truett," she said in a pained whisper.

She was going to either kick me out or kiss me. I couldn't tell which, but I wasn't leaving until I could make her understand.

Slowly, as if I could spook her at any minute, I dipped low, and brushed my lips over hers.

She tipped her chin, trying to catch my mouth, but I kept my lips a fraction out of her reach. "I deserve every bit of hate and anger and resentment you feel for me. But make no mistake, I have never, not ever, not for one fucking second of my entire god-forsaken life, stopped loving you."

Her body stiffened against me, but before I had the chance to overthink it, her mouth collided with mine in a frenzy of need. Her tongue warred with mine in a duel of longing and desperation.

"Please, Truett." She tugged at the hem of my shirt. Those words had once haunted me, but now they ignited my system with feral desire.

With a growl, I cupped her ass, the firm swells filling my palms as I lifted her off her feet. Without hesitance, her legs wrapped around my waist and I feared my cock would break free of my zipper when her core hit me.

Our tongues continued their battle, her hands in my hair, frantic to find an angle that would give her more of my mouth—more of me.

More of us.

I carried her the short distance to her desk. Paperwork littered the surface and with the slice of my hand, I blindly swept it to the floor before setting her down on the edge.

My hands roamed down her sides, exploring her unfamiliar curves. There had been a time when I'd known her body better than my own. It pained me to think of what I'd missed, the subtle changes throughout the years, but I was all too eager for the journey of rediscovery.

"Yes," she hissed into my mouth as I glided my thumb over her nipple, entirely too much fabric dividing us.

We broke our frenzied kiss, peeling each other's shirt off. I didn't bother unhooking her bra, and just stripped it over her head. It followed our shirts to the floor.

And then I froze.

Just.

Stopped.

My hands were buzzing at my sides as I drank her in. Dear God, how was she even more stunning than I remembered. From her peaked nipples to the curve of her breasts, she was fucking perfect.

It was Gwen.

It was *my* Gwen. What the hell did I expect?

Our labored breaths filled the silence of the otherwise quiet room.

"True," she whispered, catching my attention, reminding me

that I was standing there ogling her body like a teenage boy seeing a naked woman for the first time. And quite honestly, she wasn't all that wrong.

When my gaze flicked up to hers, a gentle smile played on her lips. "Come back to me."

Those four words hit me like a surge of electricity, jolting my deadened heart back into rhythm.

I wasn't too delusional to recognize that she was simply asking for me to escape my thoughts and rejoin her in a blaze of fiery passion.

And I would do that, no question about it.

But what she couldn't possibly know was that those four words would forever mark the beginning of my quest to reclaim my life—starting with her.

Come back to me.

Come back to me.

Come back to me.

I had never wanted anything more.

Palming the back of her head, I pulled her mouth to mine with a white-hot urgency.

Her nails raked down my back as I moved my assault to her neck, nipping and sucking my way down to her chest. I found her nipple, flicking it with my tongue before sucking it into my mouth. Her gasps and moans guided me lower, until I reached the waistband of her shorts.

"Gwen," I said more in warning than asking permission.

Her only answer was to open her legs, spreading them wide.

I traced my finger over the fabric covering her core. Her lids fell shut as she leaned back, propping herself up with her arms.

"Look at me," I ordered.

Her brown eyes that had owned me since I was seventeen years old fluttered open.

"I'm gonna make love to you so you can never forget how much you mean to me," I stated the absolute fact it was.

Her chest rose with a deep inhale.

I hooked my finger into the leg of her shorts, pulling them aside. My finger brushing up to find her clit.

"Oh, God," she breathed, her head falling back.

I snapped with my free hand, demanding her attention. "I'm not done yet. Eyes on me."

Her wanton gaze slid back to mine.

"Then, I'm going to make you come so hard, you will question whether you've ever had an orgasm without me."

Her mouth fell open, her shock morphing into visceral desire as I slowly pressed one finger inside her.

"And then I'm going to fuck you until the only thing you know for sure is that you are, and have always been, *mine*."

Her eyes flashed wide, and I leaned forward pressing my lips to hers before I mumbled, "Where would you like me to start?"

"Truett," she breathed, her fingernails biting into my back.

"I gotta hear you say it, Gwen. I need to know you're with me."

Her eyes got dark, heat pinking her cheeks. Her words were so quiet they were barely audible.

But I heard them.

Oh, God, did I hear them.

It was a command and plea all at once. "Fuck me, Truett."

I responded with a growl, claiming her lips. One swift movement, I withdrew my finger from inside her and tugged off her shorts. Her shoes met the same fate as her shirt and bra, haphazardly tossed in a pile at our feet.

With frenzied hands, she made quick work of unbuttoning my jeans as I toed out of my shoes. She shoved down my pants, taking my boxer briefs with them, freeing my cock.

"Jesus," she whispered, wrapping her palm around my length.

I sucked in a sharp inhale through my teeth, my central

nervous system firing a tsunami of shock waves that damn near took out my knees.

I needed to be inside her. To claim her. To make her understand, that while I'd ruined us, she had always owned me. I hadn't forgotten her. I hadn't forgotten us.

Fully naked, I lifted her onto the desk again. She clawed at my back, while kissing me with such an urgency it was almost violent.

I trailed my fingers up her heat, finding her wet and ready, and then drove into her with a quickness that leveled us both.

"Oh, God," she moaned, hooking her arms around my neck.

We moved together, the age-old choreography of desire. Her body responded to my every thrust, pulling me deeper into the abyss of our shared greed. It was a chaotic reunion of souls—a solace of ecstasy.

She was mine, even for just those minutes. Gwen was mine again. Pressure mounted inside me. Reality finally on my side. I dropped my hand between us, circling her clit with my thumb, as I continued to pump into her.

"Truett," she cried out, her heat tightening around me.

She was so fucking close.

Her breasts swayed as I worked her hard and fast like a reckless savage. Feral need overshadowed any sense of restraint or control.

I dipped my head and spoke into her panting mouth. "That's it, baby, give it to me. Let me feel you come on my cock."

"True," she breathed, my name falling from her lips like a prayer.

I wasn't going to last much longer. I'd been too long without her. Too starved for the kind of release only she could give me.

I changed my rhythm to deep calculated thrusts, my thumb never slowing at her clit. My jaw clenched painfully as I surged inside her, planting myself at the hilt.

She jerked and then her orgasm ripped through us both. She pulsed around me, coaxing my own release. I came on a strangled groan, feeling as though something inside me was tearing free from my soul. The room spun as I rode out the aftershocks, Gwen clinging to my shoulders, our hearts pounding in unison.

"Fuck," I whispered, kissing the top of her head.

Her body relaxed and she melted against my chest. What I wouldn't have given to have a bed to collapse down on beside her, holding her tight until we caught our breath. I was far from done, but her office had some serious limitations in the lovemaking department.

"God, I missed that," she confessed without looking up at me.

A satisfied smirk stretched my mouth. "Me too."

"But I'm scared."

I turned to stone, concern flooding my system. "Hey," I cooed, tipping her head back so I could get a better read on her face. "What's wrong? Did I hurt you?"

She shook her head. Her eyes were glassy, still clouded by her desire, but her eyebrows were drawn together. "That was… incredible, Truett. Something I'd dreamed about for years. But, if I'm being honest, I don't know where we go from here. I don't know how to let you back in."

I smoothed a hand up and down her back. "It's okay. It's a lot to process."

"A lot is an understatement." Her breathing shuddered as though she might cry, but the tears never formed in her eyes. "And now that we've had sex, I'm scared I'm jumping into something I'm not ready for."

"Gwen, baby, I'm not asking you to jump into anything. I hope what I said to you earlier and then what we just did shed some light on the way I feel about you and why things ended the way they did. But I don't expect the past to melt away because of it. I did this to us. I take full responsibility. You have every right to tell me to fuck off. I wouldn't even blame you. But I'm willing to do whatever it takes to keep you in my life. I just need you to give me that chance."

"But what if I can't?"

"Then you can't. It will crush me, but that's not on you. We have a history, and the majority of it played out like a tragedy. You have every right to be scared. I'm scared too. If you don't have it in you to give me a chance to be your man again, then maybe we could be friends. Or, hell, I'll be your handyman until I'm eight hundred years old if that's all I can get."

She laughed, and it was sad, but there was a modicum of relief in her eyes.

I kissed her forehead. "Some things happen for a reason, Gwen. Some things happen for no reason. And then some things just never happen at all. I haven't always been there for you, but I can't stop hoping that maybe there's a reason you bought this specific restaurant and waltzed back into my life. And maybe, if I'm lucky, that reason is us."

She swallowed hard. "When did you get so wise?"

I chuckled. "Therapy. Lots and lots of therapy."

She closed her eyes and shook her head. "I don't know what to say."

"Say that you'll think about. That's all I ask."

She drew in a deep breath, her breasts rising with her chest. It made me a jerk, but at the sight, my cock stirred back to life.

"I'll think about it," she replied, her gaze flicking down between us. "But I probably shouldn't think about it while you're naked in my office."

"Oh, I don't know. Any chance it will sway things in my favor?"

She slanted her head. "I'm terrified to find out."

I chuckled. "Okay, then. You still want me to help out around here today?"

Indecision warred on her face. "Can I maybe just have some space for a while?"

"Of course," I replied before kissing her forehead again. "You know where to find me."

We got dressed in silence, bumping into each other as we pulled our clothes on. I hated to leave her like that. It felt too much like a quick fuck rather than the full-body worship she deserved. But if she was willing to think about the possibility of letting me be a part of her life again, the least I could do was give her the space to do it. After all, she'd given me eighteen years to get my head straight.

She walked me to the door, and I didn't wait for permission before dragging her into a hug. She curled in close as if she were trying to absorb one last moment of comfort.

"I love you," I told the top of her hair before pressing a kiss to her crown.

She didn't say it back. She didn't have to. I'd destroyed the bridge that had joined our lives together, but love would forever exist between us, even in the emptiness of the divide.

It should have been harder to leave her, knowing it could be for the very last time if she couldn't find it in her heart to give me another chance.

But for the first time in over eighteen years, there was hope that I could get her back—and then never have to let her go again.

"Hey, True," she called just before I crossed the street. "Just so you know, I would have sat in that house with you for the rest of my life, completely alone, just to be with *you*."

I dipped my head and rested my hand over my heart. As much as I appreciated the sentiment, I hadn't wanted that life for her. I still didn't want that life for her.

But if wanted her to be in my life, that was all I had to offer.

I walked home with my mind spinning. Flashes of me driving inside her colliding with memories of her anger, frustration, and lastly her fears.

I'd asked her to give me a chance, but she had no idea the mess she'd be walking into.

As I stopped in front of my house, dread filled my stomach.

I didn't want to go inside. That front door was nothing more than a portal to the past, and for once, I didn't want to escape the present. My safe little existence locked inside those four walls made my stomach churn.

I'd let a whole beautiful life pass me by.

Staring at that front door, I was assaulted by visions of what could have been.

Me packing the car for vacations at the beach.

Us jogging down the steps, laughing as we headed out for a date night.

Gwen carrying bags filled with tomatoes and zucchini after a Sunday trip to the farmers market.

Me falling to my knees when she met me at the door with a positive pregnancy test.

Our daughter blowing out birthday candles as our son tried to swipe the icing.

Playing catch on the front lawn.

Kissing boo-boos when they fell off their bikes.

Taking pictures before they headed off to prom.

Cars lining the street as we hosted a high school graduation party in the backyard.

Our last child driving away for college, leaving us with a heartbreakingly empty nest, but still grinning because I knew Gwen would be forever by my side.

I hadn't just let go of Gwen all those years ago.

I'd let go of an entire beautiful future together.

And after all the tragedy I'd experienced, that might have been the most devastating reality of all.

CHAPTER TWENTY-ONE

Gwen

"OKAY. SPILL," DYLAN ORDERED, LIFTING A CRACKER covered with baked brie from her plate.

"Jeez, can you at least give everyone a minute to get comfortable first?" Angela scolded as she settled into the far corner of my sectional, a glass of white wine in one hand and a small plate of various cheeses in the other.

"What? She said it was an emergency meeting," Dylan defended.

I'd texted them around lunchtime and begged them to come over for a girls' night. Their kids didn't have school since it was spring break, and I'd promised them a cheese board, so it wasn't a hard sell.

I was fucked. Literally, figuratively, and if you asked my body, most of all, *thoroughly*.

I'd spent all morning at the restaurant trying to work but only managing to overthink all things Truett West.

He loved me.

He'd *always* loved me.

After our divorce, I would have killed to hear him say those words to me. It had taken six years for me to move on and even consider dating again. Back then, I was angry and swore to anyone who would listen that I hated him, but for too long, a part of me always assumed he'd come back. Too many nights, I'd dream that he'd suddenly swoop back into my life, sweep me off my feet, apologize profusely, explain that he couldn't live without me, and then beg me to take him back—essentially exactly what he'd done on Saturday with the addition of mind-blowing sex.

I'd just never thought it would take eighteen freaking years.

I was a different person in a different place in life now. One where I was a forty-one-year-old two-time divorcée, single mom, coparenting with a narcissist, while trying to open my very first restaurant and most recently being stalked by a producer who wanted to make a documentary about the worst day of my life. My plate was full. I had absolutely no room for a relationship with a man as complicated as Truett. And worse, I wasn't sure there was enough of my heart left to even try.

"Okay, if you're not ready to start yet, just tell me if I should run out to my car and get my shovel to hide Jeff's body or not," Dylan said.

I sighed and then took another sip of my wine. "It's not about Jeff. He's at the game with Nate."

"That producer?" Angela guessed.

"Not him, either. At least not directly anyway."

"Knock, knock!" Lucille's voice boomed from the front door as she trotted inside. "What'd I miss?"

"Nothing yet. Though it sounds like we don't need the shovels after all," Dylan replied.

"Damn," Lucille said, dropping her bag onto the kitchen counter, and then she got to work pouring a drink for herself. She didn't bother asking where anything was. She just started opening and closing the cabinets until she found what she was looking for. "I got your text earlier and went out and bought a new spade and everything."

I scowled at Dylan. "You told her to bring a shovel?"

She nodded with pride. "Yep, and Angela has the garbage bags and duct tape."

I swung an accusing gaze to little Miss Goody Two Shoes only to find her grinning too.

"We wanted to be prepared."

I blinked. "I can't decide if I'm touched or terrified."

"Let's go with touched," Lucille said, plopping down beside me. "Now, if it's not about that that asshat, why'd you send out an SOS?" Arching her eyebrow, she nudged me in the side. "More hypothetical situations?"

Dammit.

"Hypothetical situations?" Angela questioned.

Lucille crunched on a cracker, while grinning mischievously.

I sighed. Better just to get it over with. I aimed a pointed glare at my two best friends. "Before you two start in on me, just know that I am fully aware of the fact that I have lost my mind."

The two exchanged a worried glance, but it was Dylan who piped up first. "Well, this should be good."

Angela shot me a warm smile. "Just know that we're here for you no matter what."

"Thank you, I appreciate—"

"You got laid, didn't ya?" Lucille waggled her eyebrows at me.

My cheeks heated. "Jesus," I mumbled. But the only thing the women in that room heard was the fact that I did not deny it.

"Holy shit," Dylan breathed. "Who did you sleep with?"

Lucille turned her entire body toward me. "It was the hot gargoyle, wasn't it?" At that, she popped me on the hand like I was her child who had tried to touch the hot stovetop. "You slept with the hot gargoyle and you didn't bother to call me after? You treat me like I'm not even your best friend."

"Hey," Dylan objected. She swung a finger between her and Angela. "*We* are her best friends. But with a mouth like yours, I hereby name you the keeper of all her secrets from here on out."

"The hot gar—" Angela's voice trailed off as realization dawned on her. "Oh my God, you didn't! You slept with Truett? When? Why? When?"

"You already said when," Dylan deadpanned, her stare never wavering from me. "But seriously, Gwen. *When*?"

I huffed. "I didn't say I slept with him!"

"You sure didn't deny it, either," Lucille mumbled.

Angela moved to the corner of the coffee table and perched in front of me. "Are you okay?"

"I don't know," I confessed. "That's why you're here. To help me figure that out."

I scanned their faces.

Lucille had a devious smirk.

Angela's mouth was tipped in a deep frown, concern lining her forehead.

And then in typical Dylan fashion, she was a mixture of the two, no doubt wanting all the dirty details while also worried another man was about to break me.

"Start at the beginning," Angela prompted.

"Don't leave out any of the good stuff, either," Lucille added.

I let my head fall back against the cushion and sighed heavily. "The beginning? That's over twenty years ago. Which is exactly why I'm so confused. Let's just start with Wednesday."

"You had sex with Truett *last Wednesday*?" Dylan asked.

"No. Stop interrupting." I scrubbed a hand over my face and quickly recapped the incident with Folly on Wednesday night and Truett's surprise visit with the newspaper and spring rolls on Thursday. I tried to gloss over the kiss, but my best friends were having none of it.

"You kissed him? Last week? And said *nothing*?" Angela's incredulous face scanned mine.

"Well, she said something," Lucille butted in. "Just happened I was the only one who heard it."

"Dear God, woman. Can you keep anything private?" I hissed, but it was too late.

"You told Cooter?" Dylan accused. She never could hide her hurt, but she usually did a better job of covering it with sarcasm though.

"No, she sniffed it out," I argued.

Lucille shrugged. "Wasn't that hard. She was talking in hypotheticals about her ex. After meeting Captain Shit Head, I'm just happy it was the hot one she chose to lock lips with."

We all hummed in agreement.

"Okay, so you kissed him Thursday. Then what?" Dylan asked.

Angela chewed on her thumbnail as she waited for my response.

I'd known that it was going to be Twenty Questions times three, but my need for advice clouded my judgment. I'd have probably been better off confiding in the tree in the backyard, but it was too late now. "First of all, *he* kissed *me*. And it was amazing."

Dylan mumbled from behind her wine glass, "It had to have been if you slept with him." Her head popped up. "Wait, did you sleep with him that same night?"

"No. That happened when he came back to help me on Saturday. You guys know I hate owing anyone, but honestly, I wanted to see him again. Plus, he's extremely handy and knows what he's doing."

"Apparently," Dylan quipped.

Angela held a hand up. "So Saturday, he shows up and what? You just get naked?"

I shook my head. "Friday, when I talked to Lucille about the kiss, she asked a good question about why we'd gotten divorced in the first place. I spent the rest of the night stewing on the fact that I didn't have an answer, so when he showed up Saturday, I was already on edge."

Dylan grinned. "Angry sex. My favorite. Except, ya know, when it's your *ex-husband*."

"I know. I know. But one minute I was demanding an answer, and the next I was naked on my desk, his mouth all over me."

The memory of his growl when I'd tugged at his shirt echoed in my thoughts. God, how was he able to set me ablaze with nothing more than the touch of his fingers?

"You had sex at the restaurant?" Angela's mouth fell open.

Lucille laughed. "Remind me to bring bleach wipes with me next time."

How were these my friends?

Dylan canted her head. "So was this like a one-night stand, or are you considering actually going back to this guy?"

"He asked me to give him a chance and then he told me he loved me." I chewed on my bottom lip. "And that he always has and still does."

They all fell silent, a weight tamping out their humor.

"Oh, honey," Angela whispered.

"He said that, after Nathanial died, he didn't hurt as much when he was with me, and that wasn't something he deserved. So he pushed me away."

"Damn," Lucille breathed. "That's heavy."

Dylan was slightly more cynical. "But that doesn't explain why he was willing to abandon his family. He filed for divorce before the mall, Gwen."

"Trust me, I haven't forgotten. I spent all morning wondering if I'd been abducted by aliens and they'd reprogrammed me as a dumber version of myself. But I don't know how to explain it. There's still this spark between us and it scares the hell out of me, because I've never felt it with anyone but him."

"So what's the problem, then?" Lucille asked. "It sounds like he's stirred up some positive feelings that you may have forgotten over the years. Why are you questioning it?"

"Because it's *Truett,*" I explained without really explaining at all.

"Let's just say their history is...um, well, *dark,*" Angela said gently. "We didn't know Gwen then, but I wish we had so we could have helped her through it."

I wished like hell for that too. I might have been able to recover faster if I'd had the two of them to lean on. Maybe they could have even talked me out of marrying Jeff. No, strike that. Life with him hadn't been good, but I'd had Nate because of that marriage. And that alone made those years worth their weight in gold.

"Yeah, I heard about their history, but people can change." Lucille reasoned.

"Has he changed though?" Dylan asked. "I mean, he doesn't even leave his house."

"I don't know," Angela said thoughtfully. "It sounds like he's left it more this week than he has in years. *For Gwen.*"

"That's true," Lucille agreed. "I've been working there forever. Man's always shown up one day a week for one single hour. He's been there a hell of a lot more since Gwen took over. Something tells me it's not just for the sandwich he never eats."

The room was quiet for a minute as I considered the possibility. Had Truett changed? The fact that he was willing to open his damn mouth and have a discussion was definitely a step in the right direction. But the problem was I'd never been the best judge of character. After all, I had married Jeff.

Though I supposed Truett had a lot to do with that too.

When I'd met Jeff, he was the exact opposite of Truett. He was edgy and carefree, never taking no for an answer. It made sense that he was an attorney. He talked incessantly, which had been charming at first and opened up a healthy line of communication I'd always wished I'd had with Truett. Eventually, edgy and carefree turned into controlling and cruel. And the things I said during those supposedly healthy conversations became tools he used to put me down and manipulate me.

But the one thing I knew more than anything else, which was probably a good part of the reason I'd stayed with him as long as I had, was that Jeff would never leave me. His ego was too big to ever admit that kind of failure. So, in some twisted way, I'd convinced myself that knowing what to expect from my future was worth living unhappily in the present.

Truett wasn't Jeff—not even close.

Though he wasn't an emotionally abusive asshole, that didn't mean he couldn't shatter my heart into a million pieces again. Sure, he left his house more now, and he had found his voice again, but at the first sign of trouble, would he shut down again? Cast me aside? Abandon me when I needed him most?

"Yes, he's changed," I admitted. "But maybe it's too late. I've been wearing his scars for so long they've become the foundation for who I am and how I love."

And then leave it to Lucille, the craziest woman I had ever known, to ask the simplest question to ever rock my world. "Do you still love him?"

I closed my eyes, my whole body sagging.

Did I still love him? I barely knew him anymore.

Did I find him sexy and sweet and witty and gentle and funny and protective? Absolutely, but did that constitute love? It was obvious I didn't hate him anymore, but love wasn't the opposite of hate. I had love for him. It wasn't like I wanted anything bad to happen to him. Actually, I wanted him to live a life of happiness and freedom. He'd been through hell and back too many times.

But love?

Like, love *love*?

"I don't know. I love Truett from the past. This guy… I have no clue. We've had like ten conversations, one kiss, and some seriously incredible sex."

"Well, if you want my opinion, I don't like it," Dylan said bluntly. "I've wanted to cut that man's balls off for years. Jeff sucked, I hated him, but I think I might hate Truett more."

Angela's head swiveled toward Dylan, her eyes bugging. "There's no way you hate Truett more than Jeff. Truett broke Gwen's heart, but he didn't do it on purpose. Can you even imagine everything he's had to deal with? He was broken too. Jeff shattered her spirit though. That asshole relished in being the one to beat her down. There's no competition between the two. Jeff wins at being the worst, hands down."

Dylan shrugged. "All the more reason to scrap 'em both. There are plenty of other fish in the sea."

My chest got tight. "What if I don't want anybody else?"

Angela narrowed her eyes. "Is that what you're scared of? That you won't feel this way for anyone else?"

A tear slid down my cheek. "No. I'm afraid I'll lose eighteen more years with him because I'm too scared he'll hurt me again to take the chance that he won't."

The room filled with sympathetic sighs.

It was Lucille who once again put things into perspective. "Listen, you have to protect yourself. Only you can decide if the reward is worth the risk. But what's gonna hurt more? Giving it a chance and it not working out? Or never trying and spending the rest of your life wondering what could have been?"

My head swam, indecision paralyzing me. "I don't know."

"Yes, you do. Think about it. Is he your number three? Because if so, you owe it to yourself to give it a whirl. Number three wasn't perfect, but that man was mine. Sounds to me like maybe Truett is yours too. Gargoyle warts and all."

I laughed. Leave it to the most outrageous woman to live in Belton to also be the wisest friend I had.

"Warts?" Angela muttered. "Gross."

Dylan gagged. "Okay, if warts are involved, we have far bigger problems. Do I need to make you a doctor's appointment?"

Truett's deep timbre rang in my ears. *"I have never, not ever, not for one fucking second of my entire Godforsaken life, stopped loving you."*

I sat there, thinking back to the first night at The Grille. I'd gone to him when Nate hit him with that spitball instead of letting Lucille handle the cleanup. That wasn't something you did for someone you hated.

When he'd shown up the first Wednesday after The Grille closed, frantic to get inside, I'd opened that door and had an entire conversation with him, rough as it might have been. I didn't have to do that.

When he'd sat outside in the rain, I could have left him alone, but I went to him and invited him inside.

I'd worried about him when Folly had shown up and rushed to his side.

I'd kept the booth and offered him an open invitation to come back.

I'd made him a club sandwich so he'd feel comfortable.

I'd tried to protect him when Folly had shown up taking pictures.

I'd driven him home and given him a key to the restaurant.

I'd asked him to kiss me, and then only two days later, I came, crying his name.

No. The opposite of hate was not love. It was indifference. And never, not one day in my life had I ever been indifferent to Truett West.

"I think he's my number three," I admitted, the words flying from my mouth like they'd spent eighteen years poised on the tip of my tongue.

Lucille let out a loud clap and slung her arm around my shoulders. "That's my girl."

"I have no idea what that means." Angela looked at Dylan. "Do you know what that means?"

Dylan shrugged. "No clue. But it sounds like a good thing. I'm sure, if you give it a second, the motor mouth of Belton will fill us in."

"Long story," Lucille answered. "I'll explain later, but now that we've got that sorted, let's get to the good stuff. We're going to need all the dirty details. Don't you go leaving anything out, either. I want to know what he smelled like, how loud you were, and how many times that man got you off."

I wasn't sure I wanted to go that deep into details, but a little girl talk never hurt anyone.

"He told me he was going to make me come so hard I would question whether I'd ever had an orgasm without him."

"Thank you, Jesus, he's a dirty talker!" Lucille toppled over, the back of her hand over her forehead, pretending to pass out.

"Shut up," Angela whispered in awe.

Dylan leaned forward, swirling her glass of wine. "Okay, but did he?"

"You have no idea," I replied, a massive grin stretching my lips.

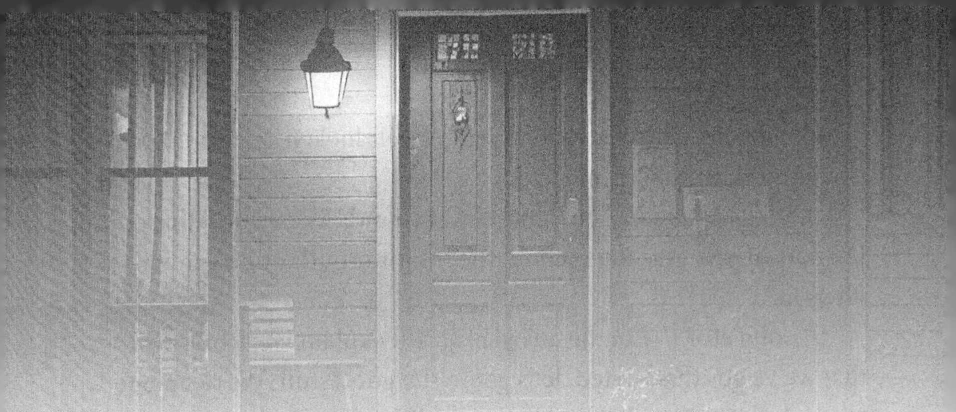

CHAPTER TWENTY-TWO

TRUETT

IT HAD BEEN TWO DAYS SINCE I'D HEARD FROM GWEN. A PART of me was coming apart at the seams, fighting the urge to reach out to her. For a man who lived locked away in his house, space was not my forte. Space from Gwen was even harder.

I'd been able to distract myself with work, but the nights were hard. Straying from my virtually unrecognizable routine, I'd stayed up late playing out all the potential scenarios.

In some, she fell into my arms, vowing that she loved me too.

In others, she told me to take a hike and never spoke to me again.

I'd refused to allow myself to get trapped in my usual cycle of doom and gloom. So for the most part, I mixed and matched all the potential highs and lows.

There was no way she hadn't felt the connection between us—the overwhelming feeling of right. The way our bodies, while technically strangers, had joined together like two halves forming one whole.

I hated that the idea of *us* scared her—and that I'd been the one to cause that.

But I couldn't let her go again.

Which then led me to the spiral of what-ifs, trying to imagine what would happen if she *did* give me that chance. The obstacles still standing in our way were not just hurdles. They were volcanos waiting to erupt, with lava so hot it could snuff out even the strongest bond.

We had so much to talk about. So much I needed to tell her, to explain to her, and I wanted to beg her to love me anyway. If she was willing to give me a chance, we could sit down and have a candid discussion the way she'd always begged me for in the past. I couldn't give it to her then, but I finally felt like I could now. With Gwen at my side, anything seemed possible.

Naively, I'd assumed that would be the second step in getting her back. Something we could deal with together, after she agreed to give us another shot.

At least that was what I thought until my phone buzzed in my pocket, an alert from my video doorbell letting me know motion had been detected on the front porch. I clicked the notification, her face lighting up the screen just as her knock sounded at the door.

"Shit," I rumbled, lurching off the couch. My first thought went to Folly, fearing he'd gone to her again. Though when I squinted at the video, she was sporting a gentle smile. It would have soothed me immediately had she not been standing *at my fucking front door.* With two large totes hooked over her shoulders, she rocked onto her toes, waiting for me to open up.

Shit. Shit. Shit.

Frantic, I swung my gaze around my living room. Realizing there was nothing I could do about any of that shit in the next thirty seconds, I glanced down at myself. I'd changed into gray sweatpants and a white T-shirt after work. It wasn't the best, but not the worst, either.

She knocked again, causing nerves to roll in my stomach.

I blew out a ragged breath, smoothed down the top of my hair, and then padded to the front door.

"Hey," she chirped.

Standing in the doorway, I smiled. "Hey. What are you doing here?"

She peered up at me, her hair fluttering in a gentle breeze. "I think we need to go on a date."

My eyebrows shot up, victory skyrocketing within me. "I think you would be absolutely correct." I swayed my head from side to side. "But are we talking about a date as friends? Or lovers? Or something more along the lines of me finishing up the wiring in the restaurant's bathroom?"

She gave me a curt nod. "Yes."

I chuckled. "Okay, but what part are we starting with?"

"If you promise to never refer to us as 'lovers' again, I would very much like to start with a romantic dinner." She patted one of the bags, and I noticed the top of a carrot sticking out. "I'll cook for you and then you can massage my shoulders. Deal?"

My smile stretched so wide my face physically hurt. I lifted my fingers and wiggled them at her. "I'll start stretching these babies out now."

She laughed. "Good. Now, move and let me in. I've got an entire pork loin in here and it's getting heavy."

The sound of my smile crashing could have been heard around the world. "Wait. Why aren't you cooking at the restaurant?"

"Because I'd rather we not suffocate from paint fumes on this date." She stepped to the side, trying to get around me but I blocked her path.

"I don't mind paint fumes."

"Quit being silly." She stepped to the right and I moved with her.

"No. We can't do it here. I, uh…" I laughed awkwardly. "It's a mess in here. I'd be so embarrassed. Just let me grab some shoes and we can head to the restaurant. It will give me a chance to touch up the edging in the kitchen while you cook."

She laughed. "Truett, your mess is my definition of

organization. I promise not to judge your one single dirty plate in the sink."

She started left, so I went with her, my frazzled mind trying to come up with any excuse to keep her from going inside. But at the last second she spun around me, ducking under my arm into the house.

"Ha! Gotcha! You gotta be faster than—"

I died right along with her words.

The bags slid from her limp arms, landing on the floor with a loud thud.

Embarrassment engulfed me, a boulder of shame settling in my gut. I didn't want her to see that. I didn't want anybody to see that.

As she stood there, her gaze sliding through my house, the obstacle that I'd feared would be a volcano erupted right before my eyes.

"What is this?" she whispered, lifting a trembling hand to her mouth.

I shook my head, not knowing how to answer. Or even if I should. After all, she'd lived in that house. And not just the same address. It was the same...exact...house, frozen in time for over eighteen years. Nothing, from the couches and tables to the pictures and paint on the walls, had changed. It was the same wood floors and tattered area rugs. Not even the TV had been upgraded.

Everything was older now, but I'd kept it up as best I could.

"Truett," she whispered, tears already in her voice. Bending over, she picked up Kaitlyn's sneaker from the shoe rack beside the door. "Oh, God," she croaked, turning it in her fingers. She looked up, catching sight of the basket of toys beside the couch. Still carrying the shoe, she walked over and squatted in front of it. She lifted a toy tiger in a doll's tutu, wearing homemade pink glitter shoes. "This isn't happening."

My throat got tight, not a syllable able to pass through.

When I didn't respond, she dropped the toy and the shoe and then sprinted down the hall as if she feared I was going to stop her.

I wasn't.

I couldn't.

Not even as I heard the door of Kaitlyn's bedroom creak open.

A mixture of shock and agony filled her chanted cries. "No, no, no, no, no, no, no!"

I knew what she was seeing. An unmade bed, a hamper of dirty clothes, a cup from which the water had long since evaporated still sitting on the nightstand. A coloring book open to a picture of a tiger. Crayons haphazardly spread around the floor. A row of stuffed animals lining the back of the bed.

I'd memorized every inch of that room, because standing in that doorway was my Friday routine.

Eighteen years earlier…

"Why doesn't she just go home?" I snapped in a shitty tone that had become the only tone I possessed anymore.

Allen Stanley, the Doogie Howser of the VA's therapists, narrowed his eyes. "What part of Gwen waiting outside upsets you the most?"

The part where I know she's out there, within my reach, for the first time in months.

The part where she fucking smiled when she saw me get out of his car, still happy to see me after the absolute hell I'd put her through.

The part where she was still wearing her wedding ring despite the fact that we were divorced.

"She shouldn't have to deal with this."

"Did you get the feeling that she thought of this meeting as a burden?"

No. Not my Gwen. She loved so damn hard she'd have sprinted

through the gates of hell if she thought there was even the smallest chance of saving me.

"I don't know," I replied.

"You want to tell me what you're feeling right now?" he asked.

"Nothing," I snapped, using the back of my hand to wipe away the sweat beading on my forehead. "A whole fuck-ton of nothing."

"Truett, if you want this to work, you have to be honest with me—and yourself."

I cussed under my breath. Not wanting to dive deeper into the topic of Gwen, I went for a distraction. "Look around. Everyone's so fucking happy."

"Does that seem unfair to you? That you can't be happy too?"

"Fair?" I barked a humorless laugh. "What part of any of this is fair?"

"You're right. It's not. You've been through a horrible tragedy. You're allowed to be frustrated and angry. But I'm proud of you for coming here today."

"Oh, goodie. Does that earn me a gold star? Free personal pan pizza? Another fistful of pills to pop at bedtime?"

"Do you think you need more meds?" His calm voice grated on my exposed nerves.

"For the love of God, stop asking me questions."

"Okay," he replied.

In his silence, my mind went back to Gwen sitting outside. How the hell that woman could still muster a smile when she saw me, I couldn't understand. I couldn't even look in the mirror without wanting to break it.

Shaking my head, my filter slipped and I blurted, "Gwen shouldn't have to deal with this. I've put her through enough."

Allen leaned back in his chair, eying me closely. "You want to reframe that?"

"Not in the least," I grumbled.

He dipped his chin, his black frame glasses sliding down his nose. "Okay, let me give it a try, then. Gwen was eager to come here today because she's heard about your incredible progress and is excited that you are so open and willing to work on yourself."

Open and willing was the stretch of a lifetime. I'd only recently gotten out of a sixty-day stint at a rehabilitation facility after I'd spent months locked in a house, dodging doctors and therapists almost as often as friends and family. If I couldn't prove I could become a functioning member of society again, I was at risk of losing everything.

Allen called it exposure therapy. I called it medically sanctioned torture. But if I wanted Gwen to trust me again, I needed to learn to trust myself.

Allen had been taking me out on "adventures" for over a month.

At first, it had been simple things like walking into a coffee shop and ordering a drink to go.

The next time we'd go out, we'd sit and stay for a few minutes.

Baby steps, he called it.

Eventually, we'd worked up to hour-long walks in the park, grocery shopping, and once, much to my absolute horror, Putt-Putt Golf.

But on that particular day, after much debate and Allen's constant reassurances, we'd decided it was time for my ultimate test—a mall food court in Watersedge, New Jersey, ten minutes from Gwen's new apartment.

"Daddy!" Kaitlyn yelled, racing over to me with a drink in her hand.

Daniel balanced a tray of food a few feet behind her.

"I got Sprite!" Kaitlyn skidded to a stop in front of me. "You want a sip?"

I smiled genuinely, as only she could draw from me. God, she looked so much like her mother it both filled my heart and emptied my soul.

I could still remember like it was yesterday, when Gwen had come to me crying, holding a positive pregnancy test. We were still in high school, irresponsible and wildly in love, but one look at that flickering heartbeat on the ultrasound and I discovered the reason for my existence. Her parents were livid, but I put a ring on her finger the very next day. While Gwen worked her ass off to finish high school early, I joined the Army, hell-bent to be the husband and father my dad had never been.

In the last six months, I'd failed Gwen in every possible way, but I was working to get my life together for Kaitlyn.

"Nah, I don't need a sip. That's all yours." I glanced up at Daniel and quirked an eyebrow. "Gwen's gonna kick your ass for giving her soda."

He shrugged. "I'll take my chances. It's a special day."

It was a special day. It was the first time I'd been out of the house with Kaitlyn in months. And in true father-of-the-year fashion, I'd had to bring a shrink to babysit me and my younger brother to babysit Kaitlyn in order to do it.

Sipping on her drink, Kaitlyn walked around the table and climbed into the chair beside me, while Daniel sat next to Allen.

Passing Kaitlyn a box of cheese fries, I leaned in close, her long brown hair tickling my nose. "Did you get an application for head chicken nugget maker while you were over there?"

She let out a giggle that momentarily soothed the searing pain in my chest. "No. I want to be a vet now so I can take care of all the cute puppies and kittens."

"Oh, so you turned six and suddenly head chicken nugget maker isn't good enough for you anymore?" I poked her in the side, and she squirmed away from me, laughing.

"Mom said it's better to help the animals instead of eat them."

I nodded. "So that means no more bacon?"

Her brown doe eyes flashed wide. "Bacon isn't an animal!"

I screwed my lips shut. "Right. Of course not. Silly Daddy."

She picked up a fry and popped it into her mouth, chewing as she spoke. "Why don't we get bacon anymore?"

The same reason we didn't live under the same roof anymore?

And why we didn't go play at the playground anymore?

And why I didn't take her to school each morning anymore?

Or read her bedtime stories? Or kiss her boo boos? Or… or…anything?

"I don't know, baby. Maybe we can go back to The Grille soon."

Her chubby cheeks dimpled as she smiled. The twinkle in her eyes was so full of joy, it illuminated the darkness inside my soul. In that moment, with that vision of her etched on my eyelids for the rest of eternity, I could have died a happy man.

Death had other plans.

Suddenly, a sharp, deafening crack tore through the air. Adrenaline exploded in my system as I recognized the gunfire immediately.

"Get down!" I shouted, diving over Kaitlyn and knocking over the table in the process. I was careful to protect her head as we hit the floor, my body covering her completely.

Chaos erupted around us. Screams echoed from every direction as people ran, a stampede of panicked feet, trying to make their escape.

My heart pounded as the boom of bullets continued, each shot bleeding into the last.

I lifted my head a fraction, searching for the source of the madness, but all I saw was Allen, still sitting in his chair, slouched over, a gaping hole in his head.

My stomach rolled, newfound panic detonating inside me. What the fuck was happening? How was I suddenly in a war zone? And in the nightmare of all nightmares, why was Kaitlyn with me?

I fought my trembling body to stay in the present.

Before I'd agreed to come, I'd mapped out the exits, and I sat so I faced the door—safety measures I'd insisted on. I'd thought that I'd prepared for the worst, and somehow, this was more horrifying than I ever could have imagined.

"Stay down, baby," I whispered, scanning the area, assessing our options. I caught sight of Daniel first. He was thankfully hidden behind a tall concrete pillar, seemingly unharmed.

I finally spotted the shooter near the main doors of the food court. A rifle hung over his chest, at least a dozen magazines clipped to his belt. But nothing was as terrifying as when I realized he was wrapping a chain around the doors—locking us in.

A new level of panic detonated inside me. I had to get her out of there. There had to be another way. It was a fucking mall; he couldn't have chained *all* the exits.

More gunfire rang through the air, screams preceding the sound of bodies hitting the floor. My pulse spiked, desperation fueling my adrenaline. With Kaitlyn still hidden beneath me, I glanced over my shoulder, spotting the service hallway a few yards away. It was partially hidden behind a cardboard cutout of a baseball player advertising his upcoming mall appearance. There was a door at the end of the long corridor, one that would have been easily missed by most.

It was my chance.

My only chance.

Utterly still, I watched as the shooter paced a path around the food court. I waited for a lull in the gunfire, every second stretching into an eternity. When I saw him stop to reload, his back to us at the far end of the food court, I decided to make a break for it. I'd only have a few seconds to get her to safety, but it was now or never.

"Baby, I need you to hold onto daddy's neck, okay?" I whispered. "I'm going to get you out of here. Just keep your eyes closed. I've got you."

Pushing myself up onto my elbows, I started to scoop her off the floor, ready to run for both of our lives. "Hang on," I ordered, but when she didn't cling to my neck, I looked down, getting my first look at her since the bullets had sounded.

It was only a second of my twenty-four years on Earth.

One blink. One heartbeat.

But I could have lived a thousand lifetimes and the vision of my baby girl, bloody and lifeless, would still be carved into the marrow of my bones.

"No," I hissed, frantically patting her down, trying to find the source of blood pooling around her. "Kaitlyn, come on. Stay with me." With the danger taking a back seat to my fears, I sat up, checking her pulse. Finding none, I immediately started CPR.

"Truett, get down," Daniel whispered from somewhere nearby.

No. I could save her. I could still save her.

Tears poured from my eyes as I started chest compressions, begging any and every God in the universe to bring her back to me. As the spray of bullets ricocheted around us, I feared she'd be hit again, so I pulled her toward an overturned table, a worthless shield in a worthless fight.

Allen had once explained to me that, when a brain experiences trauma, it reroutes what it's seeing in order to protect itself. And as I stared at my baby girl, my mind started to close in on me, dragging her from my clutches even as I fought to stay in the present.

I didn't remember when I stopped CPR.

I didn't remember when I released her.

I didn't remember when my brain decided I needed to take cover to protect myself.

The first thing I remembered of the events that followed was that a river of blood carved a path at my feet as I sat frozen—my ass on the tile, my back to an overturned table, the past melding into the terrifying present.

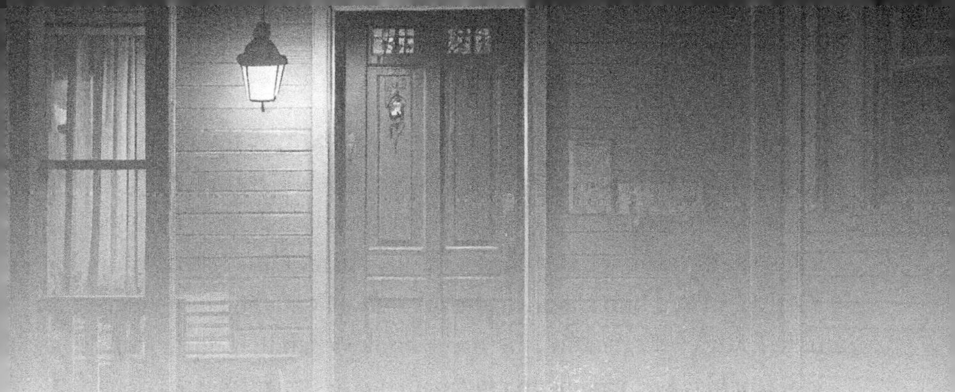

CHAPTER TWENTY-THREE

Gwen

IT WAS A SCENE RIGHT OUT OF *THE TWILIGHT ZONE*. THOUGH sadder.

Exponentially sadder.

It had been eighteen years since I'd moved out of that house and everything was exactly the same. The day he'd presented me with divorce papers, only a month after Nathanial died, I'd stormed out of that house, taking nothing more than the clothes on my back and our daughter. There was no discussion or explanation. Just Truett sitting on that same brown couch, staring off into space as my entire world crumbled.

I'd taken Kaitlyn and gone to stay at my parents' for a while. Everyone assured me that he still loved me and he was just struggling with everything that had happened overseas. That only pissed me off more, because I was struggling too and all I wanted was to curl into his lap and grieve together.

After a while, I took a job managing a restaurant a few towns over in Watersedge. He wouldn't talk to me, but I worked with his attorney to set up a custody schedule. He got Kaitlyn every other Wednesday and alternating weekends. Despite everything he was going through, he was still such an incredible dad. She loved going over there. She didn't understand why he never left the house, but she was just happy to be with him.

Out of the blue, a week before her sixth birthday, Truett checked himself into an out-of-state VA rehabilitation facility. I'd never been so happy in my life. For the first time in months, I had hope that maybe we could be a family again. During that time, Kaitlyn missed him so much she insisted on emailing him videos practically every morning before school. When he'd reply with a video of his own, it came to my email, but he never even acknowledged me with a "hi" or "hello."

Give it time, everyone had said.

But as it turned out, that was the one thing we didn't have.

I lost myself after Kaitlyn died. In a span of six months, I'd lost my brother, my husband, and my daughter. The pain was so deep my bones ached. I fell into a darkness only one other human would understand—and he wouldn't speak to me. Alone, the grief ravaged me to the point I didn't recognize myself anymore. I became so vile and hateful—angry at the whole fucking world for taking my baby away from me.

It wasn't until I found Truett passed out drunk on the front lawn on the Fourth of July that I started to heal. He was gone, and there was nothing I could do to save him. But I still had an entire life in front of me. I had no idea what I was going to do. Or how I could ever move on without her, but I knew with an absolute certainty that I didn't want to end up like him.

I fought every single day, clawing my way out of the darkness, to create a life worth living—a life that had been stolen from my daughter. I'd made a lot of mistakes along the way, but at least I'd tried.

At least I'd left the fucking house.

With my hands shaking, I walked back to the living room.

He watched my every step from the doorway as I walked over to him, my heart breaking in my chest.

I stopped in front of him, tears leaking from my eyes. "Tell me you don't seriously live like this, Truett!" I shouted even though he was standing right in front of me. "Please God. Tell me you don't live like this."

"It's not that bad," he defended, but it held no conviction. "The house, I mean. It's comfortable, ya know? No need to fix something that's not broken."

I blinked at him so hard my lashes could have fueled the winds of a hurricane. "It's not the house that's broken here. It's *you.* What the hell are you doing? It's been eighteen years. You couldn't even come to her funeral, but you've locked yourself in this house for the last two decades like some kind of time capsule? Make this make sense."

"Funerals are for dead people."

It was an odd response, which on any other day I would have questioned if I'd heard him correctly. On that day, with the scars of the past ripping open faster than I could mentally stitch them shut, I shot back, "Oh, I know. Because unlike you, I was there. I buried her alone. I kissed her goodbye alone. I watched them lower her into the ground alone. You don't need to explain funerals to me. I'm *very* well versed."

He let out a low groan and breezed past me. He sat down on the couch, planted his elbows on his knees, and dropped his head into his hands.

And then…he said nothing.

I stared at him in disbelief, an enraging case of déjà vu making the hairs on the back of my neck stand on end.

I wouldn't do it again.

I wouldn't beg him to talk to me.

I couldn't force him into that suit the day of her funeral any more than I could force him to be the man I needed—then or now.

He'd said he'd changed. I'd *believed* that he'd changed.

It hadn't taken a full twenty-four hours for him to prove me wrong.

Turning on a toe, I started for the door, ready to leave the past where it so obviously belonged.

"Do you remember when we first got married and we were so broke we couldn't afford to eat anything other than peanut butter and jelly for, like, two weeks straight?" he asked.

I froze, my hand on the door, a knot in my stomach.

"You were still pregnant, and I felt like shit because I knew you were having cravings, but we didn't have the money for anything else. Remember that game we made up?"

Pressure mounted in my chest as I slowly turned back to face him. "Eggplant Parmesan and Veggie Tacos?"

He reclined back on the couch, a soft smile playing on his lips. "Well, for me, it was Burgers and Ribs, but yeah, that's the one. You know how we'd take a bite of the sandwich and then get all loud and animated, describing something totally different until we convinced ourselves it was actually a five-star meal? We were still eating PB&J and we knew it, but to this day, those were some of the best ribs I've ever had."

"What are you getting at with this?"

His face paled and he drew in a deep breath, holding it for a long second before speaking on an exhale. "She's not dead."

"What?"

"That's what I tell myself. Instead of Burgers and Ribs, I play a little game of Kaitlyn's Still Alive."

My stomach soured, realization sinking in. "Oh, God."

His knee bounced as he scrubbed his hands over his thighs. "Come sit down. I'll talk, tell you anything and everything. Just please don't leave."

I closed my eyes. It was everything I'd ever wanted to hear from him. But after seeing that house, I wasn't so sure anymore. My emotions were all over the place, from heartbreak and sadness to bitterness and anger. I despised that damn couch for a multitude of reasons, but no matter how hard I tried to resist, I couldn't help loving the man sitting on it.

I walked over to him and slowly sank down beside him. His hand snaked out, landing on my thigh. I couldn't be sure if he was tethering me to him so I wouldn't leave or anchoring himself to me so he didn't get lost. Either way, I had a feeling we were about to travel through hell together.

He drew in a deep breath and then finally tore down the eighteen-year-old wall he'd so carefully constructed between us. "It started a few days before her funeral, when I couldn't take the pain anymore. You and I hadn't been together for a few months, so I was used to her not being around every day, and… Well, I convinced myself she was with you. Out there, smiling and laughing, baking cookies, playing at the park, living an incredible life. It's why I don't leave the house. I'm not scared of the outside world, Gwen. I'm scared of the reality that she doesn't exist anymore outside of these four walls."

My lungs burned as I held my breath, praying this was all some kind of sick joke. I felt like my skin was on fire from just standing in that house, much less living in it for nearly two decades.

How had he made it that long, frozen in time, with no reprieve or end in sight?

"I don't understand, Truett. Is this some kind of self-imposed torture like when you'd go to The Grille and sit in the booth?"

He let out a low hum. "No. Though I'm not sure you quite understand the full reason I go to that booth every Wednesday, either."

TRUETT

Eighteen years earlier…

With hollow eyes and a beard I hadn't bothered to shave in the three months I'd been home, I stared at myself in the mirror. "Who the fuck are you?" I whispered, my head spinning in a fury of panic and hatred. My teeth were clenched painfully hard, a fistful of pills in my hand. "You don't fucking deserve to be here," I snarled at the man staring back at me. "You had one fucking job and you missed the cell phone. They came home in coffins and now look at you, taking the easy way out. You fucking pussy. You fucking, *fucking* pussy." I slammed my fist down on the bathroom countertop, splitting my knuckles wide.

I didn't feel it because all I ever felt was pain. Pure, agonizing guilt stripped me limb from limb with every undeserved breath I took.

I couldn't do it anymore.

It had to end.

My existence was nothing but an insult to their memory.

I wanted somebody to yell. To berate me for all the ways I'd failed. I needed somebody—anybody—to hate me as much as I hated myself. Instead, I got pats on the back and a chain of command who called me a hero.

A hero. Imagine that. I'd all but killed four men who would have died to protect me, and I was a hero for what? Surviving?

Friends and family gave me hugs, tears filling their eyes as they droned on about how thankful they were that I'd come home. Bullshit. I shouldn't have come home at all. That support team should have left me buried in the rubble of that building, letting the birds pick away at my carcass as death took its time draining the life from my body.

The doctors called it survivor's guilt. The loss of purpose, the constant replaying of events, the detachment, and isolation. They were probably right. But I couldn't feel anything else.

It was the hardest thing I've ever done, but I'd filed for divorce. Letting Gwen go had felt like ripping away the fibers that connected my body to my soul. But when she was with me, when she touched me, it seared like a branding iron, scarring me from the inside out, because in those moments, with her holding me as though she could keep me from falling apart, nothing actually hurt at all. And that was wrong on levels outsiders couldn't even pretend to comprehend.

I didn't deserve a reprieve.

I didn't deserve *her*.

I didn't even deserve a final escape, either, but I couldn't take it anymore.

I stared down at the pills, a concoction that would finally make the world right again—a world without me in it. I waved at myself—one last goodbye for the road—and then lifted the pills to my mouth, ready and eager.

Only death never showed. It sent something far more frightening in its place—*reality.*

"Daddy," she called from somewhere in the distance.

My whole body jolted, a wave of panic consuming me as my vision snapped into clarity, bringing the world outside of my mind into sharp focus.

Kaitlyn?

Oh, God.

Kaitlyn.

What day was it? Tuesday? Shit. No. I looked down at my watch. Jesus, how long had I been standing there?

It was Wednesday. *My* Wednesday. Six p.m. to be exact.

I was supposed to be watching our daughter.

I was supposed to be keeping her safe.

Bile crawled up the back of my throat as I thought about what she would have found if I'd convinced myself to take those pills just a few hours earlier.

Shame sliced through me like a jagged knife, leaving wounds so deep they throbbed with every heartbeat. I looked back at the mirror, finding the same hollow eyes, the same unkept beard, the same question rolling from my tongue. "Who the fuck are you?"

That selfish bastard didn't bother to reply.

"Daddy?" she repeated.

Glancing around the bathroom, I frantically tried to find somewhere to hide the pills while using my free hand to dry my eyes. "Hey, baby. I'm in here," I called.

In the distance, I heard her yell. "He's here! Bye, Mom. I love you."

I couldn't hear Gwen's reply, but that was probably for the best. No use in adding salt to the gaping wound I carried in my chest.

I dumped the trail mix of narcotics into the toilet, flushing just before sprinting from the room.

Pausing in the hallway, I shook my arms out, trying to quit trembling. I cleared my throat, plastered on a smile as if I hadn't just been ready to end my life, and stepped around the corner. "Hey, pretty girl!"

She was still in the process of kicking her shoes off and shedding her backpack, ready for school the next day. When her gaze finally made it to mine, she stilled. "Were you crying?"

I chuckled, praying it sounded more genuine than it felt. "Who? Me? No way."

She watched me from across the room, not running to me like she would have only a few months earlier. But things had changed. I'd changed. Her life had changed. She'd lost her beloved uncle. Her parents were in the middle of a divorce. She'd been ripped away from her home and moved to an apartment a few towns over.

And what? I was going to make her life harder by adding the loss of her father to that list?

Take my pain and transfer it to her? Saddle her with the childhood trauma I'd vowed to protect her from?

The day she was born, I'd sworn to be a better father to her than my own had been to me. He'd been shit at the whole fatherhood thing, but at least he was alive. Jesus, what the hell was wrong with me? I'd been so damn focused on what I didn't deserve that I'd lost sight of what she did deserve—everything.

I felt the blood drain from my face.

"Are you okay?" she asked, eying me with a soul-plundering scrutiny only children possessed.

No. I was not. I was so far from okay I couldn't see the horizon anymore.

But if I had any hope of *her* being okay—better than okay, happy, peaceful, safe—I had to get my life together.

"Hey, you wanna go to The Grille?"

Her eyes lit, an incredible smile splitting her face. "*Go* there?"

Nerves rolled in my stomach at the mere thought of leaving the house with her. I didn't trust myself anymore. I didn't trust that I wouldn't miss another cell phone or whatever other dangers lurked in the shadows of my mind. But her smile… I would move entire mountains for that smile.

Or at least I'd try.

"Yeah. Why not."

She bounced on her toes and then sprinted toward me, colliding into my legs. "Can I have your bacon?"

My hollow chest filled with warmth as I smoothed down her mess of brown curls. "Uh, obviously."

"We don't have to tell Mommy, right?" She stuck out her tongue. "She made me a bean sausage for breakfast today."

Gwen was a vegetarian, so our tradition of me sneaking Kaitlyn meat had started as soon as she'd gotten the teeth to chew it. For years, we'd been making secret trips to The Grille on the nights Gwen would work. I'd always order a bacon cheeseburger. Kaitlyn would get an order of cheese fries and then swipe my bacon.

For obvious reasons, we hadn't been since I'd gotten home from my deployment. I wasn't sure I was going to be able to sit through a whole meal, but dammit, I wanted to give her some normalcy before I rocked her world all over again.

I couldn't live like that anymore. I needed help—more than just the doctors and therapy appointments I'd been dodging. I'd been told about an out-of-state rehabilitation center that specialized in veterans with combat-related post-traumatic stress. I'd brushed it off at first, not willing to admit how bad things had gotten, but now, it seemed like the only way.

If I wanted to be present in her life, it was up to me to make that happen.

It was a Wednesday night and exactly six p.m. when we slid into that booth at The Grille. Instead of my usual burger, I ordered a club sandwich, no mayo, bacon on the side, and lived in the moment the way Nutz, Steve-O, Skytrash, and S'arnt would have wanted.

Kaitlyn laughed, filling my ears with stories about her stuffed animals and the perils of kindergarten. I'd thought I'd done a pretty good job of hiding the fact that I felt like I was going to peel out of my own skin, but just as I felt like I couldn't do it anymore, she moved to my side of the booth, took my hand, and said, "Let's go home, Daddy."

Home.

Home.

Home.

Gwen

Tears leaked from my eyes as a blanket of sadness made it difficult to breathe. "Oh my God, Truett. I had no idea."

He gave my leg a squeeze, but I immediately reached down to take his hand, intertwining our fingers. When I scooted over, our thighs became flush. I would have crawled into his lap if I'd have thought I could have absolved him of even a fraction of his pain.

"You didn't know because I didn't tell you. That's on me." He hung his head. "So, yeah. She saved my life that day, and then three months later, I failed to save hers."

I started to give him a whole speech about how it wasn't his fault. How he never could have known what he was walking into that day at the mall. It wasn't going to help; I knew that firsthand. I'd spent a long time beating myself up about moving to Watersedge and subsequently paving the path for Kaitlyn to be sitting with him that day at the mall.

If only I'd moved somewhere else.

Taken a different job.

Fought harder for my marriage even when Truett had given up.

But that was the thing about life. You can only operate in the present with the experiences you learned in the past. Hindsight was no more realistic than unicorns or dragons when it came to decision making. It was simply a tool people used to convince themselves that they had control over the trajectory of their lives.

The truth was none of us knew where life was going to take us. When I'd lain in that hospital, a terrified teenager, holding the most precious baby girl God would ever put on this Earth, while the man of my dreams stood beside me, promising me the world, I never could have fathomed that six years later it would all be gone. But the future happened whether you were ready for it or not.

All at once, I released his hand and stood up.

His head tipped back, panic blazing in his eyes. "Gwen, no. Please don't leave."

I rested my hand on the curve of his jaw. "I'm not leaving you, but I'm also not staying here. And neither are you."

His eyes flashed wide. "What?"

"Truett, I can't even pretend to understand how you've done this for so long. We're going to have a lot of long talks about finding you the proper help. But you asked me to give you a chance so here it is… In this house, Kaitlyn might be alive, but *you* are dead.

This"—I waved my hands out, motioning around the room—"is the coffin you buried yourself in."

He blanched, but I didn't let it slow my roll.

"You have been sitting on that couch for so long the past has turned into the future, causing you to skip the present altogether." I extended my hand, asking for his, and when he placed it in mine, I gave him a gentle tug, urging him to his feet.

He rose to his full height, his strong body towering over me.

Looping my arms around his neck, I peered into his deep brown eyes. "I love you."

He dropped his forehead to mine, his arms folding around my hips. "Oh, thank God." His lips brushed mine, seeking a connection I couldn't yet offer him.

I leaned away, dodging his kiss. "I love you, but I can't stay here with you."

His body turned to granite. "Gwen—"

"But you can come with me. This isn't the only place Kaitlyn still exists. You just have to let me show you."

He stared at me; the weight of contemplation heavy in his eyes. "I don't know, Gwen."

"You gotta trust me, True. Do you want me to be a part of your life?"

He nodded rapidly.

My heart soared. "Then I'm going to need you to be a part of mine too."

CHAPTER TWENTY-FOUR

TRUETT

It was a monumental decision, but it wasn't necessarily hard to make. I desperately wanted Gwen back in my life—whatever that took. She was right; that house was my coffin. And over the last few weeks, it had felt like it was collapsing in on me.

Sitting on that couch, pouring out my deepest darkest secrets to her, had felt like a road marched barefoot over broken glass. Yet, still bleeding and broken, I would have followed her anywhere.

She'd patiently waited for me to change into a pair of jeans and slip my shoes on, and then together we picked up the toppled-over bags of groceries she'd brought over for our "date."

I'd thought things had changed after she'd bought the restaurant. Then again after our kiss. And most definitely after she came calling my name. But in the short time since she'd walked through my front door to the moment we walked to her car, it felt like we were two totally different people—or, more accurately, it felt like we were one singular unit again.

As we drove, I started to feel like she was more nervous than I was. She never let go of my hand, and at every stop light, she'd peer up at me and whisper, "Are you good?"

I was with Gwen, she'd told me she loved me, and she was giving me the chance I so desperately needed to hopefully win her back. It was safe to say I was the best I'd been in nearly two decades. I hadn't asked where she was taking me, because honestly, I didn't care, but roughly ten minutes later, as we pulled into what appeared to be a sleepy golf course community, I assumed we were headed to her place.

She parked in the driveway of a two-story brick home. It was new and nice, everything mine was not. I sat there for several beats, studying the front of her house. Her yard wasn't large, but the grass was freshly cut and the sidewalk that led to the front steps was lined with colorful flowers. The deep porch held two rocking chairs on one end and a bench swing on the other. Flanked by two large white flowerpots, overflowing with an assortment of plants, the door was a dark blue that matched the shutters.

It looked well taken care of, cheery, and most of all, peaceful. I imagined it was a place where laughter flowed freely and love filled every space inside and out, because before our worlds had been flipped upside down, that was exactly how our house had always been.

She cut the engine. "Are you sure you're up for this?"

I looked over at her and told her the God's-honest truth. "I don't know. But I love you, and if this is where you are, there is nowhere else in the entire world I'd rather be. Not even the past."

Her face softened and she leaned across the center console, pressing an all-too-chaste kiss to my lips. "If that changes, you let me know. No more suffering in silence, okay?"

I offered her a tight smile. "I'll do my best."

Carrying the groceries, I followed her up the steps and waited as she typed a code into the front door. The deadbolt robotically unlocked.

The minute that door swung open, I was struck by a wave of nostalgia—the familiar scent of lavender with hints of vanilla filling my senses. I remembered when our house smelled like that. When I'd come home from work after a long day, and Kaitlyn would run over, launching herself into my arms. As she walked over to kiss me, Gwen would smile so big it was like she hadn't seen me in weeks rather than hours.

It smelled like home.

But not my own.

Our home.

God, I'd missed that smell.

Misreading the shift in my mood, Gwen reached out and took my hand. "Hey, I'm right here."

I dipped low and touched my lips to hers. "I'm okay, seriously."

She nodded, so unconvinced it almost made me laugh.

She entered first, tugging on my hand as if I wouldn't follow. A pack of rabid dogs couldn't have stopped me though. As I walked inside, my attention was immediately captured by at least a dozen square canvas pictures arranged above the large gray sectional. There were shots of Gwen holding Nate as a baby, her eyes tired but shining with pride. I scanned the rest, following the progression as he grew from a chubby toddler into a wiry little boy.

The photo of Kaitlyn in a pink tutu, grinning with bright-red lipstick smeared on her face, stopped me in my tracks. In that instant, I was transported back to the dance recital she'd talked about for months only to get stage fright and refuse to go out with the rest of her class.

I walked closer to the wall of photos, noticing that images of our daughter were equally dispersed among the candids of Nate. My chest got tight as I took the time to examine each one, reminiscing over when and where they had been taken.

I froze—heart, body, and soul—when I came across a certain picture in particular.

With a front tooth missing and a mess of untamed brown curls covering an eye, she had her arms wrapped around the golden neck of Gwen's parents' dog, Jazzy. He was licking her face. Her head was thrown back, and her mouth was open in a giggle that I swear I could still hear.

"That's one of my favorites," Gwen said as she stepped beside me, placing a hand on my lower back. "Jazzy was so good with her."

"I've never seen this one before." My mouth was so dry it came out as a rasp.

"I took it when we were staying with my parents right after you filed for divorce."

Guilt swelled in my throat.

She rubbed my back, soothing me as only she could.

"I have a lot of pictures you've never seen of her."

My gaze snapped to hers. "Really?"

"Yeah. After Nathanial died and I was faced with how fragile life could be, I went out and bought one of those fancy DSLR cameras. I think I took more pictures of her over the next few months than I did in the entirety of her first six years."

"Can I see them?" I rushed out.

Her grin stretched. "Hang on. Let me go get the albums." She was only gone for a minute before she came back holding four large photo albums.

She set them on her square wooden coffee table and gave my arm a squeeze. "Make yourself at home. I'll be in the kitchen, starting dinner."

While I was still raw and reeling from the day, food was the last thing on my mind, but I thought she was attempting to give me space. I'd had space though—years of it. What I hadn't had was her.

I scooped up the albums and followed her into the large open kitchen. There was a granite island in the middle with stools surrounding two sides. "You mind if I sit in here with you instead?"

Happiness twinkled in her eyes. "I'd love that." She walked to her stainless-steel refrigerator, pulled out a bottle of wine. "You okay with Sav Blanc?"

I shook my head. "I don't drink anymore. But I don't mind if you do."

"Good for you," she praised. She put the wine back in the fridge and asked, "Can I get you anything else to drink?"

I patted the photo albums. "Nah. You've already done enough."

She sighed. "After what I saw today, I'm not sure I have."

"Don't say that."

She leaned her hip against the counter and crossed her arms over her chest. "I should have checked in on you. Through the years. I was just so angry and hurt, but I never would have let you stay in that house."

In two long strides, I moved to her. With my hands on her hips, I lifted her to sit on the counter, bringing us eye to eye. "Nobody *let* me stay in that house, babe. Least of all you. My doctors hated it. Therapists fired me over it. My brother's a psychiatrist and couldn't convince me to move. And trust me. He tried *a lot*. He once threatened to have me involuntarily committed. But I wasn't delusional or a danger to myself or others. I just wasn't ready to let go."

She looped her arms around my neck and opened her legs, drawing me closer. "That's the thing though. You don't have to let go, Truett. You just have to move forward. That house is not what keeps her memory alive." She tapped my temple. "Because she will always be alive in here." She moved her hand to settle over my heart. "And in here. She existed. She's ours. She will *always* be ours. The stuff in that house is just that—*stuff*."

"It's *her* stuff."

"It *was* her stuff," she corrected. "Do you really think that even if she was still here today she'd be living at your house? Sleeping in a twin-sized bed with pink sheets and coloring pictures on the floor? If we were lucky, she had maybe six more months before she outgrew those sneakers you keep by the door. Those toys? They'd have been discarded and sold at the family yard sale the minute she discovered eyeshadow and lip gloss. Truett, you do realize she'd be twenty-four now, right?"

My chin snapped to the side. Had it really been that long? Yes, I mean, logically, I could do the math, but my baby? Twenty-four? "Jesus," I mumbled.

She smiled, leaning to the side to recapture my gaze. "I see you're starting to get it. When I was her age, we'd already had *and* lost her. She'd be a woman now."

I bit the inside of my cheek. I couldn't fathom a world where Kaitlyn was all grown up. What would she look like? Probably like her mother; she'd always been her clone. Would she still have loved animals? Would she have gone to school to become a vet? Would she have a husband or a family? Holy fuck, would I have had grandkids? I smiled at the thought.

Yes, smiled.

But then again, I was with Gwen. I shouldn't have even been surprised anymore.

I rested my palms on either side of her on the counter, a million thoughts and scenarios ricocheting in my head. "Do you think we'd still be living in that house?"

"No." She replied so fast it was downright offensive.

My lips thinned, but it only made her laugh.

"Don't look at me like that," she teased. "If I'd let you, you would have filled every room in that house with a baseball team of kids. It would have been busting at the seams. Plus, we were lucky you got stationed at the base nearby, but the Army wasn't going to let us stay there much longer. Though, with or without that house, I know we'd still be together. Somewhere out there, still bickering over putting down the toilet seat and the temperature on the thermostat."

That sounded incredible. All of it. The kids, the family, but most of all, the together part. "I miss that life," I confessed. "The one we had and the one we never got."

"Sure." She shrugged. "But would you rather stand still in what could have been?" She swayed toward me, nipping at my bottom lip. "Or move forward with what we could still have?"

I didn't have to think.

It wasn't even a question.

I'd known from the minute she dropped the rings at my feet that, if I ever got the chance to get her back, there was nothing I wouldn't do to keep her. "I just want you." I spoke between peppered kisses. "I. Just. Want. You."

She slanted her head, taking the kiss deeper. It wasn't desperate despite the way I hungered for her. Our tongues slid against each other with the slow rhythm of comfort and longing—promises being made without the use of words.

I was lost in her until she broke our connection all too soon. "I want you too," she whispered, holding me tight. "But not like this. That whole 'love conquers all' thing is a beautiful thought, but we know better than most that love doesn't always win. You need help, Truett. More help than I can ever give you."

I sucked in a sharp breath, dread filling my stomach. It was everything I'd feared when she'd walked into my house.

"But!" she amended. "If you can work on yourself, I'd love nothing more than to work on *us* again."

I nodded, hope spiraling in my veins. "I'll do whatever it takes. I promise."

"Then I'm here, but let me make this clear. I'm not going back to that house."

As I stood in her kitchen, staring into the eyes of the only woman I had ever loved, with pictures of our daughter on the wall and a future full of possibilities, I suddenly didn't want to go back, either.

"Can I stay the night with you?"

She smiled, so much damn pride in her eyes it leaked into my chest, filling me too. "Absolutely."

CHAPTER TWENTY-FIVE

Gwen

WE'D SPENT THE REST OF THE NIGHT LOOKING AT OLD pictures, catching up, and stealing kisses like we were kids again. I'd cooked dinner, but neither of us had touched much of our food. Instead we'd sat for hours, swapping stories, alternating between laughing and crying—and sometimes a combination of the two. It was so damn surreal to have him back in my life. In my house. On my couch. His hand anchored to me no matter how we were sitting.

There was an undeniable heat between us, but a lot had happened that night, and by the time I guided him upstairs to my bed, it was well past three in the morning. Being that it was his first night away from his house in so many years, I feared he wouldn't sleep at all. But as he casually stripped down to his boxer briefs, slid into bed behind me, and held me tight, his whole strong body relaxed. He fell asleep so fast I wondered when he'd last had a good night's rest.

And eight hours later, when my lids fluttered open past eleven a.m. for the first time in my adult life, I wondered the same about myself. Though, as I unfurled and patted around the bed finding it cold and empty, I came awake with a jolt of adrenaline.

"Truett!" I shouted, flying out of bed.

I hadn't bothered so much as smoothing down my sleep-mussed hair before racing down the stairs. When I rounded the corner, I caught sight of him fully dressed but barefoot, stomping my way, a protective concern contorting his face.

"What's wrong?" he ground out.

I slowed to a stop because he clearly was not going to and I feared injury if we collided at that speed.

His hands landed on my hips and he pulled me against his chest, his worried eyes scanning my face. "Are you okay?"

"Are you?" I shot back, my heart finally slowing.

"Yeah? Why wouldn't I be?"

"I don't know. I woke up and you weren't there, so I panicked."

He grinned. "Babe. I have an internal alarm clock that, whether I get ten minutes of sleep or ten hours, I'm still up by seven. After I watched you sleep for a few hours, I came down here so I didn't bother you."

I crinkled my nose. I didn't remember so much as rolling over that night, much less if I'd drooled all over his shoulder. "You watched me sleep?"

"Yep." He gave my hips a squeeze.

"For hours? Plural?"

His grin stretched. "Yep."

"Wonderful," I mumbled.

He playfully swayed me in his arms. "It was. So fucking wonderful. I wasn't sure if it was a dream or not. Well, until you aimed that morning dragon breath at me."

I immediately slapped a hand over my mouth and spoke behind it. "Shut up."

He threw his head back and laughed so hard his shoulders shook. It was such a rare sight of beauty that I smiled up at him, so lovestruck that silly cartoon hearts probably floated from my eyes.

When he looked down at me, his laughter trailed off, but his smile never wavered. "I'm kidding. You were so damn gorgeous. I had to get out of there before I made a move I wasn't sure you'd be okay with."

There wasn't a move Truett West had that I wasn't okay with, especially not as I felt his cock thicken between us.

Morning breath be damned, I looped my arms around his neck. "Oh, yeah, and what was that?"

He answered by sliding his hand over the curve of my ass. My little blue nighty did little to cover me. I might have frantically dug it out of the back of my closet as we'd prepared for bed for exactly that reason.

Maybe.

Possibly.

Definitely.

His eyes heated as his fingers lingered, dipping beneath my panties to palm my ass. "How ya feeling today?" he asked.

Breathless, I replied, "Good."

"You still feel like giving me a chance?"

Boldly reaching between us, I slid my hand up his length. "There's nothing I wouldn't give you, True."

He let out a growl, and then covered my mouth with his. As our tongues dueled for control, his deft fingers swept between my legs.

"Fuck, you're wet," he rumbled into my mouth. "Here or upstairs?"

I fisted the front of his shirt, trying to keep my balance as he skillfully found my clit. "True."

"Here or upstairs?" he repeated with such a gentle dominance it sent a chill down my spine.

God, this man. Nobody had ever been able to light me on fire like him. Desperate for more, I took a step to the side, opening my legs to allow him more room to play.

"I'll take that to mean here."

Ravaging my mouth, he blindly guided me to the couch. It was only a few feet, but with furious hands and desperate need, we'd stripped each other naked before I felt the cushions hit the back of my knees.

Nipping at my bottom lip, he plucked my nipple, sending sparks to my core. "I've been thinking about you like this all damn morning. So fucking sexy. All fucking mine."

"Yours," I agreed, a promise and a vow that sent a second wave of heat through me. "All yours."

"Sit down, baby." His intense gaze swept over my body, appreciation for what he was seeing evident in the low growl that slipped through his lips. "Last time I didn't have the control to take it slow, but today, I want to watch. It's been too long since I've seen your face when you come on my fingers, even if it was on the back of my eyelids every time I gripped my cock."

My stomach dipped. "You thought about me when you got yourself off?"

A wry smile twisted his lips. "Gwen, baby, you are the only woman I've ever thought about. There's never been anyone else."

I blinked at him. It was a sweet statement that could very easily have been hyperbole. But there was something in his eyes that sparked a thought. "Have you been with anyone since…"

He shook his head. "No. I never felt right about using a woman just to pretend she was you."

My mouth fell open, shock mixing with sadness. "Never?"

"Wipe that pity off your face. I got two hands and one hell of a memory. I took care of myself just fine."

Oh.

My.

God.

Oh my God.

OhmyGod!

"Truett," I whispered, resting my hand on the side of his face.

"Sit down, Gwen."

"That's so long."

"Yep, and the longer you stand here talking about it, the longer I'm gonna have to wait again." He rubbed circles over my back as he explained, "Look, I'm sure I could have figured something out or met someone online over the years. But I didn't want to. When I slid that ring on your finger at eighteen, that was it for me. You have always been *it* for me." Fingertips dug into my flesh, my skin erupting with goose bumps. "I fucked it up and lost you, but I'm here now, and you're giving me the chance to make things right. You preach a whole lot about me being stuck in the past for us to be naked and standing here talking about who I *haven't* slept within the last eighteen years."

I bit my bottom lip. He had a point.

He was also naked, his cock long and hard. His dark gaze was aimed at me in a way that held immeasurable amounts of promise. Promises, I knew all too well he could and *absolutely would* fulfill.

But mainly it was Truett. If he wanted to watch, I wanted to be the entire fucking show.

Lowering myself, I reclined back on the couch and spread my legs wide, opening to him.

He sucked in a sharp breath through his teeth and dragged his fingertips up my inner thigh. "So fucking beautiful." Capturing my mouth, he sank to his knees before me, his fingers slowly entering me. He swallowed my moans, feasting on my pleasure. Seemingly fueled by the nourishment, he released my mouth and stared down at his hand—his skilled fingers coaxing and curling inside me.

I writhed as he found all the right places, even those I'd yet to discover on my own. Somehow, he knew, as if it were a secret only he had been privy to. One that he had kept for eighteen years waiting on the moment it could be revealed again.

"Yes, Truett," I breathed, arching my back. He stole the moment to fold over and suck my nipple into his mouth. It was the most overwhelming moment of pure ecstasy. His tongue swirled at my breast as his thumb caressed my clit, sensations firing in every direction, until my body had no other option than to shatter.

The orgasm tore through me like a hurricane of pleasure, ruthless and tranquil all wrapped up in one. But he didn't stop there.

Not my Truett.

"Fuck, Gwen," he rasped as I rode the pulsing waves, lost in a sea of euphoria. When the last pulse of pleasure washed through me and I felt the loss of his hand, he asked, "You want to get on top, or you want me to carry you to bed?" His lips curled in a sexy smirk. "Although, gotta say, I fucked you on a desk last time, I don't feel good about taking you on a couch now."

Head swirling, a smile curled my lips. He'd always been incredible in bed, so gentle and attentive. We weren't done until we were both fully spent, and if he got there before I did, he'd make sure I came on his fingers or tongue before we collapsed into a tangle of sated bodies.

I missed the days where I had choices, and always got to be the loudest voice when it came to when and how we made love.

Did I want him to carry me to bed and continue to worship my body as only he could? Absolutely.

But he'd had his show, now I wanted mine.

Leaning forward, I grabbed his shoulders, encouraging him to move to the couch beside me. When he settled on the cushion, I turned and threw a leg over him, straddling his lap.

A wicked grin curled his lips. "You still hungry, baby?"

"Starved," I whispered, positioning him at my opening.

He let out a groan as I lowered myself onto the tip of his length. "Then take what you need. *Everything* you need. *From me.*"

In one swift movement, I sank down, hard and fast. He let out a low curse, his head falling back against the couch cushion, as a cry escaped my mouth.

It was more than a moan, more than a vocal expression of pleasure.

It was a cry of perfection, of finally feeling home again.

A cry for time lost, and a sigh of relief as the Earth finally tilted back on its axis.

I rode him hard, greedy as if I needed to reclaim him even though he'd admitted that he'd always been mine. I hadn't always been his though, and while I regretted nothing because of the child I'd gained, I needed him to understand that there would never be a moment when I wasn't his again.

"Easy," he rumbled, his fingertips biting into my hips. "I'm not going to last long if you keep that up."

I didn't slow; if anything I sped up, rolling my hips in a relentless rhythm that ensured I wouldn't be lasting long either.

"Dammit, Gwen," he groaned as he released my hips and folded his arms around me, using me as leverage to drive into me from the bottom. "Come on, baby, give me one more. Let me feel you milk my cock."

The pressure built inside of me again, and I fought the urge to close my eyes and lose myself in the sensations. I wanted to see him fall off the edge.

Dear God, he was a beautiful sight.

Muscles straining beneath dense tattoos as his mouth hung open, his every upward thrust deeper than the last, his eyes locked onto mine, a raw intensity in his gaze that sent chills over my body.

I could feel his resolve weakening, the tension building in his body, mirroring my own. The sound of our ragged breaths filled the room, a symphony of pleasure and desire.

I raked my nails down his biceps, feeling the ripple of his muscles under my touch. "Don't stop," I begged.

His response was a deep, guttural groan that sent a surge of fire coursing through me.

With a final, powerful thrust, he teetered on the edge, his eyes closing momentarily before they snapped open, wild and blazing.

We shattered, the past dissolving, leaving us reeling and *together* in the present.

Spent, my body sagged as I braced myself with my forearms on either side of him.

"Jesus," he rasped, peppering kisses across my collarbone.

I smiled, lazy and sated. "I couldn't agree more."

His chest heaved with labored breaths. "You know we're gonna have to use a bed one of these days."

"Maybe. But we have plenty of time to get there."

A profound reverence painted his face as he drew in a deep breath. "I hope so."

Using both my hands, I framed his. "I'm here, True. No hope necessary. What happens from here with us is completely up to you."

He nodded and rested his forehead on mine. "I won't fuck this up again. I swear, whatever it takes to keep you, I'll do it."

I kissed him, chaste but filled with emotion. "I love you, True. But the things you need to do have to be done for *you* and not just to keep me."

He nodded, a grin curling the side of his mouth. "I know, but a little incentive never hurt anyone."

I laughed as I eased off of him. The loss was staggering, but my body, while tender, had never felt better. Grabbing my nighty off the floor, I pulled it on as I walked to the downstairs bathroom to clean up. When I got back, he had pulled on his jeans, but remained shirtless, casually stretched out on the couch, like a Greek God.

"C'mere," he said, patting the space in front of him. It was already late, and I had a busy day at the restaurant ahead of me, but cuddling with Truett was not an offer I would ever deny.

He flipped to his back, and I squeezed in beside him, resting my head on his pec. Contentment washed over me as I nestled into his warmth, the steady rise and fall of his chest beneath my cheek grounding me with a sense of safety and belonging, as if this was where I was always meant to be.

He pressed a kiss to the top of my head. "How you feeling?"

While I was blissed out of my damn mind, my lips got loose. "Good. Well, better than good, actually. I forgot how nice it is not to vomit after sex."

His body turned to stone and I regretted my choice of words immediately. "What do you mean *vomit after sex*?"

Tracing the black tattoos on his chest, I tried to brush it off. "Nothing. So, are you planning to come to the restaurant with me?"

Using two fingers under my chin, he tipped my head back, forcing my gaze to his. "Yeah, I'm coming to the restaurant. I called into work earlier and took a few days off so we can get you caught up. But first, you're gonna tell me who the hell made you vomit after sex."

I sighed. It was a conversation we would have to have eventually, but five minutes after some seriously incredible sex didn't seem ideal. "I just meant, I've been with someone else, ya know, after us."

He narrowed his eyes. "I know you have a kid, Gwen. I didn't figure it was an immaculate conception. But I did figure it was a man who loved and took care of you." His face flashed hard. "Is this the jackass who you said used you as a punching bag?"

Shit. "Yes, but—"

"Before you try to sugarcoat this, I need to remind you that you promised me at the restaurant that you wouldn't lie to me and you'd tell me if that fucker hurt you."

I sat up, the air between us suddenly unbreathable. "Yes, and I also told you that he did hurt me. Just not in the way you were assuming."

His eyes flashed wide, a hurricane brewing within them as he sat up, pinning me with a malevolent glare. "Then I'm going to need you to be really specific here, Gwen. Because right now, I'm assuming some pretty fucked-up shit that left you vomiting after sex."

He would have been assuming right.

It *was* fucked up.

The way Jeff had thought I owed him my body just because I wore his ring. The way he thought me changing clothes or taking a shower was an open invitation for him to grope me. The way he would use his words to beat me down, emotionally exhausting me until it was just easier to give him what he wanted rather than spend the next week living with his snide comments or the silent treatment.

Sex had been a tipping point in my decision to divorce him. I'd struggled for so long, thinking there was something wrong with me, even going so far as to go to the doctor to find out why I had no libido.

Turned out, I didn't have a problem with sex at all.

I was just having it with the wrong man.

"Gwen," Truett prompted, his patience waning.

"Look, yes. At the end of our marriage, when he'd browbeat me into sex, I would sometimes throw up afterward. But he never forced himself on me."

Truett slanted his head. "You ever say no?"

I grimaced. "There were times where I wouldn't want to do certain things, and he'd get mad, so I'd just…give in to avoid conflict. But—"

"No buts!" He lurched to his feet, stabbing a hand into his hair. "That's not consent, Gwen. That's fucking manipulation and coercion. Please, God, tell me you recognize that."

"I do," I shot back. "I absolutely do. And it sucks that it took me entirely too long to figure out how toxic he was. For years, I was so blinded by the desire to keep my family together that I missed every single red flag even when they were flown directly in front of my face. But I figured it out eventually and left him."

He planted his hands on his hips. "You call the cops first?"

"What? No."

"So this fucker just got away with taking advantage of you? Treating his woman like a piece of meat? That woman being his own Goddamn wife? That woman being the love of my fucking life?" His last statement/question was spoken only a half decibel below a yell.

His tone made my attitude slip. "Yeah, that sums it up. Thank you for the recap. But you know what? You are yelling at the wrong person right now. I let it go. I went to therapy. I did a lot of soul searching. I worked on *me*. Jeff Weaver is an asshole with no moral compass, so he is no longer in my life. My only concern with him from here on out is to teach my son the difference between right and wrong. And how to respect himself and whoever he chooses to date one day to ensure he doesn't end up like his father."

His chest heaved as he stared at me. "This is on me. I never should have let you go."

I rolled my eyes. "I believe we've more than covered that part in recent weeks, but this is *not* on you. I hate to break this to you, Truett, but not everything is about you. What was it you told me recently? Some things happen for a reason. Some things happen for no reason. And then some things just never happen at all. Through the years, I put up with a lot of shit: heartbreak, grief, turmoil, trauma—you name it, I've been there. But I have no regrets, because Jeff falls under the 'some things happen for a reason' category. Without him and all the bad that came with it, I wouldn't have Nate and all the incredible that comes with *him*."

He remained silent, and for once, it didn't piss me off.

I understood why he was pissed. Dylan and Angela had had similar reactions when I'd confessed the depths of Jeff's abuse. On some levels, it was sweet that Truett was so protective. But I'd just had amazing sex with a gorgeous man who touched me with love and care, who had promised to work on himself so we could then work on a future together the way it was always supposed to be.

The last thing I wanted was to be discussing Jeff fucking Weaver and his dumpster fire of issues.

Standing up, I slowly made my way over to Truett. I pressed up onto my toes for an all-too-brief kiss. "I love you. I'm sorry that beautiful moment we shared ended with this conversation, but it's done. He can't hurt me anymore." I patted him on the chest and pleaded with my eyes for him to let this go. "We have a lot to do today, so I'm going to go take a shower. We can grab some lunch and then head to the restaurant. Okay?"

He stood there, stone-faced as his jaw ticked at the hinges, obviously still so pissed it was hard to breathe the same air. But he didn't delay in replying with, "I love you too. More than you will ever know."

I grinned. "You shower already?"

He shook his head.

Walking my fingers up his still bare chest, I teased, "Well, I've been giving a lot of thought to water conservation recently. Maybe you should come join me. You know. For the environment."

A ghost of a smile flitted over his mouth. "You go ahead. I need a few minutes."

Disappointed, I pressed one last kiss to his lips and then left him standing in my living room.

When I came back downstairs twenty minutes later, he was gone.

And so was my car.

CHAPTER TWENTY-SIX

TRUETT

I LOVED THAT GWEN HAD SUCH A LOGICAL AND COMPOSED attitude about the way that asshole had treated her. She had her son to focus on. It was obvious he had become her beacon of light in the darkness.

I, however, wasn't so forgiving. Abuse was abuse, and it did not sit well with me that this piece of shit had gotten off scot-free. He was out there, living his life, while she was saddled with the memories of throwing up after sex.

I would never win husband of the year.

I'd failed her on every front.

But not that one.

Never that one.

A quick Google search of his name brought up a bio for a law firm only five minutes away. The prick still had a picture of her and Nate on his "about me" page.

I couldn't just stand by and do nothing, so when I saw her keys on the kitchen counter, I took it as a sign.

Fury, molten hot and unrestrained, raced through my veins as I flung the door open and stalked into the lobby. A sign that read *Weaver, Lowry, and Dixon* hung on the wall above the front desk. The older woman sitting behind it looked up with a smile on her face that fell the moment she caught sight of me.

“Jeff Weaver,” I spat, the name burning as it tore from my throat.

Her eyes widened as she glanced down the hall and then back to me. “He’s, uh, in a meeting. Can I take a message?”

The only message he would be getting from me would be delivered in person.

Veering right, I marched down the hall in the direction she had inadvertently indicated.

“Sir! You can’t go back there! Sir!” Her frantic voice echoed behind me, but I paid her no mind.

Conveniently, the first door on the right had a gold plate engraved with his name. With the door cracked open, I could hear voices coming from inside. I gave exactly zero fucks if I was interrupting something. I shoved the door open and stalked inside—a predator on the prowl.

He was the only one in the room, sitting reclined in a leather office chair, his feet propped up on a large ornate wooden desk. Behind him was a wall of framed diplomas that probably made him feel superior, feeding his apparent case of little man syndrome. I clocked the wall of windows to my right, and to the left of his desk were bookshelves, filled to the brim. They rattled when I slammed the door behind me and locked it in one swift motion.

He sat up, his feet finding the floor as he snapped, “Who the fuck are you?”

“Excuse me?” A voice came through the speaker of the phone positioned on the corner of the desk. I snatched it up, ripping out the wiring as I launched it across the room.

“Hey!” he shouted with all the confidence a five-foot-five man wearing penny loafers could possess. “Have you lost your damn mind?”

“Yep,” I clipped, rounding the desk. I fisted the front of his yuppy-ass button-down shirt with one hand and dragged him to his feet. Bending, I brought my face just inches from his and growled, "You fucking piece of shit!"

He squirmed like the weasel he was, but my hold on him was rock solid. "Get your fucking hands off me!" He shoved at my shoulders, trying to free himself, but I spun, kicking blindly at his office chair. It sailed across the room, slamming into the bookshelf as I pinned him against the wall. His head cracked on a diploma, sending it crashing to the floor.

"What? You don't like being touched without permission?" I seethed.

"What the fuck is your problem, man?" He tried again to escape my grasp, his pathetic attempts only fueling my rage. "Patty!" he shouted, craning his neck toward the door. "Call the fucking police!"

The knob rattled as who I could only assume was the receptionist trying to get into the office. Her voice was laced with fear as she responded, "They're on the way!"

"You better hope they're fast." I spoke with such an eerie calm I barely recognized my own voice.

"What the hell is wrong with you?"

"Oh, this isn't about me." I shook him, his back hitting the wall as a button flew from his shirt. Angling my face down to his, I leveled him with a hard stare. "Let me make myself perfectly clear. You so much as breathe the same air as Gwendolyn Pierce and I will rip your skull from your spineless torso."

"Gwen?" It took but a split second for him to put the pieces together, and once he did, he let out a sardonic laugh. "Truett West. We meet at last. Christ, you're even more of a lunatic than I'd heard." Spittle flew from his lips as he leaned into me. "Stupid too. Did you not see the sign when you walked in? Do you have any idea who the hell I am?"

I wouldn't have cared if the sign had said *President of the United*

States. There was nothing on my mind except all the ways I was going to make him pay for what he had done to Gwen.

"I know who you are. You're the troll under the bridge who thought it was okay to touch a woman even after she said no." With another violent shake, I slanted my head, our noses practically touching. "Let's see you force yourself on me."

He smirked. "You're not my type, but I do appreciate the offer. By the way, you got it wrong. Gwen's last name is Weaver. Not Pierce. And sure as fuck not *West*."

The fury that had been simmering in my gut grew into a rolling boil. "Big man, huh? Only way you can get some is to force yourself on a woman."

Smug arrogance coated his every word. "I've never had to force myself on anyone, least of all, my *wife*. I'm sure you remember how marriage works."

"Yeah, asshole, I do. I remember that being married meant both people consented and no one ever threw up when it was over."

He scoffed. "I don't know what lies she told you. She loved everything thing I did to her. Fucking begged for it. She's just looking for an excuse to make herself feel better about how she ruined her life when she walked away from me."

The sheer lunacy of his statement forced laughter from my throat. "You're out of your Goddamn mind if you think she regrets leaving you."

His dark eyes sparkled. His twisted ass was enjoying this. And they called me crazy.

"You're delusional, man. With me, she was taken care of. She didn't have to spend all day and night in that dump of a diner. I was the one who took care of the bills, made sure she had what she needed. Which, from what I've heard, is a hell of a lot more than you ever gave her. No surprise, she took care of me in return." A vile grin stretched across his face. "Been a long time since you were with her, but I doubt you've forgotten how good she is at satisfying a man."

Bile surged up the back of my throat as I thought about my Gwen, soft and sweet, ever having to be touched by this monster. Much less spending a fucking decade with him.

Jeff Weaver was the worst kind of human. He thought he was a smooth talker, born with a silver spoon in his ass, someone who had never been held accountable for his actions. He'd spent his entire marriage getting away with any and everything he wanted, abusing the woman he was supposed to love and protect all for his own selfish and despicable pleasures.

Like a scene from a movie playing out in my head, I thought about how I was going to relish my hands giving him back all the pain he'd caused her.

His grunts as my fist connected with his nose.

His cartilage crunching under my knuckles.

His pleas for me to stop.

I reared a fist back, my arm tingling in anticipation.

Before I could even begin to swing, the office door flew open with a crack. "Police!"

In an instant, two men were on me, pulling me away. I fought the urge to shake them off and finish what I had gone there to do, but nothing would change him. And if I was locked in a cell for the better part of my life, I couldn't protect her. It was less than a second before I was face down on the office floor, my hands wrenched behind my back.

"Don't fight me!" an officer yelled, his knee in my back. "Put your hands together and don't move."

Despite the adrenaline still surging within me, I did as I had been told.

Cuffs clicked around my wrists, and then the pressure on my back eased when two officers each grabbed a bicep, helping me to my feet.

"Anyone want to tell me what's going on?" the younger officer asked.

"He's a psycho who just burst into my office and assaulted me."

The older cop with a thick gray mustache arched an eyebrow. "Any particular reason?"

"He thought he could put his hands on my woman," I replied. "I thought he should know otherwise. You got here one swing too soon."

"Your woman?" Jeff scoffed. "You should really take him in for a psych eval before hauling his ass to the jail."

The cop hit me with a glower. "Sounds like we got here just in time. You got any ID?"

"No, sir," I said, never tearing my eyes off the pretentious garden gnome in the corner.

"You got a name, then?"

"Truett West."

The cop's eyes flared with recognition, while the other let out a low whistle from behind me.

"You screwing with me?" he asked.

"No, sir."

"Dammit. This is not what I wanted to do with my day," he mumbled under his breath. He looked at Jeff. "Do you need medical attention?"

Insult pinched between his eyes. "This pussy ruined my favorite shirt, but that's about it."

The cop frowned, his eyes narrowing. "You mind watching your mouth?"

"Actually, I do," Jeff replied like the smug bastard he was.

The cop's face got hard. "I'm not going to ask you again. Shut your mouth."

He held Jeff's stare for a long second, and unfortunately, he actually closed his gaping asshole of a mouth.

"Right." The cop nodded, tugging on my arm. "You come

outside with me. Darren, you stay here and get Mr. Weaver's statement."

My feet shuffled after him, but before I exited the office, I issued one last warning. "You come near Gwen again, and I'll put your ass in the ground where you belong."

Pure evil twinkled in his eyes as a venomous smile curled his lips. "You mean, like you did with your daughter?"

My vision flashed red, blood roaring in my ears, and the room around me disappeared as every ounce of restraint I'd ever possessed was gone in an instant.

A blinding rage detonated inside me. Stripping my arm from the cop's grasp, I bolted toward him with my hands still cuffed behind my back. I hit him with my chest, slamming him into the wall. The pleasure I felt when the fear he couldn't hide transformed his face was only second to the sound of his nose cracking as I headbutted him so hard it made my head spin.

The cops tackled me from behind again and the air rushed from my lungs as I landed on the floor, face down.

"Stay down." The older officer came down on top of me and growled in my ear, "Do not make me tase you, West. One more move and you're going to have more problems than I can help you with."

My chest heaved as I fought to catch a breath. The wild desire to get my hands on that monster ricocheted inside me, destroying me from the inside out.

"You fucking nutjob!" Jeff roared. "I swear to God, you will rot in prison for this."

"Hey!" the younger cop snapped. "Not another word or you're walking out of here in cuffs too."

"Me?" he whined.

A grin split my mouth as I caught sight of blood pouring from his nose.

As my pulse slowed, adrenaline ebbing from my system,

logical thought won out and I forced my mind to ignore the bitter outrage still churning inside me.

"Listen," the cop said. "You're gonna push to your knees and then you're gonna stand. When you do, do not so much as look in his direction. You got me?"

I grunted my agreement and the officers once again pulled me to my feet. I kept my head down, knowing that if I caught sight of him again, their threats to tase me would become promises they would have to follow through on.

Murmurs followed as I was led away, but I kept my gaze trained on my feet, focusing on each step so I could block out the sound of his words replaying in my head.

The officer guided me past a small group of employees gathered in the lobby and through the front doors.

I didn't feel guilty. Not one fucking ounce. Maybe that made me a monster too, but I'd put on a green mask and talons every day of my life if that was what was required, because no one had ever deserved a headbutt more.

As I walked to the squad car, I saw a pair of brown leather shoes trot up beside me. "Truett, would you like to comment on what happened in there?"

My head snapped up and I saw Taggart Folly beside me, a mic in his outstretched hand. A cameraman trailed behind him, trying to keep up.

Fuck.

What the hell was Folly doing there?

And how long had he been recording?

The windows in Jeff's office had been wide open. If Gwen was right and Folly was looking for something juicy to use in his documentary, my going off half-cocked would give him everything he needed.

It was only that realization that caused any form of regret to sink in.

Good Lord, I'd spent eighteen years locked away, keeping to myself, and staying out of the public eye. And now I was suddenly flanked by officers, more than likely being arrested for assault.

Though I'd also spent eighteen years without Gwen, and for ten of them, she'd been in the arms of that maniac.

As I slid into the cold plastic back seat, handcuffs biting into my wrists, an unlikely smile split my mouth.

Worth it. So fucking worth it.

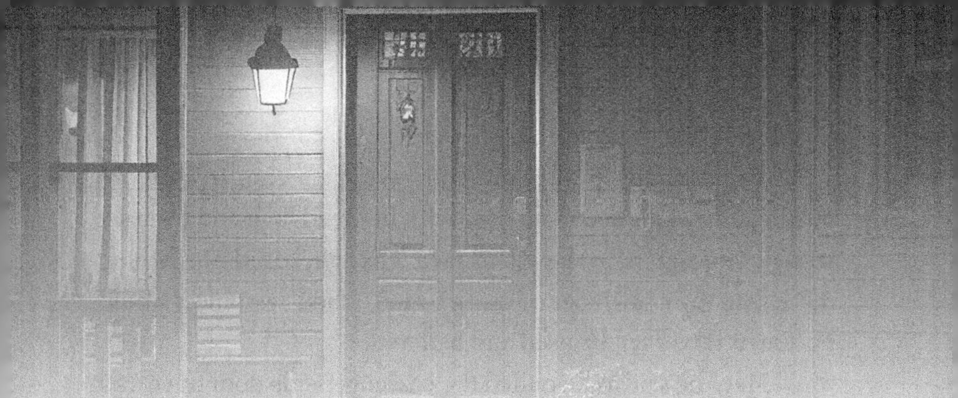

CHAPTER TWENTY-SEVEN

Gwen

I CUSSED UNDER MY BREATH AS I WATCHED TRUETT WALK through the heavy iron door of the county jail. He scanned the parking lot, looking for my car as I sat there trying to figure out if I was more pissed or concerned to be picking up one ex-husband after he'd stolen my car and gone to pick a fight with my other ex-husband.

I mean, seriously. How was this my life?

I didn't know all the details of what had gone down, just that there had been some kind of altercation at Jeff's office. He'd called me and told me a wild story in which he was as innocent as a choir boy and Truett was a maniac who had broken his nose. But Jeff was about as reliable as a snake in the grass, so when I tried to question him, he resorted to yelling and blaming me for the entire thing. I only let him call me a lying whore once before I hung up on him. So yeah, that was fun.

I'd immediately called the police station, where they had confirmed that Truett was in custody, but they wouldn't tell me anything else. So then I called Dylan, who gave me the number of her uncle's best friend's brother who just happened to be a bail bondsman. She assured me he could figure it out.

And then finally, thirty minutes earlier, I'd gotten a call from Truett asking me if I could come pick him up from the jail.

It was safe to say my nerves were *shot*.

Truett finally spotted me and gave me a chin jerk before heading my way. He walked over with his head high and his back straight, no sign of injury to his face. Though, based on nothing more than my knowledge of the two men, I didn't assume it would be Truett who'd left bruised and battered.

"Hey," he said as he pulled the passenger-side door open and folded his large body into my SUV.

I pressed my lips together and bit the inside of my cheek, hoping to find some composure. But seriously, I was picking up one ex-husband after he'd stolen my car and gone to pick a fight with my other ex-husband. I was way, way, *way* too old for this shit.

My voice dripped with sarcasm as I smarted, "Well, hello, inmate seven-oh-seven. How were your adventures in lockup?"

He shrugged. "Pretty boring, actually. They made me sit in an office and refused to change the TV channel to anything other than old game shows. They did order burgers for lunch though, so I guess it wasn't all bad."

I blinked at him. "What? They didn't throw you in the slammer and force you to use a communal toilet with all the drunks and criminals?"

He chuckled. "You look disappointed."

"Uh, yeah. That's because I am. I had to Uber to the impound lot, where they informed me they only took cash and the nearest ATM was a twenty-minute walk. So I had to call *another* Uber to take me there, get the cash, go back, and get my car, then drive across town to a bail bondsman's office. And let me just tell you, that was an experience I *never* want to repeat.

"There, they too informed me they only took cash, so I had to drive to another ATM, where it denied my transaction because I'd already reached my daily withdrawal limit, so I had to call the bank, get that sorted out, and then finally drive back to the bail bondsman's office, where I frantically begged them to get you out as soon as possible, all because I was worried out of my mind that they had locked you up in the slammer and forced you to use a communal toilet with the drunks and criminals."

I was out of breath by the time I finished, but not out of frustration. "So yeah, I guess I am kind of disappointed you got to spend the day watching *Family Feud* and eating burgers."

He flashed his eyes wide, his lips twitching with humor. "You done yet?"

I scoffed. "No! I just picked you up from *jail.* It's going to be a long time before I'm done. I highly suggest you start talking before my anger turns to violence and I unleash the world's harshest titty twister on you."

His hands jumped to cover his nipples, but that damn man grinned at me. "Okay, okay. Relax. I'll pay you back for the impound fees, and if you put your titty-twisting fingers away, Troy gave me back the bail money. It's in my pocket."

I slapped my hand on the steering wheel. "Who the hell is Troy?"

"He works for the bond company."

"And they just gave you back the money? I'm pretty sure that's not how bond works."

"It's a small town. I think they make their own rules. Besides, he's friends with Don."

"And *Don* would be who?"

He leaned back in his seat, getting comfortable, and extended his arm to prop his hand on my headrest. "The cop who arrested me."

"Oh, so you guys are all buddy-buddy, on a first-name basis now?"

"Something like that. Hey, I need to go back to my place so I can change. I smell like burnt coffee," he said with all the casual coolness of a man who'd asked me to pass the ketchup.

My temper finally snapped. "Jesus, Truett. Say something that makes sense. What the hell were you thinking, storming over there and punching him in the face?"

He lifted a finger. "First of all, I did not punch him. Secondly, I was thinking that he was a piece of shit and he needed to be treated as such."

"He's an attorney! He knows every judge in this town. You're going to be lucky if he doesn't convince them to try you for attempted murder at this point."

He barked a loud laugh. "I hope that fucker does. They issued me a trespass warning and told me to stay away from him. I hardly think I'm headed to trial."

Even more confused, I cupped my hand around my ear. "I'm sorry, what?"

"A trespass warning. It's kind of like a ticket, I guess. I don't know. I zoned out for a while when Don was explaining it. Don't worry. It won't go on my record or anything."

I drew in a deep breath, trying to find a Zen that I wasn't sure existed in a clusterfuck the size of the continental United States. "Could you *please* explain to me how Jeff ended up with a potentially broken nose and you only got a trespass warning?"

His grin fell. "Yeah, I don't want to talk about that."

I briefly wondered if anyone had ever sprained an eyelid from blinking too hard or if I was going to become the first. "Either you talk or you're walking home. I'm not sitting in the dark on this one. And I dare you to ask me to."

He held my challenging gaze for a few seconds before relenting. "Fine. Between me and you, I headbutted him. He deserved worse, but I was already in cuffs. Don recognized my name. His sister survived the mall that day, so he wasn't real happy to be arresting me in the first place."

I sucked in a sharp breath. "She was…there?"

"Yeah, and it made me uncomfortable as fuck to have him thank me. I only managed not to tear out of my own skin because it probably saved me felony assault and resisting arrest charges. After the shit your ex spewed, the whole damn police department was willing to turn a blind eye."

I sucked in a sharp breath, the desire to ask the question almost as strong as the fear of hearing the answer. "What did he say to you?"

The leather of his seat squeaked as he shifted uncomfortably. "You gotta raise a kid with that man. I'm going to need you to trust me when I say that is *not* something you want to hear."

"Oh, God," I breathed.

Truett reached out and grabbed my hand. "Now he knows I'm at your back. And I'm going to sleep a hell of a lot easier because of it."

As much as the caveman routine turned me off, there was something about the conviction in his voice that made my stomach dip. "I need you to promise me that won't happen again."

He let out a strangled laugh. "I can't promise that, Gwen. You and me make this work, I see a lot of issues in mine and Garden Gnome Jeff's future."

I pulled my hand from his. "Then you and me are *not* making this work."

His eyebrows shot up to his forehead. "Come again?"

"Truett, I despise that man. But he's Nate's dad. I swore to myself that, no matter what happened between me and Jeff, I would not let it affect Nate. Jeff is an awful human being, but I will not feed into that in front of my son. And I refuse to be with someone who can't do the same. If we go the long run, you're going to have to attend birthdays and graduations and weddings with that man. I can't have you showing up and acting a fool because Jeff decides to act like the dick he will always be."

He pinched the bridge of his nose. "Shit. I'm sorry." Dropping his hand, he reached over the center console and intertwined our fingers. "I'm not gonna lie and say that I regret it, because I think that fucker deserved worse than I could ever dole out. But I hear what you're saying and can respect that Nate's more important than whatever feelings I may have about that prick. It won't happen again."

"You sure? Jeff is a master when it comes to slinging low blows and then playing the victim."

"Oh, I more than learned that today. But yeah, I'm sure. I can keep myself in check. I can't promise I won't talk shit behind closed doors, but the last thing I want is to make things harder for you or your boy."

Relief filtered through me. Had the roles been reversed, Jeff never would have been able to do the same. And I had a sneaking suspicion Jeff wasn't going to be happy about Truett only getting a trespass warning, but I was very adept at blocking his phone number.

"I do like talking shit behind closed doors."

Truett grinned, bringing our joined hands to his mouth. "I like doing anything and *everything* with you behind closed doors."

My cheeks heated as I whispered, "I like that too."

Chuckling, he kissed my hand. "You pissed at me or are you still good if I stay with you again tonight?"

I bit my bottom lip. "Two nights in a row? You sure you're ready for that?"

His face got serious. "It's weird. In order for Kaitlyn to exist inside that house, you have to be gone. I don't know what happens from here. There's a lot of stuff that needs to be done that I am nowhere near ready for, but I don't want you to be gone anymore."

I stared at him, hope swirling in my chest. I didn't want to be gone anymore, either. "Okay," I whispered.

"Can we swing by my place and let me grab some clothes?"

"Of course." I flashed him a mischievous grin. "But just so you know, I am also still pissed at you because I got absolutely nothing done today. So if you're staying with me, you better strap in and see if you can reset that internal alarm clock, because it's going to be a late night working at the restaurant."

"Fair enough." He laughed.

We chitchatted on the way to his house, his hand anchored to my thigh the entire drive. He refused to tell me what Jeff had said, but he did give me a play-by-play of driving for the first time in almost two decades. Let's just say it is not like riding a bike, and he had some seriously big opinions about auto manufacturers replacing the gearshift with buttons.

When I pulled up in front of his house, I put the car into park and then waited for him to get out. For a long moment, he sat there staring at the house. I had no idea what was going through his mind, but I gave him the time to work through it on his own.

His voice was gruff as he asked, "Do you ever think about the last time we saw each other?" He flicked his gaze from me to the house we'd shared all those years ago. "You said you'd hate me forever as you dropped your rings on the floor. The sound of them hitting the hardwood echoed in my living room for years." He shifted in his seat so that his body was angled toward me and reached for my left hand. "I never imagined you'd change your mind."

I sighed, the pain of that memory suddenly fresh as the day it had happened. "I didn't change my mind, nor was that the last time I saw you."

"What do you mean?" His thumb rubbed circles over the back of my hand as he watched me intently.

"It was the first Fourth of July after we lost Kaitlyn. I got a call in the middle of the night that you were passed out in front of that house those college kids used to rent every summer."

Truett's eyes widened. "Oh, God."

My heart twisted as the memory of him lying in the grass, wearing nothing but a white T-shirt and ratty gym shorts slammed into me. He'd always been larger than life, a big man who had made me feel safe. But that night, when I'd arrived, he'd looked so small, as if the weight of his grief had physically caused him to shrink.

I swallowed the lump that had formed in the back of my throat. "They were doing what all twenty-something guys do: drinking and shooting off fireworks. Apparently, after you downed a bottle of whiskey, you stumbled over there yelling gibberish. One of the kids recognized you and made them stop the fireworks, and after that, you just sat down and passed out. Your phone was in your pocket and I was still programmed in as "Wifey," so they called me instead of calling the cops. Some of the guys helped me drag you back to the house, and once you were settled on the couch, I locked the door and swore that I would never answer another call in the middle of the night again."

Truett groaned, scrubbing his hand down his face. "Fuck. I don't remember any of that. I was drinking a lot back then."

"Okay, but you told me last night that you don't drink anymore."

He shook his head.

"Why not?" I asked.

"I don't know. I guess I realized it didn't help anymore. After a while, it just gave me more anxiety and made everything worse. So I quit."

"Right. So I meant what I said that day, about hating you for the rest of your life. But you aren't the same man I walked out on any more than you are the guy I had to drag off of the neighbor's lawn." I pushed my hand into his hair, gently scraping my nails on his scalp. "You're trying to get better and I can see it. That's all I've ever wanted from you, True. Effort. Just a little bit of effort."

He wrapped his hand around the back of my neck, pulling my face to his, and softly grazed his lips over mine. "I'm trying, Gwen. I swear on my life, I'm going to keep trying every single day."

His mouth was on mine in a flash, his tongue licking at the seam of my lips, begging for entry. I gave him what we both so desperately wanted. As our tongues rolled together, I relished the taste of his hunger for me. It matched my own desire for him, a fire he'd ignited a lifetime ago that had never been extinguished.

Fisting my hair, he anchored my head in place, deepening our kiss. He poured every ounce of regret for his actions that day, and all the days before, into me, his expert mouth reassuring me that he was working hard through his demons.

When he was finished apologizing through the warmth of his kiss, he gently pulled away, his eyes hazy and lust filled. The hand at the back of my head trailed down my arm before his fingers laced with mine.

"Go get your stuff." I looked over his shoulder, dread filling me as I thought about him getting out of my car to walk into his house alone. A home that was filled with heartbreaking memories and utterly empty. I paused, weighing the likelihood of disappointment in his answer before I finally said, "Tomorrow's Wednesday, True."

He flashed me a tight smile. "I know. I'll be with you. It's okay."

"And what about tomorrow night? I'll have Nate, so I won't be going to the restaurant."

His forehead wrinkled. "Oh, right. Maybe you can drop me off before you pick him up?"

"Or, you can stay. He's been begging for hot wings ever since Lucille introduced him to them. We could order dinner and just hang out."

His eyes flared, uncertainty lining his brow. "Would that be weird—I mean, for him? Meeting the new man in Mom's life?"

I laughed. "You aren't new, silly. He knows who you are."

"He does?"

"Truett, I didn't erase you or Kaitlyn from my life. Nate's always known about his sister, and in turn, her father. The two of you have never been a secret in my house."

Truett's fingers flexed in mine, his grasp growing even tighter. A sad smile crept across his face and I wondered if meeting my other child would be painful for him. Maybe I was putting too much pressure on him too soon? It had been quite the day of firsts for him already. Maybe this was one step too far.

"You can say no. The invitation is always open. It doesn't have to be tomorrow."

His strong shoulders rose as he drew in a deep breath. "I could go for wings."

Relief mixed with excitement fluttered in my belly. "Okay, then. Grab enough clothes for two nights, I guess."

He nodded, and I could tell he wasn't completely comfortable with the idea, but no one could deny that the man wasn't trying.

"I'll be right back." With a sweet brush of his lips across mine, he pushed the passenger door open and climbed out.

I rolled down the window, and as I watched him jog up the steps, I shouted, "Hey! You got any shirts with stripes? Maybe we could do a little guard and convict role-play!"

CHAPTER TWENTY-EIGHT

TRUETT

I WAS PACING GWEN'S LIVING ROOM WHEN I HEARD HER CAR pull into the driveway.

She'd left to pick up Nate about twenty minutes earlier and I'd been a bag of nerves ever since. I'd lost my only daughter, but I was no stranger to children. Daniel had two boys who occasionally came over to the house with him and I loved the hell out of those heathens.

This was different though. It was always a big deal for a woman to introduce a man to her kids. The pressure to make a good first impression. The balance of trying to be fun and witty so they like you, but not so fun and witty they didn't respect you. I'd never personally been the adult in that situation, but I'd met a few of my mom's boyfriends over the years.

I'd hated them all.

They weren't bad guys or anything. They were just random people I had little interest in getting to know.

But this was Gwen's kid. The stakes had never been higher.

"I win!" The door swung open and a little boy wearing a white T-shirt and a blue striped bathing suit came barreling inside.

My lungs seized as I took him in. He was Gwen's clone. From his dark hair and eyes to her nose and full lips, he looked just like her. Which also meant he looked just like Kaitlyn. It had stolen my breath when I'd seen him that first time at the restaurant, but after seeing so many pictures of him all over Gwen's house, I hadn't thought it would hit me as hard.

I was wrong.

"Who are you?" he asked as he came to a screeching halt in the foyer.

My throat was thick, but I managed to reply. "I'm Truett."

Gwen had told him I was going to be there the night before when they'd talked on the phone. From what I'd heard of his response, he'd been excited. That was one of the only reasons I hadn't hitchhiked home in the last twenty minutes.

He scanned me from head to toe, looking more than just a little disappointed. "No, you aren't."

Gwen came in behind him and shut and locked the door. "Dude, could you slow down? I'm getting too old to keep up with you."

He tilted his head back and looked up at her. "That's not Truett."

She twisted her lips. "I'm pretty sure it is."

"Then what's wrong with his face?" he asked as if I weren't standing directly in front of him.

Gwen bumped him with her hip. "Hey! Stop being rude. It's called a beard. I promise it's still Truett under there."

Slowly, he walked over to me, his lips pursed and his gaze skeptical. He circled around me like a guard dog sniffing someone new. He lifted my arm, inspecting my tattoos, and only then did he seem convinced.

"Oh, hey, Truett," he chirped.

"Hi," I replied stiffly.

Speak, asshole. It's a child. Don't freeze up now.

I cleared my throat. Ah yes, the bribery portion of the evening. "I brought you a little something."

"A present? It's not even my birthday! You're the best!"

I grinned as I snagged the gift bag off the couch.

It took him no time to tear out the tissue paper Gwen had added, his face falling into a deep frown as he examined the present. "Mom! Seriously?"

I cut my eyes to Gwen just in time to watch her stifle a smile.

"Truett, you shouldn't have!" she feigned surprise.

Perplexed, I stared at her. She'd sat with me on Amazon the night before and helped me pick out a gift I could have delivered the following day.

Nate turned the box over in his hands, disgust curling his mouth as he pinned his mother with a glare. "A pressed flower kit? You made him get this, didn't you?"

I flared my eyes at her. "You said he'd asked for that."

She laughed. "Well, I thought you'd like that. We haven't done one of those before."

Nate groaned but turned his attention back to me. "Uh, thanks for the gift."

I scowled at Gwen. "There's something else in there too. Something *I* picked out."

With much less enthusiasm than before, he took the present and unwrapped it slowly, a fake smile plastered on his face. But when he read the writing on the box, the smile morphed into a full-on grin. "Is this that jellybean game where some of them taste like grass and boogers?"

I proudly nodded.

"I've been wanting this!" He bounded over and threw his arms around my waist.

I turned to stone immediately, but something deep inside of me also relaxed. The hug lasted less than a few seconds, but his excitement lingered.

"Mom, look! You have to eat them and you don't know what you're gonna get!" He held it up just inches from her face. "Can we play it? After dinner? Please?"

Disgust turned the corner of her mouth down, but she skirted the question and announced, "We'll see. But first, you need to go take a shower."

"I already took a shower. I used soap and everything!"

She rolled her eyes. "You poured dish soap on an old blue tarp and then spent two hours sliding with your friends."

Serious as a heart attack, he replied, "Yeah. That's the same thing."

Gwen barked a laugh as she moved my way. She placed a quick peck on my cheek before asking, "Dear Lord, what is it about boys that gives them such an aversion to personal hygiene?"

Nate glanced between the two of us, not a sliver of concern on his face, and with that, the ball of nerves I'd been battling loosened its grip.

"I don't know, Gwen. Soap and water usually equals a shower in my book." I winked at Nate.

His eyes lit up. "Yeah, Mom. See? Even Truett agrees with me!"

She shot me a scowl, but it held no heat. "Mmhm. You still have grass on your feet, kid."

With a quick swipe of his hand, he brushed the blades onto the floor. "There. All gone."

"Get in the shower, Nate."

His head fell back. "But I wanna hang out with Truett!"

I was well aware that it was a ploy to get him out bathing, but it still struck a chord deep within me.

Gwen wasn't wrong. I'd been a boy once too and showering sucked. But it didn't have to be a total downer.

"Hey, what's the fastest you've ever taken a shower?" I asked.

He shrugged. "I don't know."

I leaned to the side and checked the oven timer. "Those wings have seven minutes left, and let me just tell you, they look incredible. Definitely not the kind you want to eat cold. Seven minutes probably isn't enough time for you to take a shower and get dressed though."

"Yeah, it is!" he exclaimed with a big goofy grin. "I can do it in three minutes!"

"No way?"

"You wanna time me?" he asked, discarding his gifts on the couch.

I scoffed. "Absolutely. How many times do people get to witness a world record in real life?"

"Yesss!" he hissed, and then right there beside me, in the middle of the living room, he got down on all fours in what I assumed was supposed to be a runner's stance. "Okay, okay. I'm ready. Tell me when to go."

I pressed a few buttons on my watch until the stopwatch popped up. "On your mark, get set…" I drew it out for a long second to rile him up. "Go!"

He took off like he'd been shot out of a cannon, nearly knocking over the lamp on the end table as he turned the corner.

As his feet pounded up the stairs, I looked back and found Gwen smiling at me.

"You do know he's not going to wash anything while he's in there."

I hooked her around the shoulders and pulled her into my side. "He's already soaped up. A rinse should still do the job."

She laughed and pressed up onto her toes, brushing her lips with mine.

I kissed her back, long and deep, sliding my hand down to her ass while we didn't have little eyes around. It was the wrong damn time to get myself worked up, so I begrudgingly released her mouth.

"Any issues picking him up?" I asked.

"Surprisingly, no. Jeff just stood at the door without uttering a word."

"Smart man," I mumbled.

"I wouldn't go that far, but here's to hoping whatever you said to him actually got through."

"How'd his face look?"

She laughed and headed to the kitchen. "A little swelling, but there was no bruising or anything. I'm gonna go out on a very short limb and say it's definitely not broken."

I followed, muttering, "Shame."

She pinned me with a glare, and I lifted my hands in surrender, pointing one finger up at the ceiling.

"He's behind closed doors, which means we're technically behind closed doors too. It's the only time I'm allowed to talk shit, remember?"

"Nate didn't mention it though. I figured Jeff would have gone home bragging about how he'd bested a maniac. He really likes to be the hero."

"Well, that makes one of us," I mumbled.

She shook her head and opened the oven. A whiff of orange came floating out as she peeked inside.

I sniffed the air. "I thought you said those were buffalo wings?"

"They are, but I decided to try my hand at spicy citrus wings too. I figured they'd be something fun I could do at The Rosewood for a trivia night or a happy hour special."

I sat down on the stool closest to her. "If they taste half as good as they smell, you'll have a line wrapped around the building."

"Fingers crossed." She turned to me and wedged her hips between my legs, resting her hands on my thighs. "It's almost six. How are you feeling about not being in the booth?"

"Jesus, woman. Stop asking me that. We discussed this. I'm with you and I don't hurt when I'm with you." I leaned forward, pressing a reverent kiss to her lips. "Unless you make me spend another four hours installing ceiling fans that outweigh you. I'm sore as shit today."

She giggled. "That's what you get for stealing my car."

"I borrowed it. Kinda like how you borrow me for manual labor and eye candy."

She threw her head back, laughing. "Damn, you figured me out."

Suddenly, there was a stampede on her stairwell, and I turned in time to see Nate leap from the third step, tripping over his own feet as he stumbled through an imaginary finish line.

He fell dramatically to the floor, panting as he asked, "What was my time?"

Grinning like a fool, I looked down at my watch.

It read: four minutes and thirty-eight seconds.

Carefully moving Gwen from in front of me, I jumped to my feet. Throwing my hands over my head, I spoke in my best sports announcer's voice and lied. "Two minutes and thirty-eight seconds. Ladies and gentlemen, we have a new world record!"

Nate pumped his fist from the floor, basking in his victory.

I froze when a flash illuminated from the corner of my eye.

It wasn't gunfire.

It wasn't Folly.

It was Gwen, her phone held high, snapping pictures of her son—and me. Memories trapped forever, all because I finally walked out of my house.

For that alone, I celebrated my own victory.

Rushing toward her, I bent low and folded her over my shoulder. "And the crowd goes wild!" I roared, carrying her around the kitchen.

Nate rolled in hysterics as Gwen slapped me on the butt, demanding I put her down. She joined me for the chorus of Queen's "We Are the Champions," so I figured I wasn't going to be in too much trouble as I added another lap around the living room.

Nate cheered.

Gwen laughed.

And I felt a piece of my soul heal for the very first time in eighteen years.

A timer sounded from the kitchen, ending our celebration, but the evening was just getting started.

"Did your tattoos hurt?" Nate asked, chowing down on a chicken wing.

"Some of them did," I answered, my fingers sticky with the most delicious spicy citrus sauce ever to be invented. People weren't just going to be wrapped around the building; they were going to be wrapped around the city.

"Which one's your favorite?" He spoke around a mouthful of food.

Gwen patted his arm. "Finish chewing before you talk, please."

He nodded and then peered at me expectantly.

"Oof, that's a tough question," I replied. "I got them at such different times in my life that it's almost like a history book about me. But I guess, if you forced me to choose, it would be this one." I wiped my hands on my napkin and then lifted the side of my shirt.

Nate hurried around the table and then squatted so he could get a better look at my side. It was a tiger, its head three times the size of the rest of its body, and a pink squiggly line acting as a tutu was wrapped around its stomach. There were only four black stripes on its entire orange body, but at the end of each stick leg were large silver dots meant to be sparkly shoes.

Nate's mouth fell open. "Is that Fiona Iona?"

Then my mouth fell open. "How do you know that?" When Gwen giggled, I craned my head back to look at her. "How does he know that?"

"Hey, bud. Take Truett to see the playroom while I start cleaning up."

He excitedly tugged on my arm, and despite the fact that I had two wings left, I was shocked enough to follow him.

He guided me down the hall, past the bathroom, to a closed

door. His nose wrinkled as he looked up at me. "It's kinda messy, but just pretend it's not, okay?"

Little did he know, I was a master pretender. "Okay."

He swung the door open, and he was correct. It was a mess, which was most likely why Gwen kept the door shut.

There was a loveseat that took up most of the room, toys lining the floor around it. But on the walls were frames holding children's art like they were being displayed in a gallery, complete with little plaques beneath them listing the title and artist. Half of them were Kaitlyn's, the other half Nate's.

I could barely breathe as I stared at them. All of them, not just Kaitlyn's.

Gwen kept her alive in a house where there was laughter and happiness, while I'd kept her locked in a home where the only sound for several years had been me waking up screaming from nightmares.

Nate jumped up onto the loveseat, pointing to the top row. "See, Fiona Iona."

It wasn't the same exact drawing as the one I'd had tattooed on my side. Different squiggled tutu, a few more stripes, but it was definitely Fiona Iona.

I stood there staring as I felt Gwen appear behind me.

She ducked under my arm and curled into my side. "I told you we didn't forget about her."

I drew in a shaky breath. This woman. This fucking woman. "I love you."

"I love you too," she whispered. "Hey, bud, this room is a disaster."

"Truett said it was okay. Right, True?"

True.

Everyone called me that. It was the logical nickname. But there was something about hearing him say it that, once again, hit me deep.

"Yeah, it's totally fine. Actually, it looks good if you ask me."

"See?" Nate giggled.

Gwen looked at her son. "Truett is a neat freak who folds his underwear. We're lucky he didn't have a stroke when he walked in here."

"You fold your underwear!" Nate gasped in pure horror.

I shrugged. "What can I say? Old habits die hard."

Gwen's face turned serious. "I want to show you something else we do, but I'm worried it might make you uncomfortable. Being that it's Wednesday and all, we might be pushing you too far already."

I narrowed my eyes. "I think you're more obsessed with Wednesdays than I am. I'm fine. Really."

"Okay, then. We watch old videos a few times a week. You up for that?"

I swallowed hard. Boy, did I know about watching old videos. Though I had a feeling Gwen didn't talk back, pretending she was still alive. "Yeah. I'd like that."

Together, we piled onto the couch. Nate insisted on sitting between us in his self-proclaimed spot.

Gwen grabbed the remote and turned the TV on, and within seconds, Kaitlyn's smiling face filled the screen. My heart lurched as her excited giggle floated through the speakers, her sweet voice calling my name.

"Daddy! I wanna ride that one!" Her stubby finger pointed toward a roller coaster she wasn't tall enough to ride.

The camera panned to a man I didn't recognize. "Aw, baby. That one's too big."

He was lean, clean shaven, with a high and tight haircut, his arms covered in tattoos. His shoulders back and his spine straight, he exuded a confidence that wasn't arrogant, but instead full of life.

I stared at him, my heart in my throat, trying to remember when that man had turned into the Truett of the present. Was it the day I'd left for deployment? The moment I'd lost my team? Or was it the second I'd let go of Kaitlyn for the last time?

"But, Daddy! Pwease! I just wanna ride a coaster." Kaitlyn's voice was laced with tears, and my heart squeezed, just as it had that day at the amusement park.

The young and happy version of Truett scooped her up into his arms and promised her that she'd get to ride a roller coaster—just maybe not the biggest one in the park. Gwen's laughter from the other side of the camera sent a wave of longing through me. I'd heard her laugh at least a hundred times over the last few weeks, but not like that. This was filled with carefree youth. Oblivious to the traumas headed our way.

The video cut, and when it resumed, Kaitlyn and I were seated in the front of a ride shaped like a caterpillar. Her eyes were wide, her mouth hanging open in a grin as we both turned and waved at the camera just moments before the ride started.

We were in the kiddie section, the rides all fairly tame. But this was her first experience, and by the time the caterpillar train came to a halt at the end of the tracks, Kaitlyn's wide smile had transformed into round eyes and a look of horror.

Nate giggled beside me. "This is my favorite part!"

Together, the three of us watched as I helped my daughter down the stairs, her lower lip quivering as we made our way toward Gwen, who was still standing behind the camera.

"How was it, baby?" she cooed.

Kaitlyn swallowed hard, and then without a hint of hesitation, she shouted, "I wanna do it again!"

Nate dissolved into a fit of laughter. "She looked so freaked out when she got off but then wanted to do it again! What a champ. That's my sister!"

The wind rushed from my lungs as though I'd been punched in the gut.

"That's my sister."

Of course she was his sister.

Gwen was Kaitlyn's mother, and she was Nate's mother.

But, until that very moment, it hadn't seemed real.

My baby girl had a younger brother. A brother who not only knew about her, despite never having met her, but one who was proud of her. I looked at Gwen who was eyeing me over the top of Nate's head. She offered me a soft smile that I returned as I reached for her hand.

Lacing my fingers with hers, I said, "She was a lot like you, Nate."

Nate tipped his head back at me. "Yup. Let's watch another."

For over an hour, we sat there watching home videos, many that I was in but had never seen. And with each one, I realized that I missed the carefree man who had taken his daughter to the park, snuck kisses from his wife when no one was looking, and smiled so much his cheeks had to have hurt.

Watching those movies transported me back in time to when life had been good and I had been fully alive. But the longer I sat on Gwen's couch, her son between us laughing and chatting away, the more I realized that what I'd been doing on my own couch for all these years was nothing more than an illusion.

I didn't want to live in that fantasy world anymore.

I wanted this.

Silly conversations about disgusting jellybeans.

Lighthearted debates over whether a shower was necessary every day.

Home-cooked meals shared around a table with people who were actually there.

I wanted reality. This reality.

The doorbell rang as the last home movie was ending, and Nate sprang to his feet. "I'll get it!"

I exchanged a questioning look with Gwen, and she shrugged her shoulder.

"Pike!" Nate squealed from the door. "Dude! What are you doing here?"

Gwen pressed to her feet, and I stood to follow her.

"Dylan?" she asked, her head tilted to the side. "What's up? Everything okay?"

Dylan's blue gaze darted around the living room until it landed on me, and her lips tipped up in a smile. "Yep. Everything is great." She stepped inside, closing the door behind her. "Pike's been begging for a sleepover, so I figured we'd stop by and see if Nate was free?"

Gwen cocked a brow. "Is that so? It just happens to be the same night Truett is here?"

"Weird coincidence, right?"

After having disappeared down the hall with Pike as soon as he'd come in, Nate returned with a bookbag slung over his shoulder. "I'm ready!"

"Whoa!" Gwen held a hand up. "Ready for what? Where do you think you're going?"

He screwed his lips to the side. "To Pike's, duh."

"Duh?" Dylan and Gwen scolded in unison.

"I mean, please?" Nate batted his eyelashes at his mother and poked out his lower lip.

I stood off to the side, watching with amusement as the two boys took turns begging for a sleepover until Gwen finally relented.

"Did you pack a toothbrush? Underwear? A shirt maybe?" Gwen asked, reaching for his backpack.

"Uhhhh… Maybe?"

With a sigh, Gwen turned to me. "I'll be right back."

When the boys started chattering about staying up all night and Nate excitedly showed his friend the jellybean game they were going to play, Dylan sent them out to the car.

"We haven't formally met," she said with her hand outstretched. "I'm Dylan, Gwen's best friend."

I grasped her hand, noticing the strength of her surprisingly firm grip. "I've heard a lot about you. I'm Truett."

"Probably not as much as I've heard about you." She grinned, pulling her hand from mine as she stepped closer. "Not all good stuff, either."

A wave of shame washed through me as I held her intense stare. "I know Gwen's told you the good, bad, and ugly. God knows there's certainly been a lot more ugly than good."

"Sounds like the ugly is water under the bridge though? Hell, I'm almost sick of seeing her smile all the time." She pressed her lips together. "But it sure beats watching her cry. And I'm sure I won't be seeing that with you around, right?"

She was asking for a promise in probably the nicest threatening way possible. Luckily, it was one I felt confident I could keep. "Not if I can help it."

Her eyes twinkled. "I heard you punched Jeff."

"I did not punch him."

"Right. Sure." She winked. "Just so you know, if you were a politician, that alone would have earned you my vote."

I chuckled, shaking my head. It was easy to understand how she and Gwen were friends.

She looked me over once more and nodded just as Gwen came back down the hall, Nate's bag full.

"What'd I miss?" Gwen asked.

"Nothing." Dylan plucked the bookbag from her hand and pulled the door open. "I'll have him back to you tomorrow afternoon. Enjoy your evening."

We followed her through the door, watching as she made her way to the car. As soon as she started it up, Nate rolled the window down and hung his upper body out.

"Bye, Truett! See you later!"

I lifted a hand in a wave as he turned his attention to his mother.

"Mwah, mwah, mwah!" He blew countless kisses—just like Kaitlyn.

And just like with Kaitlyn, Gwen reached up to catch every one, planting them on her cheeks. "Love you, baby!"

"Love you too, Mom!" he shouted.

We stood together on the porch until the car was out of sight, my heart pounding in my chest.

"Kaitlyn used to do that," I managed to utter, emotion clogging my throat.

Gwen's hand reached for mine and she pulled me into her side. "Yep. I didn't even teach him that. He just started doing it one day."

Turning so that I could face her, I wrapped my arms around her waist. "He's a good kid. I see so much of Kaitlyn in him."

She nodded as she looped her arms around my neck. "Losing Kaitlyn was the hardest thing I've ever experienced. I didn't think I'd ever love like that again. But then Nate came along. He can't replace her; it wouldn't be fair to him to expect that. But he helps keep her memory alive. He's the silver lining on the darkest storm cloud in my life."

She pressed to her toes, her lips trailing kisses along my neck until she reached my mouth. The emotions that evening tumbled from my lips as I poured every bit of love and appreciation I had for her into our kiss. Our tongues danced together; a routine learned long ago but never forgotten.

Yeah. I wanted this.

A life in reality.

A life with her.

CHAPTER TWENTY-NINE

Gwen

"WHAT ARE YOU GOING TO DO WITH IT?" TRUETT asked.

"I don't know," I whispered, emotion thick in my voice.

"Baby," he soothed, curling me into his chest. "It doesn't match. I see it. You see it. Customers are going to see it too."

"I know, but it's your booth. Her booth. Nathanial's booth. And if I'm being honest, I kind of feel like it's our booth now too." I stomped my foot. "Dammit, how am I the one sentimental over a booth that I would have trashed not even a month ago?"

He chuckled. "You don't have to make a decision now. It's not connected to the wall anymore. We can work around it for a while longer. Trashing it isn't the only option. I can take it back to the house or—"

"No," I replied quickly and firmly. "I don't even want you in that house, much less to help you fill it with more memories of the past."

He nodded, understanding in his eyes even if his face was still sheepish.

"You're right. We'll figure it out. We have too much to do today to be standing here, stressing over this."

The restaurant was a flurry of activity as the date of our grand opening grew closer. It was all hands on deck for the next couple of weeks, and having Truett there to help me was a welcome relief. While I focused on the menu and getting the new employees hired and trained, he was taking care of last-minute repairs and finishing touches.

The space had been completely transformed, and while it had taken a lot longer than I had anticipated, I couldn't have been more thrilled with the results.

When I'd first taken ownership of The Grille, it was a dated space that lacked charm or personality. Looking back, I understood why Angela and Dylan had been so skeptical.

But I'd had a vision, and as I glanced around, I realized that my dream space had come together flawlessly.

As you walked through the front door, your eyes were drawn to the back wall, where a chalkboard was centered among the weathered brick, adding a rustic feel to the entire space. I'd positioned the bar directly in front of that wall so that it would be the star of the café, with its sparkling black countertop and creamy off-white base.

To your left, there was a collection of high-top tables that would soon be surrounded by barstools covered in rich black leather, and to the right was a row of booths, all connected by a single farmhouse table.

The Rosewood Café really felt like a place where people of all ages would gather, whether it was for a cup of coffee or a hearty dinner. It felt comfortable, like a second home where stories were shared and memories were made.

I was still in Truett's arms when a man in a polo shirt with a Belton Security logo embroidered on the top right called out from near the door. "Mrs. Weaver, you should be good to go."

Truett let out a low grumble at the use of Weaver and then kissed me on the top of my head before releasing me. "Excellent."

I stood there watching, gratitude swelling in my chest. It wasn't that I couldn't have handled this on my own. There was no doubt in my mind that I would have been successful without his assistance. It was the fact that he gave it so easily, so freely, and never once made me feel like I needed to give him something in return.

Truett just jumped right in wherever he was needed and took care of what had to be done, which at the moment was working with the security company to have our new cameras and alarm installed.

There was a quick conversation between the two men, and then Truett shook his hand and escorted him out the door, locking it behind him.

Nate was still at Dylan's, so Truett and I had been there since seven. My body was sated from making love to him the night before, but I could not get enough of that man.

Finally alone again in the restaurant for only a few more minutes, I pressed my lips to his, letting out a moan when his large hand grasped the back of my head, anchoring my mouth against his. He licked at my lips and they parted for him, granting him full access to explore my mouth. He tasted like vanilla, coffee, and every hope and dream I had for this place all rolled into one.

"You have any idea how fucking sexy you look right now?" he growled, his eyes scanning the entire length of my body.

I arched an eyebrow. I was dressed in an oversized T-shirt—one I'd bought online thinking it was a crop top—that covered most of my jogging shorts. My hair was in a messy bun, and I was fairly certain I'd forgotten to remove my makeup the night before. There was no chance in hell that the way I looked could be classified as anything other than homeless, but that didn't stop me from asking, "Could you elaborate on that for me?"

He chuckled, moving behind me to wrap his arms around my waist, pulling my back flush with his chest.

His lips on my neck sent a tingle down my spine, the vibration of his low groan shooting straight to my core. His hands found the hem of my shirt before he skimmed his fingers along my ribs. "I haven't caught a case of amnesia since last night, baby. I know exactly what you're hiding under that shirt. Any fucking hotter and this whole place would spontaneously combust."

As he continued to trail kisses along the column of my throat, I arched my lower back, pressing my ass into his groin.

"Mmmm..." I moaned. "You're a tease. I have way too much to do for you to get me all worked up right now."

He spun me so that my breasts pillowed against him. "I didn't start that. If anyone's a tease, it's you."

I grinned, looping my arms around his waist as I rolled my hips. As I tipped my head back, my tongue darted out to wet my lips. "I would never tease you."

His eyes zeroed in on my mouth. "Yes. Yes, you would. And you'd enjoy the hell out of doing it too."

I laughed and pushed to my toes, giving him a quick peck on the lips before wriggling from his grasp. Chances were, another minute of our back-and-forth while wrapped in his arms and hours of my workday would be lost forever.

I walked to the bar, looked at the stack of papers, and sighed.

"What's all this?" he asked.

"The better question would be: what is it not? Applications, tax forms, sample menus, schedules, vendor lists..." I grabbed the single sheet of notebook paper and waved it toward him. "And let's not forget, Lucille's time-off requests."

"Place isn't even open and she's already putting in requests?"

I looked at her scribbled handwriting and nodded. "Yep. She needs to make sure I haven't forgotten about her standing hair appointments on the second Tuesday of each month."

He laughed. "Sounds about right. Hey, that reminds me. I called the guy about the blinds. They assured me the delivery would be here before ten this morning."

"Thank you! That was on my list of things to follow up with." I dug through the papers until I found the legal pad that held my never-ending to-do list. Making a show of it, I scribbled out the word *blinds* and beamed at him. "One down, twenty thousand to go."

He took the pad from my hands and scanned it. "Assemble barstools. I'll get to work on those if there's nothing else you want me to do?" He waggled his eyebrows and leaned in so that his mouth was at my ear. "Like, say, in the office?"

A jolt of desire ran through me. The offer was more than tempting, but I fought the urge to say *screw it* and drag him to the back.

"Later," I whispered. "I promise."

With a wink, Truett dropped the pad of paper on the counter and set to work locating the boxes of stools.

For the next hour, I placed orders with beverage vendors and followed up with emails to local farms I'd reached out to while Truett assembled barstools in record time. We worked in a comfortable silence, Truett dropping a sweet kiss on my head with every stool he completed.

When a knock at the door sounded, I pushed to my feet and scurried over, noting that it was already ten thirty and the blinds were late. But at this rate, I was just thankful they'd arrived today.

"Hey!" I said to the man standing on the other side of the door. He was dressed in khaki pants and a button-down with a tie—not exactly what I expected for someone about to do manual labor. But I didn't care if he'd been in boxer shorts as long as it meant the newspaper was finally coming down.

"Gwendolyn Weaver?" he asked.

I smiled and nodded. "That's me."

He shoved a handful of papers in my direction. "You've been served."

"I've been what?" I asked as I took the papers from his outstretched hand.

"Have a nice day." The man spun on his heel, leaving me standing dumbfounded in the doorway.

"Blind people finally here?" Truett asked as he came to a stop behind me, peering down the street. "Where'd they go?"

Still unsure of what had just happened, I closed the door and skirted around him, making my way over to the booth.

He followed, concern creasing his brow as he settled into the opposite side. "What's that?"

"I don't know," I murmured as I began to scan the document.

With every word I read, my pounding heart roared in my ears.

At the top, on the left-hand corner of the page, Jeff's name was listed with the word *plaintiff* beside it, my name directly below with the title *defendant* underneath.

The oxygen was stripped from my lungs as I realized it was a motion for an emergency custody hearing.

I squeezed my eyes shut, certain I'd misread it, but when I opened them again, the same frightening sentence was staring back at me.

"Gwen, look at me." Truett's hand covered mine.

I managed to tear my gaze away from the document in my hand and met his worry-filled eyes.

"What is that?"

My throat was dry, which made the effort to answer and say the words aloud nearly impossible. "Jeff..." I trailed off, looking back down at the court order.

A growl tore from Truett's throat. "Jeff what?"

I swallowed hard, fighting back the tears that threatened to overtake me. "Jeff's trying to get full custody of Nate."

In the blink of an eye, Truett was on his feet, the papers I'd been holding ripped from my hand as he seethed, "You're fucking shitting me."

I shook my head, my chest tight.

It didn't make sense.

Why would he try to take Nate away from me?

Truett's eyes were full of fury as he quickly read the documents. With the flick of his wrist, he tossed them back to the table. "This is bullshit."

I snatched them up and fully read them this time, going slowly, word for word.

Truett paced beside me, inventing new cuss words.

"It says that he feels Nate is in immediate risk of emotional harm or substantial bodily injury," I croaked, disbelief knotting my stomach. I kept reading, frantic for answers.

And then everything stopped as I saw Truett's name at the bottom.

And then it got worse. It stated that there was video evidence of Truett assaulting Jeff.

And then it got worse again. It stated that a PI had taken pictures of Truett at my house, claiming that Truett had moved in with me and Nate.

"Oh, God." I slapped a hand over my mouth as Truett sidled up beside me, reading over my shoulder.

Holy shit, Jeff was really going to do this. He knew all about Truett. Everything he'd been through. One of the things I'd loved about him when we'd first met was that he had been sensitive about my past and supportive of keeping Kaitlyn's memory alive with Nate.

And now, he was going to try to take Nate away from me?

I looked up to Truett, hoping he would have the answers. Instead, his jaw was set in a hard line, guilt written all over his features.

"That motherfucker."

"This is ridiculous," I said. "You're not a threat to Nate."

He laughed without humor and stabbed a hand through his hair. "This isn't about Nate. He knows we're back together. I told him you were mine. He's jealous and his ego is bruised. This is the only way that pussy can hurt me—by hurting you."

Yep. That sounded like Jeff. God knew he had no problem hurting me. But Nate? He knew that our son would end up collateral damage. And he did it anyway. This was a new low even for Jeff.

Rage surged through my veins. "No. He can't do this. He doesn't have a leg to stand on. You didn't even get charged with anything."

He hung his head. "No, and I'm sure that lit his ass on fire. But Folly was there. The windows were open. I'm sure that's the video he has." He scrubbed his beard with his hand. "You said it yourself. He knows every judge in this town. He'll have no problem getting what he wants as long as I'm in the picture." Unable to meet my eyes, he said simply, "I won't be the one to cost you another child."

For the second time that morning, it felt like all the oxygen was sucked from the room. He didn't have to elaborate. I knew that look. I knew his thought process. I knew all too well what would follow.

He was convinced that he was the reason we'd lost Nathanial and Kaitlyn. That he was responsible for them being taken from me—from us.

And then he'd left me. Making life-altering decisions that were never his to make.

I stared at him, unable to formulate a single sentence as my mind swirled. A myriad of emotions washed through me.

Anger.

Fear.

Frustration.

I'd waited for years to be able to get to a place of happiness and contentment. Just a few moments ago, I'd thought I'd finally made it.

Everything had been falling into place.

My restaurant was set to open soon. I had friends that were

more like family. My son was healthy. Most of all, I'd gotten the answers I'd so desperately needed from Truett.

And with one single sheet of paper, it was all being ripped away.

Jeff was going to try to take my child from me.

And Truett was going to walk away again to keep that from happening.

He dropped into a squat in front of where I sat frozen in the booth and squeezed my thigh. "Gwen, baby. Look at me."

I brought my gaze to his, not really seeing, as I prepared for the worst. I was going to lose everything all over again.

"What's going through your mind right now?" he asked.

"You're going to abandon me again, aren't you?" My voice was flat, the anxiety in my chest nearly suffocating me.

His head snapped back as though I'd slapped him. "Is that what you think?"

I finally focused on his face, seeing him clearly. His eyes swam with worry, uncertainty causing the lines on his forehead to deepen. "You said you weren't going to be the reason I lose Nate."

"I'm not," he said firmly, "because that asshole is not taking him from you and I sure as hell am not leaving you." His fingers flexed into my thighs, the squeeze grounding me. "I'm the reason for this mess. I'll be the one to fix it." He spoke with such conviction, I saw the man I'd fallen in love with again. The man who was confident and strong. The man who believed in himself.

"How?" I asked, fear washing over me. "The emergency hearing is tomorrow."

He pulled his phone out, typing out a quick text before shoving it back into his pocket. "I don't know yet. But I will." Sheer determination coated every word he said. "This is bullshit, and it's going to be hard. But we've faced way harder."

"And I lost you in the process," I croaked out.

He shook his head adamantly. "I lost myself, Gwen. I won't

make that mistake again. There is nothing—and I mean nothing—I won't do to hold onto you. I want this with you. I need this with you. I will never let anything or anyone—including myself—take you away from me again."

A part of me believed him.

A part of me was scared to trust him again.

And then a part of me realized that Truett wasn't the only one who needed help. I still carried my demons from the past. I wasn't trapped in a house, but the trauma of losing my entire life still lived inside me. I was just slightly better at hiding it.

"Gwen," he prompted when I hadn't said anything. "I'm gonna take care of this. I'm gonna take care of *you*. Do you hear me?"

"Yeah," I whispered.

"Good."

For several minutes, he stayed positioned in front of me, rubbing my thighs and murmuring reassurances while I tried not to let my mind spiral out of control.

When Lucille knocked on the front door, Truett pushed to his feet and dropped a chaste kiss on the top of my head.

"You good to stay with her? I've got some things I need to take care of."

Panic sliced through me. "You're not going to Jeff, are you?"

He shook his head and frowned. "I'd love nothing more than to get my hands on him again. But that would only make things worse. Besides, I think I need to start a little closer to home."

"Are you coming back?" I called after him.

He walked backward to the door. "Always. But I don't think it's a good idea if I stay with you tonight."

My heart sank, but better judgment told me he was right. No use giving Jeff anything more to try and use against us.

He placed his hand over his heart. "But I'll be there in the morning. I swear."

He let Lucille in, and before she had the chance to even say hello, he ordered, "Get on the phone and call Dylan and Angela. Stay with her until they get here, and then make sure one of you goes home with her tonight. I do not want her to be alone. Do you understand me?"

She flicked her confused gaze between us. "I hear you. Is everything okay?"

"It will be," he assured her.

I watched as he walked out the door and waited on the outside for Lucille to lock it behind him. I held his gaze. I had no clue where he was going or how he was going to fix this. Nerves rolled in my stomach, and suddenly, I felt like I was right back at that mall, a glass door dividing us as he prepared to wage war. Only this time, as he walked away, it wasn't an apology he gave me.

"*I love you,*" he mouthed.

And never had I believed something more.

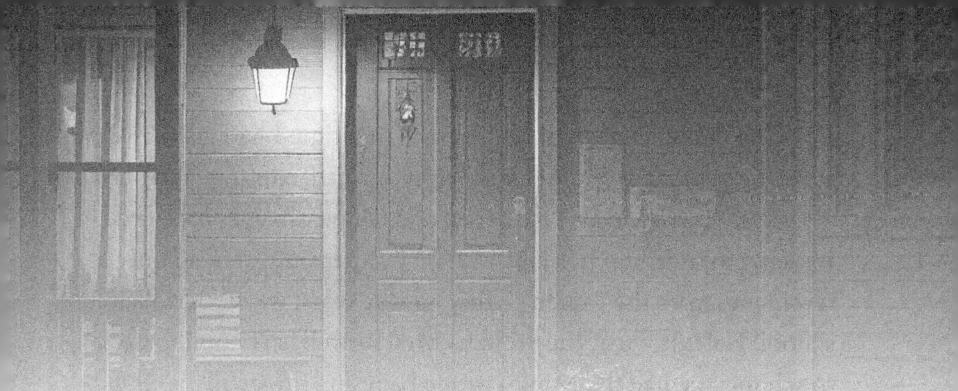

CHAPTER THIRTY

TRUETT

Leaning back in my chair, I let my hand hover over the mouse of the computer.

Kaitlyn's face appeared, but she didn't say anything as she played with a set of plastic farm animals.

"Kaitlyn," Gwen said, urging her to look at the camera.

Her head popped up, brown curls bouncing wildly. "Oh, hey, Daddy."

My finger still positioned over the mouse, I had to fight the urge to pause it.

That was how our conversations worked.

She'd talk.

I'd pause it to respond.

I'd press play and she'd talk again.

And I would be able to pretend that she was somewhere with Gwen, happy and living her best life.

Only today, I couldn't pretend anymore.

I'd sat on that couch with Gwen and Nate, reality finally feeling like a reprieve.

I had no idea where the day would take us. But I'd done everything I could think of to prepare for court that morning. Still, I worried that it wouldn't be enough. It wasn't Wednesday, but I decided to spend a few minutes with my girl before heading out.

The video Gwen had sent me the first time I had gone away to get help, months before I lost her in the mall, continued to play.

Kaitlyn's round face hardened and her brown eyes narrowed. Leaning forward on her elbows, she put her button nose only a few inches from the camera. "This was the worst week ever! I hate school. Hate. It. First, they told us Mrs. Rowell isn't coming back to school. She had that stinky, rotten baby and forgot all about us. Babies poop their pants, Dad! All of us in class use the potty like big kids. But nooooooo, Mrs. Rowell wants to stay home with that, that *baby*. And then they made Mr. Ward our teacher! He's the worst!" she cried, finally leaning back in her chair so I could fully see her again. "I hate him. I don't even want to go to school anymore. But Mom said if I stop going now, I'll never be able to be a chicken nugget maker at McDonalds when I get older. It's not fair. I just want Mrs. Rowell back."

My chest got tight, the grief damn near crippling me just like it always did when I heard her say those words. This time, however, the pain that sliced through me was sharper than ever before.

I just wanted *her* back.

I'd tried for eighteen years though, fighting against an unstoppable future in which she would never grow up. And for what? To hold the very essence of her captive in that house with me?

I'd listened to Nate laugh and talk proudly about his sister, and I'd seen my baby girl's determination in Gwen as she rebuilt that restaurant from the ground up. They were outside this house, and Kaitlyn was not only alive, but she was living—through them.

Before she'd passed away, I hadn't wanted her to spend her life trapped by my grief. I'd wanted so much more for her because there wasn't anything in this world that could stop her from being great. Except for me. It was part of the reason I'd let Gwen go—to spare them both the pain of living in the darkness of my sorrowful shadow.

But rather than trying to find the light to help me escape, I'd trapped her in the darkness with me. And that was a disservice to not only my daughter's memory, but to the entire world who had never gotten to meet her.

I couldn't do it anymore.

I couldn't sit frozen in this house, waiting for the impossible, while ignoring all of the incredible possibilities that were still out there. Kaitlyn didn't need me anymore, but the world still needed her. And every day that I sat alone in my self-imposed prison, I let her die all over again.

And that was a fucking tragedy.

"Did I show you Fiona Iona yet?" Kaitlyn asked as she lifted a plastic tiger sporting a doll's tutu around its midsection toward the camera. "She's a ballerina. Mom said she's going to get me some glue and pink glitter so we can make her shoes. I don't think the glitter will work though, because she needs to be able to take them off when she goes to work. Hang on. Let me show you her sister."

She started talking a mile a minute about her toys and their lavish nicknames, which I'd memorized over a decade earlier.

As I studied her beautiful face, working hard to commit every feature to memory, a tear rolled down my cheek. "I'm so sorry," I said as she continued to babble on. "I am so sorry Daddy couldn't save you." My voice hitched, the words feeling like razor blades in my throat as I struggled to get them out. "But I have to go now. I can't keep doing this, kiddo. I can't let *you* keep doing this. You deserve to be free. We both *deserve* to be free."

My shoulders shook, a sob tearing through me. "I need you to know that I love you. In the past. In the present. And for my entire future. I will carry you with me. Every breath I take will be for you. Every time my heart beats, it will be for you. And every smile that your mother and crazy little brother put on my face will be for you. But they need me now, baby. And I need to be there for them, the way I can't be there for you." A guttural cry sliced through me, and

I hung my head. "Just…please know that I love you. I love you. I love you so much, Kaitlyn."

"I love you, Daddy!" she replied.

Chills exploded across my body, the hairs on the back of my neck standing on end. My head popped up and I saw her through the computer screen, still frozen in time at five years old.

Oh, the cruel yet perfect timing of that video.

Or maybe, just maybe, it was a sign sent from up above.

One that freed us both.

Clinging to the thought of my girl letting me know that she was okay, that we were all going to be okay, I smiled at her perfect face as she blew countless kisses my way. I caught each and every one of them, pressing them to my tear-stained cheeks.

"Byeeeeee!" she sang as her face got really close to the camera again.

I didn't want to say it. I'd never been able to utter it before. It was always *see you soon* or *talk to you later*. But never goodbye.

Never to her.

But it was time. Time to move forward. Time to make her proud. Time to live in the present.

Time to recapture the life I'd put on hold all those years ago.

I wasn't sure I could speak at all. But I only had a few more seconds before the screen went black.

I drew in a deep breath, praying that she was somewhere out there, dancing in the clouds and watching over us all.

"Bye, baby," I croaked out.

And then she was gone.

However, my world didn't go dark.

I wasn't gone.

Gwen wasn't gone.

And I was finally ready to face the world in order to ensure Nate wouldn't be gone, either.

After drying my face and straightening my navy suit, I exited the office, not a new man but a man determined to build a new life.

My living room was full of people, and they all stood when they saw me.

Daniel walked over to me and rested his hand on my shoulder. "You ready to do this?"

"Not yet."

His gaze flashed with concern, but I walked over to the basket of toys and picked up Fiona Iona. Smiling, I heard her voice in my head. "*I love you, Daddy*!"

Yeah. I could do this.

I tucked the tutu-wearing Tiger inside the pocket of my coat and then nodded. "Now, I'm ready."

CHAPTER THIRTY-ONE

Gwen

THE AIR WAS STALE WITH THE SCENT OF OLD WOOD AND faded varnish as I nervously shook my foot. The cramped courtroom was even smaller than I'd imagined in the minuscule Belton courthouse. Two worn tables stood in front of the judge's bench, each with a pair of mismatched chairs tucked behind them. A waist-high, wooden partition separated the front from the gallery, where three narrow pews lined the back of the room.

Angela was seated beside Dylan and Lucille in the front row. She leaned forward and gave my shoulder a reassuring squeeze. "It's gonna be okay."

I wanted to believe her. But it didn't matter what happened from that point on. My son's life would never be the same. I'd sworn not to put Nate in the middle of my relationship with Jeff. We were two adults. Our child shouldn't have to deal with jealousy or revenge stemming from of our failed marriage. However, it seemed I was the only adult in this situation.

Jeff had every right to be upset about the way Truett had acted. But there were ways to handle difficult situations without dragging our child into the middle. He could have taken it up with the cops and used his legal connections to find out why they hadn't charged

Truett with more. That wouldn't have been my personal preference, but at least it wouldn't have involved Nate.

Or we could have had a discussion when he'd called me after Truett was arrested. However, that would have required him not to call me names and scream into my ear.

If the task had been too difficult to calm himself that day, then he could have spoken to me when I'd picked Nate up from his house to ask face-to-face if Truett had moved in with me.

But no, Jeff had decided to use our son as a pawn to get his revenge on Truett—and, in turn, me.

I would never be able to forgive him—or forget.

Dylan slapped me on the shoulder when Jeff walked into the courtroom. My jaw fell open as he strutted in sporting an oversized bandage on his nose and a brace around his neck. He hadn't needed either when I'd seen him two days earlier. And just to add salt to the wound, Taggart Folly entered one step behind him.

"You have got to be shitting me," I whispered, a rancid mix of nerves and rage churning in my stomach.

"Ignore him," my attorney, Marcus Cooper, ordered. Well, really, he was Truett's attorney.

Marcus had called me less than ten minutes after Truett had set out on his journey to "fix this." I still had no idea what that meant or if he'd figured out anything. But he'd sworn he was going to be there, and while there had been no sign of him yet, I had faith he'd keep his word.

"Is that neck brace a joke?" Dylan sniped entirely too loudly. I was sure Jeff heard her almost as much as I was sure that was the point.

Lucille crossed and uncrossed her legs. "That man is a joke. If we can call him a *man* at all."

"Hey, keep it down," Marcus scolded. "When the judge gets in here, I don't want to hear a word no matter what he says or does. Judge Clavet is no nonsense, and from what I've heard, he is not happy about Jeff pulling strings to get this in front of him so quickly. We are presenting a calm and supportive collective front. Do not give him a reason to believe there may be some truth to the accusations about Gwen's parenting."

The three of them immediately clamped their mouths shut.

I sagged in my chair. How was this happening? My parenting? Really? Jeff had done nothing when Nate was a baby. He was always busy at work or social engagements, trying to level up his career. He hadn't worried about "my parenting" then. It wasn't until Nate was around four and went from being a baby to take care of to a little person to have fun with that Jeff decided to be an active dad. I didn't always agree with his parenting style, but I'd never wanted to take Nate away from him.

"Ho. Lee. Shit," Lucille breathed, catching my attention.

I followed her gaze to the courtroom doors. Truett walked through the doors like it was a high fashion runway wearing a navy-blue double-breasted suit that fit him like the world's sexiest glove.

His chin held high.

His shoulders resolute.

A confidence so thick it cloaked the air around him.

He was flanked by five men. I recognized Daniel at his left, but not the others. The two behind them were in military dress uniforms, and a pair of police officers pulled up the rear.

It looked like a parade, but as hope surged inside me, it felt like the answer to my prayers.

Truett West was back.

And there was nothing he wouldn't do to protect his family.

"Hey," he whispered, leaning over the partition to kiss the top of my head.

"Who are all these people?" I asked.

He winked. "Reinforcements."

"All rise," the bailiff called out, silencing the conversation.

A bald man with a thick gray beard in a black robe took his place behind the bench. We were seated, and then he began a myriad of formalities, including reading Jeff's emergency motion aloud. When he was satisfied he'd checked all the required legal boxes, he set the paperwork down, took his glasses off, and leaned back in his chair.

"Mr. Weaver, I've reviewed the evidence you have provided to support your claims today, though I still find myself with quite a few questions about your allegations against Mr. West and the perceived danger to your son."

Jeff stood up, holding his neck as if his head might topple off without the brace. "Yes, Your Honor. I'm happy to answer any questions the court may have about—"

"I'd like to speak to Mr. West. If that is okay with you, Ms. Weaver."

Jeff went solid and my heart lurched into my throat. I mentally gagged when he called me *Ms. Weaver* and swore right then and there that, before I left the courthouse, I'd get the required paperwork to legally change my name.

Unsure how to properly address the judge, I stood with shaking legs. "Um, yes, sir."

When he smiled, he looked like Santa Claus. "No need to be nervous. Nobody's on trial here. We all just want to figure out what's best for your son."

I nodded. "Yes, sir."

"Okay, then. Mr. West, thank you for coming today. Do you mind if we have a quick talk?"

Truett stood up behind me, but it was Marcus who spoke first.

"Your Honor, before we proceed any further, I'd like to point out that there is a member of the media in the courtroom with us today. The man seated behind Mr. Weaver is Taggart Folly, a producer with Flat Line Productions who has been harassing my client in an attempt to gain her participation in a documentary he is filming on the tragedy at The Watersedge Mall. My client and Mr. West lost their daughter that day. Due to the sensitivity of this matter and Mr. West's hopes to speak freely without it being documented for entertainment purposes, we ask that Mr. Folly be removed from the court."

Folly had the audacity to look offended.

Jeff scowled before slapping on the fake confidence that made him such a successful attorney. "I assure you Mr. Folly is not here as a member of the media today. He was a witness the day I was assaulted by Truett West."

The judge arched his brow. "From inside the building? Because I watched the video you submitted and there was no sound and the sun was reflecting off the windows, making it next to impossible to make out who's who. The only thing I could tell for sure was that there was a scuffle inside, and then Mr. West was led out in cuffs. He was released later in the day with nothing more than a trespass notice. I believe I've already seen everything he can add to this case. Mr. Folly, please see yourself out of the courtroom."

"That's not fair!" Folly protested. "There's nothing that states a member of the media can't attend this hearing."

"I just did. Out!" Judge Clavet boomed.

Marcus grinned—a *huge* grin—as Folly grumbled and shuffled out.

The hinges on Jeff's jaw ticked, his ego no doubt taking a hit.

Truett's hand landed on my shoulder from behind, but I was too damn nervous to find any comfort in it.

The judge searched around his desk, shuffling through a stack of papers. "Okay, here we go. Mr. West, I have been supplied with images taken in front of Ms. Weaver's home." He paused and looked at me. "To avoid confusion, may I call you Gwen?"

"Please do," I replied, and he flashed another one of his holiday best.

"As I was saying, there are pictures of you arriving at Gwen's home with a duffel bag of sorts. Are you currently residing at her residence?"

"No, sir," Truett answered.

"Have you been in contact with Nathan Weaver?"

"Yes, sir, I have."

"Can you tell me a little about that?"

Truett drew in a deep breath. "Gwen cooked dinner on Wednesday night and I met him for the first time. We ate wings and then watched old family videos of my daughter. It was only for a couple hours before a friend came by and invited him to spend the night. He left and I haven't seen him since."

"So it was a friendly evening? No issues or problems?"

Truett smirked. "Well, he was a little disappointed with the flower pressing kit I gave him as a gift. Apparently, it was an inside joke between him and his mother, but it ended up as a joke on me. I think I redeemed myself by getting him one of those disgusting jellybean games. You can't go wrong with gross when it comes to boys."

The judge chuckled. "You don't have to tell me. I have two grandsons. Boys are a different breed these days." He cleared his throat and then sat up straighter in his chair. He swung his gaze between Truett and Jeff. "I'm going to level with you two. I did not want to take this case today. I tried to pass it off to every colleague I have. But it seemed we all had the same problem. I know who you are, Truett. I know what you did."

My back shot straight in my chair. Suddenly, I was terrified of where this was going.

The judge continued. "I remember the day when we found out about that horrible, horrible tragedy at the mall. We were all scrambling, calling our family and friends in Watersedge, checking to make sure everyone we loved was accounted for."

My stomach wrenched, and I flicked my gaze to Truett. He was standing stock-still, his arms at his sides, his face unreadable.

I tugged on Marcus's arm to get his attention. "Don't let him talk about this. Anything but the mall."

He looked at me like I had three heads and hissed, "Relax. It will be fine."

It wasn't going to be fine. If Truett had willingly put on a suit, I knew he'd committed to the cause ahead of us, but there was no telling what would come out of his mouth if the judge made his way down the path I feared he was headed.

And much to my horror, he did exactly that. "Your name and a picture of you in uniform was plastered all over the newspapers for weeks. It made national news, but no one could get a single comment from you. I want to personally say thank you. I'm sorry about the loss of your daughter. From one father to another, I feel for certain she would be proud of the hero you were that day."

Oh my God.

Thank you.

Proud.

Hero.

It was the trifecta of trigger words.

I shot to my feet. "Please stop talking."

The judge sliced his gaze to me. "Excuse me?"

There was a rumble of whispers through the room, including an arrogant laugh from Jeff.

"I'm sorry," I rushed out. "I wasn't trying to be rude. It's just—"

Truett moved forward until his lower body was flush with the partition, and he hooked his arm around my shoulders, pulling my upper body against his chest. I went willingly, hoping that whatever calm he claimed I gave him would keep him from losing his head and me from losing my son.

Surprisingly, his heartbeat against my ear was slow and his breaths even. "I'm sorry, Your Honor. That was my fault too. If I may level with you as well, Gwen knows I haven't always liked the word *hero*. But over the last few days, I've done a lot of soul searching and reflection. I'm starting to think fighting the label has been more damaging for me than just accepting that my action saved the lives of others."

In utter shock, I tilted my head back to peer up at him. I looked for any sign that he was uncomfortable or maybe pretending again. However, the brown eyes that flashed down to me were free of clouds and storms of the past.

He released me, but only long enough to fold his hand around mine. "You see, I was already a broken man the day I walked into that mall. I was struggling with trusting myself after I'd lost my team overseas. I had considered taking my own life—planned it, even. But then, this little girl—" He brought our intertwined hands up to rest over his chest. "*Our* little girl reminded me why I needed to live. Why I needed to get better. I worked hard to be the father she deserved, all of it culminating in that day when we were at the mall as part of my exposure therapy. I walked in broken, but I walked out demolished. It's a hard pill to swallow to be called a hero, because I failed the only person I was supposed to protect."

Tears spilled from my eyes, and I brought our joined hands to my mouth to kiss the back of his palm, knowing that, if his words were shredding me, they had to be wrecking him.

He continued. "It's been confusing for me over the last few days, as I've thought about how I chose to live my life after I lost my daughter. I shut myself off from the world because of the things I thought I did and *did not* deserve. I tried to keep her memory alive, albeit not in the healthiest of ways, but I wasn't ready to let go." His lips curled into a warm smile. "And then I met Nate."

I sucked in a sharp breath.

Jeff scoffed. "Your Honor, is this really necessary? The only part of his story that is pertinent to this case is when he made the choice to viciously attack me in my place of business."

Judge Clavet never tore his eyes off Truett as he barked, "Sit down, Weaver."

Lucille laughed and I leveled her with a glare, silencing her immediately.

"Carry on, Mr. West."

Truett gave my hand a tight squeeze. "Seeing him, my daughter's brother, got me thinking about all the lives that were affected that day. As I sat in that mall, frozen and lost, bombarded by the chaos, while trying to process that my daughter was gone..." His voice got thick, and he used his free hand to grip the partition as if he were having trouble keeping his knees from buckling. "I saw Gwen pounding on the glass doors. I was engulfed by the fear that she could be next. It was only then that my mind thawed enough for me to act."

I slapped my hand over my mouth, a sob escaping my throat. When I'd seen him through the doors, I'd had no idea that Kaitlyn was already gone. But I, too, had been engulfed in fear when I saw him rise to his feet. A piece of my soul withered as he mouthed the words, "*I'm sorry*," before taking off after the gunman.

If she had still been alive, he never would have left her side.

And if she hadn't been alive, he wouldn't care to be, either.

I'd thought I was going to lose them both.

Truett paused, offering me a reassuring smile. "I have no idea what would have happened that day had I not gone after that monster, but I can now clearly see what happened because I did. Nate happened."

"Truett," I whispered, warmth blooming in my chest.

He looked back up at the judge. "My brother survived that day, later making me an uncle to two incredible boys. I found out recently that Officer Don Hutching's sister survived and went on to become a driving force in New Jersey's senate. There are doctors and architects, children and grandchildren, husbands and wives, who are here, in the present, because of my actions that day. It's been eighteen years and the domino effect of the most heartbreaking day of my life is still happening. I believe one of those dominos is exactly why we are all here today. I don't think that Mr. Weaver's claims have anything to do with Nate's safety."

Truett once again brought our joined hands to rest over his heart. "I've made a lot of poor choices in my life. One of which was being stupid enough to let this woman slip through my fingers. Jeff Weaver reaped the benefits of that mistake and is now unable to accept that Gwen and I are back together. This is an act of jealousy, not concern."

Jeff let out a loud laugh. "Your Honor, you can't be seriously entertaining this nonsense."

Judge Clavet's bushy eyebrows drew together menacingly. "The only nonsense I hear right now is your outburst. One more and I will hold you in contempt."

The pure joy I felt watching Jeff get his ass handed to him momentarily dried my tears.

"Okay, Mr. West. Let's get to the point."

Truett nodded. "Yes, sir. As many regrets as I have about losing Gwen, I've seen the way she looks at her son, and Nate could never be one of them. Gwen is an incredible mother. I got to witness that firsthand for six years with our daughter and only one night with Nate. But I can confidently say she would never knowingly put her child at risk. I admit that I let my emotions dictate my actions when I went to Mr. Weaver's office, but I assure you, I have no criminal record and have never and will never be a danger to society. My mental health has been a difficult journey over the years, but violence has never been a part of that. My doctor, Lieutenant Colonel Nunnery, and my therapist, Major Wright, have been with me for years and were gracious enough to come here today to speak on my behalf should you have any concerns about that. I assure you I am not a violent man."

Finally, losing his grip on control, Jeff rocketed to his feet. "Not violent? Your Honor, as much as I've enjoyed this little story time, it's irrelevant. I don't want him around my son. The man headbutted me. I'm pretty sure that is still a crime in Belton."

The judge nodded. "You are correct. So is obstructing justice."

"Obstruction of justice?" Jeff shot back incredulously.

The judge lifted a paper in the air. "Did you think that, because you tried to rush this emergency hearing through in less than two days, I wouldn't take the time to prepare? I watched your useless video and your meaningless pictures, but I also read the police report. It's not lost on me that the arresting officers have not only joined us today, but are also sitting behind the *defendant*."

He put his glasses on and leaned forward, the paper still clutched in his hand. "It says here that you were instructed by officers not to speak multiple times, and instead, you continued to argue and provoke Mr. West. In all my years of sitting on this bench, I've heard a lot of things that turned my stomach, but never have I been more disgusted than when I read that you used the senseless death of another man's child to insult him."

I gasped, rage burning my throat as I fought the urge to throw up. He'd brought up Kaitlyn. My Kaitlyn. He was lucky Truett only headbutted him. I would have done far worse.

"This is bullshit!" Jeff shouted, his voice echoing through the small space. "I'm the victim here!"

"Enough," Judge Clavet snapped, slamming his gavel. "Bailiff, please take Mr. Weaver into custody."

A familiar arrogance flared in Jeff's face. "Are you fucking kidding me? Why does everyone in this Godforsaken town want to suck Truett West's dick?" His rabid gaze slid to mine. "What is wrong with you? He left you after he killed your brother *and* your daughter. And you're just going to run back to him? You really are that desperate and pathetic, aren't you?"

Truett's hand painfully gripped mine as he barely held himself back.

Jeff's insults were nothing new to me. I'd spent a lot of years wilting under his abuse, convincing myself that keeping my family together was all that mattered. But, eventually, I had been forced to look in the mirror and accept that I mattered more. He could call me names all day long, but his words no longer held power over me.

So, as Truett fought to maintain his composure and the judge wildly banged his gavel, calling for order, I smiled as a pair of cuffs were clicked around Jeff's wrists.

"You are a disgrace," the judge spat. "I'm holding you in contempt of court. Maybe you should spend less time worrying about your ex-wife's personal life and reflect on how you can be a better father. I find no reason to grant your request for emergency custody of Nathan Bryce Weaver. Your motion has been *denied*."

Relief flooded my veins as the room busted into a flurry of quiet celebration. I slapped a hand down on Truett's arm, my fingernails biting into the fabric of his suit, waiting until I could launch myself into his arms.

The judge let out an exasperated sigh. "Anything more from you, Mr. Cooper?"

"No, Your Honor. Thank you for your time," my virtually useless attorney replied.

He lifted his gavel, but Truett quickly rushed out with, "May I say one more thing, sir?"

He arched an eyebrow. "Go ahead."

"I think you were right." He stepped over the partition dividing us and pulled me into his side. "My daughter would be proud, and as hard as it is to admit, she probably would have called me a hero too."

With gentle eyes, the judge smiled. "You were her father. On the good days, the bad days, and every single one in between, you were *always* her hero."

Truett's breathing shuddered, his arm tensing around me, as another wave of tears filled my eyes.

"Thank you," Truett rasped.

The judge nodded, banged his gavel, and then dismissed the court.

Dylan, Angela, and Lucille cheered and clapped as Daniel, his doctors, and even the cops Truett had brought with him that day hurried to the front, patting him on the back.

But he only had eyes for me. "I'm sorry that took me so long. All of this."

We had so far to go. So much healing to do. But our future together was only a blink away.

"Welcome to the present, True."

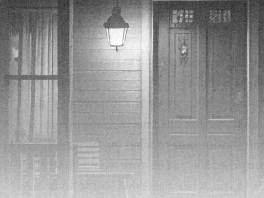

CHAPTER THIRTY-TWO

TRUETT

LIFE WAS HARD. THAT DIDN'T CHANGE BECAUSE I'D mentally committed to taking the first steps to reclaim my life. There were no fewer than a million grueling miles between where I was and where I wanted to be.

But I was trying. Little by little. Minute by minute.

With Gwen by my side.

We hadn't heard anything from Jeff in nearly two weeks. With the majority of their custody swaps being done in the carpool line after school, it wasn't necessary to see each other regularly. Thankfully, his surprise visits and nasty texts had stopped. That was as much of a win as I figured we could expect from him.

While I wanted to be with Gwen twenty-four-seven, we thought it was best to ease Nate into me being around all the time. On the weekends she had him, I'd only come over on Saturday and leave after breakfast on Sunday morning. And on the nights he was with his dad, we were either working at the restaurant or in her bed, making up for lost time.

She hated when I went home and had gone so far as to convince Cooter to offer me her guest room. That was the easiest *no* I'd ever spoken. Besides, I'd spent the majority of my life in that house. I couldn't just walk away and never look back the way she so desperately wanted me to. But I had agreed to trash the couch, so I'd at least placated her for a while.

It was finally time for the soft launch of The Rosewood Café, and for the last five days, Gwen had banished me from the premises.

She had wanted to put the finishing touches on the place herself, promising that the surprises she had in store would be worth the long hours. The nights I spent at her place, she'd come home an exhausted, sweaty, overwhelmed mess. Yet she would walk in the door, a smile stretched wide across her gorgeous face, and spend the next half hour recapping her day.

I'd never seen her more radiant.

From the moment she'd shown me her plans, I hadn't doubted for a second that The Rosewood would be every bit as amazing as she was. Gwen had decided that a soft launch for friends and family would be a good test of their preparation. As the time loomed near, I wasn't sure who was more nervous: Gwen or Cooter. They'd both thrown themselves into The Rosewood, and despite Cooter's unconventional approach to life in general, she'd turned out to be not only an incredible resource, but a great friend to Gwen as well.

As I stood on the sidewalk, waiting for our head chef to open the doors, the air was static, everyone abuzz with excitement to see what she had created inside a once outdated grease pit. Gwen was not messing around with the big reveal. The sign over the door had been covered with a tarp to keep it hidden. I couldn't help but laugh when I saw she'd used two of the old newspapers to cover the logos on the doors.

Finally, Gwen slipped through the front door, wearing a crisp white chef's jacket, her hair pulled back in a bun. Everyone cheered as she waved, her face beaming with pride. She froze when she saw the long red ribbon with silver and gold jewels that hung between the potted trees on either side of the door.

As a surprise, Nate had spent his free time bedazzling the ribbon for his mother. As much as he complained about those arts and crafts she made him do with her, I think he secretly liked it just as much as she did.

She found Nate in the crowd. "Did you do this?"

He nodded, suddenly extremely uncomfortable to be called out in front of the crowd.

"Buddy, it's amazing! I love it!" she exclaimed, opening her arms for Nate.

He glanced around before giving her what could possibly be the world's shortest hug and then escaping back to his place beside Pike and Daphne.

"Truett," she called, searching for me in the crowd. Her face lit when our eyes finally collided. Circling her hand in the air, she said, "Come up here."

With a smile that had become a permanent fixture on my face as of lately, I weaved my way to the front, but I wasn't going to stay. I dropped a quick kiss on her lips before leaning in toward her ear to whisper, "This is your moment, baby. Not mine. Embrace it."

Her face got soft. "True, I couldn't have done this without you."

"You could have, and you would have, and it would still be incredible. You'd just have significant credit card debt."

She laughed, snaking her hand out to pinch my nipple. "You mean significantly *more* credit card debt?"

"That too." I winked. "Now, come on. Give the people what they came for."

She pressed up onto her toes and brushed her lips with mine.

"Get a room!" Cooter yelled.

Everyone laughed, and I stepped away, staying close without stealing her spotlight.

"Wow," she breathed. "Thank you so much for being here tonight." She paused as a round of applause erupted. "Proud doesn't begin to cover the way I feel about this place. Literal blood, sweat, and tears have gone into this transformation. And I'm not just talking about the restaurant. The day I signed the contract to purchase The Grille, I never could have imagined how much my life would change."

Her eyes locked on mine. "It's funny. I bought this place as a fresh start, but somehow, I found a piece of my past that had been missing for far too long."

Emotion lodged in my throat, so I blew her a kiss. Midsentence, and without missing a beat, she caught it in the air and placed it on her cheek.

"I got to thinking," she continued. "I began to wonder how this little restaurant of mine might affect the lives of the people who come here to share a meal. What kind of memories might be made between these four walls? What kind of connections might be forged over a shared table, between friends, families, or even strangers? What kind of comfort might people find here? Only time will tell. But I know the memories I've made, the connections I've forged, and the comfort I never could have imagined I'd find again.

"So, with that, some of you might be surprised that things look a little different than you're expecting, but I could not be happier with the way things turned out. I could not have done this without each and every one of you. Thank you." Her eyes once again filled with tears, but she managed to keep them at bay. "Those two words are not enough, but hopefully the food will help bridge the gap. There will be a cocktail hour first so I can hopefully shake off some of the nerves. If you see me without a drink in my hand, please remedy that immediately."

Everyone laughed, but I stared at her, happiness cocooning me.

She swiped under her eyes and then clapped her hands. "Anyway, without further ado… Welcome to The Haven!"

My whole body jerked. The…wait…*what*?

Chills exploded across my skin as I stared at her. She made quick work of cutting the ribbon as the crowd cheered.

And I just stood there, dazed, dumbfounded, and so fucking filled with love it physically hurt.

She extended her hand toward me. "Come on, True. I need you for this."

I immediately became unstuck and moved to her side, lacing my fingers with hers.

With a gorgeous smile playing on her lips, Gwen stopped us just inside. Her guests eagerly flooded in around us until it was just the two of us standing in that doorway.

She squeezed my hand. "What do you think?"

I couldn't drag my stare away from the tall wooden letters spelling out our daughter's middle name centered over the blackboard menu. I took measured breaths, working to control the thick emotion that swelled in my chest.

"The Haven?" I asked.

"Yep. I had those letters cut from the table top of the booth."

"What?" I gasped.

She turned and pointed toward the hostess stand. Two benches formed an L in the corner. "I used the seats over there. I left the original vinyl and covered it with cloth slipcovers."

I was in a losing battle to hold my emotions back. "This is incredible."

She smiled. "I know you used to come here as some kind of penitence, but look at all it's given us. From now on, I want this to be our safe space, our refuge, *our haven*. Us. Me, you, Nate. And anyone who walks through that door. I want the whole world to feel the warmth and joy that was, and will always be, our Kaitlyn Haven West."

"Jesus, Gwen. It's perfect," I breathed, wrapping my arms around her waist, pulling her body flush with mine. "You're perfect."

"Okay, let's not get carried away."

We both laughed, and I bent over, resting my forehead on hers and gently swayed us from side to side. "God, I'm gonna miss you."

My chest ached at the thought of being away from her for so long. I didn't know how I was going to manage not being able to pull her into my arms whenever I wanted or hear her laughter ringing loudly every day. But I knew that making the decision to attend a residential treatment program was the only way I was ever going to be able to fully heal and move forward with my life.

With our life.

"Yeah, it's gonna suck," she replied. "But I'm so proud of you for finally making yourself a priority."

I gave her another squeeze and then cleared my throat. "You think anyone will notice if we sneak off to the office?"

"I'm pretty sure about twenty people would notice, especially those two."

I looked up and saw Dylan and Angela making their way over.

"You two done making out yet?" Dylan quipped.

Angela swatted at her shoulder. "I know this is special for you both. But, Truett, you have to share."

"Fiiine," I huffed teasingly. After one last kiss, I released her and they swooped her away.

I went back to admiring the wooden letters until Daniel patted me on the back.

"There you are. I lost you in the stampede to the bar." He tipped a beer to his lips.

He had Jacob, who was almost three, sitting on his hip, so I poked him in the belly. Wiggling as he laughed, he hid his face against his father's shoulder.

Daniel nudged Carson with his thigh. "Say hey to Uncle Truett."

Dramatic as only a five-year-old could be, he threw his head back and whined, "Can we go home yet?"

"Hey, dude. That's my line." I ruffled the top of his hair.

"I'm so bored," he groaned.

Daniel rolled his eyes. "You'll have to excuse him. He's not sure what to do when he's not being completely and utterly spoiled with things like a trampoline park or video games."

Grinning, I shook my head and located Nate across the room. "Hey, buddy," I called.

His head popped up from the game of Jenga he was playing on the floor with Pike and Daphne.

"Can you let Carson hang out with you guys for a little bit?"

"Sure," he chirped.

Carson was hesitant, but Daniel tipped his head toward the kids. "Go ahead. I'll be right here."

Reluctantly, he shuffled away.

"Where's Amber?" I asked.

Using his drink, he pointed across the room. She was standing with Angela, Gwen, and Dylan, a glass of wine in all of their hands.

I instantly snagged the beer from my brother and set it on a nearby high-top.

"What was that for?"

"That is a dangerous circle your wife is standing in. The next thing you know, she's going to be bottle deep, discussing the finer and less-than-finer points of your sex life. You, sir, are going to need to drive home tonight. Go ahead and prep for it now."

He laughed. "Fair enough." He shifted Jacob to his other hip. "I guess I'll be letting Amber know that you'll be attending all future birthday parties and holiday get-togethers. No excuses now."

I groaned. "As long as I get a couple of plus-ones, I'll be there."

The happiness and relief on that man's face made him look like a kid again. "I'm so proud of you."

"That's what everyone keeps telling me," I deadpanned. "Just promise you'll check on Gwen when I'm gone. God only knows what that asshole will pull if he catches wind that I'm not around."

"You just focus on Truett while you're gone. I'll hold down the fort. I promise."

He would. Daniel would always have my back, and it was about damn time I started having his.

"Hey, you should drop the boys off with me and Gwen one night. I'm sure you two need a break."

He quirked an eyebrow. "Is tonight an option?" He tipped his chin at his wife. "That is her second glass of wine in so many minutes. She's going to be so hungover tomorrow."

Laughing, I shook my head. "Not tonight. But definitely sometime when I get back."

"Deal." He narrowed his eyes across the room. "I think someone over there is trying to get your attention."

I turned and saw Gwen waving me over. She was standing with Cooter, so I steeled myself for whatever adventure I was about to embark on.

"I'll catch up with you in a few." I jerked my chin at Daniel and then headed her way.

Gwen reached for me as soon as I got close, sliding her arm around my waist. "Truett, baby, can you help us settle something here?"

I pulled her into my side with my arm around her shoulders. "Sure."

"Please tell her that her name tag is misspelled."

Cooter pulled at her shirt to read the tag and then looked back to Gwen. "No, it's not. Lucille is spelled with two L's. How are we best friends and you don't even know how to spell my name?"

Gwen pulled a small rectangular tag from her pocket, a mischievous grin on her face. "Weird. I always thought Lucille was spelled C-O-O-T-E-R."

A loud hoot erupted and she snatched her new name tag. In less than a second, she'd switched them out, tossing the old one over her shoulder. Thankfully, it only hit the wall.

"Thank God!" she exclaimed. "I was sick to my stomach every

time someone referred to me as Lucille. That was my granny's name. It made me feel like I was being haunted."

A tall gentleman in a three-piece-suit appeared beside her, with two cocktails in his hands. He leaned into her ear and sweetly said, "I wasn't sure if you were allowed to drink or not while you're working, but I couldn't very well come back from the bar without a drink for my best girl."

Cooter beamed up at him, taking the drink. "Gwennie, Gargamel, this is my new beau, George. But you can call him Dinky."

He smiled awkwardly and extended his hand in Gwen's direction. "Nice to meet you. This place is beautiful. Also, please just call me George." He shook her hand and then turned with it still outstretched to me. "And you are?"

I grasped his palm. "Look, I'll call you George if you call me Truett and not Gargamel." I hit Cooter with a side-eye. "Not really sure where that even came from."

"Well, you were the hot gargoyle, and ya know, natural progression is Gargamel," Cooter explained as though it made all the sense in the world.

"Isn't that the bad guy from *The Smurfs*?" Gwen asked.

Cooter shrugged. "I dunno, but it sounded good." She turned to George. "Dinky, scoot over there and check on those kids. They're awful quiet and that's never a good sign."

George gave us a salute as he quickly shuffled away, and the moment he was out of earshot, Dylan appeared out of thin air.

"Coot! Why the hell are you calling that man 'Dinky'?" She dropped her voice. "Is that a reference to something being small?"

Disgust washed across Cooter's face. "Girl, please! You think I'd ever date a man with a small package?" She looked over at Gwen and waggled her eyebrows. "Trust me, he's not dinky anywhere that counts. When I first met him, he was driving the smallest car I'd ever seen. I swear I thought I'd had a stroke, because it looked like he was sitting behind the wheel of a roller skate. So when he got out and I saw he was a piece of man meat, I marched over and asked him what the hell he was doing in such a dinky car. He replied that hopefully he'd be doing me in that dinky car, and I don't know, the name just came to me."

I couldn't decide if I was more impressed with his comeback or horrified at the fact that that was Cooter's pick-up line. Okay, that wasn't true. I was impressed by both. I had to give credit where credit was due, and while Cooter was a fiery ball of crazy on her best day, she was also a lot of fun.

Angela tapped a knife to a champagne flute and announced, "The kitchen is just about to open and our girl needs to get back there. Spoiler alert: it already smells *divine*. But before she disappears on us in search of her first Michelin star, let's have a toast."

Gwen rolled her eyes. "Oh, please. It's a café, Ang."

"You never know. I hear the club sandwiches are amazing." Angela shot me a wink.

I threw my head back, laughing. I didn't have a drink in my hand, but I did have the only woman I would ever love at my side, a bright future ahead of us, and a life I was finally ready to fight for.

I lifted my imaginary drink in the air. "To Gwen, the most kind and beautiful woman I will ever know. Be it a friendly smile at a low moment, a hot cup of coffee when the world is too cold to sit in the rain, or a hug when your soul has been starved for happiness, Gwen is a giver who has offered all of us a piece of her heart. Most especially me. So, here's to a future full of possibilities, a new beginning, and if we're lucky, maybe even a piece of bacon on the side."

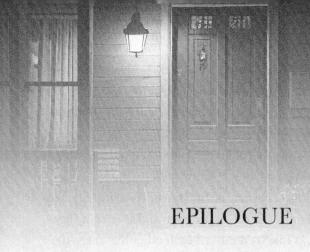

EPILOGUE

Gwen

Nine months later…

"HEY, BABE?" I CALLED, WALKING IN THE BACK DOOR, Fiona hot on my heels. "Is it on yet?"

"Just a few more minutes," Truett replied from the other side of the room.

"FeFe," Nate called, immediately dropping to all fours and patting the wooden floor.

Truett let out a grumble. "Can we not make FeFe a thing? It's bad enough your mom puts her in dresses."

When we'd gone looking for a dog to surprise Nate with for his birthday, Truett's only request had been that we didn't get a small dog. But one look at the sweet face of a four-year-old, five-pound Chihuahua mix and the tag on her kennel that read: Fiona, and I knew it was a sign.

She'd been surrendered after her owner passed away and came with an entire itty-bitty wardrobe. That crazy dog would tap dance beside her box of clothes, begging to get dressed, sometimes refusing to go outside without them.

Much to Nate's dismay, Fiona had claimed Truett as her person, preferring him to either of us. It always made me laugh when we'd take her out in public. Truett, the world's toughest and sexiest biker, toting around his pretty, pretty princess.

Right on cue, Fiona jumped on his legs, vying for attention, and he mindlessly scooped her into his lap.

"Traitor," Nate whispered at Fiona as she wallowed on Truett's chest. My son stood up and asked, "Can I walk to The Haven?"

Just days after the soft opening of The Haven, Truett had checked himself into a residential treatment program and spent nine agonizing weeks away. While we'd missed each other like crazy, neither of us could deny that those two-plus months had brought us closer together. During that time, we were forced to do the one thing we'd never done after his deployment.

We talked.

Laughing, crying, getting to know each other again, and rekindling the connection that had almost been lost, we spent hours each night on the phone. Every conversation made us stronger and healed wounds neither of us had realized we still carried.

I visited him when I could. It was a long drive, and between my commitments at The Haven and my time with Nate, those trips were few and far between. But when we did see each other, it fueled our souls, reminding us what we were fighting for and renewing the hope that had been lost so long ago.

During one of those visits, we made the decision for him to move in with me when he returned. We discussed it with an attorney to make sure it wouldn't break any rules in my custody agreement, and then we talked it over with Nate. It was Truett who insisted that my son be completely at ease with the idea before we made any moves. Not only was he okay with Truett moving in, but he was completely thrilled about the idea. His first request was a spicy food competition, the loser having to cross-stitch a picture of the winner's choice. I grinned the entire time as Truett sweated through the ghost pepper potato chips and proudly displayed the awful needlepoint he'd made after losing that read *Have a nice poop* over the guest bathroom toilet.

As we expected, Jeff was a prick of epic proportions when he was informed of our new living arrangements. However, after the dressing down Judge Clavet had given him the last time he'd tried to pull a fast one, he never once mentioned taking me back to court.

When Truett finally came home, I spent the first night marveling at the peace I felt with him by my side. He was still very much the man I'd fallen in love with—not just as a naïve girl, but years later as a weathered woman. The difference in his eyes was immense, as if a weight had finally been lifted. Those nine weeks had changed him—not yet healed, but healing.

Truett's courage and dedication to working on himself inspired me to do the same. I started going to individual therapy again to work through my own issues. But it wasn't enough for us to only heal separately—we needed to heal together.

Couples therapy had been challenging, forcing us to confront the parts of our relationship we had avoided for so many years. Some days, it felt like we were making no progress at all, maybe even slipping further away, but we kept fighting. The past—our past—wasn't something that could be fixed overnight. We both knew it would be a journey that would consume us for the rest of our lives, but we were committed to doing it together.

"Mom?" Nate whined. "Please, can I go? This place is boring now that you got rid of all the cool stuff."

I glanced around the empty living room. The only things that remained were a few stray boxes, the chair Truett was sitting in, and a TV leaned against the wall. We hadn't just gotten rid of the cool stuff. We'd gotten rid of almost everything. A week after Truett came home, we started cleaning out his house. It had been a slow and often grueling process. There were times he could only manage to part with a single item of clothing or a forgotten piece of furniture. Other times, he tackled entire rooms, stripping them of the memories that had once held him captive. Every item we discarded felt like a massive victory and a step closer to freedom.

Truett made the decision to donate the house to a charity that helped homeless veterans get back on their feet. He came to me with the idea after one particularly difficult day while cleaning Kaitlyn's bedroom. It just felt right. In a true full-circle moment, the house that had seen so much pain would now be a place of healing for others.

"Please," Nate begged. "I'm starving."

Truett smirked over his shoulder. "Wait, I thought you wanted to go because you were bored?"

Nate crinkled his nose. "Yeah, it's the worst. I'm bored and starving at the same time."

Truett chuckled, his large hand still stroking Fiona's soft fur. "Bud, if you want to go hang out with Cooter, you can just say that."

Nate nodded enthusiastically. "Yes! She's going to let me wipe down the tables today!"

I rolled my eyes. I couldn't make the kid put his plates in the dishwasher, but somehow Lucille had him bussing tables and sweeping floors.

The Haven had officially opened the day following our soft launch, and we were almost immediately overwhelmed with business. Everything I'd worked so hard to accomplish had come to fruition, and the pride and satisfaction I felt every time I walked through those doors never got old. Lucille had been spot-on with the staff she'd helped me hire. She'd told me repeatedly that she had no interest in management, but she ran the entire show with ease and expertise. My menu was a hit, the local farmers providing the produce that I dreamed of, which left customers returning time and time again.

It wasn't all smooth sailing—there were bumps along the way and a steep learning curve—but The Haven was there to stay. Truett and I had already started dreaming of future locations.

My son bounced on his toes, patience not something he was familiar with. "She's already waiting for me halfway. So can I go? Please. Please. Please."

"Fine," I relented, stabbing a finger in his direction. "But I don't care what she says. You are not allowed to cook anything again."

He groaned in protest as he bolted through the door, bounding down the front steps. I followed, watching as he raced up the sidewalk to where Lucille stood grinning at the end of the block. We exchanged a wave as he reached her, and when they turned toward the restaurant, I went back inside.

Truett was still sitting in the lone wooden chair, staring at the TV, and I couldn't tell if he was nervous or just lost in thought. Either way, we were alone, and I never missed a chance to steal a kiss.

I walked over to him and aimed my words at the dog. "Ms. Fiona, any chance I can borrow my husband for a while? You've been hogging him long enough."

Truett laughed and immediately set her on the floor. She was none too happy about it and yipped at his feet, but I slipped onto his lap without a trace of guilt.

Three months earlier, while we were cuddled on the back porch, watching Fiona chase frogs, Truett had proposed. The night was cool, the moon high among the stars. He'd been off for a few days, and I could tell something was on his mind. A million possibilities ran through my head, but a ring wasn't one of them.

We hadn't discussed getting remarried yet, but it seemed Truett had been planning it for a while. As he got down on one knee, making promises to love me the way I had always deserved, he lifted a custom-made ring in my direction.

To say it was gorgeous would be an understatement, and not just because of the design. The thought he'd put into every detail made it absolutely stunning. I hadn't known that he'd kept my old rings, the ones I'd dropped at his feet the day of Kaitlyn's funeral.

He'd had the gold melted down to make a new three-stone

setting. In the center was an emerald-cut diamond that he said represented our future. It was clear, flawless, and filled with promise. Flanked on either side were symbols of our past and present: Kaitlyn's and Nate's birthstones. Our entire lives wrapped into one stunning, never-ending circle.

There was never a doubt that I'd say yes.

Within a month, we'd tied the knot in a small, intimate ceremony at The Haven, surrounded by love, laughter, and the people who mattered most to us. And yes, even Dinky was in attendance. The Haven had become the symbol of a fresh start for me, and nothing made me happier than to say I do there.

"It's time," Truett whispered, his warm hand moving from my thigh to grab the remote.

I shifted on his lap, trying to get a better read on his face.

We were turning the keys over to charity the next day, so it felt right to watch the documentary in his house—a final act of closure we both not only needed but deserved.

"Are you okay?" I whispered, framing his strong jaw in my palms.

"Baby, you're sitting on my lap, and when this is over, we get to grab Nate, go home, crawl into bed together, and move into the future together. So yeah, I'd say I'm pretty damn okay."

My voice hitched. "You're an incredible man, you know that, right?"

"I don't know about that." His lips curled into a gentle smile. "But we do make one hell of a team."

Taggart Folly hadn't stopped harassing us until we were finally granted restraining orders against him. We'd hoped that it would be the end of his little project, but not long after he left town, we got word from our attorney that he was moving forward with a film he'd titled *The Massacre at Watersedge*. It was a punch in the gut, and we'd used every resource we could to fight it, but ultimately, there was nothing we could do to stop him from releasing what was surely going to be a sensationalized version of such a horrible tragedy.

But there wasn't a chance in hell we were going to let him have the last word. Truett and I might not have been able to control his narrative or how he portrayed the events of that day, but we had something Taggart Folly didn't.

We had the truth.

The second Truett decided that it was time to tell his side of the story, he made it clear that there would be no documentary about the shooting at The Watersedge Mall. The maniac who had ruined countless lives didn't deserve one single second of fame or notoriety.

However, the survivors did.

Each and every one of them deserved a voice—a testimony of their strength and resilience. Truett wasn't the only hero in the mall that day. There were dozens of stories of strangers banding together, putting their own lives at risk for one another. Even those who hadn't been able to be a hero for anyone other than themselves faced a different kind of hell on Earth in the aftermath of an event like that. Those were the people who deserved a platform.

With zero connections other than his name and the lore behind it, Truett was able to find a producer we felt we could trust in less than a week. Together, we focused on making a documentary with the survivors who were ready to have their stories told, never once bombarding those who weren't.

When word got out that the mysterious Truett West was involved in the project, it took on a life of its own. So many people came forward with experiences they'd never felt comfortable sharing before. Even billionaire and public figure Caven Hunt and his wife broke their silence for the first time, knowing Truett would never allow their story to be treated with anything other than respect.

By the time it was all said and done, the murderer's name was never mentioned, and *Survivors: The True Heroes of Watersedge* ended up being seven hour-long episodes—one for each day leading up to the release of Folly's film—allowing us to steal any possible momentum or shock value he might have had.

We'd already watched all the episodes—some more difficult than others, especially our own. But as the button on the streaming service changed from "Coming Soon" to "Watch Now," there was pride in knowing we got to have the final say.

Still in his lap, I nestled even deeper into Truett's chest as he appeared on screen, sitting in the very chair we were currently in. His voice was deep and resolute as he talked about mental health, emphasizing how no one can do it alone.

Overwhelmed by his strength as he spoke through the raw emotion that had destroyed us, a single tear rolled down my cheek. My emotions never lost on him, he used the pad of his thumb to wipe it away, his other arm flexing to keep me close to his chest.

On the screen, Truett drew in a deep breath. "Life after tragedy is about surviving, healing, and moving forward. Everyone has a story, and this is ours."

More tears escaped as I stared at the man on the TV while the real-life version of him held me in his arms. I'd never been more proud to call him my husband.

I tipped my head back so that I could peer into his eyes, whispering, "This is our future, isn't it?"

He pressed his lips to my forehead, lingering for a moment. "You've always been my future, Gwen. But yeah, forever starts today."

I smiled as I let my lids drift closed, the sound of his voice and the warmth of his embrace enveloping me. We'd come a long way, and we still had a long way to go, but the future—our future—had never been brighter.

"I love you, True."

"I love you too. Forever."

THE END

ACKNOWLEDGEMENTS

This book was a labor of love that took years to complete. Life's challenges and my own mental health struggles made the process slower and more difficult than I ever imagined. But now, I can say with all my heart that I've never been more proud of a story than I am with this one. So many people contributed to making this book possible, and while I'll do my best to thank everyone, please know that if I miss you, your contribution did not go unnoticed.

To the readers: You are the reason any of this is possible. Thank you for spending your time with my words for over a decade and for sticking with me through my two-year absence. This is my dream job, and I wouldn't be able to do it without you. Cheers!

To Matty: See? I told you, you didn't break me. This book has been two years in the making, and I don't think I've ever said, "I'm almost done!" so many times in my life. Yet, you cheered me on every single time…for months. HAHA! Thank you for your endless patience—not just while I was writing. You came into my life when I, like Gwen, was on a journey of healing. Thank you for walking with me through the ups and downs of both my life and career. The endless head scratching, surprise donut runs, constant water refills, instinctive ADHD wrangling, and your quiet calm during my deadline meltdowns have made you my true hero. And I know, no matter what you say, you'd still love me even if I were a Caterpiddar. Just like I love you!

To Ashley: There aren't enough words in the English language to thank you for everything you do for me. I can say with absolute confidence that I never could have finished this book—or any of the ones before it—without you. No matter how ridiculous, insane, or unbelievably outrageous things get, you're always there, ready to dive in headfirst. You're the first person I call with a crazy plot twist idea, and you don't just listen—you spend the next two weeks spinning it in your head until it invades your dreams.

Thank you for your 3 a.m. texts with "something Truett would say," and your countless voice messages as we plot out an entire book in two-minute increments. (Seriously, when will we learn to just call each other instead?) Your ability to anticipate what I need, even when I have no idea myself, is nothing short of magical. You don't just help with my books; you dive into my entire life, making sure everything runs smoothly when I'm on a deadline. I literally couldn't do this without you, and I mean it when I say Vegas is definitely on me! I love you so much that I might even be willing to give you a hug—how's that for commitment? Saint Cooter and Dinky send their deepest appreciation as well.

To T.M.: I can't thank you enough for sharing your expertise and helping bring Skytrash, S'arnt, Steve-O, and Cherry to life with such authenticity. Your insights have been invaluable, and I'm truly grateful for the time and effort you've invested in this project. Thank you for your service, and for no longer hating me. Love ya!

To Barbara: From the very start, you've embraced me as part of your family. I appreciate you reading my books and sharing them with the entire neighborhood, even if it means I can't look you in the eye for a week or two afterward. HAHA! Love you.

To the real-life Cooter: I'm sorry! You're nothing like the crazy, say-anything Lucille, but I couldn't think of a more fitting name. Please don't hate me—your son said it was okay. HAHA! Love you.

To Brittni: Thank you for all the encouragement and for taking on the challenges that come with a scatter-brained client like me. I'm still mad that you guessed the twist, but your suggestions and feedback more than made up for it.

To Megan Cooke: What can I say? You've been with me for over ten years, and I'm never letting you go. I appreciate how much you love my brand of emotional murder, but I'm still not paying for your therapy. I will, however, spring for a lifetime supply of tacos and margaritas when we get together.

To Julie: You are a saint. I honestly don't know how I'd write a book without you, and I hope we never have to find out. Thank you for always being there and fitting me in, no matter how hectic life gets. I'm so lucky to have you as a friend.

To Michele Ficht: Thank you for coming to my rescue and squeezing me in on such short notice. You're incredible to work with, and I'll forever sing your praises.

To Mickey: Ten years, thirty-plus books, and you're still willing to work with me, even when I send it in seven hundred parts. Please don't edit these acknowledgments. HAHA!

To Stacey: Thank you for always making my books look gorgeous and always being just an email away. You are always there when I need you and can't tell you how much that helps my anxiety around a deadline. HAHA! You are the best!

To Hang: I don't know how you do it every single time, but you create the most gorgeous covers with nothing more than a rambling email from me as I try to describe something that never makes sense. Your talent is nothing short of magic!

To Danielle: Thank you for still being my friend, even though I'm rarely able to hang out because I've been on a deadline for the last two years. By the way, Happy Birthday! This book is your gift because I had no time to go shopping.

To Renee: Taking you on as a P.A. was one of the best decisions I've made in my career. You've run the show behind the scenes for the last two years, always keeping me in check. I'm sorry I disappear sometimes, but don't expect that to change anytime soon. HAHAHA! I love you.

To The Author Agency: Thank you for working so hard on this release. It's been amazing to work with such kind, capable, and reliable people. I look forward to many more releases with you.

Last, but probably the most important people of all…

To my kids: Without you, my entire life would be a hollow shell. The days each of you were born, my entire world started all over again. The last two years have been a tough journey for multitude of reasons, but you four have—and will always be—the heart in my chest. Now could you please stop growing? I've had enough of it already!

Lunny: I am so incredibly proud of you. The way you've persevered over the last few years is nothing short of awe-inspiring. I wish you could see yourself through my eyes—your strength, your wit, your kindness. Your sharp sense of humor and quick banter always brighten my day, and your love for the dogs shows the depth of your compassion. I believe with all my heart that your experiences now are shaping you into someone even more remarkable than you already are. Your challenges will become the fuel for the brightest future imaginable. Keep being the amazing person you are, and know that I'm always here, cheering you on. I love you!

Tootsie Pooter: (I know, I know—I'm sorry I gave you that nickname when you were a baby, but you're stuck with it now.) From the moment you came into my life, you've been the kindest soul I've ever known. You love to help others and have never been one to back down from challenge—or an argument. Your love for food and your endless curiosity in the kitchen always bring a smile to my face—even if it does sometimes cost me a small fortune in ingredients! I know one day, all those experiments will pay off when you become a world-famous chef—or at the very least, when you start cooking me dinner! (I'm holding you to that, by the way.) Watching you grow up has been an incredible journey, and I'm so proud to call you my son. I know the best is yet to come, and I can't wait to see where your passion and talent take you. Keep being the amazing person you are, and never lose that spark that makes you so uniquely you. I love you more than words can say!

Greybae: You are such a strong and thoughtful young lady. (And yes, I know calling you a 'young lady' is cringe, but if there's one thing I've learned, it's that moms are supposed to be cringe.) I'm in awe of how you navigate the world with such confidence and excitement. The way your face beams when you're with Lacey or Elon is nothing short of pure magic. Your tenacity and sass are unmatched, and I have no doubt that you're going to set the world on fire one day. Just don't forget the little people—like your old mom—when you accepting your first Oscar or swear in as President of the United States. Keep shining, my beautiful girl—you are destined for greatness, and I'm so proud to be your mom. I love you!

Hippy Hop: You never cease to amaze me with your brilliance and wit. Every day, I get to witness the incredible combination of your sharp mind, quick humor, and those legendary sarcastic comebacks that always leave us laughing. From the time you were little, your gentle heart has been one of your most beautiful qualities, and it's been a privilege to watch you grow into a fiercely independent young lady. I have no doubt that you are going to flip this world on its head one day. Your kindness, strength, and wisdom beyond your years inspire me on a daily basis. I'm so proud to call you my daughter. (And yes, I know, you will hate every second of reading this, but hey, it's my job to embarrass you just a little!) I love you!!!

OTHER BOOKS

The Difference Trilogy

The Difference Between Somebody and Someone

The Difference Between Somehow and Someway

The Difference Between Someday and Forever

From the Embers

Release

Reclaim

The Retrieval Duet

Retrieval

Transfer

Guardian Protection Series

Singe

Thrive

The Fall Up Series

The Fall Up

The Spiral Down

THE DARKEST SUNRISE SERIES

The Darkest Sunrise

The Brightest Sunset

Across the Horizon

THE TRUTH DUET

The Truth About Lies

The Trust About Us

THE REGRET DUET

Written with Regret

Written with You

THE WRECKED AND RUINED SERIES

Changing Course

Stolen Course

Broken Course

Among the Echoes

ON THE ROPES

Fighting Silence

Fighting Shadows

Fighting Solutude

CO-WRITTEN ROMANTIC COMEDY

When the Walls Come Down

When the Time is Right

ABOUT THE AUTHOR

Originally from Savannah, Georgia, *USA Today* bestselling author Aly Martinez now lives in South Carolina with her four hilarious children.

Never one to take herself too seriously, she enjoys movies that can surprise her with a twist, charcuterie boards, and her mildly neurotic golden retriever. It should be known, however, that she hates pizza and ice cream, almost as much as writing her bio in the third person.

She passes what little free time she has reading anything and everything she can get her hands on, preferably with a glass of wine by her side.

Facebook: www.facebook.com/AuthorAlyMartinez

Facebook Group: www.facebook.com/groups/TheWinery

Twitter: twitter.com/AlyMartinezAuth

Goodreads: www.goodreads.com/AlyMartinez

www.alymartinez.com

Made in the USA
Monee, IL
14 November 2024

70125203R00193